THE FOREST KNIGHTS BOX SET
ALTDORF & MORGARTEN

BY
J. K. SWIFT

New Releases Mailing List
http://eepurl.com/hT8zU

Published by UE Publishing Co.
Vancouver, BC, Canada
Copyright© 2011, 2012 by J. K. Swift
All rights reserved.
Print Edition

This is a work of fiction. Names, characters, places, and incidents are either products of the author's imagination or used fictitiously. Any resemblance to actual events, locales, or persons, living or dead, is entirely coincidental. No part of this publication may be reproduced or transmitted in any form or by any means, electronic or mechanical, without permission from the author.

www.jkswift.com

He turned to Erich and said, "Walk."

On the road the horsemen began their second charge. A few unwise bandits raised their swords and tried to sidestep the horses but were cut down by the riders' weapons. Most fled into the trees, as did the others further up the road that came from around the bend to see what the screaming was all about. In minutes it was over.

The bearded man marched Erich through the trees. They passed Erich's three archers crumpled in the underbrush, lying in pools of their own blood with their throats cut. One of them still in his teens. Erich knew the circuitous route back to the road was taken solely for his benefit. He fought to push down the guilt building inside.

Thomas took a slow drink from a water skin and then rotated his mace arm to work out the throbbing in his shoulder. The ligaments had been stretched one too many times, but he refused to admit he needed a lighter weapon. He watched Ruedi march his captive out of the trees and force him down hard on his knees in front of the small group of men.

"This one is the leader," Ruedi murmured through his forked beard.

Thomas nodded, his dark eyes narrowing. He appeared tall because of his lean, wiry build, but he was still a full head shorter than Pirmin Schnidrig, the fair-haired titan of a man standing next to him.

"Just a kid," Pirmin said, his words strongly accented.

"Old enough to put a knife in your back if you show it to him," came another voice. Hermann Gissler, an angular man bordering on gaunt, with small eyes and black hair greying at the temples, strode forward and put the tip of his long sword in the middle of Erich's chest. "Do we hang him? Or spare the tree, and run him through now?"

"Not worth the rope," said Urs, a short, stocky man with forearms thickened by years at the forge. "Let us take him to Schwyz and turn him over to the Vogt. Judging from the size of his band they must have been quite active in this area. Might be a reward."

"Waste of time," Gissler said shaking his head. "He will only slow us down, and no village in these lands has money for a reward. Besides, they would just hang him anyway."

Thomas gave his sore shoulder a hard squeeze to get the blood moving, and looked at the dead men littering the road. He turned to the man on his knees, who looked straight ahead, head held high and eyes unseeing. A small crucifix hung from the man's neck.

He was healthy and better fed than the few people they had seen since crossing the Gotthard, nevertheless, his eyes showed no hope. He had the look of a man who knew he was going to die. And perhaps that is what he deserved. Thomas had no way of knowing how many innocent deaths this man was responsible for, and he did not care.

He had, of course, killed Christians before. But they had always been a threat in some way to the Christian Kingdom in Outremer; Saracen spies, or lowly mercenaries loyal to God only until the gold ran out. But here, in this cold valley, hidden in the shadows of rocky peaks so high and numerous you could ride for hours without seeing the sun, it felt different. Senseless. As though God had no interest in how the lives of these people played out.

"We let him go," he said.

Gissler looked at Thomas, eyes wide in disbelief. "We might not spot him next time. To show his appreciation for the mercy you have shown, he will put a quarrel in your back first chance he gets."

"You confuse mercy with indifference. We are God's soldiers, chosen by Our Lord to protect those who follow the one true faith. This man wears the cross at his neck. It is not our place to discipline half-starved ruffians."

He looked at the brigand, whose eyes had come alive and were darting side to side with a newfound hope that he may not be killed.

"You forget Thomas, we no longer fight in His army," Gissler said. His mouth moved to say more but he stopped himself.

"Bind him to a tree. By the time someone sets him free, we will be hours away," Thomas said. His tone left no room for debate.

Gissler narrowed his eyes but lowered his sword. He knew there was no point arguing with Thomas once he decided on a course of action. But then he brightened, as a new solution presented itself in his mind.

In one fluid motion he reversed the grip on his sword, stepped in and slammed the pommel into Erich's forehead. Stunned, Erich fell forward and reached out his hands to catch himself on the ground. Gissler whipped the blade onto Erich's right hand, cleanly severing away half of his first three fingers. The sword clanged as the steel made contact with the rocky ground, and just as swiftly, Gissler wiped and resheathed his blade.

Erich screamed and pulled his hand into himself, curling up into a ball.

"No need to waste rope on his likes. He will not be any good with a bow for the rest of his miserable life," Gissler said, his mouth turning up slightly.

Ruedi leaned on his larger crossbow and laughed. "Gissler the problem solver," he said, shaking his head. "Of course he could still use one of these," he said holding up his small crossbow with one hand.

Thomas let out a breath and stared at Gissler, but said nothing. It was not his fault. The others stood around drinking water, checking their weapons, or comforting their mounts. No one was surprised by Gissler's sudden action for they were all men shaped by a lifetime of war, Thomas included. It was, after all, common practice to cut off the fingers of enemy archer captives.

Finally, Anton, a small man with several earrings in his right ear who had taken to wearing perfume and bathing as frequently as the Saracens, wandered over to the writhing form on the ground and skillfully tied off the man's fingers, stemming the flow of blood. Then he began gathering kindling for a fire.

"It will not take me long to cauterize this mess. Go on ahead—I will catch you soon enough," he said to Thomas.

"Once you are done, take a moment for those on the road," Thomas said. "No man should die unshriven, but since they did not unburden their souls in confession, I am afraid a blessing is the best we can do. We leave them to God's mercy."

"Yes, Captain," Anton said. His face paled briefly as he contemplated the horrors of facing his maker with an unshriven soul, and then he remembered the groaning man at his feet who was still alive. "Max, leave me some of your kirsch."

Max, a barrel-chested man with a sour face and hair more grey than black, balked at Anton's request. "Get your own—this is one of my best batches. Who knows when I will have the means to make more?"

"Oh calm yourself. Soon you will have all the cherries you want. You are back in the land of kirsch, remember?"

Grumbling, Max rooted through his saddlebag filled with packets of saffron, turmeric, pepper, and other exotic spices he had hoarded and brought from the east. It was worth a small fortune in the right hands, and if he remembered correctly, his family in Zug had connections with buyers. He found a small flask of one of the poorer quality cherry alcohol batches he had distilled himself and tossed it to Anton.

"That should be for drinking, not burning," he said.

"Was hoping to hear that," Anton said. He popped out the stopper and took a long swig, grimacing as the hard alcohol burned its way down. Then he roughly pulled Erich up to a sitting position and forced the young man to drink a few mouthfuls. He coughed and sputtered, but managed to keep most of it down.

Max turned his back in disgust.

The men mounted up leaving Anton building his fire in the middle of the road amidst a handful of motionless corpses. Erich moaned beside him, cradling his stumped fingers.

They resumed their traveling pace. By nightfall the party would be in the village of Schwyz, where they would split up and go their separate ways. After so many years together this weighed heavily in the thoughts of each man, but with no desire to speak of it, they rode mostly in silence.

"I hate to say it, but Gissler was right Thomi," Pirmin finally said in his melodic Wallis accent. "We should have made an example of the leader and left him twisting at the end of a rope."

The way he sung his words made even a hanging sound like a cheery event. He came from the Matterhorn area and everything about the man was big, from his almost seven foot frame to the custom-made, eight-foot long battle-ax he carried. He was larger than life; an oversized blonde Adonis, both terrifying and beautiful to behold, and he was Thomas's closest friend.

"A year ago you would not have taken any chances with that outlaw. I fear you are getting soft. As usual God only knows what is rattlin' around in that head of yours."

Thomas first looked slowly at the thick woods, patches of snow still visible at the bases of most trees, and then higher up at the white-peaked Alps surrounding them on every side. He could not recall any particular memories of this road, but breathing the clear air and taking in the majestic scenery of the Alps stirred up a warm, comforting feeling that was at the same time both new and familiar.

Strange, he thought. There was no reason for him to have any feelings for this land. Unlike the others he rode with, he had almost no memories of family here. None that still lived, that is. He did not even know his true last name. For that matter, when he thought about it, he only knew two of the men's original last names. For the purpose of making record keeping matters simple, the Hospitallers gave all the boys from the alpine areas the same last name: *Schwyzer*, meaning 'one from Schwyz'. The boys were forbidden to use any other last name. Hermann Gissler refused to surrender his family name. He got around the rules by telling the monks his first name was Gissler. As for Pirmin Schnidrig, well the monks tried to beat his last name out of him, but that only made him all the more determined to make sure everyone knew he was a Schnidrig.

"Not soft. Just tired. I think I am getting too old to be one of God's soldiers," Thomas said.

Pirmin laughed and rolled his eyes. "Thomi, you were an

old man when you were five."

This made Thomas grin just enough that he could feel the scar tissue tighten and resist along the length of his face.

His saddle leather creaked as he twisted and looked behind them. A thin tendril of smoke rose above the trees from Anton's fire in the distance.

He turned back to the road ahead and wondered what God had in store for him. He had been a leader of men and a war galley's captain for twelve years, a soldier of the One Faith for over twenty. Almost a year ago to the day, Grand Master de Villaret had said, "Gather the Schwyzers, Thomas, those who remain, and take them home. This is the last order I shall give you."

In a few short hours, that order would be fulfilled.

They rode on in silence, and no one looked back when the brigand leader screamed long and hard, like he was being dragged away by the furies of hell.

Seraina was leaning against a young oak, listening to the wind, when she heard the far-off scream reverberate gently through the woods and drift up to where she stood. She opened her pine-needle green eyes and stood up straight; her long, auburn hair sticking to the bark of the oak as though the tree was reluctant to give her up. Although miles away, she could hear the scream because she stood at the edge of a clearing shadowed by the towering presence of the Mythen.

The Mythen were two mountains, standing side-by-side, one taller with the upper reaches treeless and jagged, while the shorter one had a mane of green running up the side closest to its companion. They jutted out of the earth with a statement; distinct from the low-lying hills surrounding them, their pyramidal shapes too grand and symmetrical to be ordinary. They were sentries of the ancient world, forgotten now by most, and although their rock surfaces had been ground down and large pieces had sloughed off over the millennia, they were not without power.

Seraina came to this place often to visit the Mythen, and in return for her company, they helped her listen to the wind. The wind guided her thoughts and through them, her actions. Without the voice of the wind she would be lost, her place in the Great Weave unknown.

But the messages were never clear, and today's bordered on cryptic. She had not yet seen thirty harvests, a child in the eyes of the elders. Seraina cursed her youth and lack of wisdom for not being able to discern the exact message, but just as quickly she thanked the Mythen for bringing her what they could. This day, laced together with the sound of human suffering, the warm wind whispered its message over and over. Her heart pounded in her ears.

The Catalyst's time was near.

CHAPTER 2

Salzburg

THE HABSBURG FOOL was a stringy gnome of a man, easily twice Leopold's twenty-four years but little more than half his height. He wore no hat but his purple hair was cut short and plastered to his head in a star pattern. His frilly tunic was black on the left and white on the right, while his tights were the opposite. Yellow, pointed, soft-leather shoes completed the ensemble. When Leopold approached, the Fool made a flourishing gesture with his arms and bowed to the young Duke before thrusting open the double doors to the council chambers. At the last second he stepped in front of Leopold and strutted ahead to escort him into the large room, the soft tinkling of bells on the Fool's pointed shoes marking every step.

The sound had infuriated Leopold since childhood, for somehow the Fool had complete control over the loudness and intensity of the bells and, Leopold felt, used them purposely to mock him. He could walk without making a sound when he wanted to, for despite being a garish entertainer, the Fool had always been by King Albrecht's side when he was alive and could in fact blend in when he so wished. Since the King's assassination the previous year, the Fool had attached himself to Frederick, Leopold's older brother by a year, and who now sat at the head of an ornate rectangular table in the council room.

Frederick smiled and held up a hand in greeting as his brother entered, relief etched deep in his face. Seated around him were eight older men, the advisors to his late father, but unlike Frederick, not one of them looked pleased at the entrance of the younger Habsburg Duke.

"The fool has arrived!" the jester announced.

Leopold shot him an angry glare and imagined what it would feel like to have his hands around the insufferable creature's throat, shaking him until the only sound that escaped was the tinkling of those cursed chimes.

"Welcome brother, we are happy you could join us on such short notice." Frederick 'the Handsome', as he was called, came around the table and the two brothers embraced. Only a year separated them but they looked nothing alike. Leopold was fair haired and willowy in build while Frederick was dark and stocky, like their father had been. Most women would not say Frederick was any more 'handsome' than Leopold, but there was a beatific honesty in his smile that made people feel comfortable. When under Leopold's bold stare on the other hand, people were never at ease. He had his mother's sharp features: glistening blue eyes and a high-bridged raptorial nose.

Six of the men were nobles of prestigious Austrian houses, powerful members of the German Empire, but Leopold's sudden presence made many of them shift in their seats. His open disdain for his father's advisors was well known. He trusted none of them and felt sick when he thought of his brother in this room alone with these carrion eaters. He made a point of looking at each man and noting who met his eyes and who seemed surprised to see him here. The few who met his eyes quickly looked away, but that in and of itself was not a measure of guilt.

The Archbishop was seated to one side of Frederick along with a simpler dressed monk Leopold had never before seen. Though he wore the robe of a Dominican, his face had the smugness of a merchant.

"Forgive my lateness brother. I should have liked to be here sooner but the messenger bearing your summons was waylaid on the road some miles from Habsburg Castle." Leopold let his eyes wander over the nobles, openly accusing anyone who met his stare.

Count Henri of Hunenberg, a veteran knight in his late forties who was renowned for spending much of his family's fortune on several campaigns to the Holy Lands, shook his head and said, "This is further evidence of what I spoke—even the roads in the Aargau are no longer safe since so many of our soldiers were sent north. We must have more patrols to ensure the safety of messengers and merchants. And from what the Archbishop here tells us, the monks of Einsiedeln also require enforcers in their pastures near Schwyz."

"Ridiculous," Otto, the late King Albrecht's grey-haired military adviser grunted. "Louis the Bavarian openly defies Frederick's tutelage and is marshaling his forces as we speak. We must maintain a show of force in the north. Only war will decide the German kingship now. I must be granted direct control of the *Sturmritter* if Habsburg rule is to prevail."

Leopold looked at Otto, shocked by the old general's cunning. No one understood Otto better than Leopold, for Otto had been his principal tutor growing up. King Albrecht had recognized the natural gifts of his children; Frederick, with his easy smile, was the natural politician, but in Leopold he had seen the future Marshal of the Habsburg armies, and his father had seen to his education accordingly.

Otto had just made his play for control of the most fearsome fighting force in all of Europe. The Stormriders were a cavalry force created by Leopold's grandfather, the first Habsburger to become King of the Germans. He had assembled the top fighting men in Europe, provided them with the best horses and equipment, and granted them their own castle from which they would serve the Habsburg rulers. They were full-time warriors and the highest paid knights in the known world. Competition to join the Sturmritter was intense and every year men died during the fierce tournaments that served as auditions for young men seeking to earn fame and a place amongst the elite.

Otto openly stared at Frederick, demanding a response, but before Frederick could say anything, Leopold spoke up. "I am afraid that is impossible, Lord Otto. The Sturmritter are suppressing a revolt in Schwabia at the moment."

Otto eyed Leopold with an odd mix of loathing and pride. "A peasant revolt. Hardly a situation to warrant the use of the Sturmritter."

"But a strategic location that is crucial to Austria. When they are finished their work in Schwabia I am sure my brother will make them available to your cause, if they are still required. In the meantime, surely all the soldiers of Austria, under your unfailing leadership, shall be sufficient to deal with Louis the Bavarian."

Leopold turned quickly from Otto before he could reply and addressed his brother directly. "Frederick, I need to speak with you on a topic of the utmost importance. *Family* matters."

Frederick caught Leopold's hidden meaning, and ignoring

the frustrated looks of the nobles in the room, gestured for his brother to follow him out the door. "Of course. Let us take a recess. Gentlemen, excuse us if you would."

They walked down the stone corridor to a smaller receiving room at the end of the hall. Fresh rushes covered the stone floor and a fire burned in the hearth, while a thick layer of smoke hovered, trapped near the top of the twelve-foot ceiling. Leopold reached to close the heavy door behind them, and was startled to see the Fool about to follow them in.

Leopold held out his arm. "You can stay out there. I've seen enough of your painted face for one day," he said and threw the door shut before the smiling little man could set even one of his pointed shoes over the threshold.

"You have news of the assassin? Has he been found?" Frederick asked, unable to contain himself a second more.

"I do have news of our cousin's whereabouts, but it is only a tip—nothing more. I was on my way to investigate when I heard you were to meet with the nobles alone."

Frederick placed his hand on his brother's shoulder and let out a long breath. The tension in him eased somewhat.

"And I am thankful you are here. Word is the German Princes are favoring Louis for the throne and our supporters are calling for an immediate show of force. But how can I march on Louis? He has been our friend since childhood."

"It is not Louis, but the Princes who are behind this. They fear Habsburg power—it has always been so. It was the same when our father came to power. He was not given the kingship, but had to take it, and now brother, you must do the same."

Frederick dropped into one of the intricately carved wooden chairs in front of the fire. "How goes work on the Altdorf citadel?"

Leopold grunted. "It is little more than a mound of rubble at the moment. Certainly not a citadel. I need more workers. Speaking of which, I do not suppose…"

"If I had men to spare they would be readying for battle, I am afraid," Frederick said. "Not playing with stone and mallet."

Leopold's jaw clenched, starting a tremor in the muscles under his cheekbones.

"Traffic over the Gotthard Pass doubles every month with the recent improvements the Milanese have made on the Devil's bridge over the Reuss. The Gotthard is now the fastest way for all Mediterranean merchants to traverse the Alps and trade with the Hanseatic League. Both the King of France and the Duke of Milan are scheming for its control. Protecting Habsburg land from their hungry eyes is hardly *playing*, brother."

Frederick let out a sigh and pinched the bridge of his nose between his fingers. He let his chin momentarily dip to his chest.

"Forgive me, Leo. I am tired. I do not have the patience for these games. You should have been born the elder."

Leopold forced a laugh, but in truth a chill went through him at the thought of being King of the Holy Roman Empire. Having to deal with advisers and petty petitions from nobles and commoners alike, always in the midst of the conniving German princes. No, that was not a position to covet. "Nonsense. I work better behind the lines. You know that."

"I wish father were still alive. I can understand our cousin for feeling slighted, deprived even, of his inheritance, but to go so far as to plan the assassination of the King? For the love of Christ I cannot see what drove him to it."

"Evil can be found in all men's hearts if you look deep

enough," Leopold said.

"Father was a great man. Even the Jews would admit as much. But something in him changed when Rudolph died. I know you felt it too."

Leopold knew exactly what Frederick meant. King Albrecht had had three sons. The oldest was Rudolph and it had been no secret that he was the King's favorite. After many years of scheming and brilliant politics, Albrecht had secured the throne of Bohemia for his son Rudolph. Unfortunately, barely a year into his reign, Rudolph succumbed to a fever and died.

With the death of his eldest son, the aging Albrecht's mind had come unhinged. Not all at once, in an obvious way, but to those closest to him, especially his sons Frederick and Leopold, the changes were readily apparent. He became forgetful, drank wine in the evenings, something he had forbidden his own sons to do, and appeared less frequently at the local courts he had fought so hard to establish during his reign.

Near the end, he would not be seen for days, and when he did appear, he was frequently in his cups. And then, one afternoon while crossing the Reuss River, he was attacked and killed by his nephew John and three fellow conspirators. The bloated bodies of John's accomplices were found days later miles downstream but somehow John 'the Parricide' managed to escape the wrath of Albrecht's sons and fled into hiding. Claiming Frederick had enough to worry about with being the head of the Habsburg family, and potentially the new Emperor of the Germans, Leopold had declared he would take it upon himself to find John and bring him to justice.

"You must be strong in this hour," Leopold said. "All eyes are on you now, and if the princes see weakness you will never be elected to the throne. But more importantly, you cannot trust any of those nobles in the other room. They stand with you only because they need your strength to protect their lands. Not because of any past loyalty to our father. Never for a moment forget this." *Parasites,* he thought. *Every last one of them.*

Frederick looked up from his chair, his usually smiling eyes now dark and red-rimmed. It hurt Leopold to see him this way. His brother was a simple man, honorable and just, if not overly wise. He would make a good king. Too good—the German princes would flay him alive. It would be best for all if Frederick was not a candidate for the throne, but Leopold knew that was impossible.

Their father had built the German Empire up for one of his sons to rule, and Frederick would give his life to honor his father's ambitions, no matter the cost to himself. Everyone knew Frederick the Handsome's honor and sympathy for his subjects were his greatest strengths, but Leopold saw them as weaknesses that would eventually lead to his downfall. And when he fell, as he most surely would, it was Leopold's duty to ensure the Habsburg line survived. And the longer he kept Frederick alive, the longer he would have to increase the family's private holdings. In Leopold's mind, the acquisition of land and estates in the Habsburg name was the key to maintaining power.

That, and of course, the Stormriders.

"Promise me something," Leopold said.

Frederick stared into the fire. "If I can," he said.

"You will never relinquish control of the Sturmritter to another man. Not even your military advisors." *Especially them.*

"Then I would ask something of you," Frederick said.

Leopold's head cocked to one side. It was unlike his brother to barter with him. With a great effort Frederick pushed himself up from his warm chair like a drowning man kicking to the water's surface.

"Take the Fool with you to Aargau. It seems he has a history with many of our father's advisors and I fear for his life while he is here. I cannot possibly devote the time every day to keep him from harm's path."

Leopold took a deep breath before he spoke. "Surely no one could gain from killing the Fool. This is his home. He would not be happy, nor comfortable, in our rustic country estates."

"You and I know he is no threat. But some feel he was too close to father and was privy to all types of sensitive information. Please, Leo, obey me on this one thing. Father would want to see our childhood playmate taken care of as he enters his twilight years."

Leopold forced his thin lips into something resembling a smile. "Of course. But I have business to attend before returning to Habsburg. Have him ready his belongings and send him in a few days." Even that much of a respite would be welcome.

Frederick placed his hands on Leo's shoulders. "Thank you brother. It may be a small thing to you, but knowing our Fool is safe in your care lessens much of the weight bearing on my mind." He threw his arms around Leopold and they embraced.

Then holding him at arms length he looked at his brother and said, "Besides, you may find his advice intriguing. Sometimes I think he is my wisest advisor."

Frederick broke into honest, deep-belly laughter at this, which lifted years from his face. Leopold, grateful to see the change, echoed his brother's laughter, musing all the while whether God had a hand in inflicting this punishment.

✧ ✧ ✧

The cheese hut stood alone high in the hills. To provide a level foundation in the mountainous terrain, it was built on legs of differing heights consisting of flat stones stacked upon one another. The top stone of each leg was smooth and twice the size of the others so as to create an overhang, an impossible barrier for field mice trying to climb up the legs and gain entry to the hut. A month from now, when the snow was completely gone and the grasses turned the hills green, the farmer and his wife would drive their animals up from the lowlands and live in the hut all summer long making cheese.

But for now, there was only one resident: a young man, once used to the silk and linen comforts of the noble class but now garbed in the coarse, itchy brown robe of a Dominican friar. His hair was disheveled, and dark, bloodshot eyes told of countless nights with little sleep.

As dusk approached, he stood inside the small hut with the door ajar, looking out over the hills as two riders approached. His first impulse was to flee, but he soon recognized the riders and willed himself to stay put.

Moments later, Leopold dismounted, while Klaus, a thick soldier who had been Leopold's man for many years, remained on his horse and kept a watchful eye on the surrounding slopes.

"Cousin, I thought you had broken your word and forsaken me in this damnable place," John said, his voice accusing and rough from lack of use.

Leopold untied a bag from his saddle and tossed it to John, who snatched it out of the air and immediately snaked his hand inside to retrieve a thin slice of dried meat and a crusty loaf. It had been three weeks since his last visit from Leopold and his desire to speak with another person was great, but so was his need to eat something other than the porridge and cheese he had been living on. He crammed the slice of meat into his mouth and bit into the loaf. Crumbs flaked off and clung to his shaggy beard.

Leopold screwed up his nose and shook his head. "I do not recall you being so uncouth at our last encounter. Perhaps you tire of this peaceful retreat in the Alps and are ready to move on?"

John ripped off another piece of bread with his teeth and spoke around it. "You know I am. Do not play games with me Leo—what news have you?"

"Good news cousin. You are free to go wherever you like now."

John's eyes lit up and he lowered the bag of food. "The princes will grant clemency then? I can return to Salzburg?"

"Salzburg? I suppose you could, but keep in mind you are still Wolf's head in Austria and like the beast, your skin can be traded for coin."

"What do you mean? You said I had to but wait for the princes to assemble and vote. Surely they see what a madman the King had become. I have served the German Empire and yet I hide in these hills cowering like a common criminal! You swore to me—"

Leopold cut him off by grabbing the front of his robe and pulling him close. "You are far worse than a common criminal," he said, and then disgusted by the stench of the man, pushed him stumbling back into the cheese hut's wall. "The Pope has placed you under the Holy Ban."

The effect of the words was instantaneous. Horrified, John's legs went slack and he slid down the wall to sit on the ground. Leopold rubbed his hands together and then wiped them on one of Klaus's legs. The veteran soldier kept his eyes locked on the horizon.

"Apparently I underestimated how much the Pope respected my father."

John sat on the ground hugging his knees. His mouth opened and closed several times before he finally found his voice. "No, it cannot be. I will flee to Spain. No Italia. I must go to Rome and buy indulgence…"

"Fool. How far do you think you will get when every man, child, and woman has the right to beat, rob, and kill you on sight? Under threat of excommunication, no one is allowed to aid you. I have wasted the past few months of my life building discreet relations with your connections at court. And for what? Nothing. You are useless to me now."

John shook his head slowly from side to side. "No—this is not what you promised. You said I would be granted lands and titles when Frederick became King." He pointed his finger up at Leopold. "You gave your word!"

Leopold rolled his eyes and walked over to his horse. "My word was it?"

He pulled himself up into the saddle and said, "Sorry cousin. I can deal with princes and kings, but a Papal Ban is beyond even me."

John stood on shaky legs and stumbled over to the two mounted men. Klaus grabbed the pommel of his sword, but Leo held up a restraining hand as John wrapped himself around the young Duke's boot and pleaded.

"No, do not go Leo. Please, I am sorry I accused you. I have been alone too long…my mind is not right. Surely there is something we can do. I will stay in hiding and when Frederick becomes king he can beseech the Pope…"

Leopold gently placed his hand on John's head and leaned over him. "My dear cousin, can you not see I have no choice?" One corner of his thin lips turned up in a smirk. "And besides…you did kill my father. Why would I assist the likes of you?"

Leopold pushed John away by his head, turned his horse, and jammed his heels into its side. He held up a hand in parting and called out, "Good luck on the road cousin. Beware old ladies and children trying to kill you in your sleep."

He left John the Parricide, slack-legged and hunched in front of the age-blackened shack, a man with no country and no god.

CHAPTER 3

WHEN THEY CAME to Altdorf, a town near the southern end of the Great Lake, Ruedi abruptly announced he would separate from the party.

Altdorf was a thriving town for these parts. Almost a city, Thomas thought. Easily the largest settlement they had seen since coming over the Gotthard Pass. On a rise in the distance he could even see new construction under way. It appeared to be a large stone keep beginning to take shape.

"Heard a rumor about five years back I have a sister in these parts," Ruedi said. "Course it came from a drunken Norseman, and he was not sure if he was in Burglen or Altdorf at the time. Still, nothing better to do. Might as well check it out."

"Best of luck finding her. I swear, this town has tripled in size since I saw it last. It was nothing more than a few farmer's huts clustered together from what I remember," Anton said.

"Well that is no farmer's hut," Pirmin said pointing at the keep on the hill.

Thomas remembered the Norseman Ruedi talked about. *The Wyvern* had been patrolling the waters off the coast of Turkey and they came across the remains of a burned out merchant knarr floating dead in the water. Only one man remained alive, though he hovered precariously close to death.

Thomas ordered him to be taken to the Hospital in Rhodes, where to everyone's amazement and thanks in no small part to the skill of the Order's doctors, the man had survived and spent almost two months amongst the Hospitallers. He was well traveled and a tireless storyteller, provided he was kept in his cups, and told endless tales of the far North and how most people there still believed not in one god, but in many, similar to the Greeks of old.

The seven men dismounted in front of a church, which, though small, was still the most impressive building in sight. Next to it was a recently constructed barracks, with three Austrian soldiers standing about eyeing the travelers. It was midday, the street quiet as most people were at work.

Each man said some parting words to Ruedi and embraced him in the quick emotional manner of men who had forged a bond of incredible strength over the years. As a parting gift Thomas gave him a dozen crossbow quarrels.

"You will make better use of these than I ever could," Thomas said.

"Aye. You never had much of an eye, Cap'n. I will come find you sometime—maybe take you hunting. Try not to starve before then." His voice broke slightly and the forks of his mahogany beard twitched as he clamped his mouth shut.

Thomas mounted up and the men rode out of Altdorf, leaving Ruedi standing alone in the middle of the road, the occasional townsman scurrying past, pretending not to stare.

✧ ✧ ✧

It was already dark when they rode into Schwyz, but they had no trouble finding a large inn. The village was a common stopping point for travelers who had made it over the Alps and the inn's business seemed good. The high-ceilinged common room held a dozen tables, half of them filled with patrons, when Thomas's party entered. A staircase, with sturdy treads formed from split logs, led up to several rooms on the second floor.

Faces looked up but quickly turned away again when someone from Thomas's group met their gaze. Good things rarely came from prolonged eye contact with six heavily armed men weary from the road.

The owner, a thin, tight-lipped man with strong hands, watched the new arrivals suspiciously from behind a high counter, which separated the crowd from several tapped kegs. He seemed to relax slightly when Max paid some coins up front and negotiated for rooms and horse stabling.

Soon, heaping bowls of chamois stew and ceramic mugs of ale were placed before the six men. As the owner brought the food out of the kitchen, Thomas glanced an older woman and a younger pretty girl with sand-colored hair. She stared at Thomas and his companions with wide eyes, and then the door swung shut obscuring her from view.

Thomas surveyed the patrons. A few tables of traveling merchants, and another with two grizzled and grey men and a woman hunched over their drinks, talking in hushed tones. Then he looked at his own group of dirty, rough men-at-arms as an outsider might and did not blame the innkeeper for hiding the womenfolk away in the kitchen.

While with the Order, Thomas and his men had always worn brown cloaks and tunics with the white Hospitaller cross prominently displayed on the chest or shoulder. His friends looked different now in plain traveling garb, albeit their weapons and partially visible chainmail marked them as more than simple travelers.

"Our coin will go a long way in this land," Max said, obviously pleased with the outcomes of his negotiations.

"A good thing that is. Since you still owe me for reshaping that sword you carry," Urs said. During his years of service to the Order of Saint John, in addition to being a sergeant-at-arms, Urs had been apprenticed to one of the Order's weapons-makers. A quiet perfectionist with forearms almost as large as Pirmin's, Urs was far happier handling hammer and anvil than using the quality weapons he forged.

"I told you. Once we get to Zug I will sell some of my spices at the market and buy you a new horse. A good mountain pony that will carry your bulk to Basel without balking at every slope."

Urs grunted—a noncommittal sound that meant he neither agreed nor disagreed with Max. For a moment it looked like he might say more but instead wrapped his thick fingers around the mug in front of him and drained it.

Since leaving Ruedi at Altdorf, the reality that their journey together was at an end had finally sunk in, and Thomas had been debating with himself where his own path would finish. Max had family in Zug, Urs was from Basel, Gissler's father was a steward of land in the Aargau, Anton was headed to Appenzell, and Pirmin could not stop talking about the mountains of Wallis and his family's black-necked goat farm, although he seemed to be taking the long way home by going through Schwyz.

Schwyz. This was where their journey together had begun so many years ago. It was fitting that it should also end here.

"Max, I would collect my share here in the morning," Thomas said.

Conversation within the group ceased and as one they turned to look at Thomas. When they were on campaign, Max had always looked after the troop's money. He had a mind that never forgot a sum and he could write numbers. He knew a few letters, but the only one of the group who could truly read and write was Thomas.

Money had not played a large part in the sergeants' military lives, since their everyday needs were supplied by the Order, but they were given a small salarium every month to be spent how they chose. Before leaving Rhodes for the last time, Max had collected the meager life savings of his friends together and exchanged the coins for a letter of credit from the Order of Saint John, which was redeemable at any of the Order's hospices or estates scattered throughout Europe. Many merchants took advantage of this deposit and withdrawal system offered by both the Hospitallers and the Templars, since it was a safe way to conduct business in lands rife with thieves and highwaymen.

Max had redeemed the letter at a hospice they found in northern Italia a week ago, but since everyone trusted him, he still held all the coin himself, doling it out carefully when they needed to purchase meals or lodging.

"So you will be staying here in Schwyz then?" Max asked, looking over his half-eaten bowl of stew.

Thomas shrugged. "For awhile. Remember that old man and his ferry we passed on the lake close to Brunnen? It gave me an idea."

"You will be wasting yourself here in the poor country," Gissler said. "Come with me up north to the Aargau. My father has connections—I am sure he knows someone who could put our swords to use."

Thomas shook his head. "I appreciate the offer, Gissler, but I mean to try my hand at something different. It seems the Good Lord has more than hinted that my time as one of His sword bearers has come to an end, and frankly, I have no desire to see it put to another's use."

"Thomi, Thomi. Your days on the water are over. What would you be wanting with an old rotten barge I wonder?" Pirmin said, already drinking from his third mug of ale.

Thomas's eyes came to life. "She will not be rotten when I finish with her."

Pirmin stared at Thomas for a moment while he sopped up the juices of his stew with a chunk of crusty bread. He popped it into his mouth and spoke around it, which had the effect of lessening his Wallis accent, and curiously, made his speech easier to understand.

"Well I know as soon as I get back home to Tasch my family will want to marry me off to keep the Schnidrig line going strong. And I admit I look forward to one part of that. Those Wallis women are easy on the eyes and know how to keep their men warm at night, I tell you that much."

"What do you know about Wallis women? You were eight the last time you saw one," Thomas said.

"Must be talking about his mother," Anton said.

"It is the air and the water," Pirmin said, ignoring them both. "Something about it produces the most handsome animals, and people. Similar to how the bitter water in Appenzell keeps all Anton's people small and stunted. Talk nice to me lads, and maybe I will bring some of that Wallis nectar and sell it to you. No reason your children need to be ugly—God knows you and your kin have suffered enough already."

Anton punched the giant man in the shoulder, while Gissler dipped his fingers in his ale and flicked them at Pirmin. Pirmin wiped his face and crossed himself and then held up a finger.

"But first, I think I will stay here for a time and help Thomi build his boat. Raise up gentlemen and let us drink to making ugly people better looking!"

"To new ventures," Max said, raising his mug.

They echoed Max's toast and clanked their mugs together, splashing ale over the table. They laughed hard and drank long into the night, reminiscing over thirty years of shared exploits. For the remainder of the evening, they peeled back the years until each man saw only the faces of boys before him, and the aches and pains inflicted by a lifetime of war dissolved into the night.

CHAPTER 4

NOLL MELCHTHAL sprinted up the treed slope, breathing through his nose and pacing himself carefully so the armored men cursing and shouting behind did not fall too far back. His powerful legs pumped with a rhythm all their own. These were his woods, his mountains. No foreign lapdog soldier could touch him here.

He stooped and picked up a good rock. Taking careful aim he wound up and launched it at the closest man. A boiled-leather breastplate emblazoned with the red fist insignia of Berenger von Landenberg, the Habsburg appointed Vogt of Unterwalden, protected the man's chest, but the stone hit him high in the shoulder and he let out a squeal of pain. Noll laughed and ducked behind a tree as a crossbow bolt flew past and skittered off the rock bluff behind him.

He pulled up the hood on his cloak, stepped out from behind his cover to make sure the soldiers got a good look at him, and started climbing again. A minute later he crested the rise and the path leveled out for a straight stretch through the forest.

Squatting against a tree was Aldo, a tall boy in his late teens wearing a cloak the same drab brown as Noll's. He stood up and grinned at Noll with a questioning look on his face.

Noll slowed to a walk and counted slowly to ten, then he made a forward motion with his hand and the young man pulled up the hood of his cloak and ran away through the forest.

Noll veered off the path and sat down in the underbrush. He could hear the soldiers crashing up the slope for some time before they finally appeared at the top. They spotted the figure running through the trees in the distance and, heartened by the level ground, immediately gave chase with renewed vigor. They charged by so close to Noll's hiding spot he could see the sweat on their red faces and hear the bellows of their breathing.

Seconds later, Noll stood and watched the clumsy soldiers crashing through the underbrush in pursuit of their quarry. He shook his head, then turned and began walking back down the hill to the Austrian soldiers' deserted camp.

Trees were the most vocal beings in the forest. They were kind and generous souls and although Seraina rarely comprehended what they were saying to one another, she never tired of listening to their creaks and murmurs. Occasionally, she would even understand a reference to a creature or an upcoming storm, or experience a sense of emotion such as the joy of stretching out towards the morning sun or the cooling relief of a summer rain. It did not bother her that she understood so little of their language, for the sound of their voices was comforting enough.

She tended her garden behind the small cottage she had come to inhabit three years ago. It was in thick forest that allowed only sporadic beams of sunlight to pierce the canopy of trees, and perhaps that is why the previous owner deserted it. But she was no ordinary gardener. She knew how and where to plant vegetables and herbs so they flourished.

The foundation of the cottage and lower half were made from stone, upon which rough-hewn timber comprised the walls. It was a sturdy shelter and had been built with great skill many years ago, but when she found it, the thatched roof was mostly rotted away and needed to be replaced. A nearby farmer and his wife assisted her with the necessary repairs, and in return, she helped them when they needed a healer's skill.

It was three hours from the nearest village, and the village of Schwyz easily twice that, for to reach it, one must first cross an arm of the Great Lake or walk around. Seraina could not imagine why the original owner had chosen to live so far from the towns, but it suited her fine. It was far enough away that the townsfolk could pretend she did not exist, yet near enough to seek her out when they needed help.

She had not always lived so far from her people.

Like their trees, the people of these lands were capable of great kindness and looked after one another fiercely. Yet they were a private lot and devoted Christians. For a time she lived amongst them in the small village of Tellikon, near Zurich, where her skills with growing herbs and in the healing arts became well known. Even though she did not share their Christian faith, many people came to accept Seraina as a member of the community.

Until one night, with frozen rain pelting the village roofs, she assisted in a breached childbirth that left the mother dead and the baby a cripple. Death during childbirth was a common enough affair, and all would have been fine, but the baby had the misfortune of being born with misshapen feet. The parish priest called them hooves.

He tried to take the child but Seraina refused to give her up. The next night the priest appeared at her shack with a rabble of angry villagers and they tore the child from her arms. He named her a witch and a servant sent by the Devil to corrupt the people of Tellikon. Few believed his words but even fewer were foolish enough to take the chance that a demon lived amongst them.

She was driven from the town but managed to escape her pursuers and watch from the safety of the trees as they burnt her shack and the entirety of her few belongings. The torches set to her home were lit from the same bonfire used to burn the child.

Lost in her thoughts of the past, Seraina did not hear the young man approach until he spoke.

"Pretty girls should pay more attention when alone in the woods. You never know what beast might be lurking nearby."

Seraina started and stood from her garden. She cocked her head, her ears still picking up the voices of the trees, loud and unconcerned. Noll grunted as he dropped a large sack on the ground that clanged as it hit.

The trees were extremely sensitive and Seraina could tell when people, and even some animals, approached by how they reacted. She used to think it strange that Noll's presence never disturbed them, but that was before she knew him. Before she had come to realize he was the Catalyst.

"The only dangerous beasts in this area are of the human variety," Seraina said. She nodded toward the bag on the ground. "What treasures have you liberated today?"

Noll shrugged. "Soldier provisions mostly. Bread, some cheese, a few cooking pots. Choose what you want and I will take the rest back with me to the men."

Noll walked over to a barrel of rainwater, splashed some on his face and ran his fingers back through his short dark hair. He removed his shirt and began splashing water under his arms and on his neck and chest, his wiry muscles tensing under the cold water. At least five years younger than Seraina, he was lean but wide at the shoulders. For one so young he had a rare self-confidence women found irresistible and men respected.

"Oh, and I need a refill on the ivy powder," Noll said, his blue eyes glinting as beads of water ran through his hair and down the stubble on his cheeks. She allowed herself to stare for a moment before responding.

"More? You must be using too much. Where did the last three vials go?"

Noll grinned and dried off his face with his shirt. "Been lots of bedrolls to attend. Our Habsburg lords seem to be sending more soldiers than usual out into the woods these days."

Seraina shook her head. "These are games you play Noll. Really, what good are they? You steal from soldiers, taunt them, make them angry. It does nothing for the people. It changes nothing."

"Ah, but it is entertaining. And who is to say it does nothing for the people? It shows them that if my men and me can stand up to Landenberg then they can too. Two more men joined us last month."

Seraina smiled and shook her head. "Aldo and Martin? They are boys. Boys that should be at home working farms, not running through the forest playing tricks on real soldiers."

"The boys of today make up the armies of tomorrow," Noll said.

"And what if you are caught and hung? What will your *men* do then?"

Noll laughed and pulled on his shirt. "They would have to find me first. These are my woods, Seraina. I refuse to bend to the will of a foreigner who thinks because he has soldiers and the blessing of some King I have never seen, he can take land my family has lived on for a thousand years."

Seraina felt a flutter in her breast. She liked it when Noll spoke with such conviction, but she also knew better than to encourage him. Once Noll got started he was an unstoppable force and she would rather see that energy directed somewhere that it would do some good.

"I hear you moved your camp again," Seraina said, changing the topic.

"You are well-informed," Noll said, surprised. "Spying on me are you? Jealous perhaps? No need to be, you know. We are so far away from civilization we cannot even get camp whores to come to our tents."

"So where are you now?"

Noll shook his head. "You know I cannot tell you," he said, then his eyes took on a mischievous glint. "But I could show you. Why not come with me? We could use someone with your talents and it is too dangerous for you to be out here on your own. Too lonely. Come with me and I promise you would want for nothing."

His smile was bold and tempting. The invitation was not subtle, for that was not Noll's way. He lived for the moment, and at the moment Seraina could sense his desire. As enjoyable as helping him sate that desire might be, Seraina knew she could not go with him. He was the Catalyst, and to share his bed would cloud her visions of the Weave.

He was right though. She was lonely at times. But the horrors of Tellikon had taught her that to serve her people she must maintain her distance.

Seraina shook her head. "I have responsibilities here. I cannot just leave."

Noll exhaled and held up his hands. "You have an overgrown garden and some birds that you feed. What is so important that you have to be here?"

Seraina laughed and took his arm.

"As I have told you before. I must be close enough to help you but far enough away that I can still listen to the wind. Come. Let us go get you some more ivy powder."

Noll shook his head and fixed her with a puzzled smile.

"You are the strangest woman I have ever known." And then he remembered something. "Seraina, a few miles from here I found wolf tracks—the biggest I have ever seen. He was all alone, so probably driven out of the pack and hungry. Keep an eye out and be careful, will you?"

Seraina's breath caught in her throat.

"Seraina, did you hear what I said?" Noll asked.

Her only response was a curt nod, for she was not sure her voice could be trusted.

CHAPTER 5

Aarau, capital city of the Aargau region

THE TWO ARMORED MEN, thronged by cheering spectators, circled each other. Both let their shields drop slightly to ease their aching arms and sucked in ragged breaths to prepare for the next assault. Then, one man charged forward to swing his hand-and-a-half sword down upon the other's shield.

"I never understood what the point is in hitting another man's shield," Leopold said, holding his goblet out to be refilled by a servant standing ready with a pitcher of honeyed wine. "Why not simply aim where the shield is not?"

"Intimidation," Berenger Von Landenberg, the Vogt of Unterwalden said, taking a pull off his own mead. "Shake a man's shield arm to the core and it takes the fight out of him."

He sat forward in his high-backed chair, but not because the match enthralled him. Landenberg was a large man with a rounded salt and pepper beard and the soft, blackened teeth of a noble who had eaten too much white bread. Though he wore no armor, squeezing his girth between the armrests of the wooden chair, if possible, would be far from comfortable. In his early fifties now, he watched the competitors with disdain and undisguised jealousy.

Count Henri of Hunenberg also sat on the raised platform with the young Habsburg Duke and the Vogt, albeit in a plain chair that lacked the intricate carvings of the other two men. The ever-present Klaus, Leopold's man, stood at the bottom of the platform's stairs, unmoving as an iron rod driven straight into hard-packed earth.

The crowd groaned as one of the competitors missed an overhead strike leaving himself open and his opponent brought his own blade crashing down across the man's back, knocking him to the ground and ending the match.

"Sweet Mary. Finally. This match should have been finished long ago," Landenberg said, standing to fart and stretch his joints. "Wine," he said thrusting out his mug. "I have a mind to send for my own armor."

Leopold was in no mood for Landenberg's blustering. Granted the man had his uses, especially when it came to keeping order in the backward villages and mountain settlements of Unterwalden. Violence and intimidation were all those people understood, so they deserved to be governed by a filthy boar of a man like Landenberg.

The ride back from Salzburg had been long and wearying, made even more so because Leopold had to suffer the company of the Fool. His eyes scanned the crowd and immediately picked out the little man's purple hair and white and black outfit doing a dance in front of some shabbily dressed peasants, who seemed to have forgotten their miserable lot in life and were enjoying his antics.

"Our tournament days are over, Berenger." Count Henri said, invading on Leopold's thoughts. "This is a young man's domain." Although much smaller than the hulking Landenberg, Henri still had the fit body of a knight. He had been fighting off and on in the Holy Lands for almost twenty years and had returned to the Aargau five years ago when his father died. He inherited his father's lands: three lucrative estates in the Aargau and one rocky tract of land at the head of the Gotthard Pass. Not exceptionally rich titles, but Leopold was in negotiations to acquire the Gotthard land to add to the Habsburg family's holdings. Henri's family connections with landowners in Uri, where Saint Gotthard's Pass was located, had proved valuable when Leopold had purchased land at the head of the pass last year. The same land where Leopold currently had fifty stone masons constructing a fortress that would be his new home. He needed some farmland to support the fortress, and poor though it was, Henri's small estate should do nicely. Henri's Connections would prove useful in the coming years if Leopold were to bring the pass under Habsburg control.

"Count Hunenberg is right. You have seen too many years to be playing the part of a ram so sit down and accept your place. I would wager there is not a man on this field who would not rather be one of my governors than chafing under sweaty armor."

Landenberg grunted at the rebuke. "If I had your youth, my lord, I would gladly be on that field winning my share of honors."

"Honor is a myth. The tourney was created to keep our warriors occupied in times of peace. To prevent the dogs from turning on their masters, if you will. A soldier is a tool of the nobility. One that must be stored with care, mind you, and sharpened regularly, but nothing more."

"And when that tool ages and shows signs of rust?" Count Henri asked. "What then?"

Leopold did not hesitate. "We throw it out. Or occasionally, the axe is melted down and reshaped into a hoe." He made a point in looking at Landenberg as he spoke.

Henri stood, smiling at Landenberg's discomfort, and said to Leopold, "All this talk of politics has stirred my bowels. If you will excuse me, my lord." He stepped down off the dais and moved between two merchant stalls, one selling fire-roasted sausages on a stick and the other small loaves of crusty dark bread.

Leopold motioned the next pair of combatants into the ring. Landenberg, scowling, wedged himself back down into his chair. His eyes lit up when he recognized one of the combatants, a thick young man with blonde hair and the neck of a bull whose shield bore the markings of several tourneys he had won.

"Ah. Now we shall see some sport," Landenberg said. "That is Sir Rolf of Nuremberg—saw him kill a man on this field last year. Damned fool's helm was too big and the force of Sir Rolf's blow shook his skull to pieces."

"He does appear capable," Leopold said, but his eyes were on Rolf's opponent.

He was a thin, unremarkable fellow with greying hair at least fifteen years older than any competitor on the field. And unlike the other fighters, the only armor he wore was a light mail vest that was almost hidden beneath a faded black tunic. Leather bracers covered his wrists, but there were neither plates on his shoulders or legs, nor a gorget around his throat. The older man hefted several different swords from the weapons rack and tested them for balance, shifting each one carefully from hand to hand, before finally deciding on a smaller one-handed blade with a single cutting edge.

Leopold's lips turned up in a smirk. The young duke had been raised amongst men such as this. From an early age Leopold had been sent by his father to live for months at a time in soldier barracks throughout the German Empire, France, Denmark, and Italia. While his older brothers were kept at King Albrecht's side in Austria to learn how to rule, Leopold's father shipped him off to live with foreign tutors. Not so much to learn to be a soldier, but to learn how one thinks. To recognize what motivates them and what kind of discipline it takes to control them. He learned to read men's eyes, their postures, what body types made a good horseman, and which were better suited to infantry. Who would be loyal and who could be bribed. This was his education. From the ages of ten to fifteen, Leopold saw his father only three times, at public functions of state that demanded a show of Habsburg solidarity. Frederick had visited his younger brother regularly, but both Leopold's father and oldest brother were strangers who happened to share the same family name.

"One hundred silver says the old man makes your Sir Rolf yield like a pliant serving girl."

Landenberg's eyebrows arched and he looked at Sir Rolf's opponent for the first time. He saw only an aging man with inferior equipment desperate to earn some prize money and perhaps, to hold onto a piece of his youth.

"Let us make it two hundred, and since you mentioned a serving girl, you arrange to have the innkeeper in Schwyz send his daughter to serve in my household."

Leopold had no idea who this innkeeper was, but it did not matter.

"Done," he said, waving his hand to a nearby servant. The aroma of the nearby roasted sausages had watered his mouth. He summoned a page and soon he had a hot, spitting sausage on a stick in one hand and a piece of dark bread in the other. He nibbled off a piece of the succulent meat and settled back into his chair to watch the match.

The master of the ring called the men to their marks.

"For the pleasure of our Lord Leopold, Prince of the august German Empire, Duke of Further Austria and Styria, Regent and heir—" Leopold made a cutting motion across his neck and waved impatiently at the man. He bowed stiffly and continued. "Lords and ladies, our next contest shall be between Sir Rolf of Nuremberg and…" He leaned close to the older man and asked him something. "…and…Gissler."

✧   ✧   ✧

Gissler bore no shield or helm, but walked calmly to his starting position. He avoided looking at his opponent. Sir Rolf's face visor was raised and strands of blonde hair poked out from beneath his chain coif. A green silk kerchief from some female admirer fluttered in the breeze at his belt.

"Fear not grandfather," Sir Rolf said to his older opponent in a clear tone that carried far into the ranks of spectators. "You will suffer no serious injury by my hand." Laughter rippled through the crowd.

Gissler looked up for the first time at his much larger adversary. His eyes narrowed and flitted casually over the young knight. He rolled his shoulders once and spit on the ground.

"Of that I am sure," Gissler said. He lifted his sword to a low guard.

Sir Rolf flinched at the impetuous attitude of his lowborn opponent. A few people close enough to hear Gissler's quiet response cheered. One boisterous man yelled, "Take him over your knee old man!"

"Begin," shouted the master of the ring and backpedaled away from between the two men. The crowd erupted.

Sir Rolf raised his shield and stalked forward without

bothering to lower his visor. Gissler waited for him to close the distance and then changed to a high guard. He swung his sword at Sir Rolf's head and the young knight thrust his shield up to meet the blow and set up his counter. With surprising speed for such a large man in full armor, Sir Rolf took the blow on his shield and then dipped it to the side as he swung his hand and a half sword towards Gissler. But the older man was no longer in front of him.

The moment the knight's vision was blocked by his own shield, Gissler spun around his shield arm to Sir Rolf's back, lifted his foot and smashed it down into the back of the young man's knee, then thrust his shoulder into his back to topple the man forward. The knight hit the ground hard, coughing once as the air fled from his lungs. Gissler turned and whipped his sword down onto the back of Sir Rolf's helm so hard the blade shattered like an icicle dropping onto a winter-hardened flagstone floor. Sir Rolf's eyes jerked up into his head, the color all but disappearing and leaving only vacant whites staring into the crowd. He slowly pitched forward from his knees onto his face and did not move.

The crowd fell silent at the violent and excessive blow, but once it dawned on them the fight was over the cheering began. Sir Rolf's squires pushed forward and rolled their liege lord onto his side and carefully removed his helm. He was unconscious, but came to moaning when they sat him up, and the sudden movement caused him to retch. Vomit cascaded down his chin, while a squire frantically used his sleeve to wipe the unseemly mess off Sir Rolf's polished chest protector.

The ringmaster pushed his way forward and, his eyes wide with surprise, raised his arm in Gissler's direction. "The winner is…Gessel!"

Gissler was already moving out of the circle toward the

weapon racks when he heard his name called.

"Gissler? By God, what land is this? Is that really you?" Count Henri stepped out of the crowd and clamped his hand on Gissler's shoulder. Gissler flinched, and he looked as though he might repel this new attacker, but then recognition flooded his face and he stared open-mouthed, unable to speak.

"But of course it is—I recognize your work," Henri said, nodding towards Sir Rolf's squires struggling to get their lord on his feet.

"Henri," Gissler said finally, shaking his head. "Look at you." He stepped back and gestured at the Count's richly tailored clothes and plumed hat. "A lord of peacocks if ever there was one." The two men laughed and threw their arms around one another in a rough soldier embrace.

"What are you doing here? Why are you not with the Order on Rhodes? I have word the Turks are giving the black knights an awful time on that rock."

Gissler shrugged. "That no longer concerns us. The Grand Master released us from our oaths coming on a year now."

"Us? Who else is with you man?"

"Every Schwyzer crew member of *The Wyvern*." Gissler told Henri how he had traveled back with Thomas, Pirmin, Ruedi, Anton, Urs, and Max. A puzzled look crossed Henri's face.

"But what of the others? Thomas's crew had three score of you when I was last aboard. What of Lars and Gerhard? And that pug-faced fellow who fell in love with every Saracen whore he saw?"

Gissler nodded, but his smile turned grim. "Geoff. Turks captured him during one of our raids on the coast. He was known to them, so his passing was not easy, I have been told. Lars has been dead nigh ten years, about the time the

Mohammedans stopped accepting ransom for Hospitallers. We lost Gerhard at Rhodes, and as for the others..." Gissler held up his hands and shrugged. "We have been fighting a long time."

Henri's grin faded and after a moment, he nodded.

"The mind tries hard to forget the wars in Outremer after leaving. Some memories are better left stored away, I suppose, but I shall make a point of remembering the Schwyzers in my prayers tonight. They were good lads. Some, like your captain Thomas, a little pious and headstrong, but a more loyal core of soldiers I have never known."

He winked and put his hand on Gissler's shoulder again. "But enough. I am sure you wish to put all that behind you now, so welcome home. What are your plans?"

Gissler shrugged. "I arrived only yesterday," he said.

Out of the corner of his eye, Henri noticed Duke Leopold ascending from his dais and walking in their direction, his man Klaus hulking one step behind. Leopold was looking directly at Gissler, but pretending not to.

"Well, it seems fate is descending upon you as we speak. Let us make the most of it, shall we? Come, allow me to present you to the Duke."

✧ ✧ ✧

"You were a soldier in the Holy Lands?" Leopold asked.

"Yes, my lord," Gissler said.

"He was no mere soldier. Gissler was with the Black Knights," Count Henri said.

Leopold's eyes widened and he looked a little harder at Gissler.

Ah, I see it now, he thought. The alert way the man carried himself hinted at a life of discipline, but the aloof mannerisms and impetuous eyes betrayed him. He was indeed used to being seen as more than a mere soldier. He was far above that. He was one of God's chosen warriors, a Gabriel here on Earth. These Black Knights answered to no one but the Pope and God himself, just as the Templars once did. The Church had decreed that not even kings could command these men, never mind a lowly Duke of the German Empire.

"Your Order has done a great service protecting Christendom from the infidels. You are a Hospitaller Knight then?"

Gissler's mouth twitched at the corner, and he paused before responding.

"Not a knight, your Grace. Merely a brother sergeant-at-arms. Or I was. I have recently been released from the Order."

Leopold nodded, noting the bitter edge to Gissler's voice. The Knights of Saint John were largely made up of nobles from France, Germany, England, Spain, and Italia. They were required to give up their noble rights and will their land and holdings to the Order upon their death. They also took vows of chastity and poverty, and swore to accept the poor and sick as their lords. But the title of "Knight" was reserved for those of noble blood. Despite the Order's disdain for secular titles, there existed a strict hierarchy within the Order itself, and no commoner could ever rise above the rank of brother-sergeant.

"Tell me Hospitaller. What do you think of the recent trial and condemnation of the Templar Knights by his Holiness the Pope? I understand they were rivals of your Order in a way."

Seven years previous, the Christian world had been shocked to hear the Church and King Philip of France accuse the Templar Knights of heresy. The charges included spitting upon the cross, permitting sodomy, idol worshipping, and denying Christ and treading upon his image. Templars throughout Europe were arrested, including the Grandmaster

Jacques de Molay. Subsequently, Molay and many others were subjected to the inquisition and confessed their crimes under torture. They had been kept in the dungeons of France for the past seven years awaiting their fate.

"We were both working to carry out God's will. I never considered them rivals," Gissler said.

"I have read the charges against the Temple. Incredible. And the knights have confessed to many of them. Did you know they worshipped a skull with three faces?"

"I did not," Gissler said.

"And they rubbed small cords on this idol which they then wore wrapped around various parts of their bodies. The grandmaster himself confessed that the idol was responsible for imbuing the knights with great riches. Behavior more fitting a coven of witches than a holy order, do you not agree?"

"A man will confess to much under torture," Gissler said, shifting his weight.

"Would he? Does not God dull the pain of the righteous? The Church tells us the innocent have nothing to fear from the inquisitor's tools of truth. And in fact, the courts will not recognize a confession unless it has been obtained through torture. Is that not so?"

"It is my lord."

"Well, it is in the past now I suppose, since the Grandmaster of the Temple has been burned at the stake. Ah, I see you did not know this."

Gissler cleared his throat. "The last I heard Grandmaster Molay had been cleared of all charges."

"Apparently King Philip of France decided otherwise. It is no secret that he has coveted the Templars' holdings in France for many years, but his plan bore no fruit. The Pope transferred all Templar estates to the Hospitallers. How in the world your Grandmaster convinced the Pope to do that, I cannot imagine. What do you suppose he will do with all that wealth now? Continue fighting the infidel? After nearly two hundred years it seems pointless really."

"As I said, I have no knowledge of any of this, my lord. I have been on the road for the better part of a year."

Leopold could tell the conversation was making Gissler uncomfortable, but to his credit he held the Duke's intense gaze with his own look of defiance. If he had been a normal peasant, Leopold would have had him whipped. Or worse. But he was a Hospitaller man-at-arms. A soldier forged in the wars of the Levant, and there was no finer training ground for his kind. And now, much to Leopold's liking, he was without a master.

A murmur shot through the crowd as the next two competitors made their way to the clearing and readied themselves for battle.

"Where does the name Gissler hail from? It sounds familiar," Leopold asked.

Gissler's face brightened. "Here in the Aargau, my lord. My family is steward for one of the King's estates near Sursee. Perhaps you know of my father? Hubert Gissler? Or, I suppose it possible my older brother Hugo is now chief steward."

Leopold pursed his lips and turned to his man Klaus. The old soldier thought for a moment and then cleared his throat. When he finally spoke, his voice sounded like gravel sliding down a rock slope.

"King Albrecht granted that land to a French Count years ago. Brought in his own people to run it. Man named Lafayette is steward now."

The light in Gissler's eyes faded as quickly as it had appeared.

"They may still be working the land," Count Henri said. "And if not, someone there would surely know where to find them."

Gissler nodded slowly.

The crowd cheered again as the ringmaster called the combatants to their marks.

"Come Klaus. We must be returning to Kussnacht," Leopold said.

"You will not stay and see the outcome of the tourney?" Count Henri asked.

Leopold waved his hand. "I have my wedding to prepare for, and besides, the outcome of the tourney was decided the moment our Hospitaller entered. For who can compete with someone who has God on his side?"

The young Duke held the trace of a smile in his eyes but did not wait for an answer as he turned to take his leave. At the last moment, seemingly as an afterthought, he turned back and said, "Gissler, once you have sorted out your family affairs, come to Habsburg castle. Perhaps I will have work for you."

Klaus strode a few steps ahead of Leopold, cutting a path through the crowd with wide sweeps of his tree-limb arms, as they made their way to a waiting carriage with an armed escort of a dozen mounted soldiers clothed in the Habsburg colors of black and red. Two flag-bearers, one carrying a standard with the red lion of Habsburg, and the other a black bird of prey on a field of yellow, the colors of the Holy Roman Empire, stood nearby. A lithe figure with purple hair twisted its way through the hundreds of spectators and was waiting at the carriage door seconds before Leopold arrived.

By late afternoon Leopold's predictions had materialized, for no knight at the country tourney could stand before Gissler's speed and skill. He dispatched his opponents with a ruthless efficiency, never taking longer than one or two minutes, except on those occasions when he decided a knight needed to be toyed with and publicly humiliated. Every man who faced him sustained injuries and limped, crawled, or was carried from the circle. By the final matches, Gissler's ferocious reputation did as much to defeat his opponents as his sword blows.

After the final match, while a young knight still lay on the ground, his feet twitching in unconsciousness, Gissler took his prize purse and walked away.

He left the championship cup and pennant sitting on the table.

CHAPTER 6

SPRING BURST upon the Alps like God was determined to thaw the Devil's glaciers and drive the mighty stone crags back into the recesses of the earth once and for all. The green-covered slopes erupted in golden clusters of cowslips, interspersed with patches of blue grape hyacinths. Sparkling streams of the sweetest water trickled down every hill, and what seemed like an endless assortment of wild game suddenly appeared.

To Thomas and Pirmin, after a lifetime of campaigning in the deserts of the Levant, it seemed like a miracle. They welcomed the heat and worked better in it.

Thomas had convinced the old ferryman to sell his barge for twice what it was worth, making Thomas wish Max had been there to help him negotiate. During his life with the Order Thomas had very little experience with money and business dealings had always made him uncomfortable. It did not help matters when Pirmin finally saw the old barge Thomas had spent most of his savings on.

"Thomi, Thomi. I agreed to help you fix up a boat. Not build one from scratch."

It was really no more than a rectangular raft of log floats covered with thick decking, most of which was rotting and in need of repair. It was large enough to carry five or six horses and perhaps ten men. The ferryman had connected it to a come-along system of ropes and pulleys hitched to a team of oxen on land. He was able to transport people across a narrow arm of the lake, and though it proved a safe way to cut almost two hours off the trip around the outside of the lake via the road, it could only cross at the same point every time.

Thomas knew it was not much, but he had a weakness for boats of all shapes and sizes and in his mind he saw what they could be. He meant to unshackle this barge and sail her freely. To him anything still sitting above the water had a God-given right to sail.

He was well versed in the mechanical laws that made sailing possible, but he did not credit their development to the ingenuity of men. Standing on the high side of a boat with the sails reefed in tight while she sailed almost straight into the wind was as close as one could get to God, for without His assistance, how else could a boat move forward with the wind blowing in your face, striving to halt your progress and spin you off in the opposite direction?

"A little work never killed a man, but you never were one to understand that," Thomas said, shaking his head. "Do not look down on her. She's got good bones and once we fit her with a leeboard, mast and a lateen-rigged yard, she will cut through this lake fast enough."

"You mean to sail the beast? She will handle like what she is—a pile of logs held together with pitch! At least when she sinks and we have built up an appetite from our swim to shore, we will be able to eat the oxen."

"We could have..." Thomas said. "If I had the silver to buy them."

Pirmin groaned and held his head between his massive

hands.

"And where are you going to get good planks if you already spent all your coin?"

Thomas picked up one of two old axes the ferryman had included in the deal. Holding it by the head, he pointed with the handle at the forest behind Pirmin.

"We have a shipbuilder's dream of resources. Have you ever in your life seen trees as tall and straight as that? Granted, it may take a little more effort than ready cut timber—"

"You always insist on doing it the hard way, eh Captain?"

"Ah, but the ability to work hard is God's gift to the common man," Thomas said smiling. The scar tightened on his skin, but under the hot sun and with only Pirmin standing before him, it felt good.

They worked on the barge and lived in a tent on the water's edge, rising before dawn and starting early to avoid the mid-day's heat. Every day, they would watch in silence as the sun rose above the Alps and infused the Great Lake with light, turning the deep water a glimmering emerald green. It became a breathless ritual with them; one which involved no conversation for they could find no words to express how utterly different this life was from the one they had been living only a year ago.

But they did not live in isolation. Every few days, whenever they tired of camp cooking, they would saddle up their horses and ride into Schwyz. They would buy supplies and take a meal at Sutter's Inn, the same inn and tavern that they had stopped at the first night they had spent in Schwyz those few weeks past. The inn had been in the Sutter family for generations, but with the recent traffic increase over Saint Gotthard's Pass, Sutter's business grew to be too much for his family alone and he found himself hiring on a cook and another widow to help his wife make the ale and honeyed mead.

"Sutter says he knows a man with a bitch that just had a new litter," Pirmin said one night as they rode back from the inn, their bellies swollen with stew and ale. A half-moon hung over the Great Lake, sharing its other half with the water's surface.

The comment snapped Thomas out of the hypnotic trance brought on by the rhythm of Anid's gait and he looked up at Pirmin's silhouette. The size of the big man's charger made Thomas feel like he was rowing a skiff alongside a war galley. Thomas's stallion, Anid, was a pure Egyptian, a breed many Franks would consider too light to carry a fully armored man into battle. But Thomas had found Anid to have the perfect combination of strength and fearlessness for the role. And like most Arabian horses, Anid's speed and endurance was far greater than any destrier Thomas had ever ridden.

"You remember Zora?" Pirmin asked, his features unreadable in the dim moonlight.

"Of course," Thomas said.

How could he forget? Every couple years Pirmin would bring up his childhood dog and talk about her. Usually when he was drunk. And once again, at the mention of Zora, a wave of exhaustion shot through Thomas's body as his muscles remembered the long march from Schwyz to the shores of the Mid-Earth Sea.

A blonde-haired, scowling boy walked beside Thomas and though his words were laced with an accent Thomas struggled to understand, the boy talked enough that Thomas soon grew accustomed to his speech.

He was older, perhaps eight, but already his stocky build hinted at the massive man he would become. At his side walked the biggest working dog Thomas had ever seen. She was shorthaired and largely black, with a powerful white chest and snout, and a square head with a mask of black surrounding even blacker eyes. She would have been terrifying if it were not for the rust-colored thumbprints above her eyes that softened her expressions. The draft dog was hitched to a cart that she pulled effortlessly with a nonchalant grace, as though trying to pretend it was not there.

After a grueling three-month journey by land and then sea, the army of children was marching on a dusty road, less than five hours from the gates of Acre, when slavers came for them.

An avalanche of boulders and smaller rocks careened down the steep hillside, crushing a knight and the handful of children in its path. A deafening rumble echoed all around them and dust billowed up and choked the gorge. Then, a hundred men appeared and swarmed down into the ravine like so many ants, yelling and screaming in various languages.

All around Thomas was chaos. Dust hung in the air like smoke and children were running, screaming, trying to escape the slavers who seemed to be everywhere with ropes and leather collars. Thomas saw one of the black knights pinned to the ground with a spear, and two more fighting in the distance, several bodies at their feet.

Thomas pressed his back up against the rock wall of the canyon, trying to disappear, as he watched Zora savage the throat of one of the slavers that moments before had been dragging Pirmin away by his hair. Pirmin snatched up the dead man's war axe and leveled it at a heavyset man with a full beard and dark, fleshy circles under his eyes who stalked warily towards the snarling dog.

The man raised a heavy crossbow and shot an iron bolt

into Zora's side, lifting her up and throwing her away from the dead man. She yelped, her feet scrambling briefly to find purchase on the rocky ground before her strength gave out and she toppled over on her side.

Zora raised her head once weakly to bite at the shaft lodged deep between her ribs. Shaking with the effort, she was unable to reach it, and finally her head dropped hard to the ground, as though it were made of stone. She panted a few times. Then, with a whole-body shudder, she died.

Pirmin, eyes wide and chest heaving, charged the man with his axe while screaming something in his strange accent that Thomas could not comprehend. The heavy man dropped his crossbow, sidestepped, and caught the axe shaft twisting it out of the young boy's hands. Then he whipped the butt-end across Pirmin's face. To the man's surprise, the enraged boy took the blow, threw his arms around the slaver's upper legs and drove his head into his stomach, knocking them both to the ground. Pirmin straddled the man and rained blows down upon the man's face and chest.

Although big, Pirmin was still just a boy and his adversary outweighed him by at least a hundred and fifty pounds. His blows were ineffective and once the man recovered from the fall to the ground and the surprise of the boy's ferociousness, he rolled the boy over and beat him without mercy until Pirmin's hands fell limp at his side and blood flowed freely from his mouth and nose.

The slaver stood up quickly, as though embarrassed, and produced a rope from his belt with several leather collars strung along its length. He kicked the stunned Pirmin over on his stomach and kneeled to slip one over Pirmin's head, cinching the metal buckle in place at the back of his neck. The boy coughed into the dusty ground and moaned, but other than that did not try to fight back.

Thomas stared at the big dog's still form. Zora was dead, and already at that young age, Thomas knew well the consequences that went along with death. It meant that as soon as she was out of his sight, he would never see her again. And somehow he understood, without the smallest doubt that the man kneeling over Pirmin intended to take Thomas's friend far away, to a place Pirmin did not want to go.

"Good folk, the Sutters," Pirmin said, bringing Thomas back to the moment. These days, Thomas hardly noticed his singsong Wallis accent, but others did. Especially women.

"Their girl has a fondness for you," Thomas said. "Though she is not much more than a child."

Pirmin laughed, a deep, honest sound that bubbled up from his soul and would put at ease anyone within earshot.

"I have done nothing to encourage that. And even if I had, Mera will be of a marrying age in another season."

"Do not even think it. She is a child, and you older than her father." Though, Thomas admitted to himself, Pirmin looked ten years younger than his age and his boyish good looks had faded little over the years.

"Ah but she's a beauty that one. Might be just the woman to pluck me out of this monk's life I have been living all these years."

Thomas grunted. "I think you do not fully grasp the meaning of the word *monk*. Monks do not sleep through matins because they have been out all night whoring."

"Whoa. Easy now, Captain. I would appreciate it if you did not put me in the company of the common soldier. I do not have anything against whores, a necessary trade if you ask me, but one I prefer not to support. In fact, I have paid for a woman only twice in my life, once—"

Thomas interrupted. "Once before you knew you could get it for free, and another time when your lovemaking was so rigorous you were sure you left the woman with child. I have heard the story more times than you have told it."

"Ah, yes of course. I know how you and the rest of the lads would whisper about me in the dark of the barracks after I had snuck out."

Thomas shook his head in denial, but there was some truth to the big man's words. From a young age Pirmin had developed an appreciation for the fairer sex, and they for him, and so had a tendency to stray from the converted stables that had become the boys home in Acre's Hospitaller fortress.

By the time he was thirteen he was taller than most men and seemed to know every tavern and shopkeeper in the crowded city. How he managed to escape the fortress at night after the portcullis had been dropped, no one knew, but it was well known that he was the main supplier of goods sold by Max, who ran his own secret merchant stall in the barracks. For many boys, as well as some of the monks, who had lived most of their lives inside the Hospitaller fortress, Pirmin was their link to the outside world, and he played the part well.

A natural entertainer, he told stories of tavern brawls and wild women that few believed, but they hung on every word nonetheless. And when he was led into the courtyard and forced to make what the Abbot termed the *march of shame* to the whipping post, he did so with his head held high and shoulders thrown back, like some mythical hero, as boys laughed and cheered him on. He never cried out when the strap bit into his exposed flesh and when it was done he would limp away, but not without smiling or winking at a few of the other children, as if to say *you know it was worth it.*

The Schwyzers were inducted into the Order of Saint John

as brother-sergeants; fighting men. They were required to take the Vow of Obediance, and the Vow of Poverty, but not the Vow of Chastity, and that Pirmin often said, was God's way of telling him that it was his duty to share himself with the female populace. Thomas knew, of course, it merely showed that the Schwyzers were meant to be an expendable military arm of the Order and, since their life expectancy was so very short, nothing more was expected of them.

Still, living amongst monks and priests had had its influence, and unlike Pirmin, Thomas had taken his studies seriously. Women were the origin of sin and Satan's ultimate instrument of temptation. One that Thomas had successfully resisted his entire life, though he saw little evidence of the Devil in most women.

"I wonder what he is doing now?" Pirmin said suddenly.

"Who?"

"You know, my son."

"You cannot be talking about the whore you imagined you planted your seed in?" Thomas said.

"Of course. A man can tell when he has sired offspring, you know. Wonder if he looks like me? Or his mother…cannot rightly recall what she looked like though. Comely I think."

Thomas shook his head. "If you left that woman with child she no doubt went to a witch and had it rooted out."

"No," Pirmin said, shaking his head. "I would have known. And why so negative brother? Jealous I have a son out there somewhere?"

"Probably a daughter. A seven-foot hulking brute of a daughter terrifying the countryside."

Pirmin grimaced and clenched his teeth. The possibility of a daughter had never entered his mind.

"Nah, not possible. Definitely a boy."

They rode on in silence for a while, the muted thudding of hooves on grass the only sound.

"You ever think about it Thomi? Having a family?"

"No," he said.

"You should think on it. This would be a nice place to raise one, and I do not know how much longer I will be around. Have to push on to Wallis soon, I suppose."

Thomas nodded, forgetting it was probably too dark for Pirmin to see the gesture. He would miss the man deeply when he left, though he would never let Pirmin know that. For over thirty years the Order had been his family, and it was strange to imagine being alone, truly alone. Strange, but not frightening, like he had once thought it would be.

A peace washed over him as he imagined living out the rest of his life as a ferryman on the shores of this lake, knowing he had served out his time as God's soldier to the best of his ability. Perhaps this stage of his life was his reward for faithful service. A taste of Heaven here on Earth.

"Why so quiet? What are you thinking about Thomi? You make me nervous when you get like that."

Thomas took a deep breath of the warm night air. He nudged Anid with his knees to pick up the pace. The stallion surged ahead.

They were both eager for home.

CHAPTER 7

GISSLER HOVERED at the edge of the trees looking at the small hovel in the distance. An aged man struggled across the muddy courtyard carrying a bucket of slop, each jerky step causing a foul splash down his leg. Finally, with a Herculean effort he upended the bucket into a pigpen's trough, and a half dozen dirty sows squealed with delight.

The man was gaunt, a fact even the full grey beard and baggy russet clothes could not conceal. Gissler recognized the man as his brother only on some primal, spiritual level, for there was nothing left of the proud older boy he had looked up to as a child. Hugo was only five years older than Gissler, but the bent, misshapen figure shuffling about the pigpen looked to be in his sixties. Gissler could not remember even his father looking as old, or broken, as his brother did now.

The Gisslers had been a family with stature. Being stewards of land for three generations had given them a position of respect within the community and the right to a share of the land's crops and animals. His father always talked about the peasant class as *those* people. He knew the Gisslers did not have any blue blood, but in his heart he felt they were much closer to the noble class than that of peasants.

He had been wrong. When King Albrecht rewarded a

French count the estate, the Gisslers were unceremoniously forced to leave the land they had faithfully managed for more than fifty years. It must have been a devastating transition for his father to learn to rut in the mud as just another peasant, Gissler thought, and upon seeing the sorry living conditions of his elder brother, one that his father could not have survived.

"You come to talk with my papa?"

Gissler whirled at the sound of the voice to see a small girl no older than seven years old. Dirty bare feet stuck out the bottom of her grey, threadbare dress, which may have been pale blue at one time. She had a small mountain flower pinned in her hair and a few more clutched in one tiny hand. In the other she cupped a baby bird close to her chest.

"He is just over there, if you want to talk to him," she said pointing with her chin.

"What is your name?" Gissler asked, surprised at the little girl's fearlessness.

"Sara," she said.

She had her father's large brown eyes. They were the eyes Gissler remembered from his boyhood.

"Actually, I came to see you," Gissler said.

Sara's eyes narrowed. "Why do you want to see me? I am just a kid."

Gissler laughed and the sound made Sara smile.

"A friend of your father's asked me to give him something, but I am in a hurry. I was hoping you could give it to him for me. Would you do that?"

Sara shrugged. "I guess so. But I have to put this bird back in his nest first. I saved him from a cat, you know."

"Fair enough. I will help you and then you help me. Agreed?"

"You said you were in a hurry."

"I make time for worthy causes. And I can think of no purpose higher right now than returning your friend to his home."

With only a slight hesitation, she led Gissler to the bird's tree and pointed out the nest. He asked about her family and learned her mother and brother died and she never had any grandparents. Only a papa.

After the bird was tucked safely back in its nest, Gissler hung the coin purse that he had won at the tourney around Sara's neck.

"Take this to your father right away," he said. "I think he may be waiting for it."

She promised she would and started walking back towards the cabin.

Then she turned abruptly. She ran back and handed Gissler one of the little white flowers she still held in her hand.

"Here. Take this. It will protect you from the bad elves."

Without a moment's pause, she was off again running full speed towards the house.

Hugo looked up in alarm at the sound of his daughter's calls. She ran up to him and he listened to her words stumble over one another in an excited recounting of the man she had met in the forest. His eyes went wide when he opened the purse. He looked up and scanned the woods, searching for any sign of the man.

A soft wind stirred the trees, but nothing more.

CHAPTER 8

THE FIRST HEAT of summer was upon them by the time Thomas and Pirmin finished work on the ferry. Thomas had his first customer the same day they completed rigging the sail; a goat herder moving his herd to new pasture. He paid with a bag of green apples, and the goats left their own payment all over the ferry deck. It took Thomas and Pirmin the rest of the day to scrub down the wooden planking.

That was enough of the ferry business for Pirmin. He began hanging out more often at Sutter's inn doing odd jobs for the family. Sutter would usually pay him with food and ale, which suited Pirmin just fine. But Thomas knew Pirmin would have done the work for nothing, so long as he could sit in the evenings drinking and talking with the inn's patrons. It did not matter whether they were traveling merchants or the local regulars.

Thomas had never seen another man like him. So huge and terrifying on one level, but if left in a room for an hour with total strangers, they would part as the closest friends, slapping each other on the back, and swearing to get together soon.

Pirmin set up a bed in Sutter's hayloft and Thomas saw him less and less. At first Thomas would go to the inn every other day, but lately his trips had grown less frequent. Unlike Pirmin, Thomas found little pleasure in the company of strangers. Where Pirmin saw the good in people, Thomas was deeply suspicious of almost everyone, and he found being in large groups of strangers exhausting. So he spent more time alone working on a cabin near his ferry, seeing one or two people a day, many of the locals as wary of the new ferryman as he was of them.

Thomas stood on the wharf originally built by a ferryman long before the time of the one he had bought the barge from. He wrapped the ends of a rope, making a mental note that he should replace it the first chance he had enough coin, and stowed it on the bottom of the barge.

His eye caught something moving up the road. Whoever was coming, was not moving fast. He continued with his inspection of every sheet and halyard on his ferry, and when he next looked down the road, the lone figure began to take shape.

It was an old woman, hunched over by the years and rail thin. Her threadbare cloak flapped around her bones in the breeze like a flour sack snagged on scrub brush. Slung across her back, threatening to topple her with every step, was something heavy. Her eyes were fixed on Thomas as she stepped onto the dock and made her way to the side of the ferry. Thomas picked up another rope and began running the length through his hands.

The old woman halted in front of Thomas and pushed back the hood of her cloak, letting much-needed light into eyes whitened with age. She kinked her neck up at an awkward angle to look at Thomas and stared at him, her eyes scrutinizing his face and coming to rest on the pale jagged line running down the left side. For all her physical ailments, her voice was surprisingly strong and clear.

"You would be the one they call the ferryman. They said I could tell by the scar."

"Or the ferry," Thomas said, nodding at the barge he stood on. "You looking to go to the other side old woman?"

"Not yet," she said, offended. "I have a few more years in me."

She continued to stare at the scar on Thomas's face and did not say anything else. The silence was uncomfortable. Thomas leaned over and tucked away his coil of rope, then stepped onto the wharf. When he faced the woman again he had his left side angled away.

"Something I can do for you then, grandmother?"

"Came to give you something," she said.

"Oh? And what might that be?"

The woman reached to her shoulder and struggled briefly to duck her head under the shoulder strap. She held out the pack with both hands.

"Take it," she said. Her arms were starting to shake. "Take it! Cannot hold this thing all day."

He reached out, not because he wanted anything from her, but he thought she might fall over if he did not relieve her of the weight. He took the bag and helped the old woman sit on the edge of his barge. The bag was heavy; the woman was stronger than she looked to have carried it from who knew where. He peered inside cautiously.

"It is a wheel of cheese. One of our better ones. Me and my daughter made it. Her son helped some, but mostly he is useless that one."

Within the pack, the cheese was carefully wrapped in a clean white cloth, which did little to keep the enticing aroma contained.

"It smells delicious. But why give this to me if you have no need to cross?"

She gave no indication that she had heard his question. "When my daughter was born, we did not have animals. Very few people in these parts did. Were grain farmers for years, then finally we came together as a community and got some pigs." She paused and looked out over the water for a time.

Thomas nodded and glanced helplessly around. The woman was old and had no one to talk to. But then again, neither did he.

"Pigs are good, I suppose," he said.

The woman shook her head, the movement more a quiver. "We knew nothing about animals then. Not how cruel they could be, or how a sow will deny the runts of her litter her milk."

Thomas knew little of animals himself. To keep up their strength during campaigns, the fighting men of the Hospitallers were permitted to eat meat. But since the monks and priests of the order were forbidden to consume flesh, the Order did not raise its own animals, save for a few chickens and maybe the odd goat for milk. Any meat that ended up on the trenchers of the brother-sergeants was bought at market.

The woman seemed to recognize his confusion, and explained.

"You see, she has only got so much milk and if she let the little weak ones drink, the others, well, they might not get enough to grow up strong. Some of them might even die. Better to let the little ones starve than end up with a whole litter of runts."

She was not looking at Thomas now. Her white eyes were gazing out across the greenish blue waters again.

"Me and my husband never cared much about that. We

were just happy to have some animals. Life had been much harder before we got those pigs. But every time we had to pull dead piglets out of the pen, our daughter would cry and ask us why. Every time. It is God's will, we would tell her. Every time."

"Children can get attached to farm animals," Thomas said. He remembered Zora from all those years ago and how hard Pirmin had cried when his dog was killed. He cringed inwardly at the memory.

The old woman had not seemed to hear him. She was lost in a different time.

"Eventually, we got rid of those pigs, when we could afford to. Sold them and bought a cow, couple of goats."

"And now you make cheese. Fine cheese by the smell of it," Thomas said.

There was something about the woman that was beginning to grow on him. She was a survivor and he sensed an inner strength about her. She heard him this time and when she turned to look at him, he felt her eyes probing. She wanted something from him. Something she would never ask for.

"Still, I cannot look at my daughter today and not see that poor little thing of yesteryear crying her eyes out. I wonder if she blames me. Sometimes I think I should have given those first pigs back. Kept to grain farming."

Her thin shoulders fell and she seemed to be trapped in her memories of the past. Finally, she spoke. "But the truth is, we would have all starved. We needed those pigs."

The old woman looked at Thomas, her jaw set firmly. She motioned for him to help her up. He did so and she put the hood of her cloak back up. Then, without another word, she turned and began to walk back the way she had come.

"Are you sure you do not need me to help you go somewhere?" Thomas asked, puzzled by her sudden departure.

Without stopping or even turning to look back, the old woman said, "You have done more than your bit. Enjoy the cheese ferryman."

Thomas shook his head. *Crazy old woman.*

He picked up another rope and began working it through practiced hands, squeezing and pulling, testing for weaknesses. He watched the old woman until she eventually receded into the distance and disappeared amongst the green slopes.

He heard the heavy breathing of the two men before he saw them. Unlike the hard-packed desert ground in Outremer, the grassy slopes in this country muffled the sounds of approaching footsteps. Thomas turned to see two men struggling down the hill toward him, one leaning heavily on the other for support.

Even though one man was obviously injured, they moved quickly and were at Thomas's ferry moments later. Thomas helped the one man lower his companion, a boy in his late teens, to the deck. When he took his hand away from the boy's back it was covered in blood.

"We were hunting in the woods and my friend fell off his horse," the man said, speaking quickly. "I need to get him to the healer in the woods fast."

He was only a handful of years older than the injured teen, but he spoke with the commanding confidence of one much more senior. He was used to giving orders.

"What happened to your horses?" Thomas asked.

"Bolted when I got off to help him. Somewhere in the woods yonder," the young man said without hesitation. But when he looked in the direction of the woods his eyes flicked over the landscape nervously, as though searching for something. Thomas got the impression he was not looking for his own horses.

"We better stop that bleeding first, or your friend will not make it to the other side."

The man looked at Thomas and said, "You get this ferry moving and I will see to him. The sooner we get him to the healer the better. I have double your payment here, if that concerns you." He patted the pouch at his belt, next to a short sword in a well-oiled leather scabbard. His eyes were hard, determined, but fear danced at their edges.

A soft groan escaped from the boy on the deck and Thomas turned to see him squirm onto his side.

"Get some pressure on his wound. I will cast off."

The wind was up and they were well out into the deep waters when a dozen horsemen rode into view. They sat atop a hill and watched the ferry make its way across the Great Lake. They were too far away for Thomas to make out the details of their crests, but the way they rode in formation told him they were soldiers. He shook his head as he pondered the ramifications of helping fugitives escape the local authorities. Well, he would worry about that later, he told himself. Right now a man was dying on his deck.

He trimmed the sail and lashed the rudder in place, then went to where the man dabbed at the wound with a dirty rag attempting to staunch the steady flow of blood coming from the boy's back. His ministrations were clumsy and reckless.

Thomas grabbed the man by the wrist.

"Give me that," he said. "You do not know what you are doing."

The young man snarled and pulled his arm free. He dropped the rag and grabbed the handle of his sword.

Thomas ignored him and ripped open the boy's shirt to expose the wound. "You will not be needing to use that on me.

But if you insist on cutting your own throat for almost killing this boy, I will not stop you."

"Watch your tongue ferryman. I saved his life."

"I have seen many things, but never a man who can pull a crossbow bolt out of the middle of his own back. Some unthinking fool pulled it out cutting open every blood vessel around and leaving a jagged hole bigger than some men's brains."

The young man clenched his teeth and glared at Thomas.

"Careful. We are off the bank—out of reach of Landenberg's men. I do not need you anymore to sail this raft."

Thomas pulled out his curved belt knife in one quick motion. The young man jumped to his feet, his hand starting to pull his own blade. Without paying the man even a sidelong glance, Thomas sliced a relatively clean piece of cloth off his own shirt and then pushed it hard against the boy's wound.

"Since you are up, reach in that saddle bag at your feet and hand me some of that clotting moss," Thomas said.

The man glowered, but he relaxed his grip on his sword and did as Thomas asked. Thomas pushed a handful of the moss into the wound and held it for a minute; until he was satisfied the bleeding had slowed. Then he had the man take over and keep pressure on while he went back to helm the ferry and bring her into shore.

Once on shore he cut some clean bandages and produced a moldy piece of bread from his bag along with some more moss. He put them over the wound and wrapped it tightly with the bandages. The young man watched quietly.

"You learn that in the Holy Lands?"

Thomas looked up, his eyebrows knit together. "What makes you so sure you know anything about me?"

The man laughed. "I know more about you Thomas

Schwyzer than you know about yourself. I know you have returned to Schwyz after thirty years of fighting in the Holy Lands. These are my mountains. I have eyes and ears everywhere. If I did not, the Habsburgs would have hung me years ago."

"You are the outlaw Noll Melchthal." The realization came fast. He was a favorite topic between Pirmin and Sutter at the inn, but Thomas had imagined him as a much older man. Apparently this Noll was a brigand wanted by the Habsburgs but was looked on fondly by many of the locals. They saw him as some kind of freedom fighter. The thought of turning him over to the Austrians for a reward crossed Thomas's mind.

"I am no outlaw. I recognize no Habsburg judge and refuse to be ruled by oafs such as Landenberg. He may be the Vogt of Unterwalden, but he has no authority in Schwyz or Uri. We are a free people."

Thomas nodded at the boy lying on the ground. "Talk like that gets people hurt. I know your type. You are a rebel by nature and live only to disrupt the natural order ordained by God."

"Only a fool would believe God wants these lands ruled by Austrian blue-bloods."

"What would you do? Overthrow the noble class? And replace it with what?"

"Do you find it so hard to believe that common people can rule themselves? We need no royalty, or foreign judges enforcing corrupt laws. The Habsburgs get rich from our pain and suffering. It is not right and I have a hundred men under my command that agree. We do not only want to drive the Austrians from our lands, we want justice."

Thomas blinked at the force of Noll's convictions, but then shook his head. One did not simply tamper with the divine natural order. The King and Church worked together to protect the common man from the Devil and himself, not subjugate him. God had granted the peasant class the ability to work in the fields, perhaps learn a trade. They had no capacity for politics, and thrust into that arena would prove incapable of ruling themselves. Politicking was the domain of the noble class, which in turn was under direct control of the King. Together they saw to all matters secular while the Church protected the spiritual souls of all devout Christians.

"True justice can only be dispensed by God. A hundred men is nothing but mouths to feed, for the Habsburgs could have a thousand soldiers on your doorstep tomorrow. Do not be in a hurry to throw your life away in war."

Noll shook his head. "God does not concern himself with justice. I have seen enough of this world to know that."

Thomas crossed himself and leveled a finger at Noll. "Still your tongue. I will have none of your blasphemy on my boat."

"Why not join us, ferryman? You have been back long enough to see the poverty, the corrupt soldiers that reap our lands. Help us drive out the Habsburg blue-bloods."

Thomas shook his head. "You swim in black waters, boy. This will end badly. Mark my words."

Noll scowled at Thomas and then shrugged. He bent low and scooped up his wounded friend, hoisting him across his shoulders. He stood up easily, as though he carried no more than a sack of grain. He was not a large man, but lean and efficient, and his powerful legs did not tremble in the least at the added weight.

"When you are shut up safe in your hut, in front of a warm fire, and the screams of dying country men can be heard beyond your walls, I trust you will say a prayer for them, ferryman."

"I am no priest," Thomas said.

"You talk like one."

Noll turned away. He stepped slowly but took long strides so as not to jostle his precious load. From up the path, without turning his head, he called out, "If you should change your mind and want to meet with me, mention it to Sutter. The right words travel easily in these mountains."

Thomas watched until Noll disappeared in the trees. *The Devil had a purchase on that one,* he thought, and at the same moment, he realized Noll had neglected to pay him for the ferry trip.

CHAPTER 9

"SERAINA!"

She looked up from trimming one of her plants in the direction from which Noll's voice carried. The cry was desperate and the trees marked his coming with incessant whispers, which Seraina followed with her eyes. Seconds later Noll burst into her clearing with Aldo hanging limp across his back.

"Lay him here—in the sunlight," she said.

Together they eased him down onto his side and Seraina began examining the wound on his back, fearing the worst. She peeled back the bandage and was surprised to see the moldy bread and moss covering the wound. She did not move them, but held a hand to Aldo's cheek. He was pale from loss of blood, yet not feverish, as he should be. She placed her other hand on his chest and listened to his heart rhythms while Noll fidgeted at her side. *Deep, but strong and regular.* She leaned back and looked at Noll.

"He will live," she said. "But not by my craft."

Noll, who was still standing, fell down on the ground and wiped the sweat off his brow with the back of his arm. He took in a deep breath.

"Who saw to his wound?" Seraina asked. "It was not you.

That much I know."

Noll still labored over his breathing. He had carried the boy far, and up a steep slope as well. "What? Oh, the new ferryman applied a simple poultice. A pox on his hide, he is a stubborn man that one."

"The ferryman?" Seraina's eyes widened in surprise. The dressing had been wrapped with precision and skill. The use of birch mane to stem the flow of blood and clean the wound was not well known.

She continued to quiz Noll about the man until he threw up his arms and said he knew nothing more, and if she wanted to know more about the ferryman she was going to have to ask him herself.

Noll walked to the rain barrel and ladled some water into one hand and then rubbed them together to wash off the dried blood.

"Can I leave Aldo with you until the morrow? The Eidgenossen are meeting tonight and if I am to reach the meadow in time I had best be on my way."

Ah, Seraina thought. *That explained Noll's foul mood.*

"Has the council finally invited you?" she asked. When the leaders of Uri, Schwyz, and Unterwalden met it was always in secret and strictly by invitation, for they feared reprisals by their Austrian overlords.

"What need do I have for an invitation? I merely assume my father's position, since he cannot be there himself." Noll shook the bloody water off his hands and wiped them on his breeches. "And if Walter Furst, or old Stauffacher try to deny my right to speak, I am prepared to make them listen."

Seraina met Noll's icy stare and felt her heart skip a beat. Behind her, the trees murmured their approval.

A short time later Noll said farewell and she watched him

wind his way up the slope above the tree line until he disappeared over the grassy ridge.

"He is an exceptional young man. And as headstrong as all you Helvetii seem to be."

Seraina jumped at the sound of the voice behind her. *Gildas!*

She turned to see the old man sitting on a boulder, a blade of grass between his straight teeth. The green stood in stark contrast to the downy white of his beard, which in turn, blended into the white hooded robe of the druids. She was aware of another white form, but this one as insubstantial as mist, padding through the trees to her right. Remembering her manners, she fought off the urge to run into the trees, chase after Oppid, and nuzzle his fur. Instead she held up her hand in a ritual greeting.

"Blessed be the knowledge of the Weave as passed through the Elders." She bowed her head and held her right palm over her womb, her center and link to the natural world.

The old man stood and held out his arms.

"Come now child. It is just you and I—leave the formalities of another age in the past where they belong. Give me a hug, for nothing would gladden this old heart more."

Seraina laughed, ran to Gildas and threw her arms around his neck. She was a little girl again, and words bubbled out of her before they were thoughts.

"I was so excited when I heard of your arrival. Then, when you did not show, I thought I was mistaken, and was only hearing the empty echoes of my heart. It has been so long…I thought I was alone."

"And I am sorry for that child. I wanted to come to you after your ordeal with the villagers of Tellikon but—"

Seraina stepped back. "You know of that? Then why did

you not come? I was so lost. And angry. What purpose could the burning of an innocent child have in the Weave? I wandered, desolate and alone for weeks, waiting for a sign from the Elders. But nothing. I thought something happened to you all. I had just about given up hope when the Mythen called and led me to this grove."

Gildas nodded, his face pale and taut. "And you have done well. The trees are strong here, and ancient. And a great number of these people are of the old world, although few remember. They will have need of you, before their end."

He took Seraina's hands in his. It had been six years since she had seen him, but he looked far older than Seraina remembered.

"It pained me greatly to not seek you out when you were betrayed by those under your care. But I could not. There are so few elders left, and fewer talented ones seem to be born each year. I have not found a single adept in the last ten years, though I have searched every valley and mountain village from the lands of the *Menapi* to those of the *Ausci*."

He used the ancient names of the tribes. Names kept alive only through the oral traditions of druids like Gildas. The regret in his eyes placated Seraina's anger, and she found herself feeling sorry for the man who had been like a father to her. Or what she imagined having a father would be like.

"Cease your worry Gildas. The Weave is only changing her colors. The adepts will appear again, you will see."

He smiled, and his face softened, on the surface.

"You were my greatest find Seraina and I have missed you terribly, child. Now. Tell me of this Arnold of Melchthal. You believe him to be a true Catalyst of the Weave?"

Seraina nodded and her green eyes lit up like poplar leaves backlit with the sun's early morning rays.

"It is no accident the Weave led me here. Noll was the first person I met. He stepped out of the trees, with not a sound from them, mind you. And from that first encounter I knew he was something special."

Gildas nodded. "I have no doubt he is of the old blood. In different times, he may even have been trained to serve the Weave as we do. But he was not discovered early enough I am afraid."

Seraina became excited at the observation and started to pace. "You feel it too? But of course you do! That is why you are here. Is it not, Gildas?"

"Your instincts have always been keen, my child. You will make a fine Elder one day. We have agreed the Weave is creating a powerful nexus in this area. And with every nexus there must be a Catalyst—one capable of nudging the Weave in the direction of change."

Seraina's eyebrows furrowed. "There has been something bothering me," she said. "How do we know this change will be good for our people?"

Gildas sighed. "Seraina, you are a priestess of the Old Religion. It is your place to be concerned for the well being of the people. But never forget that the patterns of the Great Weave can never be fully known. Even by us. All we can do is be vigilant and do what we think right, for both the people and the land. Now, about this Arnold, or Noll as you call him. Why do you feel he is the one?"

"The people love him. Even though he is an outlaw hunted by the Austrians. Or, perhaps that is why they love him. I have seen how the Habsburgs have come into these lands and stripped them bare. The best crops, animals, even tradespeople, are taken north and east to support the great Austrian cities. And for years they have been granting tracts of our people's land to foreign lords who send men and soldiers to desecrate it. They have no respect for the old ways, and neither the people nor the land can hope to endure much longer. They plant the same crops year after year on the same land, never allowing it to rest. They cut down our ancient groves and float the trees down the river to faraway places I have never heard of, they—"

Gildas held up his hand. Seraina's voice had been growing louder and her hand movements more vigorous, but looking into the old man's peaceful eyes gave her pause, and she took a deep breath, regaining some measure of control.

"Forgive me," she said. "It has been some time since I have had anyone to speak of these things with."

"Other tribes of our people have suffered much worse. Most in fact are no longer with us at all. But you must remember that strong emotions will only cloud your view of the Weave, and that in turn will greatly hinder your ability to help the land or those who call it home."

"I am sorry. It is just that this is *my* tribe. The last of the Helvetii. And they have already suffered so much. But I think Noll could change that. He could be as great as Vercingetorix, if only I knew how to help him," Seraina said.

The impatience and despair that had been building within her these last few months, as she watched Noll and his army of boys and beggars play with Austrian soldiers, finally overwhelmed her. Seraina's eyes glistened as they welled with the first sign of tears.

"Vercingetorix had the benefit of a full druidic counsel. He had access to all the wisdom we could offer, yet he still failed to turn aside the armies of the Romans. Do not be so hard on yourself," the old druid said.

"Please, Gildas. I beg you—tell me what I must do."

He looked like he would speak, but instead placed his hand on her shoulder. Its warmth spread into her. They stood in silence, listening to the trees together as they used to when Seraina was a little girl. In time, the feelings of despair shriveled and withered, then blossomed into something else entirely.

Hope.

Finally, when Seraina had settled and nothing could be heard but the murmurs of the forest, Gildas spoke.

"Do not worry yourself too much, my child. The Helvetii are a resilient people, and I believe they still have a place in the Great Weave. Unlike my own tribe, your people's time is yet to come."

Seraina kept her eyes closed and wrapped herself in the strength of his words. His voice was deep and resonated with power amongst the trees. She felt at peace.

As he spoke, the old man's own eyes roved slowly over the grove, drinking in every moss-coated stone and sun-dappled plant, logging the memory. Tucking it away somewhere deep enough that it would stay with him for the rest of this life, and into the next. When his gaze came to rest, finally, on the young woman at his side, his lips trembled and a single tear fled from the corner of his eye. In one swift motion he wiped it away and turned Seraina towards him. She opened her eyes and Gildas nodded towards the forest.

"Now, go and say hello to Oppid. He has missed you more than you know."

Seraina beamed and an unstoppable grin spread across her face. With a shriek of delight she ran off into the trees calling out the wolf's name.

CHAPTER 10

THE SLIVERED MOON offered little light to guide Seraina's climb up the path from the water's edge. Being careful to stay well back of torchlight and the harsh whispers of men's voices, she avoided the main route and made her way in darkness through the forest of straight pines towards the Ruetli meadow. She took her time to enjoy the clear night air, stooping occasionally to pick star lilies, a red-petaled plant with flowers that only revealed themselves at night and was the base for many of her fever suppressing remedies. Slipping silently through the woods, Seraina caressed saplings, spoke in soft tones to the old growth, and skirted around areas with new shoots poking up from the forest floor. Finally, she reached the edge of the Ruetli, a clearing nestled in a thick copse of trees overlooking the eastern shores of the Great Lake of the four forest regions.

In the meadow's center, a low fire burned, illuminating the faces of a dozen men in flickering light. Walter Furst, the Justice from Altdorf, was there, as was old Werner Stauffacher of Schwyz. She recognized a guild man from Zurich named Studer, and although she did not know some of the other men, she saw the bear crest of Berne on one of their shoulders.

"Torches coming up the path," called out one of the two

guards standing at the entrance to the meadow.

The men at the fire cast questioning looks at one another.

Walter Furst held out his hands. "We are expecting no others," he said.

"How many?" Studer, the guild man from Zurich asked.

"Six torches. At least that many men."

Werner Stauffacher walked over and peered down the path into the darkness. He was tall and very old, but he still had the loose-limbed gait of one who spent countless hours walking up and down mountain trails. "Arnold of Melchthal, and his band," he said, shaking his head.

Studer cursed. "Outlaws," he said to the man from Berne. "Stauffacher, if this is some ploy of your doing, I swear I will bring the wrath of the guilds down on you and all of Schwyz."

"No need to get excited Master Studer. Werner had no idea the young Melchthal would be joining us. None of us did, but I must admit I am not so surprised," Judge Furst said. A head shorter than old Stauffacher, Walter Furst was round in the face and had grey, wispy hair that seemed to float above his head.

Studer and the men around them had their hands on their swords. "What do you mean not surprised?"

"Arnold's father is a member of the Oathbound Council," Furst said.

"I am not sure I want to deal with the Eidgenossen if their members include murderers and highwaymen," the man from Berne said. He was a squat hairy man that Seraina did not know but who, she thought with a wry smile, resembled the bear his city had been named after.

Studer nodded. "The guilds of Zurich feel the same. We are here to discuss how we can legally benefit our towns. We have no interest in rebelling against the German Empire. And where is Henri Melchthal? Why is he not here but sends his outlaw son in his stead?"

There was a commotion at the head of the path as Noll and his men approached the guards. The two guards looked at Stauffacher for guidance on how to treat the newcomer, and when he shook his head they stood down.

Noll strode into the clearing looking as unconcerned as a man coming home from the fields for dinner. He nodded to Stauffacher as he passed. His men spread out and took up positions on the outer ring of firelight, and their torches bathed the clearing in a bright light.

"Evening Furst," Noll said, pleasantly enough. Then his voice took on a hard edge. "I believe I heard my father's name mentioned? By all means, tell the guild man why he cannot be present."

Walter Furst grimaced at Noll's tone.

"Your father paid a terrible price for his pride. We all wish it had turned out differently," Furst said.

"The charges were false. You knew it and did nothing," Noll said.

"I tried to help your father, but you know how stubborn he can be."

"You did nothing!" Noll stepped forward and grabbed Furst's cloak with both fists. "You failed to act then just as you sit in the woods now like frightened rabbits while the Austrians take our homes and our land." The guards moved towards Noll but Furst waved them off.

Stauffacher moved in and laid a hand on Noll's shoulder. "Easy lad. Henri is a friend of many a man here, as well as a father."

"Believe me Arnold, I tried everything within my power to have your father tried in my court. But Landenberg would have none of it. He has since accused me of sympathizing with rebels against the German Empire and I fear it is only a matter of time before he finds a way to remove me from my seat."

Seraina slid forward through the brush. She had no fear of being seen. The trees embraced her and accepted her presence amongst them as one of their own. A cool breeze stirred the leaves of a low hanging willow branch, rustling at her in warning, but she parted them and peered out like a curious child half hiding in her mother's skirts.

She faced Noll's back and saw his shoulders bunch up, tensing under Stauffacher's touch. Noll released Furst and stepped away from the two old men and turned towards Seraina's hiding spot, his face bathed in the wavering glow of torchlight. The pain she saw there made her cringe.

She had tried to talk to Noll about his father, tell him it was not his fault. But what Furst had said about the elder Melchthal being stubborn was equally true of his son. These men of the Alps had a willful streak to them that was at once their curse and their greatest strength.

Henri Melchthal had been accused of not meeting his annual grain quota, so Landenberg gave orders to his tax collector to seize a team of Henri's prized oxen. Noll argued with the man and ended up rapping his hand with an ax handle when he tried to take the oxen by force. The collector fled the young Melchthal's wrath with several broken fingers. A few days later Landenberg himself came with an escort of soldiers. While Noll hid in the woods and watched, Landenberg allowed his collector to burn out Henri Melchthal's eyes with the very same ax handle Noll had struck him with.

Perhaps Noll felt Seraina's presence, knew she stood only paces away and had caught him in a vulnerable moment, for suddenly he dragged a hand across his face and gave the woods a long, blank stare. She leaned back and held her breath, feeling guilty for having experienced Noll's pain without his knowing.

Noll turned back to the group of men. He stared hard at Furst and let out a slow breath before he spoke.

"I am sorry for my words Walter. I know you did what you could. It would do our people little good to have the last non-Austrian Judge removed from office."

Noll whirled to face the other men and raised his voice. "One territory cannot stand against the might of the Habsburgs, but if the guilds of Zurich and Berne joined with the Eidgenossen we could drive the Austrian dogs from our doorsteps for good."

"You are a fool," the leader of the men from Berne said. "The Habsburgs have the might of the German Princes at their command. This is nonsense. I will not listen to any more of this."

"And when will you listen? You think you are safe behind your city walls? For the time being perhaps. But what will happen once the Habsburg fortress is complete at Altdorf? They will control all trade that flows through Italia to the Hanseatic League of the North Sea. Altdorf will be the new Habsburg center of commerce and they will choke the flow of goods to your cities and tax your caravans like you have never known."

Studer, the Zurich guild leader, crossed his arms and laughed.

"And what would an outlaw hiding in the hills know of commerce, boy? What information are you privy to that the guilds of Zurich and Berne are not? We have given the Altdorf fortress much thought and when it is completed, we will survive. We will pay our tithes when they come due, but in the meantime, our guilds profit nicely at Duke Leopold's expense. One of the first rules of business is do not bite the hand that feeds you."

Noll opened his mouth to respond, but an old woman's voice rang out across the clearing before he could speak.

"Some hands you would be wise to snap at Master Studer."

Gertrude of Iberg stood at the path, leaning on an ancient walking stick, and since she carried no torch, the guards there jumped at her words, surprised as anyone at her sudden appearance.

Of course, Seraina had been hearing whispers of Gertrude's approach for some time and was relieved the woman had made the climb safely. She put her hand over her mouth lest the glint of her smile give her away to those around the fire.

"Is there anyone who does not know of this secret meeting?" one of the Berne men asked.

Furst threw up his hands. "Werner, what is your wife doing here?" Stauffacher cast him an apologetic look and shrugged.

"Werner, do not answer him. Come help me get these old bones over to the fire. And Walter keep quiet. I am sure you have said enough already tonight."

Stauffacher scurried over to take her arm and the men made room for the old woman around the fire. Few people did not know Gertrude of Iberg, but she had retreated from actual council work in recent years, so her appearance at the secret meeting of the Oathbound was unusual.

Studer bowed his head stiffly. "You look well Gertrude. The years favor you more than most."

"Time has no favorites, but I appreciate any show of civility I can get from a merchant," she said.

She bent down and grasped a piece of firewood larger than a woman her age should be attempting to lift, and flicked it onto the fire, sending a plume of sparks drifting up to rival the stars.

"Zurich and Berne would do well to listen to the likes of Arnold Melchthal. What the boy says is true. Leopold has designs for these lands and I fear none of us will prosper by the likes of him."

The man from Berne spoke up. "Berne is a free city state, granted the right to rule herself by the German Emperor before my father's time. We have no quarrel with the Habsburgs."

Noll turned on him. "As was Schwyz, and the free men of Uri. But look around and count the Austrian soldiers that patrol our towns, and the corrupt judges that sentence our people. Walter, how many of our countrymen have been sentenced to work on the Altdorf fortress now? Fifty? A hundred? How many have died? Just last week the Menznau boy was found thrown out like so much garbage. Leopold keeps that fortress clouded in secrecy so we have no way of knowing how many of our sons and daughters have suffered similar fates."

Seraina's smile left her face at the mention of the Menznaus. She wrapped her arms around herself and was suddenly aware of the coolness of the night. She imagined herself standing amongst everyone near the fire, and although the thought warmed her, her smile did not return.

"And if *you* controlled the Gotthard, just how much would you charge my caravan to pass?" Studer said, a contemptuous smile on his lips.

"Nothing," Noll said. "I would welcome every merchant at the top of the pass with open arms. Provide a warm, safe refuge to water and feed his animals, let him rest, and send him on his way when, and only when, he wished."

The men around the fire laughed. Noll raised his voice to be heard.

"Word would soon spread and merchant caravans would be lining up to use the *free* Gotthard Pass. And as they descended into Andermatt, the villagers there would also welcome them. Of course their services would not be free, but they would be appreciated nonetheless. The innkeepers would feed the travelers, the smiths would shoe their mules, apothecaries would heal them, and the resources to accomplish all this would come from the farms and trades people surrounding the town. The coin from these foreigners would travel far into the countryside. And it would be the same for every town and village the merchant caravans passed through."

The men no longer talked amongst themselves as Noll's words took hold.

"Merchants and locals alike would prosper," the man from Berne said.

"Everyone except the Habsburgs," Studer said. "Therein lies the flaw in your plan. Leopold would never allow free passage through the Gotthard."

Noll grinned. "Consider it a redistribution of wealth."

"Well this is a first. A highwayman waving folks through without charging for safe passage," the Berne man said. "But all fantasy aside, the Habsburgs are not going to pack up their Altdorf fortress and leave."

Noll nodded. "They will need persuading. And that is why we have to act soon. The Holy Roman Empire has been torn apart since King Albrecht died, and the Habsburgs are fighting to get one of their own crowned again. I hear rumors of war between Frederick and Louis the Bavarian, which means Leopold will have no money, and no soldiers to send against us." He looked at Furst and said, "But we have to move before the fortress is finished, and Leopold cocoons himself up in it."

For a few moments the only sound was the popping and sizzling of sap boiling in burning logs. Finally the Zurich and Berne leaders agreed to take the matter back to their respective cities and hold council with their guild associations. They left the clearing before the darkest hours of the night to begin the long journey home.

"I hope you know what you have set in motion," Gertrude said to Noll when the guildsmen had left.

Seraina did not hear his reply, but she could hardly contain the excitement she felt. At last, the Catalyst had awakened.

CHAPTER 11

"DID THE WITCH'S brothers give you any trouble?" Leopold asked.

Gissler shrugged, and his hand went to the fresh scratch marks on his cheek, just now beginning to scab over. "Not as much as she did, my lord."

Leopold leaned back in his upholstered chair and looked at the motley group forced to their knees before him. The three brothers were chained to one another at the neck, and their wrists and ankles were likewise shackled. All of them had black eyes or bloodied faces. One could barely walk and was helped along by the other two.

Gissler had done well, Leopold thought. *It may be time to put some men under his command.*

He turned his attention to the woman. She lay curled up on her side on the flagstone floor. Her right thumb was shackled to her right big toe, as was her left thumb to her left toe, making it impossible for her to walk. A necessary precaution, for if the witch's hands were left free, she would be able to cast spells and carry out the Devil's mischief. The guards had carried her into the throne room suspended from a thick pole, and slid her off onto the cold floor at Leopold's feet.

The young Duke let out a breath, and with it, some of the

tension of the last few days. Constructing the new fortress at Altdorf was moving far too slowly. Mid-winter was when many merchant caravans set out over the Gotthard Pass. It was crossable once the heavy snows had fallen and crusted over, but when spring came its trails became too soft for carts, and the threat of avalanches of melting snow was constant. The footing would remain too treacherous for most travelers until the first day of summer. This meant that if Leopold did not have his tollgates active before winter, he would have no revenues from the pass until well into next summer, almost a year from now. With Frederick's campaign already eating up most of the Habsburg coffers, Leopold knew he could not wait that long. The Altdorf fortress must be finished before the first snows fell.

There was still time, but he needed more workers. He had sent a messenger to his brother requesting fifty more laborers (he knew Frederick could not spare soldiers) and was confident they would arrive any day now.

Added to these worries was the pressure of his upcoming marriage only two weeks away. Lady Catherine and her entourage would arrive on the morrow and the thought of having to don his courtly mask of manners twisted his lips in a grimace. Originally set for next year, Leopold had pushed for his betrothal to take place earlier. The dowry was needed now, not in a year's time.

A moan came from the witch as she tried to shift herself into a position that eased the pressure on her thumbs and toes. She was young, with an angelic face. How did the Devil manage to recruit one so full of innocence? Yes, this was just the diversion he needed. There was nothing like the battle of good versus evil to take one's mind off matters of state.

"Shall I remove the witch and her servants to the dungeon

to await trial your lordship?" Leopold's secretary asked.

The young duke nodded.

"Take the men away but leave the woman. And summon the judge. I would try her within the hour."

"Today? But my lord, may I remind you that you have other appointments to make preparations for the arrival of Lady Catherine—"

Leopold waved his hand and brushed the comment aside. He looked at the girl and caught her eye briefly. She trembled and looked away, apparently not finding any comfort under Leopold's intense gaze. Few ever did.

"Cancel all my appointments," he said. "Keeping my people safe from the Devil's spawn must take all precedence. Now get me that judge. And summon my scribe. There may be useful information gained here today for my manuscript."

The secretary bowed and hurried from the room. A short, black and white clad Fool followed closely behind imitating the secretary's hasty shuffle, the soft tinkling of bells punctuating every step.

But for once, Leopold did not notice.

✧ ✧ ✧

"What do you know of witches, Gissler?" Leopold asked, squinting beneath a hand raised to block out the bright sun. He strained his eyes to keep track of the naked body of the girl as she bobbed in the slow-flowing river.

A guard on either bank held her in the middle with ropes tied around her waist. Her thumbs and toes still clamped together, she struggled to float on her back, gasping for air. Then the current rolled her over in slow motion like a piece of driftwood. There was a series of frantic splashes beneath the surface of the water before a guard righted her by pulling on one of the ropes. She broke the surface coughing and gasping for breath, her eyes bulging with terror. A judge, a wizened man in a black and yellow ceremonial cloak, stood at the riverbank, staring intently at the proceedings.

"I have no experience with witches, my lord," Gissler said.

Leopold's eyebrows arched and he cast a sidelong glance at Gissler. "A cautious answer. But I suppose it would not do for one of God's soldiers to admit to keeping company with Satan's kin." He focused again on the dunking, anxious to not miss any outward displays of devilry.

"Fascinating creatures, really. But this one is not as clever as some I have seen tested. Perhaps she is too young. Her craft has not matured properly."

He may be right, Gissler thought. She had indeed failed the very first test.

Once the judge arrived in the receiving hall, he had the guards strip the girl bare, and while she screamed and then sobbed quietly, he examined her body carefully looking for non-human marks. When he found something suspect, a freckle that was too large, or a swollen lump of tissue, he would poke it with a needle to see if it bled. After testing spots on her thighs, buttocks, and neck, which all bled, he finally inserted the needle into the lower part of her left breast. He pulled it out, looked at the needle, then roughly lifted her breast up and examined the location. He passed sentence immediately.

"No blood my lord. The Devil protects this one, there can be no doubt." The judge was convinced, and that should have finished it, but Leopold had insisted they perform a dunking trial as well. His scribe was to carefully record the results for Leopold's witchcraft manuscript he had been working on for the past several years.

"There! Did you see that? She floats with no aid from the ropes," Leopold said. Wonder filled his voice as he pointed at the girl whose struggles were growing less with every moment.

"I saw it too your grace," the judge shouted. He shook his head. "There can be no doubt."

"I am not King, so call me 'grace' again and I will have you flogged."

"Forgive me, your…*lordship*. I served your father for too many years and my tongue has grown careless. But I am sure it will not be long before another Habsburg sits upon the German throne."

Leopold waved the man to silence.

"Did you see that Gissler? It makes one's blood run cold does it not?"

Leopold craned his neck to get a better look at the Devil's handiwork. He walked to where the judge stood and signaled the soldiers to let go of the rope. As they did so, the girl who had now been facedown in the water for several minutes and was no longer struggling, continued to float, and drifted a short distance on the river's almost imperceptible current. The judge gasped, and both he and Leopold made the sign of the cross in front of their faces. Leopold barked at the soldiers to take up their rope again quickly.

Gissler saw nothing but a young girl drowned to death.

When Leopold turned back to Gissler, his face was alight. "You did a good thing bringing me this creature," he said.

Gissler bowed. "I am here to serve, my lord. But one question if I may…"

"Of course."

"The witch's guilt was proven beyond all doubt, because even shackled, she could float?"

Leopold nodded. "Even now, though she is most likely

dead and her stomach filled with water, she still floats."

Gissler nodded. "I see. And if she sank to the bottom of the river, it would have proven her innocence?"

"Of course," Leopold said.

"But in all likelihood, she would be just as dead," Gissler said.

"Yes, and God would have received her into his Kingdom," Leopold said, looking perturbed.

Gissler nodded, masking his thoughts. Having been part of the Hospitaller navy for twenty years, he knew very well what dead bodies did in open water. Some floated, some sank, a few drifted between the bottom and the surface. The only way to guarantee a body would sink to the ocean floor, was to cut the air from its lungs and weight it with a bag of rocks.

He searched the Duke's eyes for some sign of insanity, a glint of madness, but found nothing. They were clear, focused, and fiercely intelligent. And yet, somehow, he was convinced that by ridding the world of this beautiful young girl he had promoted himself in the eyes of God.

"Come Gissler. Time to celebrate. Tonight you dine at my table. Ah—I almost forgot," Leopold said and reached into his vestment and pulled out a purse that he tossed to Gissler. "Your payment. Stand by me and you will rise high, Hermann Gissler."

Hearing his full name spoken by a duke, and a Prince of the German Empire no less, made Gissler forget about the witch and stand a little taller.

He caught the purse in one hand and then almost dropped it because of its weight. It was easily double what he had won at the tourney.

All his life Gissler had followed orders. And what had the Knights of Saint John ever given him in return? Food, a place to sleep, and two sets of clothing. His rank in the brotherhood had never changed from brother-sergeant. He could never have been a true Hospitaller Knight, for only those of noble blood were permitted to rise past the rank of sergeant. He had given them everything; his obedience, his loyalty, his youth, even his name.

He would never again be merely a *Schwyzer*, and that thought gave him great satisfaction. For to be a *Schwyzer* in the brotherhood was to be a slave. A front line soldier sent to test the strength of the enemy, to look after the Knights' mounts and muck out the stables.

Tonight he would sit at a duke's table. Yes, he was still following orders, but he was being rewarded for his talents. And, once again, he owned his name. His true name. His throat tightened as he thought of his mother and father. If only his father were still alive to see him return the Gissler name to its past glory, all would be perfect. But his brother, Hugo yet lived.

Gissler tightened his hand around the heavy purse. Soon, he would go back to his brother's dismal hog farm and take him and his daughter away from their wretched life of poverty.

✧ ✧ ✧

Leopold stood above his scribe in the Habsburg castle library and watched him carefully transcribe his notes into the leather-bound volume Leopold had titled *Malleus Maleficarum*, 'The Hammer of Witches'. Once finished, Leopold was confident it would be the Church's greatest weapon against witchcraft ever assembled.

"Be sure you list all who were present this day," Leopold said. Reading in Latin had never been his strong point, but he could recognize names easily enough.

There was a commotion at the door to the small library and Leopold looked to see Landenberg push through, snarling harsh words at a young scribe who trailed behind him. The scribe froze when he saw Leopold look up.

"I am sorry my lord. The Vogt demanded entry and I..."

"I had him!" Landenberg shouted. "He and one of his boys walked out of the trees right in front of us. I was—"

Leopold held up a hand and cut him off. "Gather your quills, Bernard. It would seem Vogt Landenberg has some pressing matter to discuss."

Even in this place could he not find a moment's peace?

The scribe hastily blotted the page he had been working on, and keeping the manuscript open, carefully carried it from the room. He was not foolish enough to let the book out of his sight. Bernard was the only one permitted to touch Leopold's tome, and he knew his life was forfeit should anything happen to it.

"From the enthusiasm in your words, I can only assume you had another encounter with Arnold Melchthal."

"We crested a rise outside Brunnen and there he was. Him and one of his men just stood there. We stared at one another like startled cats, unsure what to do. They ran, we gave chase, and I put a bolt into his man's back. That one's thieving days have come to an end, I tell you that much. Beautiful shot. From horseback too, I might add."

"So Melchthal eluded you again? Is that why you have burst into my study? To bring news of such a noteworthy event?" Leopold said the words softly, with only the slightest trace of sarcasm. In truth, there were few things in this world he enjoyed more than seeing Landenberg squirm after being played for a fool.

Landenberg threw up his hands. "He is more rabbit than

man, that one. We lost him for a bit in the trees and when next we saw him he was half way across the lake on a ferry."

"What ferry?"

"Some peasants set up a barge that crosses the waters near Brunnen."

"Who uses this ferry? Merchants?"

"No, only locals I should think. The road runs along the water's edge and merchants tend to be a distrusting sort. They would not risk their goods on those unpredictable waters."

Leopold sat in the chair Bernard had been in moments before and steepled his fingers in front of his face as he thought through what Landenberg told him.

"Then burn it," he said.

"What?"

"Burn the ferry. As it stands now, Melchthal has beaten you. He escaped. By removing the method of his escape, you ensure that this particular tactic of his will never work again. Also, you send a message, a warning, to both Melchthal and, more importantly, to those who would harbor him."

Landenberg nodded. His thick lips spread into a grin clearly visible even through his shaggy, greying beard.

"Consider it done. My lord."

CHAPTER 12

ONCE EVERY MONTH Seraina would load up her mule and make the daylong journey into Schwyz. Once there, she would set up in the market, and sell fresh herbs from her garden, or ground up ingredients with her granite mortar and pestle to relieve people's ailments. After, she would go to the homes of anyone that was too sick or injured to come to her stall in the market. Invariably, someone would offer her a bed or at least a barn full of straw to sleep in for the night. Early the next morning she would begin the trek home to her grove.

But that was not the only time she had contact with the villagers. A few times every month someone would turn up on her doorstep looking for healing, or advice. These were usually men and women whose positions or circumstances made it difficult to seek her out in the public space of the market. Once, even a priest came all the way from Altdorf to see her when a stubborn lesion on his arm refused to scab over and heal. Seraina never refused anyone treatment, and that included Austrian soldiers that came to her stall in the market, although she was careful never to mention this to Noll.

On this day, it was already noon when she set out from Schwyz for home, which meant it would be well past dark by the time she arrived at her cabin. Unless, of course, she took the Brunnen ferry. She smiled, knowing all too well this had been the plan of her private weave all along. She had slept late and tarried at the farm, helping Gertie and her infant daughter feed the chickens and then broke her fast with them before she finally took to the road.

When she reached the crossing, she was disappointed to see no sign of the ferry. But just as she was about to go back to the road, a white sail peeked through the trees, moving steadily towards a small wharf jetting out into the green waters. The long, rectangular barge drifted up to the makeshift dock and a tall man holding a rope leapt gracefully from the ferry and tied it up to a post worn smooth and black. Unfortunately, he was not alone.

Seraina bit her lip as she recognized his passengers, old man Menznau and his wife. The wind was up and the lake simmered with small waves as the couple stepped down gingerly, their legs unaccustomed to fighting the swells.

Seraina pulled the hood of her cloak up and watched from the water's edge as the old man reached into a sack and pulled out a loaf of dark bread. He handed it to the ferryman and they exchanged a few words, then Menznau and his wife wobbled down the dock. As they came towards her, the old couple made it a point not to look at Seraina, and she felt that if she had been standing on the dock, they may very well have pushed her into the water.

Their son had died recently from the lung sickness. He had been caught stealing and was sentenced to do hard labor on the Altdorf fortress. Seraina had tried to see him, but the soldiers would not let her anywhere near the prisoners. They assured her their own doctor would look after him. He did not, and the only reason the Menznaus learned of the fate of their son, was because a relative found his body mixed with the ever-growing pile of refuse heaped against an outer wall of the fortress.

As the couple passed, she felt their grief surface and flare. Seraina watched their backs, hoping they might turn around and let her try and soothe their pain.

"You wishing to go across? If so we leave now, as I would be back at this dock before nightfall."

She turned to see the ferryman running his hands along the mooring rope, head down and focused on it like his question had been directed to it instead of Seraina. But as she stepped down onto the ferry he held out his hand and she took it.

Just then the barge lurched on the waves and she leaned into his grip to right herself. She laughed and not so much saw, but felt him smile at the sound. She looked up into his face and his eyes made her gasp. They were large and brown, with amber flecks, and would have been beautiful, but Seraina could see deeper than most people. Beneath the calm, swirled unfathomable darkness, and pain. There could be no doubt that his spirit had brushed up against evil.

She blinked hard from the intensity of the man's life. He immediately turned away, and as he did so Seraina noticed a long scar that stretched from beneath his eye to the bottom of his jaw.

Oh you fool, she said to herself. He thought she had been staring at the old wound. He kept his back to her and prepared to cast off.

"Best hold onto something. Wind has been unpredictable all day," he said. His voice scratched in his throat, like he was not used to speaking.

He pushed away from the dock with an ancient oar as scarred as his face, and then busied himself with adjusting the sail until it filled with wind. The ponderous barge plowed through the water at a slow, but steady pace. He rested one hand on the steerboard, making slight corrections now and again to keep the sail from spilling the wind, and asked where she would like to go.

"The hanging rocks south of Seelisberg, if the waters permit."

"Ah. Going to see the old hag are you?"

"Old hag?"

He shrugged. "The only reason anyone goes to the hanging rocks is because some old pagan woman lives in those woods. Trades coin for magic potions some say."

Seraina laughed and the ferryman looked at her, his dark eyebrows arched upwards.

"Magic," she said, "is the name people give to something they do not understand. Some might say what you did for Noll's young friend the other day was magic."

He gave her a dark look and crossed himself at the suggestion he might use magic.

"So, you are one of the outlaw's band, are you? One of his women?"

"Are you asking if I am a whore that passes herself amongst Noll Melchthal and his men?" Seraina's tone was light and sweet.

The ferryman's face reddened and he looked down at his hand on the tiller.

"It was not my intention to compare you to that kind of woman," he said, after a long pause.

Seraina caught his eye and tipped her head to show she was not insulted. It had the desired effect of putting the man at ease.

"Well, I am not a whore, but if I were, I would not be

afraid to admit it. For a woman who sells herself is a survivor. Most often she has simply run out of options and is doing what she can to live."

He frowned at this. "There is always the nunnery," he said. "She would be better off giving herself to God, rather than some sour-breathed drunk in an alley."

Seraina put a finger to the corner of her mouth and cocked her head. "I suppose she would be safe in a nunnery. For 'sour-breathed drunks' are never found within a House of God." One side of her mouth turned up in a smile that the ferryman could not help but match with one of his own.

"You do have a point," he said.

"You would know much better than I about Houses of God, for Noll tells me you were with the Hospitallers?"

He nodded. "My whole life. What I can remember, that is."

"Do all Hospitallers study the healer's craft?"

He shrugged. "We are all required to spend time in the Hospitals. But some take to it more than others. I suppose I was one of those."

"Your teachers were Christian monks then?"

"Some. But many of the Order's physiks were Mohammedans."

Ah, that makes sense, Seraina thought.

The Arabs were an old people with a culture stretching back thousands of years. They would have much knowledge to offer.

"Do you miss your life across the sea?"

"Do you always ask so many questions?"

Seraina laughed and said, "I have been told that I do. We all have more questions than answers, but here is one answer I give to you freely, with no question attached. My name is

Seraina." She performed a mock curtsy. "You might say I am the gardener for this old hag you mentioned."

The ferryman grimaced and once again looked down at the tiller.

"My apologies. I meant no disrespect to your mistress. I am Thomas," he said. "Thomas Schwyzer."

He said his last name quietly, like a boy admitting to a theft.

✧ ✧ ✧

It was Thomas's favorite time to be on the water. The sun was beginning its descent behind the Alps and soon the bright ball would disappear, yet enough light would remain to sail by for some time. So different from the saltwater-scented evenings of the Mid-Earth Sea, where few high mountains encroached on the coastline. There, once the sun had fled, the whole world went dark.

Curious woman, Seraina, he thought. He remembered the sound of her innocent laughter and how her green eyes opened wide and flashed when she spoke, like the world was filled solely with beauty and wonder. He envied her that.

Do all Hospitallers study the healer's craft?

All people experience a turning point in their lives. A precipice, where on one side lies the innocence of youth, and the other a sheer drop into the darkness that is life. For Thomas, that moment came when he learned to read.

It had been during the waning days of Christian power in the Holy Lands. All the great Templar and Hospitaller fortresses had fallen. Beaufort, Akkar, Safed, even the once impregnable Krak des Chevaliers.

The year was 1290 and the port city of Acre was the last Christian foothold in the Levant. Thomas was called into a meeting with a Knight Justice of the Hospitaller forces, Brother Foulques de Villaret.

Foulques had been raised within the Order in Outremer and was something of a legend amongst the other knights and sergeants, both for his skill at arms and his unwavering dedication. A Knight Justice at the age of eighteen and a Knight Commander in his early twenties, he had earned even the monks' respect because he was one of the few fighting men who was able to read and write.

So, in the summer of Thomas's fourteenth year, it was with some trepidation that he answered a summons to meet with Foulques de Villaret in his keep office. Thomas had grown into a tall, lanky boy who may have been awkward if not for the physical rigors of his everyday training. Even so, he almost tripped as his foot snagged the edge of a lush Turkish carpet when he entered de Villaret's office.

He was used to the stone floor of his own dormitory, and the only place he had seen carpets, such as the one he stood upon, was hanging from one of the Arab merchant stalls in the city marketplace. In fact, the entire room reminded him of the eastern area of the bazaar. Sheer fabrics draped from the windows, allowing in ample light but diffusing it in a way that softened the grey stone room, and tapestries hung on every wall with multicolored motifs that matched those of the carpets. Elaborate candelabras were placed throughout the room and numerous feather pillows covered a seating area in one corner.

Seated behind an ornately carved desk, even de Villaret himself looked like he had just stepped out of the bazaar. His usual black Hospitaller tunic was replaced by the loose-fitting silks and linens that the Arabs preferred, but his head was uncovered, leaving his mass of black hair to float unfettered around his head. He saw Thomas's surprise at the room's décor and his own mode of dress.

"The East has much to offer," de Villaret said, sweeping his arm across the room. "Why else would so many Franks come to these lands?"

There was an uncomfortable silence as Thomas considered how to answer the knight, or if indeed it had even been a question. De Villaret stood, walked to the window, and looked out. "Your studies go well?"

"Yes, Commander," Thomas said, finding his voice.

"Weapons master Glynn speaks highly of your abilities," de Villaret said, turning back to face Thom, his eyes probing. "Especially, with the dagger. Not the most noble of weapons though, I must say."

Thomas did not know what to say. He had no distinctive talent that made him stand out, like Pirmin's great strength, Gissler's uncanny speed with a sword, or Ruedi, who could hit figs with a crossbow from across the training ground.

"I have been told you requested extra hours working in the hospital. Do you seek to replace your martial training with something you see as less strenuous?"

"No, Commander. I would use the hours I have free in the evening after Vespers."

De Villaret nodded. "It is good you have an interest in medicine, for that is the founding vocation of our order. However, God has willed you should become a soldier, not a physician. Do you understand this?"

Thomas looked down at the ground. "Yes."

"How many patrols have you ridden out on?"

"Once a week for the past year."

"Have you taken the lives of any of the enemy?"

Thomas looked up and one of his dark eyes twitched.

"I have killed a boy," he said finally. "Though I thought him a man at the time."

A month earlier his patrol had ridden to the rescue of an Italian caravan under attack by Bedouin raiders. His horse took an arrow in the lung and threw Thomas in front of the archer. He recovered, and without thinking thrust his sword into the raider's guts, mortally wounding him. As the figure writhed in pain on the ground, his face covering came away, and Thomas saw his attacker was a young boy, no more than twelve years of age.

Both the horse and the boy took a long time to die.

"Boys grow into men. Men who would undermine the one true faith. You carried out God's will and that is the end of it. Think no more on it, for there will be more. Many more."

De Villaret turned back to the window and gazed out. "If I grant you permission to work extra hours in the hospital, then you must do something for me. You will learn to read and write. First in Latin, then Arabic."

Thomas perked up, hardly believing his ears. He was going to learn to read! But he was not sure he had heard the knight correctly.

"Arabic, Commander?"

"Of course. Latin may be the word of God, but Arabic is the language of medicine. Although Frankish doctors are loath to admit it, the Arabian *hakim* are vastly superior. The works of the great Greek and Roman physicians have been lost to the West for centuries, but not to the East."

"But the writings of Galen and Hippocrates have been translated to Latin," Thomas said. "One of the monks showed us copies."

"Copies, yes. Copies of Arabic texts. The originals are long lost, so the Latin versions are translations of Arabic works. I feel the Latin copies possess a sometimes diluting layer of interpretation that the Arabic texts never intended."

"You have read them?"

"Yes, and so should you, provided it does not interfere with your military training. But not only the works of Galen and Hippocrates. Arabic medicine is the medicine of the Islamic world, not just the Arabs. That means that the Persians and Nestorians in the east and even the Spanish and Jews in the west have all contributed to Arabic medicine. You will become familiar with these works as well."

Thomas was shocked. What de Villaret suggested was blasphemy. "Even the Jews? But they are the enemy of Christ."

"So we are told. But as His soldiers, then is it not our duty to learn from the enemy? The truth is, as Hospitallers we owe the Jews and Moslems a great deal for keeping the knowledge of the ancients alive. Knowledge long ago lost in the west, due in no small part to the Church's fear of the common man exploring the divine mysteries of the human body. The Church is content to have us refuse medical treatment and pray while sickness ravages our body, leaving our lives in the hands of God alone."

There was a hard edge to de Villaret's voice. Thomas glanced around the room, looking for any place that may conceal an eavesdropper. The talk made him nervous.

"But surely the Church's position has changed. We are, after all, an exempt Order subject only to the Pope himself. If the Church was truly against the study of medicine, why would they have allowed the Hospitallers to form in the first place?"

De Villaret's eyes narrowed as he looked at the youth before him and he shook his head. "Although both the Templars and the Hospitallers are sworn to poverty, we control vast fortunes that rival that of many monarchs. In fact, a good deal of that fortune has been earned by lending money to Kings. But often wealth is merely the illusion of power. For the moment only the Pope himself has the power to command us, but that will not always be so. Change is the only certainty in life."

He turned to look out the window, and spoke quietly. "We tread softly here. Much softer than you can possibly imagine. Especially now. The Mohammedans are not the only wolf baying at our door."

There was silence for a moment, and then de Villaret wheeled around. "But I did not summon you here to lecture. In return for me allowing you to study in the hospital, I have a task that you are to complete for me. But it is for me alone. No one is to know of our conversation today. Is that clear?"

"Yes." Thomas's eyes darted around the room once before answering.

De Villaret reached down to his desk and lifted a rolled up scroll.

"First you must learn to read the three hundred names on this list. Then you will learn to write well enough to prepare your own list of the one hundred young men you think are the most suitable. They must be strong of arm and skilled in combat. But above all, loyal. Select only those you would trust with your life, and make no mistake on it, for that is precisely what you will be doing. You have sixty days to complete your task before we depart."

Thomas's head spun. "Depart? Where are we going?"

"Our hospice on the island of Cypress," de Villaret said. His intense blue eyes dimmed and when he looked at Thomas he had a sad, faraway look. "Ready all your possessions to take with you, Thomas, for once we leave, Acre will no longer be your home."

The Alpine wind suddenly changed direction and the ferry's sail luffed, fluttering uselessly for a moment until the boom started a slow swing to the other side of the barge. So lost in thought of the past, Thomas did not see it until the last moment. He ducked, and the long beam, crafted from a young tree as thick as his leg, swung harmlessly overhead and the sail once again filled with wind.

Thomas cursed the ever-changing winds on the lake. The influence of the Alps could send breezes whistling in from any direction. He would have to pay more attention. The emerald waters were as unpredictable as they were beautiful.

With his hand clutched around the steerboard, Thomas stared out over the dark waters, but all he could really see was his quill tracing the names of one hundred Schwyzer youths onto parchment. They would become members of the newly created Hospitaller Navy, under the direction of the Order's first Admiral, Foulques de Villaret.

The other two hundred Schwyzers would perish defending the walls of Acre less than a year later.

CHAPTER 13

HABSBURG CASTLE lay a half-day's ride from the easternmost inlet of the Great Lake. 'Castle' was a generous term, for it was more a stone mansion surrounded with a low fence to keep the animals out of the courtyard. Servants and farmers that looked after the estate lived in a dozen hovels that extended beyond the grounds and were scattered throughout the surrounding woods. Leopold's father had used the estate as a hunting lodge and referred to it as his summer castle. He came here to escape court life in Vienna, however, it was not a place he had shared with his family. Neither Frederick nor Leopold had ever visited the estate while their father was alive.

Immediately upon his father's death, Leopold had masons and carpenters from Berne construct a soldier's barracks, courtroom and prison cells just far enough outside the walls to be hardly visible from the main keep. He burned most of his father's furniture and stuffed boars from countless hunting expeditions and made the castle his new, albeit temporary, home. He intended to relocate to Altdorf once the fortress was complete.

The remoteness of Habsburg suited Leopold and he could understand why his father spent so much time here. However, the past week had been anything but peaceful. French and Austrian nobles had invaded Habsburg Castle, along with their baggage trains of servants and guards, and the odd Italian or Spanish popinjay flitted about as well. They had all come to see Catherine of Savoy marry Prince Leopold. A union that Leopold had opposed for years, but after spending everything he had on construction of the Altdorf fortress, he began to develop an appreciation for Catherine's charms, along with the dowry her father Amadeus, the wealthy Count of Savoy was offering.

It was a match ordained in heaven, Leopold had assured the Count. Amadeus had agreed and blessed the marriage wholeheartedly, contributing generously towards their new life together. He knew full well Leopold planned to control the Gotthard Pass from his fortress at Altdorf, but he also knew the French King had been showing expansionistic tendencies towards the pass as well, and he had no love for the French Crown. Having his own son-in-law overseeing the Gotthard would be far more advantageous.

The Archbishop of Savoy performed the ceremony in the largest church the Kussnacht area had to offer, which was not saying much. The local clergy were awed to have His Eminence conducting a royal wedding in their humble House of God, and so they fretted to make it a raucous event to be remembered by all. For Leopold, it had been the longest day of his life. After being subjected to the insufferable pomp and ceremony of the Catholic Church for hours on end, he and his new wife had to endure the feast at Habsburg Castle with foreign crowds of fickle well-wishers and bawdy entertainers. His own jester, the Habsburg Fool, reveled in it, and performed several times throughout the day to the cheers of the spectators. Leopold swore he would slit the throat of the next man who told him how fortunate he was to have such a talented entertainer in his court.

Strange, Leopold thought, how a man with hundreds of people listening to his every word and watching his every movement could feel so alone. He had been disappointed to hear his brother Frederick would not be able to attend his wedding because war had finally broken out between him and Louis over the German crown. Frederick's presence could have made this entire farce bearable.

When he finally entered the wedding chamber and left the world outside, the last thing he felt like doing was breaking in some plain in the face, skinny virgin. But the bones had been cast and the moons read. This day had been chosen for the wedding because it was the most auspicious time for a successful consummation, and Leopold's physicians assured him it was the perfect time for his seed to take root.

So, as his new wife waited dutifully under the sheets of his four-poster oak bed, he had his servants remove his own clothes and then dismissed them. The girl was nervous, as to be expected, so he took his time. One of his two principal physicians recommended a gentle approach to intercourse to avoid loosening the tenuous purchase of his seed in her virgin womb. She cried out when he penetrated her, but quickly bit her lip and remained quiet until the Duke was spent. Afterward, he propped himself up on his elbow and caressed the young girl's hair and spoke soft, reassuring words.

"I hope to give you many children my lord, if God wills it," she said.

Leopold leaned over and kissed her forehead, noting how her eyes were spaced too far apart. Leopold hoped that trait would not show in his children.

"Nothing would make me happier, my sweet. But we have

a responsibility to more than just one another now."

"My lord?"

"Our families depend on us as much as you and I depend on one another. Your father needs a grandchild and I need an heir."

And with Frederick at war, the sooner the better.

Her brows furrowed, accentuating the division between her eyes. Leopold forced himself to not look away.

"But my father has several grandchildren already. My three sisters are all married, and father had eight children with his first wife before she died."

"But how many of those grandchildren are heirs to the Holy Roman Empire? Your son stands to be King of the largest empire in the world. You must hold a special place in your father's heart for him to entrust you with this union." Leopold stroked her cheek once with the back of his hand. "And I for one, will be eternally grateful to him."

Catherine beamed at his words. He kissed her once on the mouth, and tasted the willingness to please on her lips. Leopold got up from the bed and pulled the servant chord as he shrugged into a nightshirt. Catherine sat up.

"Are you leaving my lord?"

"I leave for Altdorf at first light. I am afraid sleep will not find me if I stay within reach of your loveliness," Leopold said. He gave her a coy smile and kissed her hand. "I will not be gone more than a fortnight."

Leopold opened the door and the hulking figure of Klaus, his faithful man at arms, entered holding a lit lantern. Gone were his usual armor and weapons, and instead, the bearded man wore a knee-length, simple woolen tunic, which hung unbelted and loose at the waist. He looked at Catherine on the bed with no emotion in his face. Unruly tufts of hair, more grey than black, poked out the top of the v-shaped neckline that extended deep down his massive chest, and with his hooded eyes, he looked like a great eagle scouring a field for mice.

Catherine gasped and pulled the sheets up to her neck to cover her nakedness.

"Our family has a tradition, my sweet. One that I must honor, though it breaks my heart. But now that you are a Habsburg, I know you will understand."

"My lord?" she said.

"Klaus is a virile man, my sweet. He has served my family for many years and has been selected for his impeccable breeding. He is a Kingmaker. Remember that."

Her eyes widened and seemed to overtake her entire face.

"My lord, no, please."

Leopold took the lantern from Klaus, and the man bowed his head. He smiled revealing a mouth full of yellowed teeth, but all seemed intact. Admirable for someone as old as Klaus, Leopold thought.

Leopold exited the room. He stood in the hall and listened at the door. He heard the bolt being slid into place, and the sound of the oak bed creaking as a ponderous weight fell into it. A muffled scream followed soon after, followed by some frenzied thrashing about and more protests from the wooden bed.

Leopold's second physician favored vigorous sexual intercourse because it made for a stronger, more robust fetus. One that would be more likely to survive a difficult birthing.

Leopold had ordered Klaus to be rough. Being a Habsburg was a dangerous business these days, and when it came to family planning, it was best to play it safe.

CHAPTER 14

HARVEST CAME quickly that year, and once the crops were in, farmers rounded up their cows, sheep, and goats from the higher meadows where they had spent the summer, and marched them into town. There, they were placed in holding pens to await the festivities and fall market.

The town of Schwyz tripled in population over the course of the week as inhabitants of nearby smaller villages came in to celebrate the end of harvest. It was the biggest gala of the year, and for many, it was the one chance they would get to see relatives and friends from some of the more remote settlements.

Pirmin stayed in town all week of course, not wanting to miss a single day of the celebrations. But Thomas had remained at his cabin on the lake, using the busy ferry business as an excuse to avoid coming to town. The week of celebrations had indeed been good for business with a vast number of travelers seeking passage across the water. Thomas saw many new faces on his barge during the week, and almost every one looked at him with suspicion in their eyes and asked what happened to the old ferryman.

As the week came to an end, the number of people on the road lessened and things quieted down. Just when Thomas was sure he had avoided the festivities, Pirmin showed up at dawn on the last day.

"You drunk?" Thomas said.

"Drunk on the love of a good woman," Pirmin said slapping Thomas on the arm with one of his huge hands.

"Found out her name yet? Perhaps she had time to shout it at your back while you were riding away in the dark."

"Why so negative brother? I know just what you need to fix that sour song of yours. Breakfast. In fact, that is precisely why I have come. To break fast with my brother and thank God for all our fortunes."

"You have come all the way out here to make me breakfast?"

"Aye, Thomi. And after that, I mean to drag you kicking and screaming into town where I will revel in your discomfort."

True to his word, Pirmin did make them a hot breakfast of boiled oats with a handful of blackberries thrown in, and several thin slices of dried meat. Of course, he used Thomas's stores, and ate enough himself for three men.

✧ ✧ ✧

Thomas did not recognize Schwyz. Brightly painted flower boxes hung from every window, overflowing with even brighter red and purple autumn blossoms of every shape and size. Freshly cut spruce and fir boughs adorned doors and hung from poles, filling the air with their scent. And people were everywhere: in the street, hanging off balconies, waving and calling from open windows, clustered in small groups on the ground, drinking mead and ale, or sharing bread and sausages smeared with spicy mustard. Children chased each other in and out of the crowd of people, screaming as loud as possible, but no one seemed to mind.

It was a time of celebration, the calm before the storms of winter set in. Women revealed dresses they had worked on in private all year and spent hours braiding and tying ribbons in their friends' and daughters' hair. Men donned short, colorful vests and put fresh feathers in their well-worn forester caps. But the real stars of the festival were the cows. Adorned in towering headdresses of pine boughs decorated with gentians, carnations, and edelweiss, their owners marched them through the main street of Schwyz like heroes returning from war.

Thomas and Pirmin watched a dozen cows saunter past, the bells at their necks announcing their passage. A group of proud farmers followed closely behind, waving at friends in the crowd lining both sides of the hard-packed earthen street.

"These beasts are pretty, I will give them that. But the cows of Wallis, now those are fine animals."

"More beautiful than the finest Arabian mares, I am sure," Thomas said.

"Beautiful? Naw, Thomi. Ugly as the Devil's arse. But strong, mean, and black as sin. Every spring we have a festival similar to this, but our farmers do not dress them up in girly headdresses and sweet smelling oils. We watch them fight."

Thomas smiled. "Fighting cows."

This was a new tale on the superiority of Wallis, the land of the Matterhorn; where the water was pure, the men brave, women descended from goddesses, and now, apparently, the cows ferocious.

"Do you doubt me?" Pirmin shook his head and wagged a finger in Thomas's face. "You are too mistrusting. I bet you only drank milk from one of your mother's teets."

"I have known you too long to start believing everything

you say, my friend."

"Well, you can believe this. We would put all our cows in a big field and watch them fight all afternoon. Eventually the herd would declare a winner. That would be the one to lead them all up into the Alps, where they would dine on the sweet grasses all summer long. Of course the Queen, as we named her, would get her choice of the bulls."

"Of course," Thomas said.

Pirmin kept speaking, extolling the virtues of being nobility but Thomas only heard every other word. Standing beyond the line of parading cows and their handlers, stood the auburn-haired woman from his ferry, Seraina. He had learned soon after that day that she was in fact the 'old hag' in the woods, and not just a gardener. But, Thomas noted, there was absolutely nothing 'old hag' about Seraina.

Today she wore a sea-green dress, belted high, with a neckline low enough to make Thomas blush. She looked up and caught him staring, then smiled and Thomas marveled that he could make out the brilliance of her emerald eyes even at this distance.

Seraina stepped light-footed into the street, amongst the rush of cows and bulls, and for a moment Thomas worried for her safety. But she paid them no mind and the throng of men and animals parted around her like water flowing around a boulder in a swift-flowing river. Smiling, she made her way towards the two men, occasionally reaching out a hand to caress an animal as it passed.

Pirmin had stopped talking. He elbowed Thomas in the shoulder. "What have we got here?" he said in a low voice as Seraina approached.

Seraina stopped in front of Thomas, to Primin's surprise, and said, "Hello again ferryman. Enjoying the parade?"

Thomas introduced her to Pirmin, who could not stop staring at Thomas with undisguised amazement.

"Thomi, when did you manage to meet such an enchanting creature?" Seraina laughed and color came to her cheeks, but she did not resist when Pirmin took her hand and kissed it.

The sight of Pirmin holding Seraina's hand and making her laugh, bothered Thomas at some level he did not understand. He brushed the thought aside. A few moments later Pirmin excused himself to chase after someone he spotted in the crowd, leaving Thomas alone with Seraina.

As she watched Pirmin leave, Seraina said, "Your friend is a charmer. I suspect he does quite well with the women."

"You have no idea," Thomas said.

She turned back to Thomas, her eyes flashing. "And you, ferryman? Are you also a man of many conquests?"

Thomas's head became hot and he was suddenly conscious of his scar. In the guise of looking at the last of the cows marching past, he angled the marred side of his face away from her.

He was saved from responding by a cow passing a few feet in front of them with a towering headdress of pine branches interspersed with brilliant yellow flowers. Seraina pointed and cooed with delight. But Thomas found himself more interested in how her eyes lit up at the sight. She stood close enough for him to smell the sunlight on her bronzed skin, and when she leaned forward to get a better view, her breast pressed lightly against his arm. He marveled at her softness and found himself rooted to the spot, afraid to move.

"That is my favorite flower in the world," Seraina said, turning to Thomas. He edged back a step and for the first time looked closely at the colorfully adorned cow.

"It is an autumn crocus," he said.

Seraina raised an eyebrow. "Some in these parts also call it a meadow saffron. But I prefer its older name," she said looking at Thomas with an impish grin.

"*Colchicum autumnale?*" Thomas recited its Latin name. In the right doses, he had seen it used to treat some types of fever. But it was more often used as a deadly poison.

"There are many languages older than that of your Church, Thomas," she said, using his name for the first time, he noted. He decided he enjoyed the sound of it on her lips.

"The name I was thinking of," Seraina continued, "is 'naked lady'." She smiled and held Thomas's eyes with her own until he looked away.

"I am sorry. I did not realize an ex-soldier would redden so easily," Seraina said with more amusement than sincerity.

Thomas cleared his throat. "I was a Hospitaller. Not a common soldier. Most of us…did not have occasion to speak with women."

"You mean it was discouraged because all women are sinful? Is that not how your priests see us?"

"Women are not all necessarily sinful, but they do tend to be more susceptible to certain temptations than men," Thomas said, realizing too late how much he sounded like one of his monk teachers.

"Ah, that would be lust? Temptations of the flesh?"

If Thomas's face was glowing before when Seraina mentioned the 'naked lady', it felt ablaze now.

"Perhaps…" he began, searching for the words that would make him look like lesser a fool than he had already proven himself.

"Strange, but I have known more than a few men to be just as lustful as any woman. And what of it? Lust is as essential as water in living a healthy life. Do you not agree?"

As Thomas wracked his mind to think of a response, Pirmin appeared out of the crowd. Thomas's relief vanished, however, when Pirmin stepped aside and revealed a man who had been eclipsed by his bulk.

"My lady, I apologize for interrupting," he flashed a smile down at Seraina, who returned it with a shake of her head. "Thomi, this here is the fellow I told you about."

The lithe figure of Noll Melchthal stepped from behind Pirmin and held out his hand. "Good to see you again, ferryman. Have you put thought to my offer?" His blue eyes sparkled like a melting glacier, and although he smiled, it came across as warm as his eyes.

Thomas gave Pirmin a withering glare. He did not take Noll's hand.

"You two know each other then?" Pirmin said. "Good."

Seraina cut in and put a hand on Noll's shoulder. "Leave the man alone. This is a festive day, and not one for recruiting. Come, let us go sample some of Gertrude's cheeses."

She performed an elaborate curtsy to Thomas and Pirmin, looking every bit a little girl playing at being a lady, then took Noll by the hand and led him away to the food vendor stalls.

✧ ✧ ✧

After the parade was over the games began. Enormous logs were rolled into the town square and men and women of all ages clambered over one another to take part in competitions devised around chopping or cutting through trees in all manners imaginable.

Pirmin lived for competition and when the ax-men lined up in front of the crowd he was standing amongst them, towering over them all. When his name was called he hefted his eight-foot war ax with one arm over his head and the crowd went crazy, cheering louder for the big man than any of the others.

The sight made Thomas smile. They had been in Schwyz for only a few months and Pirmin was already the hometown favorite.

Pirmin's first match saw him pitted against a young lad with thick forearms but the otherwise lean build of a boy stuck on the cusp of manhood. They each stood on top a log at either end, with their feet spread shoulder-width apart. The log rested across two other logs so it was lifted off the ground, effectively elevating the competitors above the crowd and providing them with a stage. Someone blew a horn and they were off.

The young man's ax glided into the wood at a slight angle, first from one side then the other. After each pair of strokes, a large chunk of wood sailed through the air. Pirmin on the other hand, at the sound of the horn, hefted his ax high into the air with one hand and looked out into the crowd. He egged them on with his other hand and they whistled and cheered. A group of young girls stood at the front and chanted "Pirmin! Pirmin!"

Only after he'd worked them into a frenzy did he grab hold of his ax with both hands. He let out a deafening bellow and brought the wide-bladed weapon thundering down to strike the log between his feet. The entire length of the log shook and wobbled, and both Pirmin and his opponent had to fight to regain their balance.

Pirmin's ax blade was embedded up to the handle in the wood. He tugged frantically but the log refused to give it up. His youthful opponent looked over and shook his head then went back to chopping. He was halfway through the log.

Pirmin cursed and jumped off the log. After several grunts

and jerks from different angles, he managed to finally free the ax by heaving and pushing against the log with his foot. Red-faced he hoisted himself back on top, but before he could swing again there was a thump, as the young man's end of the log broke off and fell to the ground.

Pirmin lowered his ax, looked up to the sky and grinned. The crowd clapped and cheered as the two competitors met in the middle of the log and clasped arms. The young girls were still calling Pirmin's name long after the two men got down.

"That did not go so well," Thomas said when Pirmin found him in the crowd.

"Bah, that was a warm-up for the two man crosscutting round. That will be where we shine."

"We?"

"You and me Thomi. Entered us already. And after all that practice this spring cutting timber for your bleeding ferry, I expect to win. So drink some water and let us be off."

Thomas protested of course, but by the time they got to the crosscutting station Pirmin's enthusiasm had infected him as well. Of course, to a much lesser degree. It had always been that way when you were with Pirmin. He not only knew how to live life to the fullest, but somehow he also managed to bring life to those around him.

As Pirmin had said it would, the crosscutting went much better than the ax event. Laboring on either end of a long flexible saw, they managed to win their first four matches and had become a crowd favorite. Thomas knew it was not due to their skill, but he did not care. It felt good to hear strangers call out his name. Children ran up to give him and Pirmin drinks of water between rounds.

Eventually they lost to Sutter and his daughter Mera, but that came as no surprise, because they were last year's champions. Apparently innkeepers cut a lot of wood, and Thomas later learned that Sutter had been a forester for years before taking over the family inn, so he did not feel bad about losing.

Pirmin began complaining over and over how they started before the horn, but when Mera jumped up and kissed him on the cheek, then ran off with her friends, he smiled and went silent enough. Of course, not as silent as Sutter.

Schwingen would prove to be Pirmin's event. A local form of wrestling, it had its own unique set of rules. The combatants each donned a sturdy pair of leather shorts over their breeches. Then by only holding the leather, they attempted to throw one another to the ground.

Pirmin had no technique but he was simply too big and strong for most of the men. He was the true hero of the crowd in this event, easily winning his way to the finals. He was to meet Gruber; a barrel-chested young dairy farmer from Seelisberg, who was shorter than Pirmin by a hand span, but almost as strong. And, despite his age, he was experienced in *Schwingen*.

Thomas stood by Pirmin as he struggled into his leather garment. On the other side of the ring, Gruber's father was helping his son get into his. His mother stood nearby, casting occasional worried glances in Pirmin's direction.

"The boy's mother thinks you aim to eat her boy," Thomas said.

"And I do," Pirmin said. "As soon as I can get these leathers on. Worse than our war kit. How many bleeding straps do these things need?"

Thomas watched Pirmin's huge fingers fumble with the fastenings on the leather shorts for a few seconds more. Finally, he had enough, and slapped his hands away.

"Give me those," Thomas said. "You never could put on your own armor."

Pirmin cursed but he let Thomas take over. He crossed his arms and looked over at his opponent.

"You ever miss wearing your kit Thomi?"

"Never thought on it one way or the other."

"Well, I do. Especially the reds. I think I looked pretty fine in those reds."

A Hospitaller brother-sergeant wore brown with a white cross on the chest, or the shoulder, in his daily activities. Only the knights were permitted to wear black. But in times of war, everyone, brother-knights and brother-sergeants alike, would don vivid red tunics over their armor. On top of this blood-red background of war, a large white cross of peace was emblazoned on the chest.

Pirmin caught his opponent's mother looking at him. He screwed up his face and gnashed his teeth at her. She quickly looked away, wringing her hands.

"There you are," Thomas said stepping back.

Pirmin twisted a few times at the waist and raised each leg once. "Feels good. You still have the touch. Maybe I should have you dress me every day."

"They will stay on for exactly half the match," Thomas said.

The wrestlers were called into the circle and the match began.

It was an intense back and forth competition, but in the end, Gruber's youth and experience won out over Pirmin's strength. Both men were drenched in sweat and their breath came in labored gasps when Gruber finally won with a dramatic hip throw.

Pirmin pushed himself up off the ground and the two men

embraced, after which Pirmin raised the victor's hand into the air. The crowd screamed and the boy's mother had tears in her eyes.

✧ ✧ ✧

The meal that evening was both simple and decadent. Teams of oxen dragged the pieces of logs away from the town's streets and stacked them to dry for a year after which they would be turned into firewood. Hundreds of brooms appeared and for the next hour festivalgoers of every age and sex took turns sweeping sawdust, wood chips and dirt from the cobblestoned square. Chatting with friends as they worked, many sweeping with one hand and holding a cup of mead in the other.

Then a hundred trestle tables appeared in the center of the square. Lids were removed from huge vats of chamois stew that had been simmering since morning and a delicious aroma blanketed the square. There was a sudden, unannounced flurry of activity as people realized it was time to feast and they began to pile lengths of sausages and slabs of dried meats on tables, followed by freshly baked loaves of dark bread and huge wheels of cheese and pickled vegetables. As the sun began to set, a group of women lit torches and placed them around the perimeter.

Pirmin and Thomas sat on upright log ends and watched as Sutter and his wife tapped a fresh keg each of ale and mead. Sutter collected cups from the two men and filled them with mead. He raised his own mug to Thomas and Pirmin and toasted Pirmin on his day's performance, and then scurried off to help his wife.

Thomas sipped the mead, detecting the tartness of plums within the honeyed alcohol. It was delicious and he was about to say so when Pirmin beat him to it.

"By God's hand, Vreni! This is the finest mead I have set my tongue to. Sutter, how did an ornery scarecrow like you, win the heart of such an angel?"

Vreni rolled her eyes and waved away the compliment. Sutter, with an amazing display of accuracy, picked up a keg stopper and tossed it at Pirmin, hitting him dead center in the forehead. Thomas thought he caught the faintest trace of a smile in Sutter's eyes as he turned away to fill someone else's mug, but he may have been wrong.

Pirmin scoured the ground for a moment, looking for the projectile, probably intending to throw it back, but his mug distracted him and he took another sip. His eyes rolled heavenward and he smacked his lips.

"Ah, this is the life, eh Thomi? Tell me you are not glad I dragged you out of your shack today."

Thomas took a satisfying pull off the mead. He knew the answer to Pirmin's question but he would never admit it. "At least it looks like we will eat well tonight. I will give you that."

"You should go into the innkeeping business. I have it on good authority the miserable sort can make a good living at it," Pirmin said.

This got a grudging smile out of Thomas. "And what would you know about making a living at anything?"

They settled into the easy, mocking banter they had known since childhood, but Thomas could sense uneasiness in his friend. He was working around to asking Thomas something. A favor perhaps. Maybe Pirmin needed money, which would not be unlike him. Finally, his curiosity won out over his patience.

"Pirmin, if you need a loan I can help. The ferry has been crowded with passengers as of late, thanks in no small part to you."

"Loan? No Thomi," Pirmin said, shaking his head. "Sutter pays me more coin than I am worth, that I know. And more importantly, all the free food and drink I can stomach."

"He must be a very rich man," Thomas said. "Well, if it is not coin you are after, out with it then. Something is on your mind. I can see as much."

Pirmin chuckled and squinted down at Thomas. "You always could get up inside my head."

He quaffed his drink and looked out over the square at the hundreds of people milling about the tables filled with food. His eyes stopped scanning and rested on one table in particular. He nodded in that direction.

"That one," he said.

Thomas followed his gaze. Noll Melchthal sat on top of a table, deep in conversation with two young men standing near one end. But Thomas only gave them a cursory glance, and found his eyes settling instead on Seraina, who sat amongst a group of children at the far end of the table. She was helping them carve lanterns out of giant beets, which the children would later parade through the nearby woods to chase away bad spirits.

"He has been talking a lot of sense lately. 'Specially for one so young."

"Who?"

"The Melchthal lad. You hearing me, Thomi?"

Thomas turned his head towards Pirmin and his eyes followed, eventually.

"He is a good talker all right," Thomas said. "I will give him that. But Noll Melchthal is nothing more than a rabble-rouser. Men will die at his feet if they walk with him. Almost saw it happen last week." He remembered the young boy with the crossbow bolt in his back. Shaking his head he raised his mug to his lips.

"I know. He told me."

Thomas lowered his mug without drinking. "Just how much time have you and Noll been spending together?"

Pirmin's face was shadowed in the low light of early evening, but Thomas saw a familiar glint in his eyes. "Ever been to Einsiedeln, Thomi?"

"The monastery? What cause do I have to go there?"

He did not know much about the large order of monks living near the Mythen mountains, only that they raised horses and were especially respected as breeders of war mounts for the German Empire. They did not deal in mules or oxen, so the locals never had much to say about them.

"Quite a place they have there. Must be a hundred monks. They built a town within their cathedral grounds. Got farriers, blacksmiths, sheep, some cows, and an awful lot of nice pasture land."

"And you tell me this because you have decided to join their ranks, I suppose."

"Not if the Lord Jesus himself begged me to. But, I think I will consider visiting them again sometime before our next feast day."

Thomas followed his eyes and they stopped on a nearby table laden with roasted lamb shoulders, dried sausages, stacks of freshly baked trenchers, and a small keg of wine. He stared at Pirmin. The big man was grinning.

"Pirmin…what have you done?" Thomas was aghast.

"You know me. When I come to a feast I feel the need to contribute."

"You stole from followers of Saint Benedict! They live in austerity—how could you do that?"

"Bah! Those monks are better off than Templars. They had mountains of foodstuffs in their cellars. They will hardly miss the morsels we took."

Thomas's eyes narrowed. There was more to this story, yet. "Who are *we*?"

"Well, you could say I asked Noll and his men to help me out on this one." Pirmin shrugged. "There was a lot to carry."

Thomas stood, sloshing half the contents of his mug onto the ground. "Are you touched? Raiding a monastery with a known outlaw could get you the noose. And if you avoid that, there is the small thing of blasphemy!"

Pirmin stared at the wet spot on the ground left by Thomas's mead. "That was Sutter's brew, not the monks'. Who are you to call me touched?"

"You have gone too far this time. Einsiedeln is under protection of the Habsburgs."

"And that is exactly why we raided it," Pirmin said. "How much do you know of the troubles Schwyz and the monks have been having?"

Thomas held his tongue and glowered at the big man sitting on his stump; he hardly needed to look down to be at eye level.

"They have been fighting over pasture land for years. Until ten months ago, when Habsburg soldiers started slaughtering any animal grazing within a day's march of Einsiedeln that did not bear the monks' brand." He waved his hand toward the nearby tables heavy with meat. "More than a few of these haunches never belonged to those cursed monks in the first place."

Pirmin had no love for monks, Thomas knew that. He suspected it was because monks always administered the beatings when they were children. And Pirmin, being the type of headstrong boy he was, received far more lashes than any other boy in the Acre hospice.

"Did you kill anyone?"

Pirmin's eyes went wide. "Of course not. We redistributed some foodstuffs, as Noll likes to call it. Nothing more. We left them with their lives and valuables, I swear. Oh, except for a few kegs of ale and cider that, as we speak, are on their way to Noll's camp for his men."

"They will petition the Duke, and the Habsburgs will have no choice but to retaliate. You realize this?"

Pirmin's grin widened. "Now Thomi, do not go all mother on me. It is a little meat, some wine, nothing more. Come—let us go fill that mug of yours."

The celebrations carried on into the night and hours later Thomas found himself helping Sutter pile empty barrel kegs onto the back of a wagon. On the other side of the road, laughter erupted from a group of revelers, and when Thomas looked up he saw Pirmin amongst the crowd. He bent low, almost in half, so a woman could whisper in his ear. As she stood on her tiptoes and placed her slender fingers on Pirmin's shoulder, Thomas realized it was Seraina.

He watched them for a moment, wondering what it was Pirmin was saying to make her smile and laugh so. He felt the scar on his face tighten as he forced a smile of his own. Pirmin was a force of nature when it came to women. Thomas had never known one to be immune to his charms. Why should Seraina be any different?

"Vreni made up a bed for you at the inn, if you want it," Sutter said.

It took Thomas a moment before he understood what the innkeeper was talking about. "No, but tell her thank you. I need to go back home tonight," Thomas said.

Sutter shrugged. "Suits me. It would just be another mouth eating my bread in the morning anyway."

The two men finished loading the wagon and Sutter dropped the end board into place. Thomas turned to see Pirmin and Seraina walking towards him, her hand lost in the huge crook of his arm.

"Ah, Thomi! Good. You have not slunk off into the night as of yet."

"As of yet," Thomas said.

"Seraina is insisting on going back to her cabin tonight, and while I offered to escort her to the end of the world if need be, she refused. Wanted me to ask you to take her. Imagine that, ferryman."

"Pirmin," Seraina said and hit his arm with her open hand. "That is not what I said."

"Oh I think it was."

"I told you I had no need of an escort," she said.

"And then you asked if Thomas was going back to the ferry tonight, and when I said 'I am sure he is'—"

Seraina cut Pirmin off. "I merely thought, since we were both going in the same direction, some company would be nice," She cast Thomas a sheepish, sidelong glance. "If you do not mind, that is."

Thomas shook his head and said, "No, of course not."

"I believe what he means to say is the thought of it horrifies him," Pirmin said grinning from ear to ear.

CHAPTER 15

THOMAS SADDLED UP Anid and they rode out of Schwyz an hour past midnight. The stars hid beneath fast-moving clouds, but enough moonlight reflected through the billowing forms that they did not need a lantern.

Thomas could tell Seraina was an inexperienced rider, but once mounted behind him, she settled into Anid's rhythm like she had been born a horse nomad of the desert steppes. Anid walked as though she was not even there.

But Thomas knew Seraina was there. Her hands rested lightly on his hips, and every so often when she leaned forward to say something, she would press against his back and he would feel the warmth of her breath on his neck.

For most of the trip they spoke of herbs and healing remedies. Quizzing each other on the different names of frequently used concoctions and compresses. They compared the medicine of the Greeks and Arabs to that of the druids, marveling at the similarities and laughed at some of history's more ridiculous treatments.

As the night wore on and they closed in on Thomas's cabin, their conversation slowed until it died off altogether, leaving only the creaks of Anid's saddle carrying on the night air. They rode in a silence that neither of them seemed to find uncomfortable and Thomas found himself wishing he lived further from town.

"Why do you dislike Noll so much?" Seraina said after clearing her throat.

Thomas stiffened.

"I do not dislike the man. I only worry what will happen to those closest to him," he said. "The fairer question might be, why is it that you have so much faith in him?" He felt her hands tighten on his hips. She was silent for some time before she spoke.

"I do not expect you to understand, but Noll is special. Every so often in history a person comes along with the potential to make a great difference in the lives of his people. The old religion would call him a Catalyst."

"And how exactly is Noll so different?"

"The Catalyst is a thread of the Great Weave, like every one of us. But most people's lives have very little effect on the Weave. Whether we live or die makes little difference. A few will mourn our passing, perhaps some will be relieved, but life goes on. The Catalyst, however, is the rarest of threads. If pulled in the right manner, it is capable of completely unraveling the Great Weave, and reworking it into something entirely different."

"Your talk hovers on the edge of blasphemy, Seraina. No man can change the world as you speak of it."

Seraina sighed. "I apologize. I did not wish to put you in such a foul mood on one of the last nights of summer. Let us talk of something else." She leaned in close as she spoke, and Thomas felt his anger towards Noll dissipate with the warmth of her pressed against his back.

Then he felt Seraina tense and she pulled away from him, snatching away that wonderful heat. Anid threw back his head and skitted one step sideways.

"What is it? What do you see, boy?" Thomas leaned over the horse's head and spoke softly. He had long ago learned to trust his mount's senses over his own.

Seraina leapt to the ground and stood next to Anid's head. She stroked his velvet nostrils and said something in a language Thomas did not understand. When Seraina looked up at Thomas she had tears in her eyes.

"I am so sorry Thomas. Please. Stay here with me."

The sky had begun to lighten, or so Thomas had thought. The smell of smoke brought back his sense of reason. Dawn was yet another hour away.

His cabin was over the next rise, and when he looked in that direction he saw a flickering orange and red glow playing along the underbellies of the clouds overhead.

The ferry.

He pulled up on Anid's reins and commanded him backwards with his knees, away from Seraina. The stallion snorted in protest but complied immediately. Thomas was dimly aware of Seraina calling out his name as he forced Anid into a gallop. They pounded up the hill and when they reached the crest, Anid whinnied and reared up on two legs, startled by the sudden bright lights coming from his home below.

Everything was engulfed in flames. The cabin, the ferry, even the wharf. Thomas's hand went to his knife handle and he spun Anid in a circle, scouring the lit up countryside for some sign of who had done this.

He saw nothing but sparks whirling in the cool night air, and everywhere, reddish grey clouds. They hung over the lake and blocked out the forest bordering the road.

He was alone.

CHAPTER 16

"IT IS A FOOL'S HOPE. The fortress will never be completed before the first snows."

"Be careful who you call a fool, Landenberg."

Leopold glanced around him, wondering where that *other* Fool had gotten to. Leopold had arrived in Altdorf an hour before, and as he stood on top of the main gate surveying the masons and their teams of oxen and peasant labor milling about the main keep, he despised the fact that Landenberg was right.

While the living quarters in the main keep were almost finished, the outer walls were nothing more than a hole encircling the grounds. Extending the wall below the ground level was necessary both to prevent its buckling from frost heaves and to deter sappers from tunneling under in the event of a siege. The main gate was finished. However, what good was a gate with no walls?

"How is the tollgate on the road coming?"

"Good. Or fair I should say. We have no portcullis for it as of yet. The iron workers had a fire in the forge and it has put them behind by weeks," Landenberg said.

Leopold squinted his eyes against the mid-day sun. He leaned over the edge of the gatehouse they stood upon. He could make out the top of the massive iron gate suspended with heavy ropes waiting to be dropped at a moment's notice.

"Yet there is one here," Leopold said.

Landenberg nodded. "You said to focus all work on the fortress."

Leopold closed his eyes. Unfortunately, Landenberg was still there when he opened them.

"Look around you. Why would we need a portcullis when we have no walls?"

The tollgate stood between Altdorf and the Gotthard Pass, and was located on a section of road that squeezed between two massive granite faces. It had a guard tower flanking either side, and could hold back an army if need be. That is, *if* it had a portcullis.

Leopold fixed Landenberg with a cold stare, and willed understanding into the dim man. Just when he thought he might have to resort to drawing a picture in the dirt with a stick, Landenberg's eyes lit up and a sheepish look crossed his face.

"We should remove this portcullis and fix it to the tollgate. Then we could begin collecting tolls immediately," Landenberg said.

Just then, the Habsburg Fool's green hair appeared at the top of the stairs, quiet as a snake.

"What a splendid idea! Is that not a splendid idea, my Duke? I wish I had thought of that one," the Fool said. He held his chin and muttered to himself as he stomped up and down the first three stairs several times. The chimes on his pointed shoes sounding more like church bells as they echoed off the stone walls of the narrow staircase.

Leopold clamped his teeth and did his best to ignore the little man. He turned to Landenberg. "Get the iron out of this gate today. Now, did you summon the local judge as I told you?"

"He waits in the hall, my lord."

"Good. Come with me. I would have both you and the judge there to listen. Then if there is some confusion, perhaps you can assist each other in understanding my wishes."

✧ ✧ ✧

"This is most unexpected my lord. To be summoned before the Duke of Styria and Further Austria is an honor an old country judge like myself rarely sees."

"The honor is mine, Judge…" Leopold glanced at Landenberg.

"This is Judge Furst, my Duke. The Crown appointed Magistrate for both Uri and Schwyz," Landenberg said.

Furst bowed and his hands unconsciously smoothed the front of his black magistrate's robe. Faded and frayed around the hemlines, it matched the old man perfectly Leopold thought. He also could not help noticing the man's robe bore none of the red or yellow markings found on the clothing of Judges of other Habsburg territories.

Leopold moved to sit down on a chair behind an ornate desk, the only pieces of furniture in the recently constructed room, when Landenberg suddenly jerked and let out a howling sneeze, showering the desk with a fine mist. There was an awkward moment while the sound reverberated off the walls of the large, but bare, room.

"Cursed dust everywhere. These stonemasons must have lungs full of the stuff. Probably piss white mud," Landenberg said.

Leopold backed away from the desk, wondering how he had become so desperate to need men such as these.

"Let us walk to the balcony, gentlemen. A little fresh air will do us all some good."

They passed through an open doorway that led to a balcony overlooking the courtyard. Although the stonework was mostly complete, no doors or window shutters were yet in place. Apparently, the same ironworkers responsible for the portcullis delay were also behind in the production of hinges and latches. There were only two locations that the doors were fully operational: Leopold's bedchambers, and the prisons, which the men could now see from the balcony. The prisons were located across the courtyard from the keep, in a low rectangular building that extended two floors below ground.

"Vogt Landenberg has told me of the fine work you do for the Crown," Leopold said, resting his hands on the stone railing and looking over some workers in the courtyard.

"Thank you, my lord. I am flattered the Vogt of Unterwalden should concern himself with the governance of Uri and Schwyz at all."

Furst obviously resented Landenberg's presence in his district. And Leopold could not blame him.

"I have asked the Vogt to assist us with a troubling matter that has come to light."

"Oh? What might that be, my lord?"

Leopold could see by Landenberg's face that he was just as puzzled, but he managed to keep quiet.

"Recently, the Abbot of Einsiedeln sent me a most urgent, and if truth be told, disconcerting message concerning some of your Schwyz countrymen."

Furst looked up. His eyes narrowed, but he said nothing. A wise man fears his own words more than those of his betters.

"It seems a band of men led by Arnold Melchthal raided the monastery. They stole a great deal of their larder, and desecrated their place of worship. The Abbot said many of the brothers feared for their very lives."

Furst began to roll his eyes but quickly caught himself, remembering whom he addressed.

"Did you know of this attack?" Leopold asked.

"I heard a rumor, my lord. But no arrests have been made. I hear Melchthal is very difficult to find."

"Bleeding ghost he is, that one," Landenberg said. "But when I catch him, the Devil will not even find use for what I leave of him."

"Bold talk," Leopold said. "For one who has chased the man for what, three years?"

Landenberg's face grew as red as the fist emblazoned on his breastplate. "He cannot run forever."

"Since Melchthal is so difficult to find, perhaps you would have better fortune hunting one of his men. The Abbot described a huge man, fair in hair color and complexion, who was instrumental in the attack. He thought the man may even be Melchthal's lieutenant. He wielded a long-handled ax."

At the mention of the ax, Furst's eyes betrayed his thoughts.

"You know of this man," Leopold said.

Furst paused for a moment before answering. "I know of a big man like that. He does some work for Sutter on occasion."

Leopold gave Landenberg a questioning look.

"Sutter. The innkeeper in Schwyz. Has a fine daughter," Landenberg said.

Leopold nodded. "Very well. Take a few men and visit the inn. Find the big man and arrest him and anyone he is associating with. But not the innkeeper. Travelers and merchants need inns."

Landenberg bowed his head but not before Leopold saw

his face light up like a candle in a prison cell.

He turned to Furst. "Judge, there will be some small changes to your sentencing system. From this day forward, all who are found guilty of even the smallest crimes will be sentenced to work on the fortress. They will be housed in the dungeons and divided equally among the masons. Is that understood?"

Furst's mouth twitched. "Of course my lord."

"This brazen attack on the defenseless monks of Einsiedeln, is a sign of just how widespread banditry has become in this area. We must make a strong stand, and I cannot expect you to rise to the occasion without help. That is why I have sent for three of my best judges from the Aargau to assist you. This is not the time for leniency."

"I will do my best, my lord."

"That is all I can ask of any man of rank and privilege, Judge Furst."

Leopold turned to send Landenberg on his way, but he was already gone.

CHAPTER 17

"THEY BURNED your ferry, Thomi. By the Devil's black arse, of course I am angry!" Vex, Pirmin's new puppy, barked twice and squatted low to the ground, distressed at his master's emotional outburst.

Thomas stood waist-deep in the lake. He had removed his boots but wore all his clothes, hoping they would retain some of his body heat. They did little to keep out the chill of the autumn water.

He finished lashing what remained of the blackened ferry deck to a mooring post on the wharf. The railings, mast, and sail had been completely consumed in the blaze, and most of the floorboards were ruined beyond repair, but the members closer to the water had been spared. At least most of the wharf remained.

"Noll says it was Landenberg. His cousin's boy saw him and a dozen red-fisters on the north road that night," Pirmin said, leaning on his ax and shaking his head.

Pirmin stood well back from the water lapping gently at the fine-pebbled shoreline. He had never enjoyed water. In fact, Thomas believed, it was the only thing in this world the big man feared. Curious that a man who served on a war galley for twenty years should be so cursed. But then again, with time, water could bring down mountains.

Thinking Thomas was not listening, Pirmin hefted his ax and shouted from the shore. "Did you hear that Thomi? Landenberg did this! I say we go visit him in his sleep tonight. You and me. With all the love we can muster." He smiled grimly and ran a thumb as thick as a broom handle over the blade of his ax, testing its edge.

Thomas had been furious the night he and Seraina had come upon his burning home. If someone had been there, Austrian soldier or not, he had no doubt he would have made them pay dearly. But now he was once more under control, and thinking straight.

"Noll would have you believe it was Landenberg. That suits his purpose fine. For all we know Noll burnt all this himself just to sway us to his cause."

Pirmin's face went from red to purple. "By God, you are a stubborn worm!" He lifted his ax and strode towards Thomas, but stopped instantly when his foot splashed into the water. He danced back, as did Vex, but not before snapping at the water's edge.

Pirmin cursed Thomas in his native Wallis dialect, and although Thomas could not understand the words, he was glad ten feet of water separated him from the enraged giant.

"I cannot understand what you have against Melchthal. He talks more sense than you do recently."

"You had best stay away from that one Pirmin. I have told you as much already."

"Or what?"

When Thomas did not reply, Pirmin threw up his hands in disgust. "This country has turned you into a cowering Dominican. Or worse, if there is such a creature."

Thomas shrugged. "If it is as you say, and the Vogt's men

burned my home, he did it because he thinks I helped Noll escape his men. The boy is playing you Pirmin. Any way I look at it, this whole mess is Noll Melchthal's fault."

Pirmin shook his head. "I have said it before, and will not shy from saying it again. You are a stubborn worm, and you get more so every day. I need a drink and a woman. And the order is not important. When you finally crawl out of your monk's cell, you come find me and I will talk reason into you."

Thomas watched Pirmin swing into the saddle of his war mount with the grace of a much smaller man. He looked around for Vex, and found him at the shoreline, gingerly testing the water with a paw disproportionately huge compared to the rest of his growing body.

"Vex! Get away from there! We are going home."

Without waiting for the dog, Pirmin nudged his horse into a gallop over the green-covered slopes. Vex cast one last look at the water, whined, and then bolted after Pirmin.

Thomas stood in the water, and shivered.

CHAPTER 18

PIRMIN AND NOLL stood completely still, hardly daring to breathe. The forest too had gone quiet, as though it sensed what was to come.

Noll sighted down the length of the crossbow bolt with both eyes open. He was an instinctive shooter and never used sights. He preferred to look at a small point on his target and will his bolt to that very spot.

A hairy mass exploded from the thicket with a squeal and charged directly at the two men. Noll flinched but then controlled his breath and waited.

"Shoot!" Pirmin said, stepping away from Noll and reaching for his knife.

Noll picked his spot and eased up on the tickler until the crossbow jumped in his hand and the bolt sprang forward. Noll followed it with his breath and saw it penetrate deep into the boar's chest. The animal veered off course, snorted, and took several steps towards the underbrush. Then it dropped.

"Fine shot!" Pirmin said standing upright and releasing his grip on his knife. "That would have made any Genoese crossbowman proud. Thought for sure we were going to be wrestling pig."

"Pray that never happens. I have seen boar smaller than

this one rip men up pretty bad," Noll said.

He walked over to the boar and touched it with his foot to make sure it was dead, then leaned over and removed his bolt.

"Did you know any Genoese bowmen?" Noll asked.

"Know any? The Levant was full of them. Highest paid mercenaries in the Holy Lands. We used them when we could afford them. I do not recall ever losing a fight when we had the green and red of Genoa with us. Except for Acre…but that fight was lost before it was ever started."

"Perhaps that is what we need—more crossbowmen. If I could get my hands on more of these," Noll held up his crossbow, "we could take the fight to Landenberg. Maybe even Habsburg castle."

Pirmin grinned and shook his head. "I admire your spirit, Noll. I really do. But that crossbow you have is a hunter's weapon. A bolt from that would bounce back from chainmail and stick you in your own eye. A true war bow capable of skewering a man at two hundred paces in full kit is what you would need. But a weapon like that costs more coin than I can drink in a year."

"A full year? By God, Pirmin, you know how to squash a man's dreams."

Pirmin leaned against a tree and plucked a long blade of grass. He chewed on it thoughtfully. "No, what we need are more men. What have you got now? A hundred?"

"I could have a hundred fifty in two days," Noll said.

Pirmin laughed at how proud Noll looked.

"A hundred fifty? Come talk to me when you have a thousand. We could work with that. In the meantime, I suppose we will have to stick to fighting monks."

Noll went silent. He pulled out his knife and cut two lengths of twine, then thrust his knife into the dirt. He began tying the forelegs of the boar together.

"You must know others that would fight for our cause. Do you have any connections?"

Pirmin shook his head. "Lost track of them all. All save Thomi."

Noll groaned. "Do not mention the ferryman again. We have no need of cowards like him."

"Watch your tongue boy. His kind is exactly what you need."

Noll grunted and Pirmin could tell by his face he was not convinced.

"He is a different sort that one. I know it, and the Grandmaster of our order knew it. That is why he made him captain of the Schwyzers."

"What do you mean by 'a different sort'? I've seen plenty of soldiers in my time and they all take to killing much the same in my eyes."

Pirmin shook his head as he stared off into the trees. How could he explain to someone who had never faced the true horrors of war?

"Not that one," he began. "The battle furies have no hold over Thomi. You see, most men survive in war by letting their animal side loose. Fear and anger rise up and give a man strength. They allow him to survive the loss of a limb or fight like a madman long past total exhaustion. Warriors of old called this being possessed by the battle furies."

"I know of the furies," Noll said.

Pirmin looked at the young man's eyes and could see a hard glint there that made him think Noll was perhaps not as green as he thought.

"Well our Thomi does not. You see he has never been visited by the furies. When the killing starts, his pulse never quickens, his guts do not boil up in the back of his throat. He might as well be at home eating soup as caving in a man's head with his mace."

"And why is that useful? You just said rage lends a man strength when he most needs it," Noll said.

"Let me tell you a story," Pirmin said, shaking his head. "We were boys and the Hospitallers had marched us out of Schwyz weeks earlier. Our ship finally put ashore in Outremer, a days march from Acre. A few hours after leaving the port, slavers set upon us. Ripe we were for their kind, what with five hundred children and only a handful of guards. The black knights fought like devils and managed to beat them off, but not before the slavers made off with near two hundred of the young ones."

Pirmin paused. He had not thought on that day for a long time. But he could still smell the sun-baked earth at his feet as they marched, and feel the cool relief as they entered a canyon, the stone walls providing shade from the relentless sun. Then the rockslide came, and relief changed to confusion and terror as dust blotted out the light and made breathing difficult. Screams followed. And soon a new scent for Pirmin, one he would never get used to: the smell of blood spilling onto hot sand and stone.

"Me and Thomi should have been amongst those taken. Fighting was all around us, and a fat-jowled man tried to grab us. Thomi was only five at the time. I was eight." Pirmin grinned at Noll. "But I was big for my age."

"You are still big for your age. What did you do?"

"I jumped on the whoreson and fought for all I was worth. I had a dog too, and she helped some. Before the bastard put her down."

Pirmin was silent for a moment. Thinking of Zora was

never easy for him.

He quickly pressed on. "The slaver thrashed me good. I lay on the ground bleeding and hurting everywhere and he was about to tie my hands and drag me away when Thomi threw a rock at him. The slaver looked up and started laughing. And I tell you, I almost did too." Pirmin shook his head and chuckled at the memory.

"What was so funny? What was he doing?"

Pirmin wiped some moisture from one eye and continued. "That skinny little waif was using every muscle in his feeble body to point a crossbow at the slaver as he tried to haul me away. Not a toy like yours, mind you. It was a real war bow like I was talking about earlier. It weighed as much as him, I am sure. But you want to know the best part?"

Noll smiled. "He shot the man through the stomach?"

Pirmin laughed. "No, that he could not do. He had no bolt. The string was not even stretched. Thomi might as well have been pointing a stick at the bastard."

Noll shook his head. "Stupid boy."

"Ah, was he now?"

Pirmin grinned and took a drink from his wineskin before continuing with his story.

"He held that crossbow on the man, but his eyes were looking into my own. The slaver was laughing so hard as he walked over to Thomi, he had trouble drawing his knife, but what he did not see was Thomi leading me with his eyes to the man's axe lying in the sand behind him. The whoreson slapped the crossbow out of Thomi's hands and, just to teach him a lesson, slashed Thomi across the face."

Pirmin dragged two fingers down the entire length of his face. He was no longer smiling.

"He just stood there? Why did he not run?"

Pirmin used the same two fingers to tap the side of his head. "The plan. With Thomi it is always about the plan. Always has been. You see, Thomi lay on the ground crying and bleeding like a half-slaughtered goat. And when the man leaned over to slip a tether around the boy's neck, I drove the bugger's own ax between his shoulder blades, right through his spine. He died right then, no doubt, but his leg twitched for ten minutes. I will never forget that."

He took another pull off his wineskin and held it out to Noll, who did not seem to notice.

"You killed a man when you were eight?" There was awe in Noll's voice.

Pirmin shook his head. "This is what I have been trying to tell you, boy. I swung the ax, but truth be told, it was Thomi that killed his first man that day. If not for that skinny little boy, I would have spent my life rowing in the bowels of a Turkish slave galley."

CHAPTER 19

BERENGER VON LANDENBERG and seven of his men thrust open the heavy double doors to Sutter's inn shortly after mid-day. While Landenberg sat down in the middle of the room and put his booted feet on the table in front of him, his men forced the few patrons out and then rounded up Sutter and his family. Sutter, his wife Vreni, and daughter Mera, stood in front of Landenberg, displayed in single file.

"Fine place you have here," Landenberg said, waving his hand over the simple room. Behind him a stairway led up to several guest rooms. "I suppose you serve ale?"

"Yes, my lord," Sutter said, wiping his damp hands on the white apron tied about his waist. "And mead as well."

"It is a dusty trip from Altdorf, and I find the honeyed wine…unsatisfying. Perhaps I could bother you for a flagon of ale?"

"Of course," Sutter said, turning towards the bar.

"No, not you. I would have your daughter fetch it."

Sutter was tense before, but now his back jerked upright like a cold iron rod had been laid alongside his spine. He turned to his daughter. Her pale blue eyes looked at him for guidance. He nodded once and tried to smile.

Landenberg watched Mera with hooded eyes as she

stepped behind the bar, and tipped a clay mug under the spout of the oaken keg. She looked up once and something in Landenberg's stare caused her to tremble. Frothy, warm ale flowed onto her hand. She carried the sticky mug over and placed it before Landenberg on the table. Without taking his eyes off her he raised the ale and drained off half, then set it down and dragged the back of his arm across his face to remove the foam from his heavy beard and moustache.

"Very nice," he said. Mera inched closer to her mother and stared at the floor.

Landenberg turned back to Sutter. "Tell me innkeeper. How is business these days?"

"Fair my lord. Could be better, but you will not hear me complain."

"And when was Arnold of Melchthal last here?"

"The outlaw? Surely my lord, we would not—"

"Oh shut up Sutter. I know he and his men frequent this place. Do not fret. I can hardly blame you if a band of outlaws choose your inn to quench their needs. But I would be remiss in my duties as your lord if I were to allow your innocent daughter to be exposed to such unscrupulous men."

Sutter opened his mouth to say something, but Landenberg held up his hand and continued speaking. "Fortunately, so to speak, a member of my own household's serving staff has recently left this world and must be replaced. Your daughter seems capable. What say you my child? Would you have the honor of attending to your lord's household?"

"You are not our lord," Sutter's wife spoke up. "Schwyz is not part of Unterwalden and you are not our Vogt. You have no right to—"

Landenberg nodded to one of his men and he stepped forward and backhanded the woman hard across the face. She fell back into some chairs and another soldier yanked her to her feet.

"Vreni!" Sutter tried to go to his wife but two men grabbed him and another held Mera, who began to shake and sob quietly.

Landenberg stood up. "I may not be Vogt to Schwyz or Uri, yet, but Duke Leopold charged me with keeping the peace in all lands north of the Gotthard. And you, woman, have been harboring outlaw scum in your inn."

He grabbed Mera from the soldier holding her and said, "Show the innkeeper's wife what could happen when one gets too close to outlaws."

The soldier's lips parted into a gap-toothed grin and he nodded to the two men holding Sutter's wife. They lifted her by the arms and slammed her back onto one of the tables, its trestle legs swayed unsteadily but held. The soldier drew his belt knife and starting at the bodice, sliced open the woman's dress. She fought and shouted obscenities at the men, surprising them with the crudity of her curses, and they laughed.

"Right bit of dirt in this one's mouth," one of the men said as he removed his sword belt. "Time to take the fight out of her."

Landenberg held Mera tightly around the neck from behind, as he watched his men take turns at the girl's mother. When Mera called out and tried to struggle free he clamped down, cutting off her air. Her struggles lessened and he eased off the pressure, but kept the soft skin of her face pressed up against his own. He leaned himself into the young girl and felt his loins stir.

His intention had been to get the girl back to his estate and have his way with her then, after she spent some time as a servant in his household. But as she squirmed against him and cried out again and again, he found himself becoming hard and knew he could not wait any longer.

CHAPTER 20

WITH THE FRESHLY killed boar at their feet, Noll and Pirmin crouched in the trees outside Sutter's inn looking at the two soldiers standing on guard outside the main doors.

"What are they doing here?" Pirmin said.

"Looking for me," Noll said. Over their armor, the men wore tunics bearing Landenberg's crest. He fingered the pommel of his sword wondering how many men were inside, and cursed himself. He should never have frequented Sutter's inn, but who would have thought Landenberg would send his soldiers this far from Unterwalden in search of a common outlaw? He must be getting to Landenberg. And while that thought pleased him to no end, it was not right that Sutter should pay the price. Or his family.

Lord God, please let Mera not be inside.

"We have to go in. Sutter is in trouble."

"What do you mean? He does not know where your camp is so there is precious little he can tell them. They will kick around the chairs, ask some questions, maybe drink some of Sutter's mead, and then be on their way."

"Vreni and Mera are in there."

Pirmin was oddly quiet for a moment. "Point taken," he

said, and then gritted his teeth and blew air from between them. "This is turning out to be one hunting trip I wish I had lugged my ax along for."

The big man grabbed the dead boar by the scruff of its neck and dragged it close with one hand. "I will go first and you come when you have a mind to. I will not begrudge doing the lion's share of the work, but I will be right pissed if I need to do it all."

"What? That is your plan? You have no idea how many men are in there," Noll said.

"Bah, you sound like Thomi," a scowl crossed Pirmin's face. "Sometimes you just got to have at 'er. Do something, anything, and push your way through until the job is done."

Pirmin hefted the boar onto his shoulders, stepped out of the bush, and walked straight towards the two guards at the main door to the inn.

"Inn would be closed," one of the soldiers called out to Pirmin when he spotted him. The other one had his hand up inside his chainmail, scratching at something under his arm with a tortured look on his scrunched up face.

"Oh? For how long?" Pirmin said, stopping at the bottom of the steps leading up to the front doors. He shifted the boar on his shoulders and grunted, bending low under the weight.

"Go get your swill somewhere else, man. This tavern is closed until the Vogt decides otherwise."

"That so? Suppose I will leave Sutter's meat on his porch then. Which one of you has my payment?"

The soldier laughed and turned to his companion. "This one is either funny or daft as a stone. Do not know what smells more, him or his pig." Smiling he turned back to Pirmin. "Take your pig and your own stinking hide away from here, now."

"All right, all right. No need for a tongue-lashing. But I would leave this boar here."

"Put it downwind on the far side of the porch," the second man said. His hand was still under his armor but was now raking at the area near the small of his back.

Pirmin nodded and climbed the stairs on unsteady legs, and when he got to the top he bounced once and hefted the boar over his head in an incredible show of strength. Then, he launched it at the furthest soldier, the one with the rash. It hit him square in the chest, knocking him into the guardrail. His legs flipped out from under him, and he tumbled clear over the railing. He hit the dirt hard and a split second later the dead animal landed on top of him.

Noll sprinted out of the bushes and stood over the man in an instant, but there was no need. The man was unconscious.

Meanwhile, the other guard snarled and reached for his sword. Pirmin grabbed his wrist with one hand and his throat with the other. He lifted the man three feet off the deck and slammed him against one of the log posts supporting the porch roof. He grunted and his eyes glossed over. Pirmin let him slide down the post and then used it to pull himself into the man, and delivered a bone-jarring knee to the man's sternum. Chainmail was designed to turn aside the points of blades. It did nothing against the full strength and momentum of a three hundred pound giant. The breath rushed out of the man and his ribs crackled like dry kindling. Pirmin held the man up long enough to take his sword and then tossed him away.

He glanced at Noll to make sure he was coming and then charged through the doors to the inn, screaming in a voice that froze Noll in place and chilled his blood. It was a wail filled with the anguish, hatred, and fear of war. It was the most terrifying thing Noll had ever heard, and it took a moment for its paralyzing effect to release its hold. God only knew the effect it had on the men Pirmin attacked.

By the time he made it through the door, one soldier was on the ground unmoving and Pirmin was exchanging sword blows with two others. Across the room was a flurry of movement as two more soldiers were struggling with Sutter, one of the men had his breeches down around his ankles, and Vreni, Sutter's wife, lay behind them curled up on top of a table, her dress torn and tattered. Sutter had his hands around the breech-less man's throat, while the other one had a handful of Sutter's hair and was punching him in the back of the head. Then he stepped back and drew his sword.

Noll jumped over a chair and knocked the man's blade aside before he could skewer Sutter. He slashed at the soldier's side but his armor protected him. In his peripheral vision Noll caught movement and risked a glance to his left. To his surprise, he saw Berenger Von Landenberg himself holding Mera from behind, and at that moment, the Duke's Vogt also saw Noll. His eyes went wide.

Landenberg's face reddened and twisted. He looked like he was going to charge Noll, but he saw Pirmin swatting his men aside like gnats and he hesitated.

Noll yelled out Landenberg's name in rage, but was forced to parry an attack and he lost track of the Vogt. All he could think of was how he had to get to Mera. Fury lent Noll strength and he sent a flurry of blows against his opponent. The soldier's face blurred and was replaced with that of Landenberg. He heard the Vogt's voice saying the same thing over and over.

His boy broke your fingers, so have your justice. Take the old man's eyes. He heard his father scream and men's laughter.

His father's cry turned into a wet gurgle and Noll realized his sword was stuck in the throat of the soldier he was fighting. He pulled it free and scanned the room for Landenberg. He was nowhere to be seen, but Noll offered up a silent prayer when he saw Mera embracing with her parents. A dead soldier, his face blue, lay crumpled at Sutter's feet as the innkeeper held his sobbing daughter and wife.

Another man was dead on the floor near Pirmin, and the last soldier was on his knees begging for his life. Noll dashed through the kitchen to the back door. The stable gate was open and several horses were moving about some distance away in the woods. Landenberg had scattered them before taking flight himself. Far away up the road Noll saw a lone horseman receding into the distance. He kicked an empty milk can next to the door, grimacing as he felt the hard metal against his toes.

God had granted him a rare opportunity for justice today, but Noll had missed his chance. He had failed his father three years ago on the family farm, and he had let him down yet again here today.

Take the old man's eyes.

Noll kicked the can once more and screamed.

CHAPTER 21

SERAINA EASED the door to Vreni's room closed and made her way softly down the stairs to the inn's common room. Sutter, Mera, Pirmin and Noll sat around a table. They all looked up with pained, expectant faces and awaited her news.

"She will be fine. In time," she said.

The relief on everyone's face told Seraina she had chosen her words well. Vreni was a strong woman, but Seraina doubted she would ever be truly fine. Seraina had seen too many scars left on women by men to ignore the truth. The physical healed quickly, but those of the spirit ran deep, and in most cases, could only be concealed. Wounds of the spirit may scab over, but they never fully heal.

When Seraina had arrived at the inn, she had found Vreni on her knees praying to her god, thanking him over and over again for sparing her daughter the rape she had suffered. The sight had infuriated Seraina, but she allowed the woman her prayers, while inside she seethed at the uselessness of worshipping a god who would subject his faithful subjects to such torture.

Sutter stared at her, his eyes dull and the sockets around them black with exhaustion. The usually taciturn man could not conceal his gratitude.

"Thank you Seraina. I know your presence means a lot to Vreni. And to me. You have always been a friend to this family."

Seraina's vision clouded briefly with the beginnings of tears, but she blinked them back. She would be strong for them. She had suffered nothing, after all, and had no right to subject them to her own childish tears. She forced her lips into what she hoped was a smile, and stalled until her emotions were under control, and she was sure her voice would not quaver when she spoke. She handed Sutter a vial.

"Give her five drops in tea every night. It will help with the dreams." She wanted to say 'nightmares'. "Mera, your mother will need more help with her work than usual for the next few days."

"Of course." The young girl's eyes were still glossy with her own tears. "She spoke against the Vogt on my behalf. Perhaps if I had agreed to what he wanted none of this would have happened."

Noll stood up from the table, banging it with his hand. "Mera! Do not even think on that."

Mera flinched and Pirmin shot Noll an angry glare. He placed his hand lightly on her shoulder. "What Noll means to say is this is not your fault. Nothing you could have done would have changed this."

Chastened, Noll eased himself back onto the bench.

"Yes, forgive my abruptness, Mera," Noll said. He flashed her a weak smile.

"Please, Noll. Do not apologize. If you and Pirmin had not risked your lives to help us…" Mera could not bring herself to finish the thought.

"My daughter is right. I owe you more than I can ever pay,

but I swear to damn well try my best," Sutter said.

Mera placed her hand over her father's for a moment and then stood slowly from the table. "I had best put something on the stove for our customers tonight. People need to eat," she said. The men watched in awe as she left them.

"Brave girl, that one," Pirmin said.

Seraina took Mera's seat at the table. She sensed anger rolling off the men in waves. Pirmin and Sutter both looked at Noll, their faces grim.

Noll said, "We live in Landenberg's shadow, cowering behind his back where his arms cannot reach. Where we pray he will not find us."

Noll stood from the table and drew out his bone-handled hunting knife.

"I, for one, am ready to once again feel the sun on my face." He drove his knife into the center of the table. It continued to quiver after he removed his hand.

"And I can see by your eyes, that your thoughts echo mine."

Seraina's breast swelled with both fear and hope for what Noll had in mind.

CHAPTER 22

GISSLER STOOD in the antechamber to the main hall in Altdorf.

A runner had come for him in Habsburg yesterday morning. Leopold requested his appearance in Altdorf immediately. He had made the trip with all due haste, not only because he sensed he was on the verge of a breakthrough with the Duke, but also because he was bored. He had never been one to sit around idle.

He stepped closer to the door and listened to the Duke and Landenberg arguing in raised voices. Or rather, listened to Leopold reprimanding Landenberg for botching a simple task.

A few minutes later, the door opened and Landenberg blustered out. He cast a contemptuous look in Gissler's direction.

"So, you are here. Leopold said to send you in, but I warn you. His mood is fouler than usual. Hold your tongue if you know what is good for you."

Gissler fought the urge to unleash his tongue on the Vogt at this very moment, and managed restraint. He appeased himself by imagining how he would talk to the fat man if he were knighted, and settled for locking eyes with Landenberg as he pushed past the man into the hall.

Landenberg held his gaze, but stepped aside without a word.

CHAPTER 23

THE STARTLING BLUE eyes of Abbot Ludovicus went wide when Thomas took the quill from his hand, and instead of scratching an 'X', began writing his full name on the bill of sale.

Thomas took his time and formed the letters carefully. It had been some time since he had set ink to parchment, and if truth be told, had never achieved a high skill level in it. Reading and writing were as different as walking and riding to him. But the mere act of writing his own name was something even most bluebloods were incapable of performing.

Thomas set the quill down. Pleased with himself, he stepped back to appraise his work. He turned, and when he saw Anid, his good mood fled. He stepped in and let the horse nuzzle the left side of his neck; for some reason he always favored the side of Thomas's scar.

"Easy boy. The monks will treat you well. You will have all the mares you could ever wish for and food aplenty."

Thomas ran a hand one last time over Anid's long, black head, to his velvety nostrils. He patted his neck and relinquished his grip on the bridle. Abbot Ludovicus took the reins and passed them off to another monk quickly, as though the worn leather were crawling with lice. The monk bowed his head to the Abbot and led Anid away.

Thomas watched until they disappeared through Einsiedeln's gates into the monastery courtyard. His throat tightened, but he reminded himself he had no need of a warhorse. It had been selfish to keep Anid for as long as he had. He was a ferryman now.

"He is a magnificent beast and will be in fine hands here, I promise you. Our farriers are the best in the Empire."

The Abbot of Einsiedeln was a round man with a fleshy neck and cold blue eyes that continuously wandered, as though he were impatient to be somewhere else.

"Remember, per our agreement, he is not to be sold," Thomas said. "I want him to finish his days here, on these green slopes. Stud him out all you like but Anid is not to leave these meadows. Understood?"

Ludovicus bowed his tonsured head. "As agreed. But we will of course have to rename him. We cannot allow a heathen name within our walls."

Thomas disliked the Abbot more with every passing second.

"He will not answer to another name," he said.

"How is it a good Christian like yourself came to possess a pure-blooded Arabian like him in the first place? I know horseflesh well enough to say that his kind can only be found in the stables of princes. *Infidel* princes."

Thomas looked into the Abbot's eyes and said, "A friend gave him to me. A heathen friend."

The Abbot's eyes flicked over Thomas, and his nose wrinkled. "Well, he is small for a destrier. But fast, and strong. Coupled with the right mare, he should produce excellent stock."

Thomas nodded. The man did know horses. In fact he

reminded Thomas more of a horse trader than a monk. "When can I expect delivery of my lumber?"

"In five days time. Now if you will excuse me, I must make arrangements. Brother Titus will be along with your new mount shortly."

Ludovicus picked up the parchment from the low table and turned to leave, but Thomas interrupted him.

"It is a long way back to Brunnen. I had planned to partake of your hospitality this evening. Perhaps a hot meal, and a place to sleep would not be too much to ask?"

The Abbot turned and smiled, but his eyes were cold and unsympathetic.

"I regret that we are unable to accommodate you. Bandits recently ransacked our stores and we have little enough to see us through the winter. The brothers have taken up a vote and decided not to allow outsiders into the grounds for the time being."

Thomas bit his tongue and resisted the urge to lash out at the man. A traveler would never be denied refuge in a Hospice of the Knights of Saint John. In the fields behind the monastery he had counted over a hundred head of horses, most of them bred to be destriers, the ultimate weapons of any army, and each one worth more than a farmer in Schwyz could make in ten years.

Thomas looked at the high walls surrounding the monastery's keep. This was no true house of God; it was a house of war. He idly wondered what ruse Pirmin and Noll had used to get past the main gates and into the courtyard.

Thomas let out a breath to calm himself before he spoke. "The man who gave me Anid would see his own children go hungry before refusing a guest food and shelter."

The Abbot smiled and nodded sagely.

"Such is the way of the Infidel, I am told." He looked towards the gate and said, "Ah, here comes your mount."

Thomas turned to see a monk pulling a squat mule through the gate. The animal balked, reluctant to leave the courtyard and the comfort of the stables. Its long ears twitched and it let out an offensive snort, which sounded more like a donkey's bray than the proud whinny of a horse.

Thomas could not stop his hand from balling up into a fist. "Our deal was lumber and a *horse*," he said.

Ludovicus scrunched up his face. "Was it? Oh, well let me confirm. I would hate to be mistaken."

The Abbot held up the parchment and made a show of examining it carefully.

"No, I am afraid it simply says you will receive four wagons of lumber and one 'mount'. There is no mention of a horse." He held out the parchment to Thomas. "Written in Latin, the language of God, and witnessed here by your very hand."

Thomas glowered at the Abbot. He thought of the Schwyz harvest festival and suddenly wished he had had the foresight to stuff his belly with enough pork to feed ten men.

✧ ✧ ✧

By the time Thomas coaxed the mule back to the remains of his lakeside cabin, the sun hovered behind the tallest surrounding peaks. In the twilight, he saw a shadowy figure move near the entrance to his tent.

He reined in the mule and his hand drifted to the knife at his belt. He scanned the area, while the mule plodded ahead, ignoring Thomas's leg commands. Smoke rose from a small cooking fire, and since Thomas doubted anyone wishing him harm would first prepare dinner, he allowed himself to relax.

As he approached his camp, Thomas recognized the figure as Seraina. His pulse quickened and he urged the mule ahead.

The beast increased his pace to a bouncing trot and Thomas found himself sliding around on the animal's back like it had been slathered in olive oil. He berated himself for not having the business sense to keep his saddle. Knowing how ridiculous he must look with his long legs wrapped around the underbelly of his long-eared mule, Thomas was surprised to not be greeted by a stream of laughter from Seraina.

She stood when she saw him approach and paced to and fro until he dismounted and stood before her. When she looked up he saw the trails of recent tears on her cheeks. She said not a word, but walked to Thomas and threw her arms around his neck, put her head on his chest, and let out a deep breath.

"Seraina, what is it? What has happened?" He tried to lean back and turn her head up but she only clung to him all the harder. Her slim frame shook with a few silent sobs and he surrendered, reaching his arms around to hold her close.

He realized he had yearned to be this close to her since that first day she had appeared on his ferry, but now, holding her tight, he experienced a paralyzing sense of dread. He squeezed her gently and was overcome with the scent of wildflowers and warm, dark earth. Finally, he moved his hands to her shoulders and eased her back.

Hesitantly, Seraina told him how Landenberg's men had beaten and raped Vreni and would have done much worse if Pirmin and Noll had not intervened. By the time she was finished, her voice had risen and a quiet anger flashed in her eyes.

"Why do men talk of honor and god yet feel they can take a woman anytime they wish? Is that something your god teaches?"

"What happened at Sutter's was the Devil's doing. Not God's."

"You are wrong, Thomas. It was men who raped Vreni. Men with power given to them by other men. Men from foreign lands who treat us like animals, because in their eyes, we are not true people."

"I do not condone their actions, but Sutter must have done something to incur Landenberg's wrath."

"What could he possibly have done to deserve such a punishment? What did Vreni do?"

"They harbored outlaws. Everyone knows Noll is close with Sutter."

Seraina took a step back. "Noll cannot be blamed for this. The Habsburgs are a festering wound on our people and Noll is but the dressing."

"I do not understand how you can have such confidence in a common thief."

Seraina's tone softened, but her eyes still burned with conviction. "You underestimate him Thomas. I do not know when, or how, but Noll will make all the difference. Our people, your people, will remember his name for centuries."

Thomas shook his head. "History is the words of conquerors. That boy will conquer no one, but he will make the lives of many short and painful. Just ask Sutter and Vreni if you doubt—"

Seraina slapped him across the face. It was so fast and sudden Thomas doubted for a moment that it really happened. But then the residual heat of her hand registered on the left side of his face, and the skin burned everywhere, except of course, for the chord of scar tissue. It felt as cool as ever.

Seraina's eyes widened and she stared first at Thomas's

face and then at her own hand. She shook her head and backed further away.

Thomas stepped towards her and reached out.

"Seraina, wait."

"No," she said, her voice breaking. "I was wrong to come here."

She opened her mouth to say more but it caught in her throat. Then she turned, and fled into the trees like a startled deer.

Thomas stood alone. His eyes scoured the dark woods for the slightest hint of someone's passing. But all he had for company was a stinging handprint on his cheek, and the soft scent of wildflowers dissipating into the cool night air.

And one long-eared mule.

CHAPTER 24

TO PUT SERAINA from his mind, Thomas threw himself into rebuilding his ferry. He had decided the ferry would take precedence over the cabin, for without the ferry he had no source of income. He would live in a tent all winter if need be.

Thomas was so focused on peeling the charred layer from a log with his double-handled drawknife that he did not hear a man and horse approach. When a voice called out, he jumped, gouging a long divot in the wood.

"You. Peasant. I am searching for a man feared in the lands of Islam. A leader of men and a keeper of the One True Word. Perhaps you know where I might find this man."

Thomas put the drawknife down and straightened up. He wiped his blackened hands on his breeches, squinted into the sun, and pointed southeast.

"You will find him a thousand miles from here. That way I believe."

Gissler leapt down from his horse laughing, and the two men embraced. Thomas made a show of not touching Gissler's clothes with his charcoal-covered hands.

Gissler turned in a full circle and surveyed the burnt-out remains of what had once been Thomas's cabin and ferry.

"What in God's name are you playing at here?" Gissler

said.

"Nothing that cannot be put off until we are sharing a meal and some drink. Let me wash up. Then, what do you say we ride to the local inn?"

"Only if we spend my coin, Thomas. I have been fortunate and come into a position."

"So it would seem," Thomas said, giving a nod to Gissler's outfit. He wore a thick, burgundy traveling cloak and a white, finely embroidered tunic, which almost completely covered his light chainmail vest. On his head was a sleek cap with a peacock feather stitched into the hatband. Thomas had seen similar caps on well-off merchants and nobles, but he thought it looked ridiculous on Gissler.

"You found your kin then? Well, I look forward to hearing it all."

Gissler's eyes blackened for the briefest moment. "Better than that. I am now a member of the Duke's household."

This news caught Thomas by surprise. He turned his back on Gissler and ladled water onto his hands from Anid's trough. Or what used to be his horse's trough. It now belonged to an ornery mule.

"And which Duke would that be?" he said, rubbing his hands together. Rivulets of water cut trails through the charcoal dust on his forearms and dripped off his elbows in blackened streams.

"Which Duke?" Gissler said, incredulous. "Your Duke. The only Duke this land knows. Duke Leopold of Habsburg."

"Duke Leopold's man then? You have indeed done well for yourself, Gissler." Thomas ladled more water over his arms, scrubbed them once more, and gave them a vigorous shake. "So would you be here in an official capacity?"

Gissler laughed, and the sound set Thomas on edge. Gissler was never a man to be so receptive to humor.

"Yes, and no," Gissler said. "The Duke has been happy with my service, I suppose, and when I mentioned I knew of a Captain of the Order living in his lands, he suggested I seek out my friend and offer him a position. I thought that rather generous of our lord, would you not agree?"

"I am done with soldiering. I told you that before."

"I do not talk of guard duty for some noble's spoiled children. This is the Duke's household. And not just any Duke, mind you. Leopold is one of the most powerful princes of the entire German Empire."

He paused and put his hand on Thomas's shoulder. "He has the power to grant us knighthood, Thomas, and has promised as much."

"Knighthood? What use to me is a title? What I really need is some solid timber to rebuild my ferry."

Gissler's eyes clouded over and his top lip curled upwards into a snarl. In a way, this relieved Thomas, for it meant the Gissler he knew was once again standing before him.

"Ferry? Are you daft? I offer you a chance at a noble life, something all men dream of, and you would rather sit in the mud cutting wood?"

"You do not need to be a knight to live a noble life. We have both known enough knights to recognize the truth in that."

Gissler threw up his arms and began pacing. "If you wish to wallow in mud, I will not beg to change your mind."

Thomas eyed Gissler. "Is that truly the reason you came to Schwyz? To offer me a position with your Duke?"

Gissler stopped pacing. His lips stretched into a thin smile. "You have an uncanny ability to hear things people do not say. Very well. I also seek an outlaw. Arnold Melchthal. Do you know of him?"

"You are the Duke's manhunter then? Once a soldier of God, now you chase outlaws for rich men. Is that the glorious position you dangle before me?"

Gissler's face clouded over with the dark grey of a winter storm. "You dare to mock my path?" Gissler stepped back and held his arms out to the sides. His fine velvet cloak fanned out and floated in the breeze, and the sunlight glistened off his calfskin gloves.

"My lord keeps me in the finest livery and comfort I have ever known. I have my own quarters in the Habsburg castle itself. Servants cook my food and bring it to me whenever I desire. And meat, Thomas. I eat meat every day, on trenchers baked from flour whiter than snow."

Gissler's eyes were wild now. He had always been volatile and easy to anger, but Thomas saw something there that made a tremor run up his spine.

"And this is but the beginning. Look at the rags falling off you. What right do you have to say your life is so superior? The Hospitallers whispered half-truths and lies to us as children so they could use us. They lulled us into a dream. They twisted your mind and stole your life, Thomas. They did it to all of us, but I have woken up. And you had best do the same."

Thomas watched Gissler carefully. His agitation had grown as he spoke, and years of resentment for the Hospitallers, the Church, and perhaps Thomas as well, poured forth from the man like froth from the maw of a rabid wolf.

Thomas shook his head. "You scoff at the Divine Order. God made you a soldier, not one of the ruling class, and He has a reason for everything."

Gissler laughed, but it was built upon anger.

"I hear nothing but the voices of monks in your words. I should have known you were too far-gone to reason with. Well, I will not waste any more time, for I have a life to live."

He walked to his horse, a dun mare, grazing nearby. Gissler grabbed her reins and jerked her head up. She whinnied in alarm and danced a few steps as Gissler leapt into the saddle.

"When you change your mind, come to Altdorf and ask for me at the fortress. I will be staying there for a time."

Thomas looked up at Gissler. "Why is it that everyone always thinks I will change my mind? Am I so fickle in my ways?"

With one last stare at Thomas, Gissler whipped the ends of his reins on his horse's neck and jammed his heels into her sides. She took off, eager to be away from the source of her master's ire.

CHAPTER 25

CURSE THAT man's self-righteous hide.

Gissler sat with Pirmin, sipping at his first flagon of mead, while the behemoth across from him was already half through his third. Only the lip of the tall, clay mug peeped out of Pirmin's heavily scarred hand.

Gissler tried to focus on all that spewed from Pirmin's mouth, but the memory of Thomas's disproving face kept stealing his thoughts. Thomas was trapped in the past. No longer a captain of the Order, he was nothing now. Worse than nothing—a ferryman! He had no right to press his will on a member of the Duke's household. All those years being captain of *The Wyvern* had swollen his self-worth far beyond his station. Gissler had every right to have him tied to a post and lashed.

"What brings such a smile to your lips?" Pirmin's words cut through his musings. "Have you got a woman to tell me about?"

Gissler looked up from Pirmin's scarred, misshapen hands to his grinning, chiseled face and twinkling eyes that only the strongest of women could hope to resist. It was a face that had been spared the ravages of war, but there are always roads leading back through a man's past, if one knows where to look.

It had been an easy matter to find Pirmin. So easy in fact he regretted ever going to Thomas first. He should have known Thomas's view of himself was too elevated to ever accept a master other than God.

Gissler had found Pirmin in the same worn out inn they had all said farewell in not so many months ago; the same one they sat in now. It was mid-afternoon and the two men were the only customers in the place. Gissler had no doubt that if he were to return in ten years, he would find Pirmin astride the very same bench. Such were the lives of men without ambition.

He had thought it better not to tell Pirmin about his employment in the Duke's service, opting instead to say he had been traveling throughout Austria and France competing in the tournaments. Pirmin had not doubted him for a moment. The best lies were always the ones harvested from a seed of truth.

"I may have met a woman worth remembering," Gissler said.

"Ah, well out with it then."

"It is true the tournaments have more prizes than shields and coin," Gissler said. "But you will not trap me into moaning over my conquests like some lovesick courtier."

"Conquests? More than one then, and sounds like a battle more than a tumble with a sweet maiden. Pray, tell the tale, Gissler!"

Gissler declined a few more times, and finally, Pirmin gave up, concluding it was going to take a great deal more drink to loosen the man's tongue.

"It looks as though the tourneys have indeed been good to you," Pirmin said, nodding to the velvet cloak draped over a nearby rack. "Would take me two years of cutting Sutter's wood to get one of those."

He quaffed the rest of his drink and wiped his mouth with the back of his hand.

"Maybe three," he added grinning. "If I keep drinking my wages away."

"Coin is easy to come by for men like us," Gissler said. "You could just as easily hire out your ax and make a fortune. But you do not, and I believe I know why."

Gissler emphasized his words with what he hoped was just the right mix of admiration and jealousy to pique Pirmin's interest. And it seemed to work, for the hulk's eyes brightened at Gissler's words. He leaned forward on his bench and it groaned under his weight.

"And why is that—oh wise man with the fancy cloak?"

"You have a good thing here Pirmin. You are fulfilled."

Gissler gestured around the room and nodded to the bar where Sutter was stacking wooden mugs and bowls onto a shelf. The door to the kitchen was open and someone was preparing a stew for the evening meal. Savory smoke trailed from the doorway as cubes of mutton sizzled and browned in a pot. The scene was tranquil, and the inn spotless. Amazing really, Gissler thought, considering the mess Landenberg and his men must have made mere days before. But then again, what choice did peasants such as these really have?

"You have built something here. These are good people. What more does a man need?"

"A fine cloak would be a start," Pirmin said leaning back against the wall. But his eyes had lost their smile. "You are right. A man could do much worse. But truth is I mean to leave Sutter's inn shortly, and most likely will not be coming back."

"And why in God's name would you do that? You just said

how happy you were here."

"Had some trouble a few days back."

"Woman?"

Pirmin shook his head and looked to his hands. He stroked a crooked finger, which had been broken many times over. It was the thickness of a woman's wrist.

"Soldier trouble, if you catch my meaning. Staying here puts these people at risk."

"What have you got yourself mixed up in this time Pirmin?"

"Nothing I regret, that much I know." His tone was fierce.

Gissler let the silence build, before he broke it. "Well, I find myself with time and coin, both in abundance for now. If you want my help, you need but ask."

Pirmin looked up and stared at Gissler's face for a long moment, his eyes narrowing. Feigning interest in his drink, Gissler avoided the man's stare and let his ponderous mind reach its own conclusions. It was critical that Pirmin believe the next thought to be his own.

Finally, Pirmin spoke.

"I myself need nothing, you understand. But, there are those who need help, and we would welcome a man like you."

"What scheme do you have cooking Pirmin?" Gissler said.

"There is someone who can answer that better than me, if he will agree to meet you. He is young, but I warn you, do not take him lightly. He is as sharp as a Spaniard's dagger."

"He would have to be to have you speak so highly of him. Who is this man?"

"His name is Noll Melchthal. Have you heard the name?"

Gissler pursed his lips and fixed Pirmin with a stony look.

"Never," he said.

CHAPTER 26

"THOMAS—WELCOME. We have missed your face around here for some time."

Sutter was caught off guard by Thomas's sudden appearance at the inn. "Little early for dinner, but I got some nice mutton stew Mera made yesterday."

"Thank you. That and some mead would make me a happy man," Thomas said.

He sat at a table in the corner and watched Sutter drift off to the kitchen. He was a man going through the motions; a gaunt shadow of his usual surly self, always full of energy and quick with his tongue.

He returned with the stew and a tall tankard of mead, and when Thomas held out a coin, Sutter shook his head. He looked at Thomas with the dark, red-rimmed eyes of a man barely holding on.

"Your coin is not welcome here. But you and your friends always will be," he said, glancing down and leaving words unspoken.

Thomas tried again to pay the man, but Sutter was adamant in his refusal.

Thomas thanked him and after an awkward silence said, "I am sorry Sutter. How are Vreni and Mera?"

The innkeeper shrugged. "Well enough, I suppose. Lots of folk are worse off."

Thomas nodded, not knowing what to say. He offered up a silent prayer for Sutter and his family, and took a mouthful from the tankard. It tasted of happier times.

"I need to find Pirmin. Know where he might be?"

Sutter cocked his head. "Too bad," he said. "You just missed him and an old friend of both of yours, or so he said."

The spoon stopped halfway to Thomas's mouth. "Friend?"

Sutter nodded. "Man named Gessler, or Gissler, or something like that. Pirmin said you was all together over there in the Outremer. You know him?"

Thomas put the wooden spoon back in the bowl, and willed his heart to stop hammering in his head.

"Where are they now?" Thomas asked.

Sutter caught the flustered look on Thomas's face and sat down across from him.

"What is it? He not the friend he makes himself out to be?"

"Worse. Gissler is a manhunter working for Duke Leopold. He was sent here for Noll Melchthal."

Sutter leaned back in his chair and closed his eyes. He raised a shaking hand to his temple and let out an anguished breath.

"Well, he found him then. I set up the meeting myself." His eyes were haunted when he finally opened them and looked across the table at Thomas.

"Where? When?"

"This morning. But the location was Pirmin's picking. They could be anywhere."

"Sutter, listen to me. Gissler is an extremely dangerous man. Noll and Pirmin are both in more trouble than you can possibly imagine. If you know anything about where Noll might be, or the location of his camp, you have to tell me now."

"God preserve me, Thomas, I know nothing! I swear it. I arranged meetings at coded locations between Noll and his men. They move their camp all the time and I have never known where it was. I swear."

"Who would? You must know someone who does."

"I leave signals in secret places and then Noll or one of his men contact me. That is how it has always been done in the past."

Thomas stood from the table and Sutter jumped in his chair.

"Then get a message to them now. Tell them of Gissler."

"What will you do?"

"I have to find Pirmin. And since you do not know where he is, I must find someone who does."

By the Devil's black hand, how could I not have seen what Gissler was up to?

In his heart of hearts, Thomas knew the answer to that question, and it was a disturbing thought riddled in sin. Thomas wanted Noll out of the way, and that desire had blinded him. Noll Melchthal was a danger to those Thomas cared for most: Pirmin…and Seraina.

He pushed through the inn's doors and the afternoon light temporarily blackened his vision. When it cleared, he saw his long-eared mount leaning against the tether rail. The beast tried to stretch its neck down to some lush grass without giving up the comfortable support offered by the railing.

Thomas whirled around and his boots shook the floorboards as he stomped back inside. Sutter was still sitting at the table, his eyes focused on the uneaten bowl of stew. He looked up, puzzled at Thomas's reappearance.

"Sutter, I need a horse."

CHAPTER 27

Pirmin waited at the top of a treeless slope for Gissler to catch up yet once again. Vex whimpered at his side, eager to be off. Pirmin crossed his arms and looked at the pup.

"Easy boy. He may be a terror in the tournaments, but Gissler is not used to running through these hills like us. Give him some time."

He watched Gissler scramble up the slope like a cat walking on ice; his feet slipping and sliding several times before finding firm purchase. Noll would not have approved, for he left the ground chewed up behind him. Pirmin knew the constant climbing and descending of the Alps' meandering trails was difficult for someone unaccustomed to them, but Gissler had always been light on his feet. Far lighter than Pirmin had ever been. But, perhaps following Noll these past few weeks, as he goated through the mountains, had strengthened Pirmin's own lungs and legs more than he realized.

They had set out an hour before dawn and three hours later arrived at a meeting spot Pirmin and Noll often used. Pirmin turned his back on Gissler and looked down into a shallow bowl at the bottom of three hills. To the east was thick forest, and that was the direction from which Noll would approach.

Shifting his ax to his other shoulder, he made his way down the grassy slope with Vex bounding before him.

Once Gissler caught up to Pirmin and Vex, the two men eased themselves down onto flat boulders to rest. Pirmin broke a loaf of dark bread in two and produced a wedge of cheese from his pack.

"How long before your friend arrives?" Gissler asked.

Pirmin shrugged. "Never know for sure with him. Could be somewhere in the trees watching us right now for all I know."

Gissler glanced up at the hills they had just come over.

"Not that way," Pirmin said shaking his head. "He will come through the trees, yonder."

"Ah, yes of course," Gissler said quickly turning his head and looking where Pirmin indicated.

Pirmin sensed a change come over Gissler in the last hour of their journey. Whenever Pirmin looked at him through the corner of his eye, there seemed to be a tightness in his face twisting Gissler's dark features. It registered a memory somewhere deep in Pirmin's mind that he could not place.

Gissler stood and stretched his legs. He saw Pirmin's ax leaning against a rock beside him.

"The great ax," Gissler said. "It has been a long time since I have stood beside her in battle."

He leaned over and lifted the weapon from its resting place, grunting with the weight of it. Unlike most axes, the elongated handle of Pirmin's was made from a hollow tube of forged steel, all eight feet of it. The blade on top flared wide on one side and narrowed to a vicious pick-like point on the other.

"How well do you know this Arnold Melchthal? Is he a man to be trusted?" Gissler asked, resting one end of the heavy ax on the ground.

Pirmin looked at Gissler's face and realized what his subconscious mind had been trying to tell him. The change in Gissler, his dark expression; it was the same tight-lipped disdain that Pirmin had seen on the man's face a thousand times before. It was the mask that covered Gissler's face just before battle.

Gissler saw him staring.

"You called him Arnold," Pirmin said. "I have never called him that. He goes by Noll."

Vex began barking. Gissler smiled, but his eyes hardened.

"Perhaps Noll to his friends," he said.

"You were not lagging behind all morning. You were leaving sign." Pirmin stood and shaded his eyes. He scanned the hilltops.

"You mean to collect the price on Noll's head."

He could not stop his words. They flowed out of him, his voice deep and ragged. The signs had been there all along, but Pirmin had refused to see them. He had been a fool and allowed Gissler to use him. He had to warn Noll before it was too late.

Gissler's eye twitched and he took several steps back. He hefted Pirmin's ax with both hands and launched it as far away as he could manage.

Pirmin ignored him and instead jumped atop the closest rock. He turned towards the forest and held one closed fist high into the air. He heard Gissler make a shrill whistle sound behind him. Pirmin continued to hold his arm up until he heard steel clearing scabbard.

He turned to face Gissler, who held his sword in front of him. On the hill behind him he saw a solitary man, walking, crest the rise. He sauntered over the ridge and began winding his way down towards Pirmin and Gissler, like he had all the time in the world.

The tracker, Pirmin thought, flexing his fists.

And then the ground trembled. Fully armored soldiers on horseback began flowing over the hill, one after the other, like rapids over river boulders. One rider carried a standard with a flag bearing a red lion; Habsburg soldiers.

Pirmin glanced around and weighed his options. The forest edge was too far away. The riders would be on him in less than a minute.

"Too late Gissler. I have sent the signal. Noll and his men are long gone by now." In truth there was no such signal, but Gissler did not need to know that. Pirmin prayed Noll had the sense to stay clear.

"Not all his men," Gissler said, leveling his blade at Pirmin.

Animals, especially dogs, sometimes display senses only their masters understand. Vex must have received at least a small portion of the hate and betrayal Pirmin was feeling towards Gissler, because before either man could speak again, the young pup growled and launched himself at Gissler.

He snapped at Gissler's thigh, and although his jaw muscles had not yet fully developed, his teeth were sharp. Gissler cursed and knocked Vex away with the pommel of his sword, but not before the dog had torn a hole in his breeches and drawn blood.

Pirmin shouted at Vex and ran at Gissler.

Gissler's eyes went wide as he saw the enraged giant charging at him. Even though he was unarmed, he knew what Pirmin was capable of. Ignoring the dog, he stepped to the side and almost eluded danger, but Pirmin reached out one tree-sized arm and snagged Gissler. The two men crashed to the ground, and Gissler lost his sword. Pirmin grabbed the small man and flipped him onto his back like he was nothing more than flatbread on a grill.

Gissler reached for the knife at his belt. The two combatants did not speak, or curse, or utter idle threats. That was the way of farmers in a fistfight after a night of drinking. For Pirmin and Gissler, each man knew he was in a fight for his life. Vex ran circles around them, barking and whining in distress.

Gissler freed his knife but Pirmin grabbed his wrist and head butted him flat on his nose. Blood splattered each man equally, like a giant mosquito had been crushed between them. Pirmin pushed against Gissler's broken nose with his forearm to create space, and moved into a sitting position on Gissler's chest. He began raining blows down on Gissler's head.

A noose slipped around Pirmin's wrist, and another around his neck. He had run out of time.

He screamed in outrage as men on horseback with pole nooses lifted him off the bloodied Gissler. Grabbing the end of the staff holding the noose around his neck, he twisted and yanked the man on the other end off his horse. Pirmin ripped the man's helmet off with a flick of his hand and then crushed his head with a knee drop.

Gissler pushed himself up from the ground and staggered to his sword. He stepped in and thrust it through Pirmin's shoulder. Pirmin grimaced and turned on Gissler. He tried to reach him but Gissler jumped back and the void was filled with more riders with heavy staves and nooses. They beat Pirmin's arms and legs into positions so their ropes could be slipped on his feet, his wrists, or over his neck. Like hunters trapping a dangerous animal, they immobilized Pirmin's limbs one by one.

The blonde giant twisted and fought, and although several unmanned staff nooses dangled off his neck and limbs, eventually a fresh soldier would gain control of it once again. Pirmin was forced to the ground, where they stretched him out and beat him mercilessly with their staves.

Eventually, bloodied and battered, he was splayed wide on the ground with his face turned to heaven. He fought back no more.

"Enough!" Gissler had to yell to be heard above the grunts and cursing of the soldiers, but the effort caused a painful vibration in his smashed nose. He held a cloth to his face to stem the flow of blood and walked over to where Pirmin was held down by a dozen men, every one of them sweating and breathing hard.

Pirmin turned a hideously swollen face to Gissler. He had to spit blood from his mouth before he could speak.

"You worthless bastard, I piss on you," he said.

Gissler pulled back his leg and kicked Pirmin in the face.

Vex appeared out of nowhere and latched onto the hem of Gissler's cloak. He shouted and spun around while Vex growled and clamped on tighter, but Gissler found his range and kicked the dog hard in the ribs. Vex seemed to fold in two and yelped from a type of pain he had not felt in his short life. He stumbled back out of harm's reach and bared his teeth.

Gissler looked down at a tattered hole in his cloak. He drew his blade and walked towards the dog.

"Vex get out of here! Go home!" Pirmin shouted and thrashed against his bonds.

Vex's ears perked up at his master's voice and he looked at Pirmin with hope in his eyes. Then he wined in confusion at Pirmin's tone.

"Vex, go home!"

The dog bared his teeth once more at Gissler and then loped a few steps away. He turned back and did not move further until Pirmin yelled at him again.

"Come here, boy!" One of the soldiers called out. Several of the men laughed and started calling the dog. A thickset, older man came forward with a loaded crossbow and lifted it to his shoulder.

"Leave him be," Pirmin said. His voice sounded strange to his ears, as he forced the words from his swollen mouth. "I have coin in my pack."

The man with the crossbow sighted down the length of his weapon. "Is that so? Good. I will get that as soon as I shoot your dog."

He pulled the release. More men laughed and Pirmin closed his eyes.

"Give me another bolt," the man said.

"You better take a few," someone else said and laughed.

Pirmin opened his eyes and saw Vex standing further away. He paced back and forth at the forest's edge.

"Take three men and search those woods for any sign of Melchthal," Gissler said.

"Waste of time," Pirmin said, his voice barely a whisper.

"And kill that damned dog."

The four men mounted up, grinning at each other like boys about to get into mischief. They took off after Vex like nobles on a foxhunt. When the dog bolted into the woods, the soldiers dismounted and followed on foot.

✧　✧　✧

"Here, boy. Got a nice biscuit for you." The grey-haired soldier held out his hand and Vex raised his head, catching the scent of the biscuit.

"That is the way boy, come on out from behind that tree."

He tossed the biscuit to the ground half way between himself and the large tree sheltering the dog. He heard his men move into place behind him, making far too much noise. He waved them back with one hand behind his back, and then raised his crossbow to his shoulder. He was determined to be the one to put a bolt between the mutt's ribs.

A youth stepped out from behind the same tree, but on the opposite side of the dog.

"Hello," he said raising a hand in greeting.

The soldier hollered in surprise, re-aimed his crossbow, and pulled the tickler. But the boy had already ducked back behind the tree and the quarrel tore off a heavy piece of bark as it glanced off the trunk.

"Shoot! The outlaws are—"

"Right behind you," Noll said, finishing the soldier's sentence.

The man-at-arms whirled at the sound of the voice and saw Noll standing with his sword drawn. It was red with blood and there was no sign of the other three soldiers. He threw the crossbow to the ground and reached for his sword, but Noll was faster. He stepped in and held the man's wrist, preventing him from drawing the blade. Then, taking his time, he thrust his own sword into his throat.

The last sound the soldier heard was the bark of a dog.

CHAPTER 28

"WOULD YOU SAY he was one of the more virtuous brethren in the Order?" Leopold asked.

"Pirmin? Virtuous?" Gissler could not help himself. His half smile turned into a chuckle before he could gain some measure of control.

"What I mean to say, my lord, is Pirmin was never one for following rules. Whether they be those of his superiors or God."

"Ah, that is unfortunate," Leopold said.

He turned to Bernard, his scribe standing behind him. "Be sure to make a note of that before we begin tonight."

The scribe bowed his head and did not look up until Leopold addressed Gissler again. "But he was initiated into the Brotherhood of Saint John. There is no doubt in that, correct?"

Gissler grew tired of all this talk of Pirmin. Forced to breathe through his mouth because Pirmin had broken his nose, Gissler wanted to forget about the man. He had arrested him, his task was complete. Why did the Duke insist on pestering him with all these questions?

"Yes, he was ordained as a brother-sergeant. As were we all."

"How old were you at the time?"

The answer to this one did not come easily. It took Gissler a few moments to respond.

"Sixteen, my lord? I cannot say for sure but Pirmin and I both share an age, and I believe the ceremony was that year."

"So both of you served with the Black Knights for more than twenty years." It was not a question. "Excellent. You have done well, Gissler. I know it must have been difficult to bring a brother in arms to justice after serving together for so long. But he knew where the path would lead when he chose to follow Arnold Melchthal."

"What will happen to him my lord?"

Leopold shrugged. "He will be judged and punished according to his crimes. He is in God's hands now."

"As it should be," Gissler said and crossed himself.

Leopold held out his hand and the scribe placed a rolled up piece of parchment in his hand. Red wax held the roll in place.

"For your place in bringing a dangerous outlaw to justice, I have arranged to have twelve mares and a stallion transferred to your estate."

Leopold placed the scroll in Gissler's hand. His eyes grew as he accepted it and his fingers felt numb and awkward in handling such a light and brittle thing. The wax bore the mark of the Duke's own lion seal. He looked up at Leopold, who smiled and nodded.

Thirteen horses. It was a fortune in Gissler's eyes. He stood up straighter as the generosity of the payment overtook him. Then he remembered something.

"This is most Generous, my duke. But, I have no estate. No land to raise horses on."

"No, of course not. For I have not given you any, yet. But worry not Gissler. You will have ample opportunity to earn yourself that land. In the meantime, I have arranged for you to keep your horses in the stables at Habsburg. Of course, you will have to hire your own farrier to see to their care. And pay for their keep from your own purse."

"Of course, my lord," Gissler said. He could not believe what he was hearing. "Thank you."

Leopold pointed at him. "I told you before. Our futures are entwined Gissler. You serve the Habsburg line well, and we will raise you up from the crowd."

Thirteen horses! All manner of thoughts ran through Gissler's mind. He saw himself driving his herd onto his brother's filthy pig farm and introducing himself. Then he would take Hugo and his daughter Sara with him to his own estate, where he would give his brother a job. Together they would rebuild the Gissler name. But before that, Gissler would have to hire one of the best farriers he could afford. He knew a fair bit about handling horses but almost nothing when it came to breeding them. But with a good farrier to tend the herd, in time, Gissler was sure he would have the most respected horse farm in the Aargau.

Caught up in his own daydreaming, he realized the Duke had just asked him something.

"Gissler? Did you hear what I said?"

"I am sorry my lord. My head is still shaken up from the fight this morning."

Leopold nodded. "Your face does tell a story. I wish I were there to see it. You said the four men you sent into the woods were all hanging from trees when you found them?"

Gissler nodded. "And their eyes were cut out."

Leopold sighed. "A nasty habit Melchthal picked up from Landenberg. I told the Vogt to be careful what he teaches these peasants."

"Judging from the tracks, I would wager it was six men that got them."

"And you followed them?"

"For a half hour, my lord. Then the tracks started crossing and doubling back on themselves. The men got spooked in the woods, and I did not want to walk into an ambush and lose any more, so I gave up the chase."

Leopold smiled. "And that is why I sent you this time instead of Landenberg. He would have chased Noll and his men over a cliff. The preservation of an army is often more important than victory. I appreciate your reasoning."

The praise was a little too sweet for Gissler's ears so he changed the topic. "What would you have me do now, my lord? Return to the Kussnacht?"

Leopold glanced at the scroll clutched in Gissler's hand. "In a hurry to inspect some horse flesh are you? I am afraid you will have to wait another day or two. I have some business to finish here, but then you will accompany me back to Habsburg. In the meantime, stay near. I may need you."

Gissler bowed, "As you wish."

Leopold dismissed Gissler and after the newly mounted twelve-foot doors closed behind him, he turned to his scribe.

"Get the manuscript and meet me at the dungeons in one hour. Bring a priest and one of *my* judges. Be sure Judge Furst knows nothing of tonight's proceedings."

Bernard bent his grey head and scurried from the room, looking like a nursemaid who had left her child unattended for too long.

CHAPTER 29

THE YOUNG BOY had pressed himself up so tightly against the wall in the far corner of the cell that Pirmin, half blinded by his swollen eyes, thought he was a stone at first.

"No need to fear me boy. It is your jailers who wish you ill. Not I."

His throat, dry as rock dust, made Pirmin's voice come out as little more than a rasp and did little to reassure the boy.

Pirmin tried his best to look as harmless as a seven-foot giant covered in blood chained hand and foot to a wall could. When that did not work, he shook his shackled arms to demonstrate he was going nowhere. This seemed to relax the boy a little, and he lowered himself into a squat but kept a watchful eye on Pirmin.

Pirmin's chains had enough play that he could stand or sit, but neither comfortably. The beating he had suffered at the hands of Gissler and his soldiers had left him bloodied and sore, but he had known worse. His main concern was the sword wound to his shoulder. Although the bleeding had stopped, there was no way for him to clean the wound. Being an ex-Hospitaller, that thought disturbed him as he glanced around the filthy cage he and the boy shared.

"What would be your name lad?"

The boy eased himself down onto a pile of blackened straw.

"You can talk to me, or just listen to me. Either way suits me fine," Pirmin said. "I suppose the bastards already got your tongue then, eh?"

"My name is Matthias," the boy finally said.

"Is it now? Well, a good name that one. Right from the Holy Book itself."

"You talk funny," Matthias said.

Pirmin started. He turned his better eye toward the boy and looked closely. He wondered if the boy was a trick of the mind, like when men saw an oasis in the desert. Perhaps he was hurt worse than he thought. Maybe even dead.

"What did you say?"

"Your words, you say them strange."

Thomas had told him the very same thing when they had first met. The memories of the long march came to Pirmin and he smiled, grateful to have them. For a moment they took him away from his dank cell and the pain wracking his body.

"A good friend said those same words to me when I was about your age."

"What happened to him?"

"What do you mean?"

"Is he dead?"

"No. Why would you say that?"

The boy shrugged. Pirmin grunted and changed the topic. "Tell me what you did to land in here Mathias."

"Why should I?" The boy looked at Pirmin and stuck out his jaw. Pirmin noticed the beginning of a black eye and the remains of a handprint on the side of his face.

"Because you and me are going to be friends. Whether you like it or not."

Mathias squinted at the big man across the dark cell. "I stole three bottles of wine," he said.

"Wine?" Pirmin started laughing, but forced himself to stop because his ribs hurt something fierce. "Thought you were going to say bread, or a chicken, or something sensible. But wine? A lad like you is too young for wine. Who was it for?"

"I am plenty old enough. I was nine at winter's end. And I drank a whole half before the Duke's men found me." He puffed out his skinny chest and sneered at Pirmin.

Pirmin laughed, and this time he welcomed the pain.

CHAPTER 30

THOMAS RODE west from the village of Schwyz until he hit the road leading south from Brunnen. A wave of anger passed through him as he thought of how much time he could save if only his ferry were operational. A half day at least. For now he would need to turn south at Brunnen and follow the road all the way to the end of the lake. From there he would curve around its lower arm until the road turned north once again towards Seelisberg.

It was well after dark by the time he came to the overgrown path branching off the main road that led into the grove where Seraina had her cabin. Thomas never would have found it if Sutter had not given him detailed directions.

The path itself was virtually invisible, but it was marked with a menhir, a man-sized, cylindrical rock moved to this location centuries ago by people long since forgotten. Some said the menhir were markers that warned of places best avoided, others said they were waystones that helped the dead pass from this world into the next.

Thomas dismounted and set flint and steel to the wick of his lantern. Pushing aside some low-hanging branches, and holding the lantern aloft before him, he led Sutter's sturdy mountain pony into the bushes. Even though Thomas believed the stories surrounding menhir were nothing more than ridiculous Pagan beliefs belonging to another time, he found some measure of comfort in how his horse plunged onto the dark path without hesitation.

Fifteen minutes later the path branched off in three directions, forcing Thomas to choose one. Minutes later it branched again, and the trails seemed narrower. Another thirty minutes and Thomas was forced to admit he was lost.

At some point he had become turned around, and was no longer sure in which direction the road lay. Without the sun as a reference point he had no way of knowing. He slapped his open palm against the rough bark of a tree, one of many that crowded his path, and cursed himself for being so careless.

Thomas realized he had no hope now of stumbling upon Seraina's cabin in the darkness, so he hung his lantern on a high branch and began scrounging for firewood. He would have to wait until morning.

Some time later, with his horse unsaddled and hobbled nearby, he huddled in front of his campfire. He rubbed his hands together and when he looked up a figure stood before him on the other side of the flames.

Startled, Thomas jumped to his feet, drew his knife and took a step back from the fire. Unfortunately, a low line of saplings tripped him up. With a yelp he crashed over backwards and landed in the undergrowth.

Lying on his back, with plants crisscrossing all around him like a spider's web, he heard a woman's surprised laugh.

"Seraina?"

He was answered by more laughter and finally, when she had herself under control, Seraina said, "Oh, Thomas. I am sorry, but the look on your face was wonderful. Something I shall never forget."

Thomas sat up from his mattress of ferns and Seraina, after stifling another giggle, held out an arm and helped him to his feet. In her other arm she held a wool blanket.

"I thought you might need this tonight," she said. "And when you failed to turn up at my door, for some reason or another, I decided to come to you." Her eyes glistened in the dark with playful mischief, and Thomas was reminded of tales of men being seduced by beautiful creatures of the Fey.

He took the blanket, mumbling his gratitude, and for the first time in many hours felt himself relax. He had found Seraina, or rather, she had found him, and looking at her reflected in the flickering light of the fire, he felt a great weight lift. Then he remembered why he had come.

"Seraina, I need to find Noll. He and Pirmin are in trouble."

The playfulness in her eyes faded, and as sorry as Thomas was to see it go, the concern for his friend took precedence.

"Well look no further ferryman," a voice called out from the darkness, and this time Seraina jumped as high as Thomas. Her hand latched onto his forearm and stayed there.

Noll slipped out of the woods and walked towards them. "Noll, if I did not know better, I would say you were spying on us," Seraina said.

"I wish I had time for that," Noll said, stopping in front of them. He dropped his pack near the fire and leaned some sticks against it to shield the light. "Your fire is inviting every wanderer on the road for miles around."

He avoided looking at Thomas. There was more movement behind Noll, and Vex wandered out of the woods. He made a circle around the campsite, hot on the trail of some forest creature, and then came to sit at Noll's feet. Seraina's nails bit into Thomas's forearm.

Thomas looked down and something different about the dog caught his eye. The fur around his mouth seemed much darker than he remembered. He glanced at the dark woods, expecting Pirmin to come bursting through at any moment.

"He is not coming, ferryman," Noll said, shaking his head.

Thomas looked back at Vex's mouth, and in the flaring firelight realized it was lined in dried blood. A lot of blood.

If Seraina did not still have her hand on his arm, he would have killed Noll where he stood.

"Where *is Pirmin?*"

CHAPTER 31

THE JAILER, a compact, stoop-shouldered man with a tired face came for Pirmin and the boy that evening. Six Habsburg men-at-arms accompanied him; stern, disciplined soldiers who methodically locked Pirmin in a set of walking irons and then unchained him from the wall. As they hammered the bolts into place on his ankle cuffs, Pirmin eyed the jailer. He squinted and tried to bring his puffed up eyes into focus. He knew the man from somewhere.

"Heller. That your name? We met at Sutter's in the Spring."

The jailer raised his head and straightened up slowly, like a man with a secret who had just been found out.

"Was hoping you forgot," he said.

"I never forget someone I drink with," Pirmin said. "Unless he joins in late and I am so far into my cups there is no climbing out."

Heller started to say something but was interrupted by the shrill hammering of a soldier driving a pin into place on one of Pirmin's cuffs. When the hammering died off, Pirmin said, "I recall now, you said you were from Altdorf."

Heller nodded. "Wish I could say I was glad to see you here Pirmin."

Pirmin held out his manacled wrists. "So unfetter these and we will both feel much better."

One of the men-at-arms stepped in and backhanded Pirmin across the face. "Enough talk, outlaw." The blow dislodged a tooth loosened during his capture and opened up a cut on one of his gums. Blood trickled out of the corner of his mouth and then slowed to a standstill, like a hillside stream in the dead of winter.

The man who hit him wore a patch over one eye and he was bigger than any man in the room save Pirmin. His eye took on a mad glow when he saw Pirmin bleed and spit out his tooth. He laughed and Pirmin, smelling decaying meat on his breath, turned his head away.

He saw Mathias still standing against the far wall, shivering; his thin arms wrapped around himself and his eyes wide in fear.

"Hey, Mathias. Did you just run over here and slap me?"

The boy almost grinned, but the soldier's face twisted and the glow in his one good eye turned to fire. He punched Pirmin in his wounded shoulder. Lightning coursed through Pirmin's blood, sending a shockwave of pain throughout his entire body, and he doubled over, grimacing.

"That better big man? That feel like a boy's fist to you?" The soldier grabbed the mallet from the soldier putting on the shackles and raised it over Pirmin's uninjured shoulder. "Maybe we should even out the pain a bit so you can stand upright."

"Put that down or the Duke will hear how you crippled his prisoner," Heller said.

He strode between the men-at-arms and snatched the mallet from the one-eyed soldier, though he needed to raise himself on his toes to do so. The soldier glared down at Heller, but the threat seemed to register with him, and after a series of chest-heaving breaths he calmed himself. Turning back to Pirmin he grabbed a handful of his hair and yanked him upright. He leaned in close.

"Hear that, big man? The Duke wants to see you." He pushed Pirmin towards the door, but with his ankles hobbled by the short length of chain between them, Pirmin stumbled and fell. He reached out with his hands to break his fall, but his shoulder caused him to scream out in pain. His arms folded and he collapsed onto the flagstone floor amidst a pile of filthy straw.

He closed his eyes and clenched his teeth, pretending he had a strap of leather between them. He would not give these bastards the satisfaction of hearing him scream again.

The pain lasted an eternity. When it finally subsided, he did not have the strength to get to his knees, so he remained with his cheek pressed against the damp floor and breathed through his mouth to minimize the stench of human waste.

"Come on Pirmin. Let us get you up," Heller said softly. He placed his hands on Pirmin's uninjured arm and tried to lift him. "You," he said, nodding at one of the men-at-arms. "Give me a hand here. The Duke awaits."

It took three of them to finally get Pirmin to his feet. The one-eyed soldier put a rope around Mathias's neck and they marched the two prisoners out of the dark cell.

They went down a long corridor lit by flickering torches in metal sconces on the wall. Cells branched off on every side and faces peered out between iron slats. A few voices called out, but most knew better, and remained silent.

"Where are you taking us, Heller?"

"To the Duke. That's all I know."

Pirmin worked his tongue over his split lip and around the

inside of his mouth. He looked at the shadows of men moving in the crowded cells.

"More men in here than a slave galley. What are you doing here, Heller?"

"They have all been sentenced to labor on the fortress. Work day is over and they are back for the night now."

"No, I mean you. Why are you here?"

Heller shrugged, and kept his eyes fixed straight ahead down the long corridor. "I follow my lord's orders. Is that not what we all should do?"

The hallway ended in a high wooden door, reinforced with strips of iron riveted in place. Heller fumbled with a ring full of long iron keys and unlocked it. The door swung inward on protesting hinges and light spilled into the corridor. The air pouring out of the room was thick and damp, and as Pirmin felt the moist heat on his face, a shiver ran through him.

The men-at-arms herded Pirmin and the young boy through the doorway. Torches lined the walls and a single cell occupied the center of the large room. A table with leather restraints took up one corner, a weapons rack filled with flails, hammers, and pointed poles of differing lengths took up another. But what held Pirmin's attention, as he shambled into the room, was a large iron cauldron suspended above the ground on four sturdy iron legs. Flames from a healthy fire licked at the undersides of the metal pot. Steam rose above the cauldron and obscured the faces of four men standing on the other side.

Mathias looked at Pirmin, his face registering alarm. Pirmin did his best to calm the boy with a nonchalant nod, but he wondered what comfort he could really offer with his bloodied teeth and stringy hair. And added to that, was the fact that Pirmin was probably more terrified than Mathias, for he had a much better idea of what was to come.

The soldier leading the boy jerked on his rope and led them around the simmering cauldron to the four men. One was a cleric, who clutched a bible to his chest and chanted a constant stream of Latin. Pirmin tried to block him out.

Another man who could have been the priest's brother, stood at a podium with quill in hand. A thick leather-bound book lay open before him. The third man wore the black robe of a judge, and standing beside him, with his hands behind his back, was Duke Leopold. He ignored the boy but watched Pirmin closely with the inquisitive eyes of a hawk. The prisoners were forced to their knees in front of the Duke.

"Pirmin Schnidrig. I am told you hail from Wallis," Leopold said. "That is a long way from Altdorf, and beautiful I hear. I suspect you wish you where there now."

Pirmin looked straight ahead and tried to blank his mind, but it coursed off on its own. The snow-capped Matterhorn flashed in his head, a small cloud skewered by its sharp peak, and then an image of him as a boy slitting the throat of a black-necked goat. He saw a field, and perhaps the face of his mother, but he could not be certain that it was she. Her features had faded over the years.

The priest's intonations and the sound of sap bubbling and spitting in burning logs drove away the few memories he had.

"You may yet return there if you answer my next question wisely," Leopold said.

Pirmin looked closely at the Duke for the first time and was shocked to see he was no older than Noll. But the similarities ended there. Noll was quick to anger, but he could be just as fast with a joke that would leave men laughing, or a smile that would have women swooning. Leopold, on the other hand, had the look of a man who had been angry his entire life. But he kept it deep, simmering, and let only bits and pieces of it out at a time. He had no light side.

Pirmin glanced at the cauldron and then met Leopold's gaze. "I expect this will be one hell of a question," he said.

"Where is Arnold Melchthal?" Leopold said.

"I will not fall in your hole," Pirmin said, nodding towards the boiling water. "You think I do not know the makings of *Lex Salica* when I see them?"

"Your Latin is good," Leopold said, and the way his face lit up made Pirmin cringe.

"As a lad, I learned enough to keep the monks and their sticks satisfied. Nothing more."

"You truly do not know where Melchthal is, do you?"

"Ah, now, you would like me to say that. But I will not give you or your cursed priest any statement of mine to test."

Leopold shrugged and gestured to the table in the corner. "We could simply torture a confession from you if you prefer."

"Go foul yourself. I would rather die on that table with my guts spilling onto the floor than play your game."

"Very well," Leopold said, and turned to Mathias. "Boy. Did you steal from the food stores of the Holy Roman Empire?"

"Do not answer that!" Pirmin said. But it was too late. The boy's words came out in a torrent of fear.

"No my lord, I swear. Please! Do not cut off my hands. I need them to help me mam. Without them we will both starve before the first snows…"

Leopold nodded to the boy's handler, and the man jerked the rope and forced the boy towards the steaming cauldron.

"Bring a stool for the boy. And something to set the rock upon. The boy's arm is too short to reach the bottom,"

Leopold said to the jailer.

Heller's face lightened to a shade of grey, but he did as he was told. Moments later he lowered a metal stand into the bubbling cauldron and dropped a round stone the size of a man's fist into the boiling water, jumping back as he did so to avoid the splash. The rock landed on the stand, and rolled to a halt a foot below the water's surface.

"Come now! The boy cannot even lift a stone that size," Pirmin said. He made to stand up but three men forced him back down to his knees.

Mathias, bewildered, turned his dirty face from man to man. "Please, lords. Do not cut off my hands," he said. "I took the wine, but I did not know it was the Empire's—I swear!"

Leopold leaned over the boy. "A moment ago you said you did not take the wine. How can I be sure you tell the truth?"

"I swear, I did not know it was my lord's. I would never take something belonging to m'lord. I swear it to God."

Leopold stood up straight and put his hands on his hips. "Well that is a comfort. For God is indeed the only one who can prove the truth of your words. Perhaps you can keep your hands, and we will send you home to your mother. Would you like that?"

Mathias nodded, but his eyes narrowed. "What must I do?"

"A simple test. If you pass, you go free." Leopold turned to the black-robed judge. "Explain the conditions."

The judge cleared his throat and, in an officious voice, recited from memory the rite of *Lex Salica*.

"You will be tried by the *Ordeal of Water*. You must reach your arm into boiling water up to your elbow, grasp the stone, remove it, and place it on the ground outside the cauldron. Twenty-four hours from the Ordeal, a priest and myself shall examine your limb. Some redness is to be expected, but if we perceive any blistering of the skin, or worse, we shall conclude you did not warrant God's protection, and shall deem you guilty in Our Lord's eyes, and therefore, guilty in this court. Do you understand the conditions of your trial?"

"Enough!" Pirmin shouted. All eyes turned to the man. Pirmin glared at Leopold.

"You are a snake, not a man." He turned his head and looked at every man in the room in turn. "All of you. A nest of god damned vipers spitting and hissing, and weaving about the feet of a young lad for your own bloody entertainment." His eyes stopped on Heller, and the jailer quickly looked away.

Leopold's lips spread into a tight smile.

"Perhaps you would prefer to take his place? Surely a Hospitaller does not fear one of God's trials?"

Pirmin closed his eyes and nodded once. "I will submit to the Ordeal. But the boy goes free first and all charges against him are dropped. There. You have what you wanted."

"And why, pray tell, would I negotiate with a thieving outlaw?"

"Because you are a pox-carrying minion squeezed from the Devil's own arse. Now let us get down to it."

Leopold's eyebrows arched up at the insult but other than that he showed no emotion. The man had the features of a hawk, but the blood of a snake, Pirmin thought. Trusting someone like him would be a fast road to hell.

"Bernard, make a note that the Hospitaller offered to volunteer for *Lex Salica* to spare a young boy its discomfort," Leopold said to the scribe. He gestured to the soldier holding Mathias. "Take him outside the walls and release him."

"No. Heller takes him or our arrangement is off. I will not have your Cyclops giving the boy a farewell bugger at the walls."

The man holding the boy's rope, growled and stepped towards Pirmin with his arm raised, but Leopold cut him off and stared him down.

"Very well," Leopold said. "But remember, we can hunt him down easily enough if need be."

Pirmin nodded. His mouth was suddenly too dry for words.

Heller loosened the rope from around Mathias's neck, grabbed a handful of the boy's shirt, and guided him to a door opposite the one that led to the other cells. When he opened it fresh air blew into the room and Pirmin was sure he glimpsed a far off star.

Mathias spread his arms and legs in the doorway and cast a long backwards glance at Pirmin before Heller said something and propelled him through the opening into the cool night beyond. The door slammed shut and Pirmin was once again trapped in his inferno.

The guards put ropes around Pirmin's neck, tore the remains of his shirt off, and forced him to the cauldron's edge. Seeing that the cauldron's top stood at the same height as Pirmin's navel, the judge removed the unnecessary stool. When all were ready, they took off his hand chains. The soldiers spread out like the spokes of a wheel and kept firm grips on their ropes.

Finally, the judge took a long set of tongs off the wall and used them to retrieve the stand from inside the cauldron. The polished rock fell off and came to rest on the cauldron's iron bottom, four feet below the surface of the water.

Pirmin looked over the edge into the roiling water. Steam wafted up and flattened his wavy, blonde hair tight to his head. Through the steam and bubbles breaking the water's surface, he could see the distorted shape of the rock lying on the bottom. The thought of refusing to go through with The Ordeal flitted across his mind, but he knew that was just fear creeping into his soul. If he backed away now, they would simply find some other method of torture. And the Devil only knew what they would do to the boy.

He stared into the swirling waters, and for the first time in many a year, mumbled a heartfelt prayer. He took a deep breath.

Sometimes you just got to have at 'er until the job is done.

With a scream that vibrated the iron cauldron, Pirmin plunged his left arm into the boiling water.

✧ ✧ ✧

Leopold watched Pirmin with rapt attention. He was an ordained member of the Hospitallers, a soldier of God, absolved of all sins in this life by the Pope himself. If anyone had a chance to survive the Ordeal of Water it was this man.

Morbid fascination gripped the room in silence as everyone watched the giant thrust his arm up to his armpit in the scalding liquid. He yelled bravely going in, but the pitch of his voice soon turned into a howling scream as he floundered along the bottom of the cauldron for the rock. Then he yanked his arm out so fast, the white-hot stone slipped out of his hand and flew straight at Leopold's head like it had been launched from a ballista.

The Duke managed to lean his head away in time to avoid the missile, but the man behind him was not so fortunate. The steaming rock caught him flush on the side of his face, sizzling as it made contact. He went down in a heap, cradled his head in his hands and began screaming from the pain of the burn.

Pirmin too was on the ground, moaning and thrashing in

agony, tossing the guards around on the ends of their ropes like kites in a windstorm. The room was in chaos for almost a minute until, finally, Pirmin passed out and the guard's own suffering reached its climax and his uncontrollable screams changed to muttered curses and groans.

Leopold leaned up against a wall and observed the room. He tapped his foot and waited for some semblance of order to return. Everyone breathed easier when the big man's thrashing eased and then stopped altogether.

The judge was the first to regain his composure. "Quickly now, gather straw to his arm and bind it to keep the heat in."

As the soldiers gathered dark handfuls of straw from the floor, Leopold walked cautiously over to Pirmin and inspected his arm. At first it appeared only ruddy, and he thought God had indeed intervened on the Hospitaller's behalf. But then the skin blackened before his eyes, and when the soldiers moved his arm to wrap it in straw, the whole outer layer of skin separated and the arm twisted inside it like a sword in a sheath that was too large.

Leopold backed away just as the first scent of burnt flesh watered his eyes. There would be no need to wait twenty-four hours. The Hospitaller had failed The Ordeal by Water. Disgusted, and more than a little disappointed, he turned and strode to the courtyard door. He threw it open and left the judge and soldiers to their pointless tasks.

Pirmin remained unconscious as the judge gave specific directions on how to pack straw around the arm and tie it in place. Once finished, they dragged Pirmin into the cell in the middle of the room. Before locking the door, the one-eyed soldier loosened his breeches and, to the snickers of his fellow men-at-arms, relieved himself on Pirmin's straw-covered limb.

CHAPTER 32

"WHERE ARE you going?" Seraina asked.

"To get Pirmin. Where would you have me go?" Thomas threw the under pad over Sutter's pony and then bent down and hefted the saddle. The horse regarded him with suspicious eyes. Being saddled after dark was not a normal occurrence for her.

"Did you not hear what I said ferryman? They have him in the fortress. You cannot simply march in and ask the fifty guards watching him if they will hand over their prisoner."

"What choice do I have?"

Seraina stepped in front of Thomas. "You mean what choice do we have. I am going with you. Noll would not get near the jails without someone recognizing him, but I can."

Thomas scowled at Seraina but she met his look with firm resolve. She would not be swayed and Thomas knew better than to attempt it. "Very well. I could use your help."

"Seraina is right when she says I cannot go with you, but that does not mean I cannot help. Pirmin is my friend too."

Thomas could take no more. He dropped the saddle and shoved Noll in the chest with both hands. Noll stumbled backwards, cursed, and had to leap over the fire to avoid falling into it.

"Thomas, please!" Seraina said, coming between them and putting her palms on Thomas's chest.

The heat of the moment passed, and when Thomas looked at Seraina his breathing slowed. "He is not welcome here. I want him gone."

"Or what ferryman?" Noll stood across the fire smiling, taunting. "What will you do? Sink down into the grass like a spotted fawn and pray danger passes you by? As you did when Landenberg torched your home?"

"We both know why he burnt my ferry," Thomas said.

"Just how much suffering do you need to experience before you see the truth? How many friends do you need to see hurt? Or raped?"

"Enough!" Seraina's voice boomed through the dark night like a thunderclap. Both men froze, then turned together and looked at her in surprise.

"You are both acting like children," she said, her voice once again her own. "And selfish children at that. Our friend is in trouble. We must do all we can to help him, and that means working together. Thomas, Noll has connections, and if he offers help, it would be wise to accept."

She kept speaking. Her words were soft, and much slower than Thomas remembered her ever speaking. Yet soothing, the way a warm bath is after a hard day's ride. His anger subsided, and Thomas once again felt in control. Seraina made perfect sense. He needed Noll. They would sort out their differences another time.

Thomas cast a doubtful glance at Noll across the fire. "Can you get us into the jails?"

"Perhaps. I will talk with Walter Furst. He may have an idea."

Thomas saw the beginnings of a plan coming together.

Not a good one, but if he could get past the guardhouse and into the jails there was hope. He would have the long trip to Altdorf to worry about getting out.

"To the house of Furst then," Noll said. "If we leave now, we can be there by dawn."

Thomas glanced at Seraina and was surprised at the look of concern on her face. She turned quickly away when she caught him staring. No, not *concern,* he realized. For all her previous talk of selfish children, she had, for a moment, worn the expression of a child caught in a lie.

CHAPTER 33

"QUICKLY NOW. Get inside and bar the opposite door. It leads to the main cells and is where the guards will be patrolling. I have to get back to the gatehouse and make sure no one notices that key ring missing."

Walter Furst, dressed in his magistrate robe, ushered Thomas and Seraina through the heavy door and closed it behind them.

Seraina pushed back the hood of her cloak and allowed her eyes to adjust to the torch-lit room. The moment she stepped into the chamber her heartbeat quickened to a painful crescendo and the air stuck in her throat; every fiber of her being screamed at her to flee. The energy of the room was terrifying. She swayed on her feet and leaned against Thomas for a moment to catch her breath.

When she looked up into his face she saw him staring at a large cauldron on the far side of the room. It was blackened with soot. The remains of a burnt-out fire lay below it, now nothing more than a cold pile of ash. Before Seraina could speak, Thomas was moving. His long legs carried him across the room in a few quick strides. He stopped at a cell in the room's center and fumbled with the ring of keys Furst had given him. Seraina joined him and peered into the blackness of the cage. Someone was chained to the floor.

Someone huge.

She ran to the nearest wall and pulled a lit torch from its sconce. By the time she returned, Thomas had the door open and was crouched in the darkness at Pirmin's side.

Seraina's torch bathed the two men in light and what she saw made her gasp.

Pirmin, his ankles chained to an iron hoop embedded into the stone floor, lay on his back unmoving, his arms splayed out from his sides like a giant bird fallen from the heavens. One was wrapped in a thick layer of straw held in place by twine cinched tight in several places. His once handsome face was beaten and swollen beyond recognition, and his blond hair was caked and matted in blood and dirt.

"Oh God, what have you done?" There was panic in Thomas's voice, and although it frightened Seraina, it also shocked her into action. She jammed the torch into a holder inside the cell and dropped to her knees beside Pirmin.

"Pirmin! Can you hear me?" Thomas said. He pulled his knife and began cutting the twine encircling Pirmin's left arm. His hands shook.

Seraina put one hand to Pirmin's forehead and the other to his heart. He stirred under her touch and moaned. He whispered something that sounded like a name. *Mathias? Who was Mathias?*

Although Pirmin lived, he was burning with fever. His right shoulder had a wound that had soured. Even in the low light, she could see his upper arm beginning to darken. Soon the poison would drain into his torso and then it would be too late. She dug into her pouch and removed a small knife and several vials. They did not have much time.

Distracted by the task at hand, she was unaware that

Thomas had unwrapped Pirmin's other arm, until a rotten stench assaulted her nostrils, forcing the contents of her stomach into the back of her throat.

She turned to see Thomas sitting with his head in his hands, his knife on the ground beside him. He looked at her with vacant eyes.

"Oh God. Seraina…"

She looked down at the source of the odor, already fearing the worst. A blackened log of flesh, bloated to three times its normal thickness, had replaced Pirmin's left arm. Scattered over his arm, a demonic harvest of straw poked up from the congealed mass. Seraina realized that what she had thought before was dirt and filth on the left side of Pirmin's chest, was actually rivers of decay flowing through his blood.

Thomas stared at her. His dark eyes big and round, begging her to do something for his friend. She put her hand once again to Pirmin's heart, though she did not know why.

"I am sorry, Thomas," she said, shaking her head.

He closed his eyes, and after a moment, nodded.

Pirmin moaned again and his leg spasmed.

"Can you do something for the pain?" Thomas asked.

But Seraina was already reaching into her pouch. She popped a handful of ditch nettle leaves into her mouth and chewed them quickly, taking care not to swallow. Once moistened, she spit the leaves into her hand and formed them into a ball.

"Help me open his mouth," she said. Together they tipped Pirmin's head back and Seraina wiped his gums and the insides of his cheeks with the leaves.

Pirmin coughed once and his eyes fluttered. "Mathias?" he said.

Seraina held the big man's head in her lap and Thomas

scrambled around to his side.

"Pirmin. It is me, Thomas."

He grunted and his eyes opened halfway. "No need to yell at me," he said.

His voice was thin, not much more than a whisper. He closed his eyes and opened them again.

"Thomi? Ah, Thomi. I was wondering when you would appear."

"Save your strength, Pirmin. I am here. So is Seraina."

"Stay still," Seraina said, using the power of her voice to bring him some small amount of comfort.

"They put me to the Ordeal," Pirmin said and tried to move his left arm, which only caused him to grimace in pain.

"I know," Thomas said.

"It did not go so well."

Thomas's mouth stretched into a smile. "You did well enough."

"Had to use my sinister arm. Right was hurt too bad."

"That explains it then," Thomas said.

He closed his eyes for a few heartbeats, and when he opened them they appeared clearer. Seraina could see the ditch nettle was in his system now.

"They got Vex."

Seraina placed her hand on Pirmin's forehead and said, "No, Vex is fine. Noll saved him. Do not worry yourself over him, Pirmin."

Relief washed over his agonized face. Whether it was because his dog was safe or the herb was dulling his pain, Seraina could not be sure.

"I wish to confess," he said.

"And I will hear it," Thomas said, his voice breaking around the edges. "Go ahead."

"I did some bad things. But I did a lot of good things too. I hope God will take that into account."

Thomas waited for Pirmin to continue. After a long pause Pirmin said, "Say your piece Thomi."

"That is your confession?"

"One other thing." He turned his head and looked at Thomas. "I lied to you, Thomi."

"That does not matter."

"I never intended to go to Wallis. I would have missed your miserable face too much. I think I made up most of those stories…"

Thomas nodded. His eyes glistened in the torchlight.

"The fighting cows?"

"Nay. That one is true," Pirmin said. He ground his teeth together against a fresh wave of pain. Thomas held Pirmin's right hand and the big man clenched with what little strength he had left. His face cleared after a moment, but was a shade whiter. Even though he took a deep breath, his next words shuddered forth like his lungs had all the air of a spent bellows.

"Do not mourn me, Thomi. I lived enough for ten men…just promise me you will live enough for one."

Pirmin's eyes slowly closed. His breathing became less labored, and the muscles in his face relaxed.

"I will," Thomas said under his breath.

Seraina felt tears building as she watched Thomas make the sign of the cross above Pirmin and then go on to absolve him of all the sins he had committed in this life. It was a ritual she did not understand, but she appreciated seeing the comfort it brought to Thomas.

Pirmin never opened his eyes again. When he died a few moments later, Seraina felt a great saddening within the Weave; a collective tremor that only occurred with the loss of one who had touched a great many. The world would be a poorer place without Pirmin Schnidrig, until the Weave could usher in the likes of him once again. It may take years, but it would happen.

They sat with him for a few minutes more and then Seraina convinced Thomas they had to leave. Judge Furst would see that Pirmin was removed from the cell and buried properly, not simply thrown on the garbage heap outside the walls. She promised.

Seraina led Thomas out of the cell and back to the door that opened into a corner of the fortress's courtyard. She threw open the door and pulled Thomas behind her into the bright mid-day sun.

Into the midst of a dozen armed soldiers with crossbows and bristling spear points leveled their way.

"Welcome to the light," Duke Leopold said.

CHAPTER 34

"THAT IS NOT Melchthal," Landenberg said, disappointment heavy in his words. He rammed his sword back into its sheath.

"Bring them before me," Leopold said. A page stood behind him holding two saddled mounts, one for him and the other for Gissler. Leopold was to return to Habsburg this day, but when he got news that Walter Furst had been caught stealing keys to the jails, he decided to postpone his journey for a short while.

"Wait!" Gissler stepped forward and shouted at the soldiers surrounding Thomas and Seraina. "No one take another step. Remove your belt knife, Thomas."

"You know this man?" Leopold took a closer look at the man and woman who had emerged from the prisons. He had seen the girl before, but could not place where. The man however, he was sure he did not know. His scarred face would not have been easy to forget.

Gissler nodded, but did not look at the Duke. His eyes were fixed on the man he called Thomas.

"Aye, my lord. And he is not a man you want within arm's reach of a dagger."

At first Leopold thought the man might be simple, the way

his head was bowed, and his movements unsteady. But when he turned his face up and met Gissler's eyes with a cold glare, Leopold immediately recognized him as a soldier.

"Yet another Hospitaller? It is no wonder the Holy wars go badly—you are all here."

"Pirmin is dead," Thomas said. The words, quiet and menacing, were directed at Gissler.

Leopold was not surprised by this news. He had seen the man's wounds, but Gissler flinched, and did not immediately respond.

"He chose his path," Gissler finally said. "Do not make his mistakes your own. Resist and it will not go well for you," he nodded in the girl's direction, "or your pretty friend."

Thomas assessed the situation with fresh eyes, seeing the spear points within thrusting distance of himself and his companion. Leopold had no doubt that if Thomas were alone, his actions would have been quite different. As it was, however, he edged his hand away from his knife handle and undid the clasp on his belt. He held it out and a soldier hooked it with the point of his sword and backed away. The soldiers pushed them to the center of the courtyard, where Leopold, Gissler, and Landenberg stood.

"On your knees. You are in the presence of your rulers," Landenberg said, he sidled closer to Leopold, giving the girl a lascivious stare. She held her head up high and refused to meet the eyes of either man. Leopold smiled. Landenberg would have his hands full indeed if he tried to take this one.

"Bend your knee," Landenberg repeated. When neither the man nor the woman moved to do so, a soldier forced them down by rapping each one in turn between their shoulder blades with the butt end of his spear.

A crowd was beginning to gather. Work on the walls had

come to a standstill since Landenberg had pulled some of the guards away to ambush who he had assumed was Arnold Melchthal, come to rescue his outlaw lieutenant. It was a motley group: condemned men and women, paid laborers, master masons, and even the parish priest of Altdorf milled about curious to see what the commotion was about. It was also market day in Altdorf, so the town was busier than normal. Since the fortress was situated just outside of town, vendors had been coming and going from the fortress with their wares since early morning.

"They caught the witch!" a woman said. "As I thought, she is in league with the ferryman."

Leopold turned to see an old woman pointing at the auburn-haired girl on her knees. "I knew God was listening," the woman continued. She ran forward and spit at the side of the girl's head. She flinched and regarded her assailant with a hurt look in her striking green eyes. People began murmuring, and the word 'witch' traveled through the mob like wildfire.

Interesting development, Leopold thought. He turned to Gissler.

"Return to the stable master and procure a cage wagon, with two guards provisioned for the road. And find Bernard. Tell him to pack my manuscript in the wagon and follow us as soon as he is able."

The soldiers opened their circle and Gissler pushed away into the crowd.

"She-Devil!"

The old woman took another run at the girl, but Landenberg intervened and pushed her away.

"Get the Menznau woman away from here," he said to a soldier. The man turned his spear sideways and was about to push the woman away when Leopold spoke up.

"Hold on. Mother, are you accusing this girl of witchcraft?"

The old woman fell to her knees and clasped her hands before her chest. "I do my lord. She said she would help my son, instead she fed his soul to the Devil!"

Gasps could be heard from the onlookers.

The girl shook her head, her eyes wide. "No, it is not so. I never even saw—" Landenberg cut the girl off with a hard slap, and her hand went to her mouth. His breathing quickened at the sight of a thin line of blood from her lip and the remains of his handprint on her skin. The man, Thomas, reached out to her, and simultaneously narrowed his dark eyes at Landenberg.

"Do not speak in front of your betters, girl." Turning to Leopold he said, "Perhaps we should search her for the Devil's mark, my lord."

"Seraina is no witch!" Thomas said.

Landenberg raised his arm and stepped forward.

"Stay your hand, Vogt," Leopold said. "The man is a Hospitaller. He has earned the right to speak."

Landenberg grunted and stepped back.

"So tell us. Why do you defend this woman when she has so many accusers? A man of God should know better." Leopold said.

"She has done nothing. I demand you set her free."

Landenberg laughed. "Not bloody likely. Better chance of pissing uphill in a föhn."

Thomas slowly eased himself off the ground to his feet and locked eyes with Leopold. The soldier next to Leopold followed Thomas's every move with his crossbow.

"I am Thomas Schwyzer, a Captain of the Knights of Saint John of Jerusalem, subject only to the commands of His

Eminence, the Pope. In His name and that of our Lord Jesus Christ, I demand you set this woman free and trouble her no more."

The crowd was silent. More than a few crossed themselves. Leopold was impressed with the faith and conviction he heard in Thomas's words, but he also sensed something else. *Desperation perhaps?*

"Well, Thomas...*Schwyzer* was it? Hardly a blue-blooded name. I would think someone of your exalted rank could do better. But putting that aside for the moment, I certainly do not wish to upset the Pope, in the off chance you do indeed have His ear."

He raised his voice and addressed the crowd. "So I offer you a chance to prove yourself. Here, in front of these good people of Altdorf and in the presence of God."

The crowd erupted into a chorus of shouts and cheers.

Now, where was that damned Bernard?

CHAPTER 35

SERAINA'S KNEES ached and although her lip had ceased bleeding, her face still throbbed from Landenberg's blow. She heard someone curse her name, and the word 'witch' rang out all around her. The energy of the crowd was dizzying and she felt herself panic. She closed her eyes, but found no peace in the darkness, for the image of the villagers of Tellikon feeding a crippled newborn into flames only became so much more vivid.

She thought of running. If she could make it to the trees she would have a chance, for they would conceal her. But her heart fell when she craned her neck and saw nothing but broken walls and open land in all directions. *Killing fields*, the engineers called them. It had been a moment of fantasy, for she knew she could not leave Thomas.

"Do you know the story of Palnatoki?" Leopold asked Thomas, but he spoke in a voice that carried throughout the crowd. A soldier at each of his arms held crossbows loaded and aimed at Thomas's head. Others formed a circle to keep the crowd of people in order.

"It was a favorite of mine as a child, told to me by my father's greatest military advisor. His storytelling abilities, I must say, rivaled his military genius."

Thomas glanced at Seraina. His hard expression melted for the briefest of moments.

"I think I like this one," Landenberg said. "Palnatoki was a warrior in Dane's Land, am I right?"

Leopold blinked, obviously surprised.

"Right you are. But he was much more than a simple warrior. He was the bravest, fiercest, most skilled soldier in the land. So skilled, that his own king became jealous of his exploits and plotted against him."

As he spoke Leopold began walking. The guards opened up the circle for him.

"One day, when Palnatoki was drunk, the king overheard him boasting about his archery abilities. He claimed he could shoot an apple off the end of a stick at a hundred paces. The king called him on his claim, saying he would not have liars in his personal guard."

Leopold stopped beside one of the saddled horses his page still held, and rooted through its saddlebags.

"The king arranged a test." Leopold pulled out a red apple and held it up for all to see, and then pushed his soldier's spears aside and re-entered the circle. He stopped in front of Seraina. He reached down and put his fingers under her chin like he was caressing a lover. Seraina twisted her head away and averted her eyes. She heard Landenberg's deep-throated laugh.

"Stand her up," Leopold said. A large, one-eyed soldier grabbed her left arm and a smaller man her right, and they jerked her to her feet. Her legs ached as the blood returned to them and she stumbled. The soldier with the patch put his arms around her from behind and chuckled as he ground himself against her. Seraina broke free of his grip and pushed him back. He winked at her and grinned with a mouth full of broken yellow teeth.

Landenberg had watched her brief struggle with interest.

"Think your legs are weak now, girl? Wait till you spend the night in my jails." He laughed at his own joke until he caught Leopold staring at him.

"I will continue my story," Leopold said, "if your courtship is over."

Chastised, Landenberg nodded and stared at the ground.

"The king called in Palnatoki's young son and placed the apple on his head. He then told Palnatoki he had one shot to prove himself. The archer removed three arrows from his quiver, and on his first try, split the apple in two. The king then asked him why he took three arrows when he was allowed only one."

Leopold tossed the apple up once and caught it. He turned to Thomas. "And do you know what he said?"

"To avenge myself on thee, in the event that I caused harm to my boy," Thomas said, as though reading the words. "It is a common enough tale."

"It is good you are familiar with it," Leopold said. "As you may already suspect, we shall use it as the basis for my test."

Seraina could see Thomas's jaw muscles twitch, but he said nothing.

"You and I together shall play the part of Palnatoki. There will be no evil king in our story." He smiled and held up the apple. "Only two heroes."

"This is how it shall work. We place the apple on the witch's head and take turns shooting until one of us hits it. The apple, I mean."

"You are mad," Thomas said.

"God will protect the girl if she is truly innocent. If, however, she is a witch, well…we will just have to see. Now, since you are in my future home, I give you the choice. Would you prefer to shoot first or second?"

"I refuse," Thomas said. "This is utter madness. The girl is innocent."

"Fine. I will shoot first." Leopold grabbed a loaded crossbow from the nearest guard and as he did so his hand brushed the tickler and the bow went off. Everyone within earshot of the loud twang ducked or flinched not sure where the bolt was going. But Leopold had had it pointed at the ground and the heavy shaft thudded harmlessly into the hard earth.

Leopold smiled at Thomas. "I suppose it has been some years since I last shot one of these. But I expect it will come back quickly enough. Someone load me another quarrel."

Seraina knew what Leopold was doing, as, she suspected, did everyone else watching the young Duke.

"Thomas," she said.

His face turned and their eyes met. The weight bearing down on each of them lifted for the briefest of moments. She stepped away from her captors and walked to stand in front of Leopold. Ever so slowly she reached out her hand and plucked the apple from Leopold's grasp. His lips spread into a thin line and he mocked her with a bow.

"Seraina, no…" Thomas began, but she leaned in and put her finger to his lips.

"Do not let him choose my fate," she said. "I would leave that to the Weave. And you, Thomas."

She backed away a few steps and then the guards were on her arms once again. They led her in the direction of the main keep and left her standing in an open work site with shattered rocks and dusty ground chewed up by the hooves of oxen. The only flower she could see was a half-trampled autumn crocus.

A *naked lady*, bent and withered.

Leopold handed Thomas a drawn crossbow with no bolt and showed him where to stand. Anticipation was growing in the crowd, and Leopold could feel the people's excitement building and mixing with his own. Gissler had returned with the cage wagon, and he now stood holding the horses, a scowl on his face. He was not a man who appreciated theatrics, Leopold decided.

He set a spearman on Thomas's left and a crossbow wielding guard on his right, with his weapon trained on Thomas's head just a few feet away.

"Precautions you understand. I hope they do not interfere with your concentration," he said to Thomas.

"Give him a bolt. *One* bolt," Leopold said and someone snickered.

All conversation died down as a soldier stepped in and held out a black, leather-fletched quarrel, to Thomas. He took the bolt in his hand by the iron tip and let out a deep breath. In his other hand he held the crossbow down at his side. Still holding it by the point, he raised the bolt to eye level and sighted down it, checking for defects. Satisfied he turned towards Seraina.

As he turned towards the crossbowman at his side, Thomas reached out with the leather vane end of his arrow and flicked it against the tickler on the underside of the man's bow. There was an audible click and the crossbow jumped in the man's hands as it ejected its missile.

Thomas leaned his head an inch to the side and the bolt whirred by his ear, taking the spearman on his left high in the chest. Thomas stepped inside the dying soldier's spear and drew his belt knife before he slumped to the ground. A spin and a step later, the crossbowman's throat was cut, but with a crazed look on his face, he continued squeezing the trigger on his spent weapon until he finally collapsed.

Leopold did not recognize what was happening until both men were dead on the ground and Thomas was moving unerringly towards him, his black eyes focused on Leopold's throat.

Fortunately for Leopold, a young soldier, with reflexes better than his lord, jumped in front of him with his sword drawn. His death gave Leopold enough time to back out of immediate danger. Other soldiers rushed in.

Thomas sliced a man's leg in three places and sent him screaming to the ground. One soldier shot at Thomas but his bolt missed and hit one of his comrades in the shoulder.

"Hold your fire!" It was Gissler, sitting atop his horse with his sword drawn. "Give him room. Back up, but close the circle."

Thomas stood in a half crouch, one hand stretched out before him and the other one clutching the knife close to his body. Leopold was shocked at how calm he appeared. He had just killed at least three men, but he wore the unconcerned expression of a man sampling cheeses in the marketplace.

"Give up the weapon, Thomas," Gissler said.

Thomas heard nothing, for his eyes were fixed on the same thing most everyone else was watching.

Seraina had suddenly appeared outside the circle of spears and crossbows. She reached out one slender hand and lifted the point of a spear enough to allow her entry. She stepped over a wounded man as easily as a breeze blowing through deadfalls and walked slowly up to Thomas. She raised a hand to his face and held out the other. He looked into her eyes, closed his own, and with only another moment's hesitation, he set the knife in her palm. She let the blade fall to the earth and then pulled Thomas's head to her breast.

The soldiers were on them a second after Thomas's knife hit the ground. They pulled the couple from each other's arms and began beating Thomas with fists, hobnailed boots, and spear shafts. The girl screamed as leering soldiers manhandled her into the cage wagon and padlocked the door.

Gissler rode his horse into the midst of the soldiers beating on Thomas and drove them back.

"The next man to put a boot to him will find himself quivering on the end of my blade," he said. He gestured with his sword to emphasize his words. The soldiers grudgingly backed away from the prone figure in the dirt.

And while all this was happening, Leopold sensed a shift in the crowd about him. One that he did not care for.

"The ferryman is right. Seraina is no witch. She is a gifted healer. Nothing more," Leopold heard a voice saying.

He would have paid it no heed, except it was the parish priest of Altdorf doing the talking. Others nodded their heads and murmured curses at the soldiers under their breaths.

Leopold beckoned Landenberg over from the cage wagon.

"Send the Hospitaller to Habsburg by boat. Then disperse this crowd. I do not like the looks of it. Gissler and I will take the wagon and the witch to Habsburg now."

Landenberg's face fell like that of an unwanted child.

Leopold rolled his eyes. "Very well. Follow us tomorrow. We will wait for you before we proceed with the girl's trial."

Leopold was well aware that sometimes you had to let your dogs run wild.

CHAPTER 36

GISSLER'S MEN marched Thomas down the steep slope to the edge of the lake where their boat was tied to the dock. It was a sleek craft designed for speed and to carry no more than seven people, one steersman at the rear and the other six crowded onto three bench seats spaced out equally down the length of the boat. It had one large triangular sail, lateen-rigged to a twenty foot mast and the bottom to a ten foot boom that swung from side to side depending on the wind, and which caused the passengers to sit slightly hunched over to keep from banging their heads on the heavy wooden beam.

It was a new boat; its overlapping plank hull not yet darkened with age. Even though Thomas's head throbbed and his wrists burned where the ropes were cutting into the flesh, he still found a moment to pause and appreciate her fine workmanship—until 'One-eye' jabbed him in the center of his back and sent him stumbling. Thomas caught himself with his tied hands on the side of the boat, but a shooting pain burst through his shoulder to match the one in his back.

"Something wrong? Afraid of the water? Get moving Schwyzer scum."

Since there were already seven soldiers, One-eye pushed

Thomas down to the floor of the boat at the helmsman's feet, on top of several spare coiled up lines, and sat backwards on the first bench to watch him. The rest of the men clambered into the packed boat. It had one set of oars in the middle and with a man on each side heaving to, they pulled away from the dock.

They soon stowed the oars and the helmsman shouted curses at a soldier in the middle as he fumbled with the sail. Obviously not a sailor, he finally succeeded in trimming the sail properly and the boat shuddered to life. It creaked for a moment, until the sail filled completely, and then the boat sprang forward and picked up speed. The helmsman skillfully pointed the bow as close to the oncoming wind as the boat could manage while still making good forward speed.

Thomas kept his eyes on the floor of the boat as he flexed his fingers trying to work some circulation into his wrists. The rope binding his hands was slick with blood. He could feel One-eye staring at him, looking for any excuse to hit him again. He wracked his mind to come up with a plan to escape, but could not focus. He was too worried about Seraina. She had been accused of witchcraft, and as sure as there was a god in heaven, she was headed for a painful, horrible death. And Gissler knew that all too well. He had betrayed them all. Thomas, the entire crew of *The Wyvern*, and of course Pirmin....

Thomas cringed and felt grief and rage course through his blood in equal measures, paralyzing his mind. He tried to blank them out and concentrate.

Think, man. Think!

He squeezed his eyes shut and took a deep breath. For a moment he was on his own ship, with the smell of saltwater and the heat of the Palestine sun on his face. He saw Pirmin's laughing face, and heard the cry of a sea gull, and when he opened his eyes he heard it again.

But this was no local sea gull—it was the shrill cry of a black-crested gull.

Ever so slowly he raised his head to look over the side of the boat. *Either there was one very lost bird out there or....*

One-eye cuffed Thomas across the face.

"Stay down there. I do not want any good folk to see me traveling with a dog like you." The helmsman laughed at this, and Thomas grunted and eased himself up to his knees to face the man.

The helmsman was the only true sailor on the boat.

Thomas raised his hands up over his head and groaned as though injured, then, lowering them until they were level with the helmsman's face, he traced a slow cross in the air.

One-eye laughed and said, "Looks like you just got blessed by a witch lover. Or maybe he cursed you."

The man shook his head and swatted Thomas's hands away.

"Save your prayers for—"

His words were cut short by a hiss, followed by a wet plop, like the sound a smooth, round rock makes when thrown into a pond. A high-powered crossbow bolt had entered one side of his neck and exited the other, leaving no trace of its existence save for a plume of blood spurting from the exit wound.

The helmsman's eyes rolled up inside his head and he pitched forward. As he fell away from the steerboard, the boat began a lazy arc off course. One-eye stared dumbfounded at the helmsman until another crossbow bolt whistled through the air over his head. He threw himself backward to the floor of the boat and yelled, "Ambush!"

Thomas leaned over the helmsman's body and fumbled

with his bound hands to draw his belt knife. He could hear One-eye shouting at his men as they scrambled over one another in confusion. Two more bolts pounded into the side of the boat near the front. He tried to focus on cutting his ropes with the knife, but the going was awkward with his hands tied. He glanced up to see One-eye glaring at him and drawing his sword. The heavyset man crouched and stepped over the seat separating them. He tried to cut his bonds again but the knife slipped out of his hands and clattered to the bottom of the boat. Thomas realized he was out of time.

He grabbed the dead man's body and pulled it between himself and One-eye. The soldier hacked at it once with his sword and screamed obscenities at Thomas.

"A corpse will not protect you for long, Schwyzer!"

As he attempted to clamber over the body in the narrow confines of the boat, Thomas grabbed the steerboard handle and pushed hard, keeping his eye on how the sail fluttered and died as the boat came around. He felt the wind move to the other side of his face and he ducked. With a groan of protest the heavy wooden boom holding the bottom of the sail swung from one side of the boat to the other, catching One-eye square in the chest and launching him and one other man out of the boat. Dressed in full chainmail, they screamed and hit the water hard, surfaced once, thrashed silently for a moment, and then disappeared below the surface, their heavy armor dragging them down.

The four men in the front of the boat managed to avoid the boom. One pointed at Thomas and shouted something to the other two. They all drew swords and began moving towards Thomas in a crouch. Thomas looked to the shore and estimated they were over three hundred yards away; far out of crossbow range.

They had been moving steadily towards deeper waters since the helmsman had been killed, and that was why there had been no bolts hitting the side of the boat for some time. There was only one man in a thousand that could have made the shot that took out the helmsman, but Thomas could expect no further assistance from his benefactor on land.

Thomas glanced briefly at the dead helmsman's sword, still in its scabbard, and then dismissed the idea just as quickly. Four armored men against one in the cramped space of a rocking boat would be a glorious but stupid death. He gritted his teeth and felt the scar on the side of his face tighten.

If he knew Seraina was already dead he would not have hesitated. But so long as there was a chance she yet lived, he would do everything in his power to survive. Yes, he could jump off the boat and swim for the shore. He might survive the cold water, and looking at the awkward swaying of the four soldiers he doubted they had the skill to turn the boat quickly enough and catch him, but he could not take the chance. Besides, Thomas had to get to Seraina quickly.

And for that, he had need of a fast boat.

Thomas stood in the back of the boat, his hands still bound in front, and watched the four armed soldiers close the distance. They would be on him in seconds. The time for planning was over.

He took a deep breath and reached his tied hands down to snatch up the helmsman's knife resting on the coils of rope at his feet, then raising his arms up high, he drove the blade deep into the helmsman's wooden seat. He rubbed his bonds up and down once against the sharp blade and his hands snapped apart.

He was free.

He picked up one of the coiled lines, put it over his head

and shoulder, and then pulled the steerboard hard to one side, wedging it in place with the helmsman's body.

The boat began turning across the wind again and the boom began moving across. The soldiers were past the midpoint of the boat now, and when they saw the boom swinging around they ducked beneath it, well aware of how it had knocked their comrades over the side of the boat. Grim-faced, they continued their approach. A few more steps and they would be in sword range.

But Thomas had no intention of waiting. As the boom reached the end of its arc and slammed into place, the boat leaned dangerously. With the rudder locked in place and the sail filling with wind, all she needed was the slightest encouragement and she would go over. Thomas hopped up onto the side of the boat, took a couple of quick, agile steps and jumped out just past the mast as high in the air as he could. As he hurtled by the mast he reached out with one arm to snag the tall pole, letting his body weight tip the boat even further into the direction it was already leaning.

"You fool! You will capsize us," the nearest soldier shouted. There was a moment when the boat resisted, but the combination of Thomas's weight and the wind blowing into the sail, proved too much. It swayed, faltered, and then fell over sideways, slowly at first, but soon picked up speed, until the mast and sail slapped the water throwing up a wall of spray and tossing everyone into the cold alpine lake.

The cold water shocked the breath out of Thomas. This was no Mid-Earth sea, and he knew water this temperature could sap the strength out of a man in minutes. He needed to work fast, but at least he was not in as much peril as the armored men around him splashing, fighting for their lives to keep their heads above water. Swimming with thirty pounds of steel and leather dragging one beneath the waves was no easy feat. It was for this very reason that the crew of *The Wyvern* had adopted the use of the Saracen's lightweight Damascan mail shirts for their own armor.

As the soldiers thrashed and kicked, struggling to remove their heavy armor or swim to the side of the tipped over boat, Thomas fastened one end of his line around the narrow top of the mast. He swam back to the boat and clambered up onto the side sticking high out of the water, and then took up the line's slack. Gradually, like a man climbing a rock wall, he leaned back and heaved on the rope. With his body parallel to the water, the mast began lifting out of the water, encouraging him to ignore the pain in his shoulder and pull harder. The line dug into his hands, bloodying them, and every muscle in his body felt like it was going to snap off his skeleton, but still the boat would not turn over that last bit to right herself.

"Come on girl," Thomas said, his voice a hoarse whisper. "Do not let us down now." He could feel himself weakening. He leaned back further, his hair brushing the water, and pulled for all he was worth. The boat shuddered, but refused to flip upright. He did not have the strength, or the weight.

A strong hand grabbed his hair, twisting his neck painfully and dunking his head under the water. He lashed out blindly with one hand and felt it connect with a fleshy nose. The hand released him and as he pulled his head up he caught sight of One-eye reaching an arm out to grab him again.

Somehow, the veteran soldier had managed to remove his chainmail hauberk and boots, and with the frenzied strength of a drowning man, was now clawing his way through the water towards Thomas. Thomas knew he did not have the time, or the will, to fight off the crazed man. But perhaps he could enlist his aid.

Still holding the taut mast rope wrapped around one arm, he leaned back and extended his other arm. One-eye latched on and began dragging himself up Thomas's limb. Thomas screamed and with all the strength he had left, pulled One-eye as far out of the water as he could while simultaneously heaving on the mast line.

The extra weight lifted the entire length of the mast out of the water. The sail followed, shedding water as it rose, and then the boat popped upright like it was the most natural thing in the world.

Thomas half-rolled, half-collapsed into the boat as she righted herself, but One-eye remained hanging over the side still clutching Thomas's arm. The boat creaked and rocked from side to side, showering them with lakewater that hid in the folds of its canvas sail. Both men remained motionless breathing hard through their mouths, exhausted.

Finally, Thomas forced himself to his knees and leaned over the edge of the boat. One-eye had both his arms wrapped around Thomas's arm. His skin was ashen and his lips thick and bluing around the edges.

Thomas hit him hard in the face once, twice, and finally, after a third time, the one-eyed soldier slid off his arm like an over-ripe carcass from a meat hook. He sunk below the water without a sound, his eyes wide in terror.

Thomas collapsed backward into the boat and wrapped his arms around himself. He groaned and tried to rub some feeling back into them. He felt like he had been pulled apart by horses.

Finally, once his chest stopped heaving, and he could feel the blood moving again in his limbs, he poked his head up and surveyed the situation.

He immediately picked out a bearded figure waving on the

shore. One Habsburg soldier still clung to the side of the boat. There was no sign of any others.

"Please…help me up," he said. "I was only following orders. Please…"

Thomas leaned over and undid the chinstrap on the man's helmet.

"I got nothin' against you Schwyzers." The man spoke faster when Thomas did not answer. "Nothin' against you, or the girl. It was just orders."

Thomas removed the man's helmet and threw it into the boat. There was a lot of water in the boat and he would need something to bail with. Then he retrieved one of the two stowed oars.

He stood up and stared down at the man. He clung to the side of the boat with only the tenuous grip of his fingertips.

"No please! I got a family. Like I said, it was just orders." He was so cold he no longer shivered, but his words flowed slowly, like winter cream.

Thomas shook his head. "Orders you *chose* to follow. You have taken sides, and I can respect that." Thomas hefted the heavy oar in his hands. "But forgiveness is another matter."

"God, please…" Thomas cut off the man's words by bringing the oar down hard on his head.

✧ ✧ ✧

It took only a few moments to set the sail and get the boat moving towards the figure standing on the edge of the lake. Thomas worked the steerboard with one hand and used the soldier's helmet to bail water from the bottom of the boat. Soon he was tossing the bowline to Ruedi, who deftly secured it around the exposed roots of a crooked pine tree growing too close to the water's edge.

"This was not exactly what I had in mind when I suggested we go hunting, you and I Cap'n. But I must say, you do flush out interesting game."

Thomas stepped ashore onto a large flat rock and the two men embraced, and then Thomas wasted no time in quizzing Ruedi on what he knew of Seraina's whereabouts.

"You saw what happened in Altdorf?"

"Saw enough. I came very close to shooting Gissler through that mutinous heart of his."

Thomas shook his head. "If you had I would still be in chains on this boat, and you beside me. Did you see where they took her?"

"Aye Cap'n. Gissler threw her into a cage wagon then him and the Duke took the north road out of Altdorf. They will be taking her to Habsburg I imagine."

Thomas nodded. With the fortress in Altdorf still under construction, the Habsburg castle was the safest place for a member of the royal family. If they reached the castle with Seraina, Thomas knew he would never see her alive again. Leopold and his clerics would try her as a witch and torture a confession from her. And if she survived the tortures, she would be burnt at the stake. He had to get to her before they reached Habsburg.

As though reading his mind, Ruedi said, "We had best be off then. She looks to be a fast boat. If we leave now we may be able to cut them off at the Kussnacht. Be just like old times, eh Cap'n?"

Thomas placed a restraining hand on Ruedi's shoulder to stop him from climbing into the boat.

"I would like nothing more old friend. But I need this boat as light as possible. She will not make the speed with two of us."

Ruedi looked at the boat and then back at Thomas with a hurt look in his eyes. But he knew Thomas was right. Gissler and Leopold had too much of a head start. He removed his belt, with its dangling hook on the front for working a crossbow string, and gave it to Thomas. Then held out his crossbow and two bolts.

"These are all I got left. Gissler and Leopold were riding, and there were two soldiers driving the wagon."

"Thanks, friend. You have come through for me more times than I can count."

Ruedi's lower lip trembled just enough to be visible beneath his red moustache and beard.

"Now you listen to me Cap'n. This is the best crossbow I have ever owned. Made by a Genoese master, and I will be expecting it back, so you heed what I tell you. You shoot Gissler with your first bolt. You shoot from behind cover and without him ever seeing you. If you miss your first shot you take him out with the second. Pay no mind to the other three until Gissler is down. You hear me Cap'n?"

Thomas looked into Ruedi's pleading grey eyes and was overwhelmed with the impression his friend was saying goodbye.

CHAPTER 37

SERAINA SAT hunched in the low wagon, her eyes fixed on the narrow, hard-packed road through the carriage's barred rear door. Occasionally she heard voices above her but could never make out the words as the iron-rimmed wheels rattled and ground out the miles, snaking a ponderous route along the heavily treed coastline of the Great Lake.

She closed her eyes, ignoring the pain of her cracked lip, and focused on the trees. It took a great deal of time to still her mind and tuck away the emotions clawing to the surface, demanding to be acknowledged. Mile upon mile passed, and she knew with every passing moment she was careening closer to Habsburg Castle. Further from Schwyz, her people, and from Thomas, if he yet lived.

She clenched her teeth and bit down on her split lip, letting the pain clear her mind and refocus her energies. He was alive. She was sure of it, but she needed all her strength if she were to ever see him again.

She focused on her breathing and allowed her body's rhythms to merge with the swaying movement of the wagon. Then, when she was ready, Seraina closed her eyes and reached out to the trees.

She pushed her essence beyond the rolling cage that would

keep her imprisoned, and found herself hovering outside the wagon; free, but unable to move, as though still tethered to her physical self. Her spirit kicked and screamed, grasping at every branch and leaf whipping past in a desperate attempt to disengage her spirit form from her body. She grew weak, and felt the cold iron bars press up against her back, threatening to pull her back within her prison of flesh and bone once again.

Then wind caressed her cheek. It danced through her hair, and brushed away her tears, and without warning, snatched her away, sweeping her straight up the side of a tall pine. Breathless, she floated high above the world on clouds of green.

The strength of the natural world replenished her spirit. Invigorated, she leapt and pirouetted from one lush dome to another, rejoicing in her freedom. On some distant plane she was aware of her physical body collapsing onto its side, and the scent of moldy straw and human excrement invaded her senses for a moment. But then she turned her face to the sun and leapt to hover above the leaves of a giant cherry tree. She laughed and gazed over the canopy of the forest. The tops of the trees undulated far into the distance like gentle hills, but then they began to move and reform. The treetops took on the shapes of heads, in a crowd of giants, gathered to admire the azure waters of the Great Lake shimmering below. And off to the right, rising higher than them all, were the ancient Mythen Mountains, majestic mates of stone and earth.

Seraina felt herself whisked forward along the green-topped crowd until she hovered a thousand feet above the shore, the edge of the forest rustling at her feet. Movement caught her eye. Farther away than any human eye should be able to see, a speck marred the perfect blue-green waters. Tiny, inconsequential, yet Seraina could not pull her eyes away. She tried to avert her gaze, but there was something about that speck she knew she should remember.

Thomas.

She fell to her knees. The stink of the prison wagon filled her nostrils once again and the bruises and cuts on her body sapped her strength and called out, begging her spirit to return. She clasped her hands together at her chest, and not knowing what else to do, called upon the Mythen.

✧ ✧ ✧

The wind was not with him. Thomas angled the bow of the boat as close to the wind as she could manage and sat high on the edge to keep it flat on the water as he pulled the sail in tight. After a few minutes of making decent headway across the water, he pushed the steerboard away from him and ducked under the boom to sit on the other side of the boat. The boat shuddered as the heavy boom swung across the boat and snapped into place with the sail once again filling with wind.

He continued tacking back and forth across the point of the wind, his eyes fixed on a stand of trees on the shoreline far ahead in the distance, at a spot where he knew the road ran close to the water's edge. If he had any chance at all of catching up to Gissler, it would be there.

At that point the road narrowed before branching into two, with one route continuing along the shore of the lake and the other pushing east, leading away from the water and further into the Kussnacht, and eventually, to Habsburg Castle. If Gissler made it past that fork, Seraina would be lost to Thomas forever.

He focused on making the tightest turns possible, making the most of the feeble wind. Only the faintest tendrils of white floated across the blue sky and the slight breeze rippled the top of the water without breaking it. The horizon was not coming fast enough. In his heart he knew he would not make it. The boat was fast and well built, but he was running out of time.

Still, he would not give up. His mind raced with calculations and angles, trying to come up with alternate scenarios that would get him across the lake faster.

At the front of the boat, tucked into the bow was a cache of supplies stored under an oiled leather tarp. Most probably water and foodstuffs, perhaps a few tools for making emergency repairs. Whatever the items were, they were heavy and keeping the bow of the boat low in the water. They had to go, but he could not let go of the rudder without losing speed. Sailing into the wind required constant minute adjustments on the steerboard to keep the speed up, or worse, to prevent the boat from capsizing. What he really needed was a steerboard extension.

After tacking yet again, he wrapped the sail line around a cleat on the side of the boat to hold it in place. He picked up one of the oars and lashed it onto the steerboard, effectively extending it by the entire length of the oar. He tested it by moving a few feet away and steered the boat to see how she responded. Satisfied, he freed up the sail, tacked once more, and cleated the sail into place once again.

Moving quickly, he picked up his sword and scrambled to the front of the boat. He cut the restraints on the tarp and threw everything overboard he could with one hand, while he held the steerboard steady with the other hand. It was awkward and a balancing act, but it worked well enough. The items turned out to not be foodstuffs after all, but were sets of mason and carpenter tools: mallets, chisels, drawknives, and such. Thomas threw out half the items before deciding he needed to go back to the rear of the boat and tack again in order to stay on course.

The bow rode higher now that it was lighter, and after one more trip up it would ride higher still. Thomas tacked and was scrambling under the sail to the leeward side when the boat leaned heavily and almost capsized as a sudden gust of wind caught the sail. He eased off on the steerboard and scrambled to the high side to bring her back into contact with the water. The boat settled down and flattened out with the redistribution of his weight.

Thomas allowed himself a breath. It took a moment for his heart to stop hammering. If he capsized the boat now, there would be absolutely no way to make up the time.

He had almost lost her.

Looking around him, he noticed the ripples in the water had grown into small whitecaps. Preoccupied as he was, he had failed to recognize the change in weather. Turning his face to the sky he was shocked to see a bank of clouds rolling in fast. There had been no sign of them earlier.

Within minutes the entire sky was smothered in billowing grey clouds with dark, swollen underbellies. This was like no storm he had ever seen. It had to be a föhn, one of the unnatural warm winds that blew over the Alps. The locals had warned him to never be caught out on the lake when a föhn appeared.

Well, it was too late to heed that advice.

He felt the first drop of rain and tightened his grip on the sail line. The whitecaps grew and the water bubbled like some great titan stirred it from below.

I have my wind now, Thomas thought, his face grim. He looked out over the churning water and swallowed.

The gale blew so fierce it drove the rain hard against his

skin, leaving painful welts like one of the sandstorms of the Levant. He had seen all manner of weather in twenty years on the sea, but never the likes of this. One moment the sky had been clear as far as the eye could see, and the next the storm waged around him, the unnatural wind changing direction and swirling without notice.

Thomas was convinced God had set his wrath against him. Was it because he fought to save Seraina? Was she truly Lucifer's servant as Leopold had called her? Thomas threw back his head and shook the water from his eyes. He shouted into the gale in defiance, his voice registering in his ears as a whisper.

Thomas made his way to the center of the boat, using the long oar extension to steer. Then he jumped up onto the side of the boat, balancing there for a moment to get a feel for the wind. He took up the slack in the sail line and looped it under the backs of his legs in a makeshift harness. When he was ready, he trimmed the sail and adjusted the steerboard until the boat lurched ahead and its one side lifted out of the water. With his feet perched only on the four-inch wide side of the boat, Thomas leaned flat out above the water in his harness. He tweaked the steerboard in small increments, and the boat leveled out and shot across the waves.

Thomas yelled in terror and exhilaration.

If this was God's attempt at sending him to Hell, He was about to be disappointed.

A wave caressed the back of Thomas's hair, as though reaching for him, but he raced by far too fast. With the dark waters heaving and jumping around him, a terrible laugh escaped from his lips.

He screamed at the elements and at God, both in equal measure, like a man possessed by some malevolent spirit.

CHAPTER 38

"SHE IS A QUIET ONE. Hardly made a sound since we took her," Gissler said to Leopold.

The two men rode side by side in front of the wagon. The Duke had kept to himself since Altdorf, and Gissler had hoped the long ride to Habsburg castle would have afforded him the opportunity to broach the subject of when he could expect to see his new horses. His first task would be to hire a farrier, as Leopold had mentioned before. He needed someone dependable, who knew about breeding, but would not drain his purse too quickly. He would have to ask around, for he knew very little about what constituted a good farrier.

"What did you say Gissler?"

"The woman. She's been quiet, my lord. Perhaps we should check on her condition?"

Leopold grunted. "No need. She lives, for her kind do not leave this world so easily."

The forest road was narrow, more a path really, that had been carved into the sloped land by centuries of use. As the driver slowed the wagon to navigate a switchback, a crossbow bolt caught him high in the chest, lifting him off the bench seat and depositing him deep into the foliage where he disappeared from view.

When Gissler heard the distinctive twang of a crossbow tickler being released, his instincts forced him low over his mount's neck at the same instant the guard took the quarrel in the chest. Ignoring the panicked shouts of the other soldier in the wagon, he scanned the woods and whispered to his horse to keep her calm. Thirty yards to his left he saw a man bent over. He stood up stiffly, using his body to pull a heavy crossbow string back with a hook on his belt. The man straightened and Gissler found himself locking eyes with Thomas.

Impossible.

Leopold was shouting something but he did not comprehend the words. *How could Thomas be here?*

Thomas slotted a bolt into the crossbow and raised the heavy weapon to his shoulder. He pulled the trigger. The second man on the wagon screamed as the quarrel tore into his abdomen, slamming him back into the seat and careening off the side to land on the hard road. Thomas threw his crossbow into the woods and picked up a sword at his feet.

After a quick glance around, Gissler relaxed slightly and sat up in his saddle. Thomas was alone. Leopold pulled alongside Gissler and grabbed his arm. The Duke's eyes were wide and wild.

"That man is all that stands between you and a life of nobility. Finish this, here and now and I swear you will be ordained a Knight of Austria on this very day."

Gissler looked into Leopold's face, searching for deceit, but saw none. The young Duke gave him a knowing nod and gestured at the wreck of a man running to the back of the prison wagon. He cleaved the lock off the door with a single swing of his blade.

Gissler stared at the man who stood between him and his

future. He looked like a survivor of a hellhound savaging. Water and sweat ran off him in torrents. His tunic was in tatters and did little to cover the bruises and cuts on his arms and upper back that he had suffered at the hands of his captors. His left eye was hideously swollen, and a crusted-over cut above it threatened to reopen at any moment. Added to this was the ever-present scar marking the entire side of his face. He appeared more apparition than man.

The soldier with the bolt in his belly lay on his side and groaned. His hands pressed over the entrance hole of the shaft, while the bulk of the wooden missile extruded from his back with only the leather vanes still lodged somewhere within his torso. Every few moments he would let out a gurgling scream of pain.

The noise was beginning to irritate Gissler.

Thomas kept his eyes focused on Gissler and Leopold while he walked over to the pain-ridden soldier. He placed the tip of his sword in the hollow between the moaning man's collarbone and the left side of his neck. He leaned on the blade, and the woods became silent.

The girl stumbled from the wagon like she was drugged and Thomas went to her. He caught her as she collapsed, and eased her to the ground. He gave the two mounted men a dark stare and took a few steps toward them, moving remarkably well, considering his appearance. Ten paces away he set the point of his sword into the hard-packed earth of the road and rested his hands on the pommel. Leopold's horse whinnied, and danced to the side a couple steps until the Duke reined her in.

Gissler dismounted and drew his blade.

"What happened to you Thomas? Since when did you become protector to the Devil's spawn?"

"Say what you will, Gissler. But we both know why you are doing this. And it has nothing to do with the Devil."

"Spare me your lectures, *Captain.* Is it so wrong to want a better life for yourself? I have served God as well as any man and I will not be judged by the likes of you."

"You have traded your allegiance to God for that of a man."

Gissler laughed. "And you think serving the Hospitallers was so much more? We fought and died for French nobles, not God. The knights were all blue-bloods who saw us as little more than dogs."

"So, you would raise arms against a brother just to be welcomed amongst the ranks of those you despise?"

Gissler raised his sword to a low guard and said, "You consort with witches. And you are not my brother."

Gissler struck first: a straight thrust followed by attacks to either side of Thomas's head. Thomas knocked Gissler's blade aside easily, with quick, deft blocks. Gissler danced back and smiled.

It had been an exploratory attack to get a feel for how comfortable Thomas was with his weapon. To any normal observers Thomas would seem highly skilled, and they would not be wrong. However, in Gissler's mind, Thomas had taken the second slash too near the tip of his blade, where it had no stopping power.

Thomas had always preferred fighting with mace and dagger, much shorter weapons. He was nowhere near Gissler's equal when it came to the long blade, and Gissler saw that very thought mirrored in Thomas's eyes. The man was smart enough to know when he was outclassed.

"I will say this only once. Drop your blade and submit or I *will* kill you. But I believe you know that," Gissler said.

In response, Thomas yelled and charged at Gissler, swinging left and right with powerful overhand attacks. Gissler backpedaled and brought his sword up in a series of awkward blocks until he managed to sidestep the frontal assault and regain his balance. The quick attack had caught him off guard and he cursed himself for being so lax. Thomas was no ordinary opponent. He would not underestimate him again.

Gissler attacked. Two straight thrusts at Thomas's abdomen followed by a reverse cut to his head. Thomas parried them, but then Gissler swept his blade down and drew a line of blood across Thomas's thigh. Thomas grunted and stepped back. He dropped his sword to a low guard and met Gissler's next attack with a parry and two counter strikes of his own.

Gissler blocked the attack with ease and stepped around the left side of Thomas. His blade flicked out and he sliced Thomas across the ribs. Thomas leapt back lessening the depth of the cut, but not the pain. He grimaced and backtracked further to gain some room. Thomas was breathing heavily now, and looking into his eyes, Gissler knew the man was finished. But to Thomas's credit, he did not give in. He launched a flurry of strikes, but Gissler was ready.

He moved in circles and casually met his blade with crisp blocks at the end of each swing's powerful arc, and when Thomas stepped in too close, Gissler raised his elbow and smashed it across his mouth. Then he stepped away to create distance and slashed Thomas across his sword arm's shoulder. Thomas screamed and his blade flew through the air, landing on the ground near one of the dead wagon guards.

Breathing heavily, Thomas limped after his weapon, one hand pressed against his shoulder to stem the flow of blood. Gissler watched the pathetic man with a detached calm. *So this is how Thomas Schwyzer, Captain of The Wyvern, the finest* fighting ship in the Levant, was to meet his end. What would Grandmaster de Villaret say now of his favored son?

Gissler allowed him to pick up the sword with his left hand before attacking again. Thomas was on the defensive immediately but he was far too slow and clumsy with his off hand. Gissler slashed his chest and then rode the length of Thomas's blade with his own all the way to the handle's crosspiece. With a flick of his wrist he snagged Thomas's sword and sent it spinning from his grip. He placed the point of his blade against the front of Thomas's throat and forced him to his knees.

Thomas gulped in air through his bloody open mouth. His dirty tunic was now soaked in red and he had the forlorn eyes of a man who had lost everything. To Gissler, Thomas had already been dead a long time. His life had been spent in blind servitude. He could not bring himself to feel sorry for his old captain because Thomas had accepted his fate with open arms. Never had he fought to better his position or change his lot. He was little more than a slave to be used by those God truly favored. Those who struggled to further their station in life.

Thomas looked up at him and pulled the neck of his tunic to one side exposing the hollow between his collarbone and carotid artery.

"Make it fast," he said, his stare defiant to the end.

Gissler nodded. "You deserve that much."

He lowered the point of his sword from the front of Thomas's neck and stepped to the side to deliver the killing thrust. But his sword would not move.

Thomas had thrown his arm over Gissler's blade and held it pinned under his armpit against his side, while his hand gripped Gissler's wrist. His other hand snaked towards the body of the caravan guard next to him and yanked on the crossbow bolt protruding from the dead man's back. It came free with a wet pop and before Gissler had time to react, Thomas leaned back reaching far behind his head with his right arm holding the crossbow bolt, its iron point and shaft slick with dark blood.

With a loud cry, Thomas drove the hardened iron point into the base of Gissler's throat, just above the spot at which his chainmail vest ended. The wind blew out of his lungs and Gissler stumbled back, dropping his sword while his hands wrapped around the base of the thick bolt protruding from his upper chest.

Gissler stared at the shaft with wide eyes and his head shook back and forth in disbelief. Blood poured from the wound and seeped under his chainmail, only to emerge at his waist to turn his white under-tunic a vivid red. He stumbled to his knees and his eyes lost all focus before he fell onto his back. He looked up at nothing, still clutching the crossbow bolt.

✧ ✧ ✧

Gissler's lips moved, and with his ruined lung, he had hardly any wind left to make words, but Thomas heard them all the same. Though, like most men's last words, they made little sense.

"No... I must... hire a farrier..." Gissler gave a last shudder and his hand fell away from the crossbow bolt's shaft.

Thomas pushed himself to his feet and looked down at his boyhood friend. They had traveled to the end of the world together, faced the mightiest Saracen warriors ever assembled, and survived when so many others, most in fact, did not. Only to come back here, where it all began, and kill one another.

Where was God's Will in all of this?

A horse whinny caught his attention and he looked up.

Leopold stared at him, disbelief blanketing his face. Thomas raised a blood-soaked arm and pointed.

"You," Thomas said. His voice rasped in his throat. "You… are *poison*."

Leopold looked once again at the fallen bodies on the road, then back to the specter walking towards him. He reined his horse in a tight circle away and kicked his heels into her side.

Long before the sound of galloping hooves had disappeared into the distance, Thomas collapsed face-first onto the hard road, amidst an ever-growing circle of crimson.

CHAPTER 39

THE MOONLESS NIGHT allowed the twenty figures to crawl over the barren landscape of the fortress's killing fields like darkness overtaking a desert. They flowed through gaps in the half-built walls, shrinking well back of the torchlight from the main gates, and continued inexorably forwards, until they came before the walls of the prison. There, they merged with the night, and waited.

A door opened, and Heller, the jailer stepped out. He glanced about, craning his neck to take in all corners of the courtyard, and then beckoned to the shadows. Noll and his handpicked group of men and women passed by him wordlessly and poured into the depths of the large stone prison. It took only seconds to overcome the three sentries in the guardroom, but a full half hour to unlock the countless cell doors and manacles of the hundred condemned wide-eyed inhabitants.

They armed themselves with chains, flails, torches, pointed staves, forceps, sharp cones of iron, and other tools readily available in a house of torture. When the distant sounds of fighting could be heard at the main gates of the fortress, Noll and Heller opened the doors of the prison and set their army free.

There were less than forty Habsburg soldiers at the fortress that night. Eleven survived to be thrown into the very cells they used to guard. Vogt Berenger von Landenberg was amongst their number. He had been found in his room in the keep, hiding in a wardrobe.

Noll had him dragged into the courtyard, and at first the man cursed and screamed, demanding to be set free or he would bring the wrath of the Holy Roman Empire down upon them all. But he sang a different tune when Noll held a hot iron up to his face.

Noll wanted nothing more than to take the Vogt's eyes, as he had taken those of Noll's father. But Landenberg was the only true bargaining piece he held. He needed him to trade for Seraina, and perhaps the ferryman, if he yet lived. And a fat Vogt with no eyes would make a poor offer, indeed.

Impromptu fires had sprung up all over the courtyard. His army had found the keep's stores and people all around Noll were singing and feasting. Children and wives had raced up from the town to welcome their previously imprisoned loved ones back into the world.

Yes, Noll was now in control of the Altdorf fortress, something far more valuable to the Duke than Landenberg. And if Noll knew relinquishing it to the Austrians would ensure Seraina's release, he would have given it up in a heartbeat. But it was not Noll's to trade. It belonged to the people.

In the end, he threw the poker aside and settled for whipping Landenberg's back until it frothed with blood, and the man's screams faded into unconsciousness.

The mess on his back was nothing a good tunic would not cover.

CHAPTER 40

AFTER RIDING all night, a road-weary soldier from Altdorf limped into the Habsburg throne room early the next morning. A purple-haired Fool trailed along behind him, mimicking his inebriated-like gait, with an added flourish or two.

The bells on the Fool's shoes seemed especially loud to Leopold on this day.

The Duke, with the hulking and grizzled form of his man Klaus standing once again at his side, listened to the soldier's report. Leopold sank further into his chair with the telling of every detail. The Fool pulled up a chair beside the Duke and began copying Leopold's posture.

The soldier was in the midst of describing how Vogt Landenberg had been captured by the villagers, and was perhaps even dead, when Leopold sprang from his chair and wrapped his hands around the Fool's throat. They fell to the floor kicking and thrashing, and by the time Klaus managed to break his lord's grip on the jester, the little man was blue in the face and a crowd of servants had gathered at the door.

The soldier stood straight, his wide eyes fixated on the coughing Fool still lying on the floor. Leopold straightened his clothes and ran his hands through his hair once before turning to Klaus. He looked refreshed, like he had just stepped out of a bath.

"Make arrangements to leave at once," he said.

"To what destination, my lord?"

"Salzburg. And send runners before us. I want an entire War Council convened before we arrive."

Klaus bowed and turned on his heel. He waved his arms at the gawking servants and they fled before him as he left the room.

The Fool jumped up from the floor and began to follow them.

"And where do you think you are going?" Leopold said.

The painted man turned and faced Leopold with one hand on his hip. "Why to pack of course, my lord. For what War Council would be complete without a fool?"

He flashed Leopold his best entertainer's smile and scurried from the room. The bells on his shoes made not a sound.

CHAPTER 41

*T*HE SUN WAS out but it did little to cut through the searing cold frosting the beard and mustache of the old trapper as he made his way towards the one-room cabin in the distance. His rhythmic breathing drowned out his muffled footsteps as his snowshoes floated in and out of the fresh powder. As he came down out of the trees and started across a hillside clearing that would be a field in the spring, the trapper paused and leaned on his walking stick.

A thunderous crack boomed through the woods behind him and echoed throughout the forest. The sap in a tree had frozen, and expanded freeze after freeze, until finally, the trunk gave in and exploded.

Without looking back in the direction of the sound, the old man pushed off on his walking stick and headed to the cabin.

The door was stuck, frozen in place. He chipped away at it with his walking stick until it yielded to his shoulder. Air considerably warmer than the outside temperature rushed past him, carrying with it a stagnant odor. Against the far wall, a spruce-bough bed held two still forms, covered up to their necks with a single threadbare blanket. A man and a woman; her head on his chest and him on his back with his white, beardless face turned toward the rafters.

The trapper crossed himself and then covered his nose with the same hand. Idly, he wondered why it was so much warmer in the room than it should be, until a flicker of light caught his eye. On the small table in the center of the hut, burned a single tallow candle. And just past the candle, peering out over the rough table, a pair of dark eyes stared back at him.

A boy, who looked to be around four, stood at the edge of the table and did not move. The pupils of his already dark eyes were dilated so wide they appeared midnight-black.

The trapper attempted to speak, but his voice came out in a croak. He had not used it for speech since the summer. And then only once, while he traded for supplies. He cleared his throat and tried again.

"Nothing to fear, boy. Tell me your name."

The dark eyes narrowed and bored into the trapper's own for so long the trapper thought the boy could not understand him. He was about to try again, but in French this time, when the boy's chest heaved and he finally spoke in a voice as dry as the trapper's own.

"Thomas."

"How long you been here like this?"

The boy turned to look at the figures on the bed. He pointed at them.

"They look cold so I covered them. Might be they are still sick."

The trapper's eyes followed the frail little arm to look at the gaunt figures embracing on the handcrafted bed. The fever got them long before the cold ever did.

The old man crossed himself again and averted his gaze.

"The cold cannot reach them anymore, Thomas."

Thomas came awake with a jerk that sent a spasm of pain

racing down the length of his arm and under his ribs. The old trapper's face hovering above him faded and was replaced with Seraina's. Her auburn hair fell across one of her green eyes and he could make out the light freckles on her sun-browned skin.

She smiled and held a cool hand to his forehead. She smelled of violets and spoke words he did not understand, but were comforting. His body became heavy, and staring up at her, he fought hard to keep his eyes open, wanting nothing more than to remain lucid in the moment. But within seconds, her skin and hair blurred together and those brilliant eyes faded like stars on a cloudy night.

The scent of violets, however, remained with him long after the darkness returned.

MORGARTEN
THE FOREST KNIGHTS BOOK 2

BY
J. K. SWIFT

THE BATTLE OF MORGARTEN

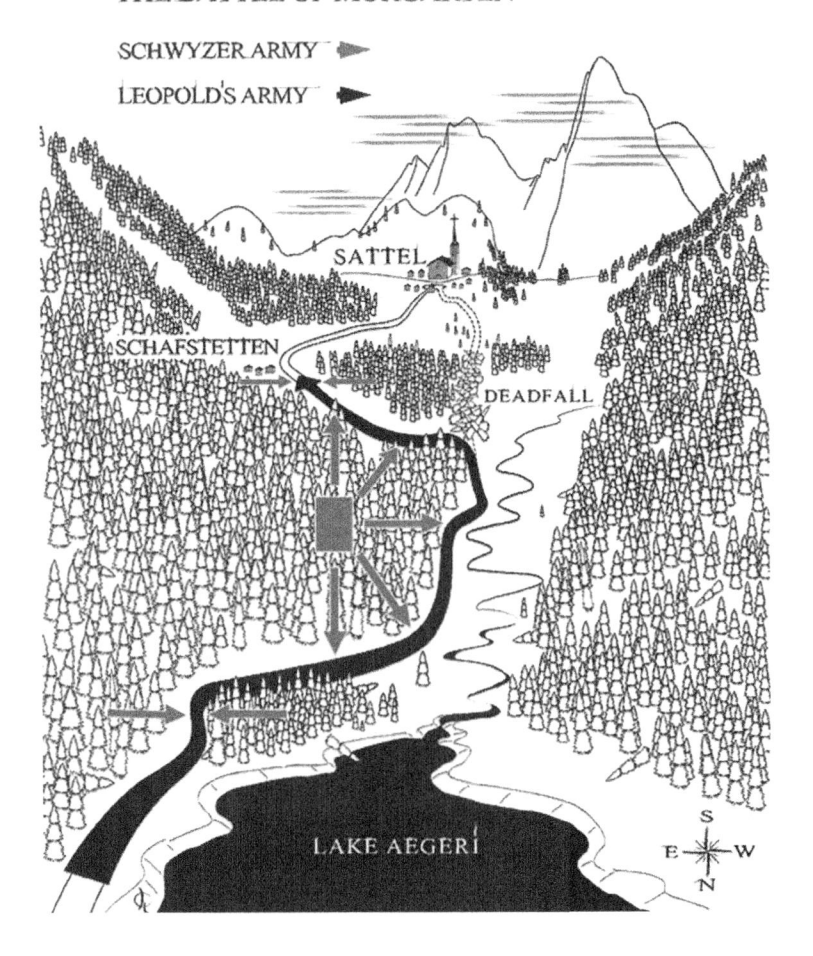

SCHWYZER ARMY
LEOPOLD'S ARMY

SATTEL
SCHAFSTETTEN
DEADFALL
LAKE AEGERI

CHAPTER 1

ERICH STOOD OVER GISSLER'S body and absently stroked the three stumps on his right hand that had once been fingers. A crossbow bolt protruded from Gissler's upper chest. Erich took a moment to admire the unknown archer's skill, for if the shot had struck a fraction of an inch lower, Gissler's chainmail vest may have spared his life. Or, perhaps it was merely luck. That was far more likely. Luck, or rather, its absence had killed far more people than skill ever would.

Erich's brows furrowed and he crossed his arms. There was something odd about the angle of the bolt. And the entire shaft was crusted in dried blood, all the way to the tips of its leather vanes....

A crash and the sound of splintering wood caught his attention. He turned away from the corpse and saw Reto climbing down from the top of the cage wagon. The bald, leathery-faced man cursed as he dropped to the ground.

"Nothing here. Found a strongbox but no coins," Reto said.

He pulled something flat and heavy that was tucked under his arm and tossed it into the trees.

"What was that?"

Reto shrugged. "Parchment. Maybe a book. That one got

anything good on him?"

Erich nodded. "A fine sword. Take it and the mail vest, but leave the clothing." They were too stiff with old blood to salvage.

Reto scurried over and picked up Gissler's sword. He whistled in appreciation and tucked it into his belt. His small eyes darted over Gissler's corpse. "And what is wrong with those boots? Look broken in and comfortable to me. Might be my size, too."

Erich held up his hands. "Take them. But if you do, you offer up your own boots to one of the other men, if they want them. And you can carry that sword for now, but when we get back to camp it goes into the pool."

Reto flashed his teeth for only a second before bending to pilfer Gissler's corpse. Erich watched as his man tugged off the corpse's boots and ripped off his tunic to get at the chainmail vest.

Erich told himself he should be enjoying this moment more. This was, after all, one of the bastards who had killed most of his men those many months ago. The past half-year had been beyond difficult. But that was nothing new for him.

Erich's father had been a grain farmer until his wife died when Erich was ten. Life had been hard while she was alive, but with her passing, Erich's father and even the land itself seemed to give in. The crop shriveled and the next year blight finished it off. They starved for a season, earning what they could by begging, and, unknown to his father, some minor thefts. The next year the community hired Erich's father as an *alper*. He was to take everyone's animals up high into the Alps to forage for summer pasture and would not return for three months. He left in early spring, leaving Erich alone on their rocky land to fend for himself. When his father returned in late summer, Erich was gone.

He fell in with rough men, and realized that to survive, he would need to be rougher yet. After ten years, and many a hard lesson learned, he formed a brigand band of his own. They did well, flourished even. Until he lost half his men when they made the mistake of ambushing Gissler's group.

Erich had built his band back up to twenty men, but he needed half again that number if he had any hope of seizing even the smallest merchant caravan. Especially considering the quality of his current followers.

He looked at the sword sticking out of Reto's belt and wondered if it was the same blade that had cut off his fingers. He could not remember the look of the sword, for it had happened too fast. The man behind the weapon, however, was another story. Erich could still hear the contempt in his words: *He will not be any good with a bow for the rest of his miserable life.*

He was right, of course. Erich also could no longer grasp a sword handle in his right hand, and had resorted to practicing with his sinister hand. It was still clumsy and awkward, but he knew with time he would adapt. What other choice did he have?

Erich wandered to the side of the road and peered into the trees at the leather-bound object Reto had discarded. Turning his head to protect his eyes, he squatted and retrieved the book from beneath a prickly bush. He turned it over in his hands, surprised by its weight.

So, this is a book.

It was the first time in his life he had ever held one. He unfastened the intricate buckle and fanned through the first few pages. He grunted with disappointment at the lack of pictures, then squinted at the flowing script and wondered at its meaning.

Reto was right. The book was worthless to men like them. He closed it and ran his hand once over the smooth cover. But there were others who valued these curiosities more than gold.

Erich tucked the book under his arm and walked over to a horse grazing at the side of the road. She cast him a sidelong glance as he approached and snorted, but did not consider him enough of a threat to give up the sweet tufts of grass overflowing into the road from the forest floor.

Someone had unhitched her from the wagon and left her to roam free. Her coat still bore harness marks, and unfortunately, a prominent Habsburg brand on her rump. Erich would have to leave her behind. No horse trader within a thousand leagues would buy a stolen Habsburg mount.

Four years ago Erich knew of another group of brigands that had been brazen enough to take three of Duke Leopold's horses from a stable in Andermatt. Habsburg soldiers hunted them for weeks, and when they found them, the horse thieves were hung and quartered. Their torsos were dragged through Andermatt until they fell apart. Their limbs received a similar treatment in various villages to the east, and the thieves' heads were sent to Altdorf to be placed atop poles in the town square. The Habsburgs placed a high value on their horses—much higher than the lives of men such as Erich.

He glanced around, wondering where the other half of the two-horse team was. *If someone had been fool enough to steal one, why stop there? Why not take them both?*

His eyes picked up two skid marks carved into the surface of the road. They were the width of a man's shoulders and led from the wagon to the forest edge. Puzzled, Erich followed the trail a few steps into the trees where the dense brush swallowed it up.

Reto came to Erich's side and scratched his stubbled head. "Looks like someone stole a horse and dragged something in there. What do you think it was? Another strong box maybe?"

Erich could see where something large had brushed aside branches to enter the woods, but then he could make out no further trail. He pointed to a single drop of blood on a rock at the road's edge.

"It was a person. Someone on a stretcher made of branches. Someone hurt."

"Should we follow them?"

"Follow what, exactly?" Erich said.

He stared into the trees. Their trunks swayed and creaked in the breeze. He swore he could feel them staring back.

He shook his head. Like the crumbled bits of a dried leaf on a windy day, the trail had simply vanished.

✦ ✦ ✦

The whispers came for Seraina in sleep, as they often did. Some time ago, or perhaps only moments before, she recalled sitting down against a giant spruce and closing her eyes. Seraina could still feel the ridges of rough bark pressed against her back. That sensation was a tie to the waking world and she latched onto it, resisting the pull of the voices.

Her visions were rare and, so she was told, a gift from the Great Weave. Something to be treasured. But these voices calling from afar, differed from the ones she had heard before. They grew, both in volume and quantity, and as they became louder, they seemed to insist that Seraina listen. No, they *demanded* to be heard. Finally, Seraina understood.

They were screams.

Wails of terror, pain, fear, and rage. The realization tore Seraina completely away from the waking world. The comforting reassurance of the tree's bark against her back was gone. She found herself hurtling through gray mist that clogged her nostrils and filled her mouth as she drew in deep breaths to ease the frantic pace set by her heart. The screams became louder, the anguish so unbearable, she clapped her hands over her ears knowing full well it would do little good.

She had to help them.

The mist cleared. Not gradually, but all at once, like the goddess Ardwynna herself had banished it from her forest realm with a clap of her hands.

Altdorf.

Seraina floated high above the ramparts of the Altdorf fortress. A great host encircled the keep, pouring through and over broken sections of the outer walls. In the distance, the sky glowed with the heat of a thousand fires as the town burned.

The winds carried Seraina lower, in an erratic swoop like a swallow chasing mosquitoes. But this bird had no control over her descent and Seraina soon gave up trying to direct her flight. She took a deep breath and surrendered herself to the Winds of the Weave, knowing full well where they meant to take her. She closed her eyes, but that only brought the gruesome images of war into focus. There was no way to shield one's eyes while trapped within a vision.

She watched as a man with a two-handed sword cut another in half from shoulder to hip-bone, and he in turn was skewered from behind by another man's blade. They fell, and other men ran over their bodies, howling, their faces red and twisted by the furies of battle.

Seraina winced as she felt their rage, their need to kill, and the great relief as a man slid his blade into the open mouth of another. His teeth dragged against the steel, ringing out a long, grating note. Tears filled her eyes and she tried to look away, but it was futile. The winds were merciless. They whisked her throughout the battle, from one gory scene to the next, like she was some wealthy patron of a macabre series of plays.

An old man sat astride a young soldier and pummelled his head with a bloody rock. A young girl, not yet in her teens, attempted to crawl through dirt muddied with blood, as two men tore the clothes from her back. Nearby, a group of soldiers laughed and passed around a wineskin. They watched a man grind against an unmoving naked woman, her arms and legs tied to stakes thrust into the ground. No sounds came from her broken lips, but Seraina could hear her screams. Shrieks that mingled with all the others, forming background music for the chaos.

Finally, relief, and no small measure of guilt, washed over Seraina as the winds took her away once more. They left her standing on top of a crumbled section of the outer wall.

In front of her, stood Thomas.

His tunic was drenched in blood, dripping with it, like it had been freshly pulled from a dying vat. He looked directly at her, and smiled. The scar, extending from the corner of his left eye all the way to his jawline, was so white it hurt Seraina's eyes.

He took a step toward Seraina but a man appeared between them. Thomas crushed his skull with a quick swing of his mace. More figures climbed onto the wall. Thomas stepped over the dead man at his feet and slashed with the sword in his other hand. Another man fell, only to be replaced by two more.

Seraina blinked. It occurred to her then, that of all the people she had seen thus far, Thomas was the only one she recognized. She had sensed the others' terror and pain, felt their need to kill or maim, but, thank the Goddess, she did not know their faces. And while she knew Thomas's face, when she quested out to him from within her own mind, she felt... nothing. No emotions whatsoever.

Thomas opened the throat of another and, when the dying man fell to his knees, Thomas brought his mace down upon his head. With every death, Thomas took one step toward Seraina. But he could never close the distance.

Seraina called out his name, and Thomas heard. He lowered his mace and sword and stared at her. He shook his head slowly.

Enemies flooded around him. A dozen swords pierced his body and he stumbled. His dark, almost black, eyes never left hers until he tumbled backward over the wall.

Seraina gasped and leaned out between two crenellations. She watched his body fall, and though she was too far away to see his face, she knew he wore a contented smile. A moment before his body smashed against the rocks below, she felt the first hint of emotion emanate from Thomas's mind. It was only a simple pause, like a breath before sleep, and was gone in an instant. But she recognized it for what it was.

Relief.

Tears clouded her eyes as she stared at the blood-red form lying broken below. The Weave came for her then. Seraina shouted in protest and reached toward Thomas, but the winds plucked her from the walls and sent her spinning back into the mist.

Seraina woke with a start and she fought back a cough as breath poured into her lungs. She pushed her spine hard against the tree, and let it cradle her, as she allowed her senses time to recover from her vision.

The mist was gone, but now she was surrounded in darkness. Two sets of eyes stared at her, reflecting the glowing coals of a dying campfire. One set was blue and ancient, the other gold and wild.

"What have you seen, my child?" Gildas asked.

The violent images were still too fresh in her mind and they stole her voice. Suddenly cold, Seraina wrapped her arms around herself and shook her head. She stared into the hissing embers, jealous of their warmth. It took several minutes before she was able to answer the old druid, but Gildas waited patiently and did not press. He knew better. The wolf at his side, however, whined at her silence.

Eventually, Seraina forced words from her throat.

"Something is wrong," she said.

CHAPTER 2

DUKE LEOPOLD RODE at the front of a squad of fifty soldiers. Klaus, his ever-present man-at-arms, was at his side. The gray-haired veteran's hooded eyes swept back and forth on the road ahead, like a wary bird of prey waiting for a field mouse to break cover.

The only sign of movement came when a cold wind pushed its way through the trees and breathed life into a scattering of dead leaves, whipping them into a frenzy. They rose a foot into the air and hovered there for a moment. Then they began to turn in a circle, slowly at first. As the momentum built, they rose higher off the road and formed a column of spinning gold and tawny debris. The whirlwind floated back and forth across the road, in an erratic pattern that resembled a drunkard stumbling between taverns.

"Look!"

Leopold cringed as the sound of the Habsburg Fool's voice came from somewhere behind him. Much too close.

"The carpenter's fart!"

The little, purple-haired man sat sideways on a shaggy Norse pony. The Fool's face was split down the middle with white and black paint, a design his clothing also followed. Every now and then, when his pony stumbled, the Fool's pointed shoes tinkled with the sound of bells.

The Fool pointed at the twirling leaves. The soldiers nearest him laughed for everyone knew the story of the carpenter who had traded his soul to the Devil in exchange for two wishes. In a remarkable feat of balance and agility, the Fool stood on his saddle and acted out the entire story while standing on his moving pony's back.

"For the first, he asked for riches," he said in his best stage voice. It carried easily to the last soldier in line. "And the Devil made appear a kettle of gold coins! Far more than any man could spend in a lifetime. But the crafty carpenter paused before he made his second wish, knowing full well the Devil would own his soul once it was granted. 'Make your second wish,' the Devil demanded."

The Fool lifted his leg, screwed up his face, and farted; a necessary skill for any respectable court jester.

"My wish is for you to catch that and return it to me," he said, then he pointed at the spinning leaves. "And there goes the Devil now! Chasing the ever elusive carpenter's fart."

Most of the soldiers laughed, and more than a few crossed themselves when the Fool pointed out the Devil in their path. The Fool bowed in all directions, and then feigned to lose his balance. He fell split-legged onto his saddle, his eyes rolled up into his head, and he doubled over in mock pain.

That was enough for Leopold.

"I think the men at the end of the line have not had their fair share of you this trip. Go ride with them. If I see your painted face again, or hear your voice, I will have the men eat your pony and you can walk back to Habsburg."

The Fool clamped one hand over his mouth and covered his eyes with the crook of his other arm. Somehow, he managed to turn his pony around and plow his way through the soldiers all the way to the back of the formation.

Leopold did not balk when Klaus raised his fist and brought the column to a halt before the bridge spanning the Salzach river. Klaus had been responsible for Leopold's safety for all twenty-four years of the young duke's life, and his dedication to the task was genuine. He was one of only two people in this world that Leopold felt he could trust. The only other was his brother, Frederich.

Klaus stood in his stirrups and his head turned from side to side on his thick neck. He motioned for Leopold and his soldiers to remain where they were. He spurred his horse ahead and rode up to the narrow bridge. His horse hesitated, at first, but Klaus nudged it forward onto the wooden planks.

Leopold watched as Klaus examined the bridge and the far bank for any sign of treachery. A slow moving barge floated down the water. It was piled high with blocks of salt from the nearby mines. Klaus waited until it had passed beneath the bridge and faded into the distance, before he took his eyes from it and continued his inspection.

The old soldier had not yet forgiven himself for being absent when Leopold and Gissler had been ambushed on the forest road in Kussnacht. Ever since then he had been especially diligent when it came to his lord's security. Each of the twenty soldiers in Leopold's personal guard had been hand-picked by Klaus for their loyalty to the House of Habsburg. Although that thought did little to comfort Leopold, the fact that Klaus trusted each man did.

Leopold was confident Klaus would never betray him. He could never hope to gain a better position than the right hand of the Duke of Further Austria. Especially at his age. Leopold heard the whispers at court. Many thought Klaus was already too old to serve Leopold and they were lining up to suggest friends, sons, or cousins that would swear undying loyalty to the Duke.

But Leopold understood well the transient nature of loyalty. He pinched the top of his high-bridged nose and closed his eyes.

Damn that Schwyzer Hospitaller.

Gissler would have been the perfect replacement for Klaus. Unconnected at court and with not a trace of blue blood in his veins, his loyalty would have been easily bought. Owning a man with Gissler's skills would have been a great boon to the House of Habsburg.

And what would he have done with Klaus?

Leopold had not even thought about that. Of course he would have to keep him near, for the gruff veteran knew more Habsburg secrets than almost anyone. Perhaps even more than Leopold himself. But Klaus had served the Habsburg line well, and Leopold would ensure he lived out his last years in comfort. Still, he would need to be watched and kept near. For the man's own protection, Leopold told himself.

Leopold opened his eyes and stared at Klaus as he rode back toward them. For such a big man he rode well, and his body was as fit as any knight twenty years younger. Leopold realized it would be a few years yet before he would need to be replaced. That was a small measure of relief, for Leopold had no shortage of problems that required his immediate and full attention.

Chief among them, of course, was Arnold Melchthal and the ragtag army of peasants he had managed to raise. He had assumed it was Berenger von Landenberg's ineptness that had allowed the outlaw to remain at large for so long. But now that Melchthal was in full control of the new fortress in Altdorf, Leopold had to admit that he had underestimated the young man from Unterwalden.

He would not do so again.

The iron shoes of his own mount clattering against the wooden planks of the bridge pulled Leopold from his thoughts. He realized they were on the move again. Up ahead in the distance he saw the beginnings of Salzburg's Low-town, and perched five hundred paces above it, on a dramatic rock outcropping, stood Salzburg Castle; home to the Prince-Archbishop of Salzburg who, Leopold hoped, would be the solution to all his problems.

Farms and garden plots lined the road leading to Salzburg, and gradually gave way to the simple bungalows of the common classes. The grand Church of Saint Peter loomed high over these, and seemed to serve as a buffer between the cramped quarters of the simple townsfolk and the more elaborate two and three-story houses of the nobility. As Leopold and his escort came nearer to the base of the castle mountain, the houses became larger and more ornate; many with fenced off grounds of their own.

Leopold and Klaus dismounted in front of a stone gate-house that seemed to grow out of the rock itself. Two soldiers snapped to attention in its arch and several crossbowmen leaned over the wall above to get a look at the new arrivals. The gate was the only access to the serpentine path that wound its way up the rocky slope to the main keep of the Castle.

Leopold ignored the guards and motioned for Klaus to follow him. Klaus grunted something to the captain of Leopold's men, then he followed Leopold through the great archway.

The Archbishop's steward stood waiting for them. He held the reins of two long-maned horses draped with silk blankets of red and white. On their heads they wore towering feathered headdresses to match.

The steward folded at the waist and held out the reins of the horses.

"Welcome to High-Salzburg, Duke Leopold. The Archbishop apologizes for being unable to greet your arrival in person, but commands we attend him immediately. He has supplied fresh horses to spare you the long climb to the castle."

Leopold did not even glance at the offered reins. Instead, he fixed the man with a withering glare and removed his gloves, one finger at a time.

"That command was intended only for you, I assume. For one prince does not command another," Leopold said. "Come, Klaus. We will take the rope-carriage. My arse has been beaten enough by horse flesh for one day."

The two men walked past the open-mouthed steward and approached the Archbishop's carriage. Decorated with ornate red and gold carvings, it had only two small wheels at its front, which made it list against the mountainside at an odd angle. The metal-rimmed wheels rested on iron rails and a series of ropes stretched from the carriage up the side of the mountain, disappearing far above.

Leopold made a show of opening the door for Klaus and gestured for him to climb in. Klaus hesitated and his usually emotionless face creased with the discomfort of having his lord open a door for him.

"Come now, Klaus. The good Archbishop would not have us thumping up these meandering paths on the backs of beasts when we could ride in comfort. Wipe your boots and climb in."

The steward managed to awaken from his stupor and scurried over. "My Duke, perhaps I could call another carriage from the keep if the horses are not to your liking."

"When there is a perfectly good one here? Nonsense. Why bother your stable hands?"

Klaus's huge boots had managed to collect enough dirt and manure to nurture a small garden, and when he scraped them off at the base of the door, more fell inside the carriage than without.

"It is just that... the rope-carriage... is reserved for the Archbishop's personal use. No one is permitted—"

Leopold held up his hand to silence the man.

"I understand completely. But, do not fret. I will be sure not to lend it out to any unsavory characters," Leopold said.

He resisted the urge to help the slow-moving Klaus squeeze through the narrow doorway with a shove. When the big man finally fell into a seat with his back to the mountain, Leopold stepped in and slammed the door shut behind him. He reached his arm through the half-door's opening and slapped his hand against the outside of the carriage like he would the rump of a horse.

"Do not stand there gaping, man. Get those oxen spinning their wheel. The bishop awaits!"

The steward puckered up his face and replied in a small voice. "The *Arch*bishop, Duke Leopold."

Leopold narrowed his eyes at the man. "The *aged* Archbishop. In fact he is getting so old he may no longer be with us by the time I get to the top of this mountain. You, on the other hand are much younger, and if fortunate, will be on this earth much longer than your bishop. I wonder who your next lord will be?"

The steward took a step back and bowed his head. He turned and shouted at the wheel house. "Hitch up the oxen! Send runners to the top. The Archbishop's cart is coming up!"

Leopold leaned into his upholstered seatback, out of the sun's heat, and tried to ignore the stench of disturbed manure wafting up from Klaus's boots.

CHAPTER 3

NOLL MELCHTHAL FOUND HIMSELF alone in the Altdorf keep, and he did not like it.

He sat on the lowest step leading up to the throne platform and kept his eyes locked on the stone floor, for every time he looked around the cavernous room he could not help but be overwhelmed by its man-made grandeur. Four tall men could stand atop one another's shoulders and still be unable to touch the timber supports of the floor above. The cold, flagstone floor, white with the recent dust created by mason chisels, stretched far into the distance.

He stared across that gray sea with an unfocused gaze. The cracks between the blocks of stone faded away the nearer they came to the dark alcove of the main doors, and once again, Noll could not keep his thoughts from settling on Seraina.

He had sent messengers to Habsburg Castle proposing a trade. Landenberg, Vogt of Unterwalden, for Seraina and the ferryman, if he yet lived. His messenger had returned two days ago with the news that Duke Leopold had refused to see him, and rumor had it that the Duke had departed for Salzburg.

Noll was crestfallen. If Leopold had taken his prisoners to Salzburg, they could at this very moment be in the hands of the Archbishop's confessors. A vision of Seraina defiantly holding back her screams as Leopold's torturers worked their dark trade forced Noll's stomach into the back of his throat. He clenched his eyes in vain and ground the heels of his hands hard against his temples.

Crippled by the strength of his own imagination, he could not bring himself to look up when the great doors grated on their hinges. He waited for the sound of boots on stone, the inevitable approach of someone who needed him to make yet another decision. But the footsteps never came. Whoever it was, must have recognized this was not a good time to seek Noll's counsel, and had left him alone with his grief.

Noll let out a breath, thankful. But as he breathed in, he sensed a presence. There was a life besides his own in the cold stone room. And it smelled of pine.

The realization that he was not alone saved him from jumping when a warm hand touched his shoulder.

"Noll," Seraina said.

He raised his head, and although he did not jump, his heart almost burst in his chest when he saw Seraina standing before him. Her green eyes flashed, filling the keep with more life than if it had been packed shoulder-to-shoulder with people. For the briefest moment, he thought it was the cruelty of his imagination at work once again, but when she smiled and pulled him to his feet, he knew it was no trick.

"Seraina!" He pulled her into his arms and laughter flowed from her lips. The sound settled over him like a hot bath. He closed his eyes, and breathed in great mouthfuls of the pine and sunshine from her auburn hair, hardly daring to believe she was there.

"I thought you lost," he said, and pulled her in even tighter. He would have been content to stay that way, but Seraina gently eased out of the embrace.

"Gissler is dead," she said. "Thomas found me."

Noll nodded, and let her escape from his grip.

Then he remembered Leopold had been together with Gissler when they had taken Seraina. Perhaps that was why his messenger could not make contact with the Duke. Perhaps he too was dead.

He could not keep the excitement out of his words. "And Leopold? What of the boy tyrant?"

Seraina shook her head. "He escaped. The Red Lion lives. The Habsburg threat is still very real."

He should not have let his hope go unchecked. Leopold would not give up his place in the world so easily. "But the ferryman is still alive as well. Your face tells me as much."

"I would have come sooner, but Thomas was badly injured. I have been by his side these many days past," Seraina said.

"He is here then?"

"No. Thomas is still too weak to move. I left him in good company, but I cannot stay long."

"Why come at all then?"

He could not keep the hard edge from creeping into his words, as it always did when he spoke of the ferryman. Was it the man himself who he disliked so much? Or was it the way Seraina spoke his name? Noll closed his eyes and shook his head. This was madness. His people were now at war with the Holy Roman Empire. A war he had started. And he was fawning over a girl like some fresh-faced boy yearning for manhood.

"I had to see you Noll." Seraina paused before continuing. "I had another vision."

Noll studied her face. She tried to smile, but it was an awkward attempt. "I would wager the omens were not good," he said.

Seraina turned away. Her nose crinkled as her eyes swept the room from the flagstone floor to the heavy timbers supporting the next level of rooms high overhead.

"There is something wrong," she said. "Something I do not understand."

"There is plenty wrong," Noll said. "For starters, I have an army of only five hundred men. Farmers and woodcutters, with only one sword for every ten men. The defenses of this fortress are only half complete and all my master builders have gone back home to their families. The Austrians could march in here with a thousand real soldiers and take this pile of stones before nightfall. And now, I have word that he has gone to Salzburg, where he will surely demand that the other princes rally to his cause. What about this situation is *not* wrong?"

The lines of worry that had creased Seraina's face only a moment before, faded. She stepped in closer to Noll and pulled one of his waving hands out of the air and covered it with her own. As always, all concern for her own troubles vanished when confronted with someone else in need.

"There is still so much to be thankful for," she said. She let go of him and spun away, her dress swirling with the sudden motion, and began pacing. Her steps were light and silent. "We have all this," she said sweeping one arm around the room. "Whereas, only a short time ago, we had nothing. You have awoken our people, but even more than that, you have shown them what is possible. Surely, that is worth more than a few soldiers?"

"But have I woken enough of our people? There is still no word from Berne or the guilds of Zurich. Nor has Lucerne offered any support for the Eidgenossen."

"Do not worry about them. More will come. I have seen it, remember? There are many yet who wish to awaken and climb out from under Habsburg rule."

Noll shook his head. "I hope you are right, Seraina. I truly do. But I also know it is impossible to awaken a man who only pretends to sleep."

Seraina laughed. "This is a fine turn," she said. "It is usually you accusing me of talking in riddles. We become more alike everyday." She took Noll's arm. "It is damp and lifeless in here. Come, my mushroom-man, let us put some sun on that frowning face."

She led him to the balcony overlooking the courtyard and they stepped out into the fresh air. Noll squinted into the afternoon light, and a soft breeze tousled his hair. He immediately felt better. Seraina was right, Noll thought. Shutting himself away in that cave, trapped alone with only his self-doubts for company, had dampened his spirits.

"Now tell me. What preparations have you made and what can I do to help?" Seraina asked.

Noll pointed to the gatehouse. "I have directed most of the work, so far, on finishing the gatehouse and the outer walls. But as it stands now, there are still a dozen breaches."

"How long before Leopold comes?"

"That is the only good news in all of this. The first snows will be here in another six weeks, so he has missed his opportunity for this year. He could possibly attack in spring, but the passes will still be too soft for an army. And besides, Leopold is too practical. He will wait for us to bring in the first crops so he has food for his men."

"Midsummer then?"

Noll nodded. "Those are my thoughts."

Seraina's face brightened. "So we have time. Time to find

more allies and prepare. You see, things are not as bad as you feared."

Noll rolled his eyes. "Perhaps. But I will feel much better when I have Pomponio."

Seraina frowned. "What is a *pom-pony-o*?"

"Not what, who. Giovanni Pomponio. He is a Venetian, and a master swordsman. I have contracted him to come and train the men."

The way Seraina's eyes narrowed told Noll she was not keen to the idea.

"How much is this mercenary charging you for his services?"

"Not just him. He says he will bring a dozen of his best men as well. And it is Habsburg gold anyway, for we found a small chest in Leopold's room."

"How much?"

Noll hesitated. "All of it," he said.

Seraina shook her head and stepped away from the balcony railing. "Noll, you could have bought swords for your men with that money. And really, do you think it wise to bring in outsiders?" she asked.

Noll felt his jaw tighten. He grabbed Seraina by the arm.

"What good is a sword in the first place if a man does not know how to use it? Ten months from now, an army of battle-hardened killers will be at our doorstep. We need to surround ourselves with men like these, learn from them, if we are to survive. And the sooner the better."

He let go of her arm. "I am sorry," he said. "I forget myself at times."

"It is all right, Noll," Seraina said. "I understand. Outsiders make me nervous, that is all. But, you may be right."

Seraina had once told Noll that it was his fire that made

him who he was. She could no more blame a cat for eating a wounded bird. And that so long as his laughter came just as often as his bursts of anger, he was living the life the Weave had intended for him.

But it had been some time since Noll had last laughed.

Right or not, it was done. The Venetians would be here tomorrow, or the day after. It did not matter how much gold it cost, Noll was not going to ask any man to fight beside him if he was not prepared.

"Will you stay here for the night?" Noll asked.

Seraina stared out over the courtyard. Her green eyes were fixed on a section of the outer wall. She seemed to not have heard him.

"Seraina?"

She blinked, and turned toward Noll. "Yes? No, I cannot stay here. I must head back to Thomas tonight."

Noll nodded. "Of course," he said. "How far do you go? I can get you a horse…"

"An hour north of White Elk Glade. It is easier to go on foot."

Noll felt the previous worries over Seraina's safety begin anew. "Stay off the roads, then. Habsburg patrols have begun to blockade the northern ways. It will not be long before they close them down completely."

"I have little use for roads," Seraina said. "You should know that by now."

CHAPTER 4

THE BLACKNESS CLEARED, one dark layer at a time, and Thomas forced his eyes open. His chest heaved and air rushed into his lungs, which sent his heart thrumming like the wings of a hummingbird.

"Easy now. The Weave welcomes you back, but no need to rush into her embrace."

The voice's owner, an old man, appeared above him and, for a moment, Thomas thought he dreamed again of the trapper that had taken him in after the death of his parents. But this man's long, powder-white beard and wizened eyes did not belong to the trapper of his memories. The man placed the palm of one leathery hand against Thomas's chest and within seconds the palpitations slowed.

Glancing around him, Thomas saw he lay on a bed of spruce boughs covered with a plush lambskin blanket. Another heavy skin was on top of his naked body and pulled right up under his chin. Though he could not see them, he felt the snugness of bandages wrapped around his middle and one leg.

At first he thought he was in a large tent, but then realized his head was inches from the base of a giant spruce, and the walls of the tent were, in fact, the tree's overgrown limbs stretched down to the ground. A tiny, smokeless fire burned on the far side of the natural room, and beyond that was an opening in the evergreen wall just large enough for a person to squeeze through.

The old man held a wooden bowl to Thomas's mouth. The lukewarm broth, thin but pungent, flowed past his cracked lips and traced a route clear down to his stomach. The man pulled the bowl away before Thomas could drink his fill.

"Enough. For now. It would not do to sodden your roots just yet."

After working the saliva around in his mouth and swallowing, Thomas found his voice.

"Seraina?"

The old man smiled. "She is fine. Do not fret over her whereabouts, as I suspect she will be along shortly."

"Who are you?" The strength and clarity of his own voice surprised Thomas. Starting at his toes he began flexing his muscles one by one, in an attempt to gauge the severity of his injuries.

"Some names are worth knowing, Thomas Schwyzer. Mine is not one of those. I did not kill you in your sleep, so I suspect you can tell that I am a friend, and that should be enough."

A rustle to Thomas's right made him risk turning his neck, and what he saw sent his heart hammering off the walls of his chest once again. An enormous wolf, its fur the same downy white as the old man's hair and beard, sat on its haunches less than two strides away. It caught Thomas's sudden movement and turned its great head toward him. Its lips curled up to bare pink gums and jagged teeth longer than a man's finger. A guttural warning echoed up from somewhere deep in the back of the beast's throat.

Thomas found himself scrambling back to lean on his elbows and his head banged against the trunk of the giant spruce. Pain lanced down his side and his leg throbbed as blood coursed through the limb.

"Oppid! Get back. Our patient does not need to see the likes of you just yet."

He reached out and pressed his hand against Thomas's chest. Thomas risked a glance at the old man and wondered if he had been saved by a hermit touched by madness. But there was something about the way the man spoke and the rhythm of his words, and before he knew it, Thomas was once again lying under the warm lambskin. His eyes, however, remained fixed on the snarling wolf.

The old man began talking to the beast as though Thomas was no longer present. "Even if he meant us ill, a man in his condition is no threat to either one of us. Surely you can see that? Settle down now."

The beast kept its amber eyes fixed on Thomas and slowly lowered itself onto its belly. After a moment it rested its massive head on top of paws the size of full-grown rabbits.

"Is that your animal?" Thomas asked once he could speak.

"Oppid is my companion," the old man said. "You have to forgive him. He is not the trusting sort."

"But he is tamed?"

"Tame?" The old man looked at Thomas and laughed, revealing straight teeth even whiter than his beard. "By Ardwynna's Grace, of course he is not tame. He is a wolf."

That did little to set Thomas at ease. He could not keep his eyes from the wolf, and finally the old man sensed his discomfort. He said a few words in a tongue unfamiliar to Thomas and the wolf padded to the doorway. But before he exited the tree shelter, he turned his golden eyes on Thomas and gave him one last blood-curdling snarl, as if to say, *I will not be far.*

With the wolf gone, Thomas relaxed. He continued the self-assessment of his injuries. He felt the stiffness of stitches on his thigh, as well as his torso and chest, but there were no severed muscles or ligaments from what he could tell. Even though he was concealed beneath the blanket, his nakedness was uncomfortable. The Knights of Saint John were forbidden to sleep naked, and it was a rule that was strictly enforced.

"I owe you my life," he said.

"Not me. Seraina is the one that tended your wounds. And she did a fine job, I should say. You were already on the mend when I first saw you."

Thomas glanced down at the line of stitches stretching down his side. "It would seem her skill rivals that of Hildegard of Bingen," Thomas said.

One side of the old man's mouth turned up in a smirk. "Ah, you mean Sibyl of the Rhine? Your church did well to claim her as one of its own, I will give you that. But tell me, why has she not been ushered into Sainthood when so many undeserving ones have?"

The hostility in his words caught Thomas off guard. "It was meant as a compliment. I know very little of Hildegard. If not for her texts on healing, I doubt I would even know her name."

"You know only what the church would have you know. Nothing more."

"I know God saw fit to imbue her with great healing skills. Is that not enough?"

"Why is it that you Christians are so eager to attribute all the good in this world to God and all things evil to the Devil?"

"God sets us all on the path He sees fit," Thomas said.

"Well, your god had nothing to do with Seraina's skills. Seraina worked hard for her knowledge. I have never seen a disciple so devoted."

"You were her teacher?"

"One of many."

There was a slight rustle at one of the makeshift branch-walls and Seraina slipped through. Her eyes went wide when she saw Thomas sitting up.

"You are awake!"

She dropped the sack in her hand and was at Thomas's side before he could speak. She took his hand in hers and placed the other on his forehead.

"How do you feel?" her eyes glowed in the half-darkness of the shelter and Thomas found himself unable to look away.

"Good," he said. "Better than good, all things considered."

Seraina took his hand in both of hers and lowered herself onto the edge of the bed. "And you will feel even better soon. The worst is over." She turned to the old man. "Gildas, give him some broth."

Gildas cleared his throat. "I already did."

"He needs more," Seraina said. "I can feel it in his heart rhythms."

The old man grunted. "Very well. He is your patient, after all." He held out the bowl for Thomas to take. "But if he needs more he should be strong enough to feed himself."

Thomas began sipping at it slowly, and his hands shook at first, but once the liquid reached his stomach he drank in greedy gulps. Before he could empty the bowl, Seraina laughed and reached out her hand to cover his own. She took the broth from him and he fell back into the bed.

"That is enough," she said. "For now. I can see Gildas is about to throw a fit."

"How long have I been here? And, for that matter, where is here?" Thomas asked, glancing around at their cave-like shelter of tree branches.

"Six days," Seraina said. "We are only a few miles from the hollow in Kussnacht where you found me. You were too injured to move any further. But no need to worry. We are well-hidden. Leopold's men could never find us here." The words bubbled out of her and she seemed to take great delight in wiping the remains of broth from Thomas's chin with the sleeve of her dress.

Six days? Thomas clenched his fingers and flexed his leg muscles. They responded well and did not feel like they had been inactive for six days.

Gildas seemed to sense what was going through Thomas's mind. "Seraina exercised your limbs for you, when you could not. Your recovery may seem *miraculous* to you, but it is nothing of the sort. It is thanks to Seraina's hands keeping your blood flowing from your heart to your extremities and back again."

Thomas stopped flexing his thigh muscles and was suddenly very aware of how naked he was under the lambskin blanket. He looked at Seraina.

"You have my gratitude," he said. "I hope it was not too… much trouble."

She shrugged. "You would have done the same for me, I am sure."

Thomas caught the trace of a smile on her lips before his eyes dropped to his hands. A breeze rustled the walls of their shelter, and a few green needles drifted down onto his bed. He was grateful to have something to focus upon.

"And my clothes…?" he said, to no one in particular.

"I burned them," Seraina said. "They were ruined and bore

the stink of memories best forgotten." Her eyes dimmed for just a moment, and then flared to life again like a candle burning too hot for a thumb and finger to extinguish. She pointed to the sack on the ground. "I have brought you all new clothing. It is time to make some new memories."

Her words came too late for Thomas. His mind had latched onto the colossal form of his boyhood friend lying still and filthy in a dark prison cell. Thomas closed his eyes to shut it out, but that was a mistake, for the image only grew more real. He could see Pirmin's swollen face, beaten beyond recognition. Bruises and great purple welts in the shape of hobnailed boots lined his chest and ribcage, and his once muscular arm lay blackened at his side, seeping puss and a foul, cloudy liquid. He snapped his eyes open before his mind could force him to relive the rotting stench that went along with the death of his best friend.

Thomas looked at Seraina and worked the dryness from his mouth. "And Pirmin? Do you know what became of his body?"

Seraina nodded. "Noll saw to him, but do not worry about that now. You should focus on your own recovery."

Thomas pushed himself up on one elbow. "Was he buried on holy ground? I saw to his shrivening, but it would all be for naught if he is put to rest anywhere but church land."

"I have not yet visited his grave," Seraina said softly. "But I am sure Noll would have seen to it."

Thomas grimaced as he raised himself higher. "I must go and see for myself. Will you take me there?"

He attempted to swing a leg out from under his blanket but the movement pulled at his stitches. Pain swept up his side and his head pounded.

Seraina placed her hands on his shoulders. When she

spoke her words were soft but firm. "I will take you, in time. But not until you are strong enough."

Thomas resisted for only a moment before he felt his strength drained away by the effort. He collapsed back into the blankets and closed his eyes until the throbbing in his skull subsided. He had to see Pirmin's resting place. He would not risk his friend being turned away at Saint Peter's Gate because Thomas had neglected his duties. But, he also knew his limits.

He opened his eyes and stared at the green canopy above. "Tomorrow, then," he said.

Seraina leaned back and lifted her hands from his shoulders. "That is not for us to decide. You have been through a great deal and we must allow the Weave time to welcome you back into her fold."

"I will be capable of travel tomorrow," Thomas said.

They stared at each other, locked in a battle of wills, until Gildas spoke up. "Ready or not, he means to set out tomorrow, Seraina. I suggest we be prepared to accompany him."

Later that afternoon, with a little prodding from Gildas, Seraina agreed to let Thomas stand. After pulling on his new breeches, Thomas stood with Seraina's help. With his arm around her shoulders, the two of them shuffled between the bed and fire until a light sheen covered Thomas's brow and the breath rattled in his chest.

Gildas and Oppid sat together on the ground and watched. The old man, with his back pressed up against the trunk of the tree, chewed thoughtfully on a blade of grass. The intense way the pair eyed Thomas made him nervous, but he tried to dismiss the feeling and concentrate on taking one painful step after another. After all, who *would not be* uncomfortable limping about in front of a giant wolf?

When Seraina finally eased Thomas back into his bed, he

grunted with relief. As darkness settled in, Gildas stoked the fire and they ate a simple meal of cheese, blackberries, and crunchy white tubers Thomas had never before seen. Although suspicious at first, he found them to be delicious and, because of their high water content, thirst quenching.

"He eats well. That, at least, is a good sign," Gildas said.

Seraina smiled at Thomas and nodded. "His body has begun to take over the healing process. I suppose I am no longer needed. Of course, I suspect someone will have to help him into his boots in the morning."

Thomas smiled weakly. The exercise had exhausted him, and his body demanded sleep as it attempted to digest the simple meal. He fought off the closing of his eyes once, but could not find the strength to resist when they shut a second time.

Later, he was woken by a hair-raising howl that belonged in the coldest hours of a full-moon night. Confused and disoriented, Thomas tried to sit up. He clutched at weapons that were not there.

But Seraina was. She stood over him and placed a hand on his bare shoulder.

"Shh… it is only Oppid," she said.

There was still enough light from the fire for Thomas to make out the fine features of her face, and of course, her eyes. "Lay back now…"

Somewhere outside their forest shelter, Oppid cried out to his kin once more. This time it was longer and, it seemed to Thomas, filled with anguish. Despite the comforting sound of Seraina's voice, and the warmth of her hand on his skin, Thomas felt a chill roll up his spine.

Sleep finally overtook Thomas, for Oppid did not howl again. Nor did any wolf answer his calls.

CHAPTER 5

THE MEETING CHAMBER was on the uppermost floor of Salzburg Castle. It was a long, rectangular room with high ceilings and smooth leather over the lower half of the walls. Wooden panels with intricately carved golden rosettes covered the wall's upper reaches. At one end of the room, upholstered benches lined the three walls. At the moment, a half-dozen men sat on them, doing their best to appear comfortable and relaxed.

The architect had had a good sense of court politics, and Leopold appreciated the irony of the room. The horseshoe seating arrangement allowed no obvious head of the table position and every person in the room was able to press his back up against a wall. The design was meant to put members at ease, but Leopold thought everyone looked small and feral the way their eyes darted around at one another when he entered the room. One by one they slid themselves up their respective walls and stood to greet the Duke.

There was not a prince among them, Leopold noted. They had all sent stewards or marshals on their behalf, as was the minimum requirement when summoned to a war council by another prince. Leopold had expected as much. The other princes had no love for Leopold, or loyalty for that matter. But they would obey the King's Law. However, there was one man present Leopold had not expected to see: Sir Henri of Hunenberg.

Only one person remained seated: a portly man of late middle years, but with the powder-gray hair of someone much older. His deep red robes splayed onto the bench on either side and contrasted with the dark leather of the walls. He made no effort to leave his seat in the center of the horseshoe.

Leopold briefly acknowledged the greetings of the other men then strode directly to the Archbishop.

"Duke Leopold," he said holding out a hand bearing only one single ring of gold, but mounted with an almond-sized gem.

Leopold dropped to one knee and kissed the ring. "My dear Archbishop," Leopold said, raising his head. He seemed to notice the red robes for the first time. "What is this, your lordship? Has the Pope finally welcomed you into his house and promoted you to a cardinal?"

The Archbishop eventually smiled at Leopold, but it took some time to appear on his lips, and there it died without ever reaching his eyes. The Arse-bishop of Salzburg, as Leopold liked to call him, held the position of *Legatus Natus*. It permitted him to wear red, although a different shade than that of a cardinal, even in the presence of the Pope.

"Your eyes deceive you," the Archbishop said. He held one arm out to the side. "This is not the scarlet of a cardinal. Merely the red vesture of my station."

Leopold squinted. "Ah, so it is. Now that I look more closely I see that it is a much deeper shade. My mistake. Still, I am sure your time must be near. Frankly, I do not know how you do it."

"Do what, exactly?" the Archbishop asked.

"Labor in the shadows of the church, of course. I should think it would drive most men to the brink of insanity to devote one's life to a cause and never be justly recognized for it."

"On the contrary. I am the First Bishop of all German lands. His Eminence has entrusted me to preside over the Princes of the Holy Roman Empire. I imagine you, better than most, can appreciate the significance of this."

"It seems you have lost half your flock, then. For half of the princes side with Louis the Bavarian," Leopold said.

"For the time being, perhaps. But they will come to reason, for Frederich is the rightful King. I have the utmost confidence that, with our help," the Archbishop made a grand sweeping gesture around the room, "your brother will prevail."

"I am sure he will," Leopold said. "But that could be years in the making. In the meantime, we have a responsibility to our future King to ensure he has a kingdom left to rule once Louis is defeated."

"Of course, Duke Leopold. Is that not why all of us are here today? Come, take your seats councilors."

There was a commotion on the other side of the heavy chamber door. Words in raised voices were exchanged, followed by a short period of silence. Then someone eased the door open. The Archbishop's Chief Steward, the man who had met Leopold and Klaus at the entrance to High-town, stepped into the room.

Every man in the room stared at him. To his credit, he stood at attention, unflinching, looking straight ahead, and waited to be acknowledged.

"Well," the Archbishop said. "What is it?"

"A messenger, my lord, he—"

The Archbishop waved him away. "I will see him after we

are done here."

"He is a King's Eagle, my lord."

The room went from quiet to complete silence.

"Show him in, of course," the Archbishop said.

The steward had just enough time to open the door, before a bearded man garbed all in black, with a huge yellow eagle emblazoned on his chest strode through. His hair and face were coated in dust from the road, and streaked darker in places wet from sweat. He took two steps into the room; large clumps of mud fell from his boots. He dropped to one knee, and locked his eyes on the floor. The only thing about him that moved, were the saddlebags that swayed off one shoulder. As was the custom of all King's Eagles, he kept his messages, and anything else of value, in two small bags joined together with a flat piece of leather. That way, when he changed horses at an outpost, no time was wasted in transferring his supplies to a fresh mount. If his horse died from exhaustion, the Eagle was expected to take his saddlebags and continue on foot until he could expropriate a horse from someone. And if he should ever lose his bags, well, there was a reason for the saying 'a bagless King's Eagle, shall fly no more.'

"You bring the King's word?" the Archbishop asked.

The man reached into one of his saddlebags and produced a small scroll. He stood, asking permission of no one, and stretched out the roll between his hands. In a strong, clear voice, he began to read.

> *Princes of the Realm and Loyalists of the Holy Roman Empire:*
>
> *We are beset by dark times, for treachery approaches from all sides. Pretenders threaten to usurp our Divine Right to Rule.*
>
> *I am forced to take up arms against my own cousin,*

who I am convinced, acts upon misinformation supplied by unscrupulous advisers. Meanwhile, on the other side of the Empire, in Further Austria, you are faced with your own challenge; an open rebellion by the peasants of the Forest Regions.

You may be tempted to consider your situation less grand, or not as worthy, as my own. However, if this were truly so, I would not have taken the time to send this decree.

On the surface, this rebellion appears to be nothing more than mountain peasants laying claim to Habsburg lands and defiling property of the monks at Einsiedeln. But this is no benign threat and I urge you, do not take it lightly. Much is at risk.

From Paris, comes word of a diseased class who call themselves "bourgeois". Their guilds grow in power and greed everyday, threatening to topple the Divine Order, the very pillars upon which society is built. These mercers would raise themselves up and be your equals. Mark my words. This movement is a plague waiting to spread.

If we stand by and allow the peasants of Schwyz, Uri, and Unterwalden to take even one farmer's field, we are remiss in our duties as Lords of this Land. For, in the end, they will only succeed in abusing God's gardens and destroying themselves while doing so. But even worse, by not acting, we are in direct defiance of God's wishes. For, by His Word, "Kings are to rule the hands of men, and the Church, their hearts".

I deeply regret my absence at your council, but as you know I fight another battle. The Empire faces war on two fronts, and neither poses a more dangerous threat than the other.

As these are my thoughts, I exert my right as your vassal lord, and call upon each and every one of you to fulfill your oaths of fealty. It is my wish that you raise from your lands the prescribed number of infantry and mounted knights as set out in your Oath to the Throne, and make them available to my brother Leopold, the Sword of Habsburg, at a place and time of his choosing.

It may be Habsburg lands today, but mark the words of your King, if this threat is not properly addressed, tomorrow it will be yours.

The messenger cleared his throat and looked up. He threw his shoulders back and drew himself to full height.

"Signed and dated by his Grace, Frederich of Habsburg, King of the Germans, and Rightful Emperor of the Holy Roman Empire," he said.

The room was silent. The Archbishop beckoned the Eagle to him and accepted the scroll. He studied it with narrowed eyes. Eventually, he nodded.

"It is indeed the King's seal. I did not know your brother was capable of such eloquence, Duke Leopold."

Of course he is not. They are my words, and my scribe Bernard's script. You and I both know it.

"Unlike myself, Frederich was gifted with a golden tongue. I have always envied him that," Leopold said.

Even you, my Arse-bishop, cannot refute the Royal Seal. I am sure it will drive you mad wondering how I got my hands on that.

The old cleric handed the scroll back to the Eagle. "You discredit yourself. I am sure you have your own set of talents that we have yet come to appreciate, Duke Leopold. Or, would you prefer I call you *Sword of the Habsburgs*?"

One of the stewards chuckled until he saw the young Duke looking at him. It was the Count of Kyburg's man. Leopold fixed his face in his memory.

A deep voice broke in on the conversation. "My lords, may I have leave to speak?" Count Henri of Hunenberg asked.

Leopold was glad the man had spoke up. A veteran of the wars in the Holy Lands, Henri was the only lord in the room, except for the Arse-bishop, who was there in person to represent his own title and lands. But, he looked uncomfortable in the council chambers. He had spent too much time in the Levant and seemed out of sorts with court politics.

Why was he here, anyway? None of the other counts or princes had come themselves. Why should he?

Leopold suddenly recalled that he still owed Henri partial payment for one of his estates near the Gotthard Pass. Surely the man had better sense than to come looking for a handout here. Leopold would pay him when he had the funds, and not a moment before.

"Of course, Count. You require no man's permission to speak in this council. We are grateful for your presence," Leopold said. He gestured for the man to retake his seat.

Count Henri bowed his head but remained standing. "We all understand the King's message. But we have not yet heard from the man who is to command this army we raise. Perhaps you could tell us what you plan, Duke Leopold."

"Plan? I think it should be obvious. I will march into Schwyz, punish those responsible for the attack on the Einsiedeln monastery, and rest up my men. From there, I march to Altdorf, retake the fortress, kill all who resist, and put the mountain peasants to work repairing the damage they have caused."

"Enslave them, you mean."

"Ah, Henri. I believe I know where this is headed. You knew some of the rebels in Outremer, did you not? You fought alongside them and counted them friends, I imagine."

"Aye. I knew both Pirmin and Thomas. But friend is not the exact word I would use to describe Thomas. Pirmin maybe, but not Thomas."

"And what of Hermann Gissler? The man this Thomas Schwyzer cut down before my very eyes. Would you count him as a friend, if he yet lived?"

Count Henri shifted his weight and stared at the Duke. "I just think there may be a better solution to this mess than marching through those villages with a full blown army. I have seen what an army can do to a land and its people. It will take years for them to recover."

"I appreciate your forthrightness and will take your concerns under advisement. Now, I trust you will heed the commands of your King?"

Henri cast his eyes downward at his hands. They were heavy, with thick digits and a crescent shape to them that looked permanent. He let them drop to his side and one slowly curled into a fist.

"I am bound to the Crown for fifty knights and fifty infantry, and I will honor it. However, I will be commanding the men myself. As is my right," Henri said.

"Of course. Having a man with your experience in my army will be most welcome," Leopold said, and he meant it. Henri may have a sentimental streak but when it came time to fight for his King, he would do what was required. His sense of honor would permit nothing less.

He did a quick mental calculation. Adding Henri's soldiers to those the other lords would be required to furnish, came to just shy of two thousand men. Leopold's own force consisted of three thousand, and how many would the Archbishop be required to contribute? Another two thousand? Perhaps three? The Salzburg Barracks was home to full-time, battle-hardened soldiers, who had seen active duty all over the Empire. They would be the best trained of them all. It was shaping up to be the ultimate punitive force.

"Archbishop. Do you recall what the size of your contributory force shall be?" Leopold asked. He kept his eyes wide and innocent, and was proud of himself for not allowing a trace of smugness to creep into his voice.

The older man steepled his fingers in front of his face.

Was the old goat actually hiding a smirk?

The Archbishop opened his mouth to speak, and then stopped himself for a moment before finally continuing on. He looked like a man about to eat a roast pheasant, but could not quite decide which wing to tear off first.

"Regrettably, all of Salzburg's military forces are already committed to the King's cause. I have my own writ from the King that I must follow. You see, Salzburg is to be kept as a place of strength should Frederich need to withdraw from the war with the Bavarian for a time. The King has commanded me to ensure all of Salzburg's soldiers are available to him at a moment's notice. All of them. God forbid that should ever happen, of course."

You dung-eating buggerer of....

"So the answer to your question, Duke Leopold, is regrettably, not one."

The Archbishop leaned back into the leather of his bench and crossed his arms. He shook his head in a display of regret, but the thin smile on his lips told another story entirely.

✧ ✧ ✧

"In all your years, have you ever known a more repugnant, holier than thou, greedy, arse licker? Have you?" Duke Leopold asked.

"Yes, my lord. Several," Klaus said.

Dressed in only his nightshirt, Leopold paced laps around his assigned room. Klaus was sure it must be the smallest guest quarters in Salzburg Castle. He thought of mentioning that to the Duke, but quickly changed his mind. Klaus did not know of another man Duke Leopold hated more than the Archbishop of Salzburg, and fanning those flames would not be wise.

Leopold puffed up his face and squinted his eyes. "*So the answer, Duke Leopold, is not a one.* How long did he practice to get that pompous tone just right? And what cruel bastard ever decided someone could be both a prince and a bishop?"

"Your grandfather, I believe," Klaus said. *God rest his soul.*

"Well, that explains it. Yet another failing of dear old grand pappy that I have to live with. If I did not need the Arsebishop's cavalry I would have spit in his face right then and there. And watched it drip down his double chin onto his precious red robes. Really, why should a cleric be in charge of some of the best soldiers in the Empire? Who decided that?"

"Your grandfather as well," Klaus said.

"The man was truly an idiot."

Klaus said nothing. He stood ramrod straight, with his hands behind his back, and eyes in front.

"Well, what do we do now Klaus? Go back to his holiness tomorrow and beg for his cavalry?"

Klaus shook his head. "We do not need his soldiers, my lord."

"No, we do not *need* them, Klaus. I *want* them. When we march into Schwyz and Altdorf, we must do so with a full display of Habsburg might. I want drummers, trumpet men, infantry, and if I can't have the Sturmritter, I want the next best thing. And that, sadly, is the Arsebishop's cavalry. And now that he has told me I cannot have them I want them even more!"

Leopold grabbed a pitcher of wine from the bedside table and filled a mug. He lifted it to his nose and sniffed it. He was about to take a drink and then groaned and threw it against the wall.

"Probably poisoned," he said. "Would that not be the perfect end to a perfect day? Or the perfect week for that matter? What do you think, Klaus?"

Klaus paused before answering. "I think the Ars... Archbishop did not believe the messenger was a true Eagle."

"I could care less what he thinks, as he obviously does not spend much time catering to my wants. He does not care if Louis trounces my brother in this war. He will still be the High Bishop for the German Empire. The only person's favor he really needs, is that of the Pope."

Leopold paused. He stared at Klaus and cocked his head. Klaus had seen that look many a time. He let out a deep breath, and waited.

"The Pope..." Leopold repeated. "Klaus, why is it that I get some of my best ideas while yelling at you?"

Klaus gave no indication that he had heard the question. But he had, in fact, heard everything. Not many men could say they had served two kings and outlived them both. Klaus suspected he knew which plan Leopold was about to hatch.

It was going to be a long night.

CHAPTER 6

THEY SET OUT mid-morning with Thomas riding bareback on their one horse and Seraina and Gildas walking alongside. Thomas was grateful that Gildas had sent the wolf away earlier when he saw how much Oppid upset the horse, for Thomas doubted he had the strength to control a fidgety animal. And Gildas too, mumbling something about towns filled with small-minded people, seemed to relax when Oppid bolted off into the woods.

They emerged from the trees onto a road some time later. Thomas knew it was for his sake that they avoided the forest trails but he wished Seraina would stop looking at him every time he winced or shifted to a more bearable position on his mount. He kept one arm pressed tight to his side, as it lessened the jostling of his stitches. He was weak, he knew that. But the pounding in his skull had subsided to a tolerable level and he was actually beginning to feel the first pangs of hunger.

"Do you need to stop for a rest?" Seraina asked.

"No."

"We have time. I know of a place we can spend the night and push on to Schwyz at first light."

"I said no. I would see us at Sutter's inn before dusk."

"Very well. But we will stop here for a few moments. You

may not be tired but your horse is. You ride with all the life of an iron anvil."

Thomas began to grunt back a reply but the vibration of speech sent a shiver of pain rippling up his side. He settled for a dark look.

Gildas stopped and leaned on his staff. "A rest sounds good. You set a swifter pace than I am accustomed. Whatever happened to the little short-legged girl of yesteryear that used to have to run to keep up with me?"

Seraina laughed. "Why I willed my legs to grow, of course, because I was sure there must be more to see in the world than thinning white hair and a crooked back."

"It seems that a great deal of that will was directed at your tongue as well," Gildas said.

Seraina was still smiling as she looked at the road before them. It rose up a steep hill and turned to the right.

"I think there are heidelberries nearby. Gildas, help Thomas off his horse and I will be back in a few minutes."

She was already several strides up the road before either man had a chance to voice their thoughts. Thomas watched as her lithe legs carried her away from them. Her strides were long and graceful, and although she was no taller than an average woman, the way she moved was more feline than human. She crested the hill and, with one last glint of sunshine off her auburn hair, Seraina disappeared around the bend.

Thomas realized he had been holding his breath. He looked down and saw Gildas staring at him. The old man shook his head.

"She is not for you, Thomas Schwyzer."

"What are you talking about?" Thomas met the old man's stare with one of his own.

"Deny it if you will. But your eyes are the scouts of your

heart, not its spies. They cannot conceal what you feel."

Thomas looked down at his horse's neck. "You are full of crazy talk, old man." He swung his right leg over and eased himself to the ground. His pulse beat at a furious pace.

Gildas looked up the road.

"I tell you this to spare you. Not because of some fatherly need to protect a daughter." He turned back and Thomas tried to avoid the man's fierce blue eyes, but they were a current that he could not fight against.

"Seraina is much more than a daughter to this world," Gildas said. His eyes softened to reveal a sadness that had perhaps always been present, but hidden. "Your priests tell us women are sin. My own people view them differently. We say *woman is life*."

"Then what do you say of men?" Thomas asked.

Gildas smiled. "*Man is the servant of life*. Fitting is it not?"

Thomas shook his head. "I do not understand what you are trying to…,"

Thomas blinked, and caught a sense of motion from the top of the hill. At the same time, Gildas too seemed to register a change of some sort, for he turned and looked up the road.

Seraina rounded the corner in the road and was coming toward them at an all-out sprint. She slipped as she started down the hill, but without slowing down, she reached out one hand, pushed off the ground to regain her balance, and continued running. The sight of her reddish-brown hair, streaming behind her as she ran, had a much different effect on Thomas now than it did earlier. It filled him with dread.

He reached to his belt for his knife, but it came away empty. He looked to his horse, but realized its back was bare, save for Ruedi's crossbow wrapped in a sheepskin blanket. The quality weapon was worth a small fortune, but now, with no bolts, it was worse than worthless. But even if he had a quarrel, Thomas knew he would be unable to cock the weapon without the assistance of a belt hook. The heavy draw weight of the string would sever his fingers before he could pull it even half way.

"A sword," he said, looking at Gildas. "I need a weapon." Gildas stepped away from him and shook his head. Thomas's eyes locked onto the walking stick Gildas held. It was crooked and worn smooth from a lifetime of use, but being made from hard, solid oak, it was heavy enough. He reached out and tore it from the old man's grasp before he could protest.

Seraina was there much sooner than Thomas thought possible. She walked the last few paces with her hands on her hips to catch her breath. Her cheeks were flushed and the sides of her hair wet with sweat. One unruly strand curled over a cheek and fluttered with every exhalation.

"Habsburg soldiers," she said. "And I think they saw me. Quickly! We must take to the trees."

Gildas put his arm on her shoulder. "It is too late for that now." He nodded toward the road. Two riders, the sun glinting off their helmets, trotted toward them. They seemed to be in no rush, but they were obviously focused on the three travelers standing directly in their path.

"We must run," Seraina said.

"We cannot." Gildas nodded toward Thomas. "He is in no shape to flee. I doubt he could even get back onto his horse in time."

"He is right," Thomas said. "You and Gildas go. I will be fine. They will not know who I am."

Seraina's voice rose to a frantic pitch. "Are you mad? Of course they will know who you are. You killed the Duke's soldiers and stole one of his horses!"

Thomas looked at his mount. The Habsburg brand jumped out at him. Cringing, he pulled the bundle holding Ruedi's crossbow forward so it covered the mark. By the time he turned around, he was greeted by the pattering of hooves on hard earth. He tightened his grip on the walking stick.

"You there. What cause do you have to run from your Duke's patrol?"

Gildas stepped forward. "Please forgive my daughter, my lords. She is mute and scares easily. She mistook you for highwaymen and rushed back to warn us."

The riders pulled up before them. The one that spoke was much younger than the other, and the way he barked out his words, made Thomas think he was eager to impress the veteran he rode with.

"Show me your trade pass," the younger man said.

"Trade papers, my lord?" Gildas said.

"This road is closed to all but those certified by the Trade Commissioner."

"Since when?" Thomas asked. "I have not heard of these roads being off limits to locals." He regretted speaking almost immediately. Not because the younger man turned on him instantly, but more so because he felt the older soldier also take an interest in him.

"Do you expect to know all that transpires in the Commissioner's office?" the young soldier said. "Are we to knock on every hovel's door and deliver each command of his lordship personally? Who are you, man, to speak so out of place?"

"He is my daughter's husband, my lord," Gildas said, shooting a scowl at Thomas. "He is a miserable man at the best of times, and often speaks out of turn to make up for his wife's eternal silence."

To emphasize the old druid's story, Seraina punched

Thomas in the shoulder and flashed her teeth at him.

"Well, if he speaks again without my leave, I will have his tongue at my belt. That should make the conversations at their dinner table more balanced."

He chuckled at his own threat, and Thomas forced his eyes to look at the ground. The older soldier nudged his horse forward and slowly began circling around to the rear of Thomas's own mount.

The young man continued questioning Gildas. "If you have no trade papers, then you did not pass the checkpoint. How did you get on this road?"

"Not far from here, there is a trail in the woods that leads to our farm," Gildas said, his words seemed especially slow to Thomas, and as he spoke he stepped toward the young man, holding his hands low and out to the side. "This path meanders between lichen-coated rocks, and under trees draped in giant-beard. The sun appears, now and then, and when it does, its rays warm your skin, and if you listen carefully, very carefully, the sound of running water hums in the background…"

Gildas continued speaking and if Thomas had been standing closer to the old man he doubted he would have been able to focus on anything but his words. But, with effort, he shook off the sound of Gildas's voice. He took hold of his horse's halter, then angled himself toward the other soldier walking his horse behind them.

"A word of caution, my lord," Thomas said. "This horse likes to kick out at others that come too close from the rear."

The soldier drew his sword. "I shall have to be careful, then," he said. "What do you carry under this blanket?"

Seraina stiffened beside Thomas. He could tell it was all she could do to hold back her words.

"Firewood," Thomas said.

"Firewood," the soldier repeated, like it was some exotic foreign word.

"And a few onions," Thomas said.

The soldier nodded. And then thrust his sword point between the blanket and the rope securing the bundle in place. The rope sprang away, the horse skittered sideways a step, and the load slid off and crashed to the ground.

Ruedi's Genoese-made war bow flipped out from its concealment and skidded to a stop at Thomas's feet. The veteran's eyes picked up on the horse's Habsburg brand in the same instant.

He raised his sword, and then screamed in pain.

Seraina was on his other side. She had thrust her hand behind his knee and had a hold of something, a ligament or tendon, or God only knew what, but whatever it was, the soldier's face was pale with agony. He dropped his sword and leaned in his saddle to get away from her. Thomas shuffled over and obliged him. He grabbed his arm and yanked him from his horse. Thomas grimaced as his stitches stretched to their limit, but held.

Thomas heard the ring of a sword being drawn from its scabbard. He looked over his shoulder as the young soldier, seemingly no longer under Gildas's trance, kicked the old man to the ground.

Seraina screamed the druid's name and rushed to help him. Thomas gripped the walking stick in his hands and brought it down on the head of the soldier lying at his feet. He hit him again for good measure, then turned to help Gildas and Seraina.

But he knew he was too far away.

As Seraina ran at the two of them, the young soldier, with

a wild look in his eyes, hefted his sword high above his head. Gildas, having pushed himself up to his hands and knees, looked up as the sword began its downward arc toward his neck.

Then Thomas saw fear twist the ears of the soldier's horse. Its eyes went wide, and before it could bolt, its master was carried clean out its saddle by a blowing cloud of white fur.

Oppid's momentum carried him and the soldier twenty feet away from the terror-stricken horse. The white wolf had his massive jaws wrapped over top the soldier's helmet, so he lived long enough to know he was in a nightmare. The man screamed as Oppid stood over him, snarling, his yellow teeth dripping streams of thick saliva. Then the wolf snapped him up by the throat, lifted him off the ground, and shook the soldier back and forth like he was nothing more than an old dusty blanket. The cracks of his neck and spine splintering made Thomas look away.

The older soldier let out a groan, so Thomas hit him again with the walking stick. Then he retrieved the soldier's sword and turned back to finish the man, but Seraina stepped in front and put her hand on Thomas's chest.

"Thomas, no," she said.

"He will bring others," Thomas said. "They said there was a checkpoint near here."

"We have two more horses, now. We will be in Schwyz before they can send others," Gildas said.

Thomas watched Oppid drag the broken corpse of the other soldier into the woods. "God have mercy. Is he going to do what I think he is?"

"At times, nature may appear cruel," Gildas said. "But look at it through Oppid's eyes. True cruelty lay in letting a perfectly good set of entrails rot in the sun." The old man's eyes sparkled. "Come, Thomas Schwyzer. Let us be on our way, and leave an old wolf his privacy. For, as those of your faith are fond of saying, it is God's Will."

As they came over the last series of low, velvety green slopes, and Schwyz lay at the head of the valley below, Gildas slowed his horse and began to stammer excuses for not going any further.

"Why not come in with us?" Seraina asked. "Sutter has a warm, comfortable inn with even a few private rooms, and the best chamois stew—".

Gildas shook his head and the downy white hair of his beard and head floated in the breeze. "No. It is time for me and Oppid to be on our way."

He slid off his horse, stroked her neck once, and whispered something in her ear that sent her trotting off back the way they had come. Thomas and Seraina also dismounted and, after Thomas removed Ruedi's war bow, they too sent their mounts away. They would not risk any harm coming to Sutter by bringing the Duke's horses into his stable.

Gildas whistled and Oppid loped out of the woods, turning his massive head warily from side to side as he crossed the open grassland between them.

"Luck is not one of my beliefs. But, I will wish it to you all the same, Thomas Schwyzer." The old man held out his arm and Thomas took it.

"How long will you be gone?" Seraina asked. Her voice was small and Thomas could hear the fear of abandonment in her words.

Gildas shrugged. Oppid was at his side now, and the old man absently grabbed and released great handfuls of the wolf's white coat. "As long as it takes. The others are scattered and will be difficult to find. But I will. And when the time is right, you must meet us on the Mythen."

Seraina nodded once, and then dropped her chin. The old man looked at her and his face softened.

"I will be back, my child. Remember, I too have no small touch of the sight, and that much I have seen."

He reached out and lifted her head. She looked up and her eyes shimmered. A tear broke free and crawled down one cheek. The sight of her in pain made Thomas avert his gaze.

"Ah, Seraina. Your eyes remind me so much of the waters we lived on when you were a child. Do you remember our lake?"

"Yes… I think so," she said, dabbing at her eyes with her sleeve. "But only bits and pieces. I was so young."

"And so full of questions for one just learning to speak. Why, why, why! How, how, how! It could have been the most peaceful place in the world, if not for your endless nattering."

Seraina smiled. "I do remember. I was happy there," she said.

"You were, and so was I. Happier than at any other moment in my long years. And when I look at you now, it gladdens me to see that green lake reflected so clearly in your eyes. Somehow, you have preserved the same wonder and innocence as back then, but like those waters, I see the strength of steel as well. There has never been a prouder man, than the one that stands across from you now."

Seraina hugged him and buried her face against his white robe. Her shoulders shuddered and he kissed the top of her head. After some time, he eased her to arm's length.

"Come, now. You will upset the wolf. It is best you say your goodbyes."

Seraina wiped once more at her eyes and nodded. She called the wolf by name, then dropped to her knees and threw her arms around his neck, her fingers not even close to touching. She forced a laugh and whispered strange words into his ear.

Thomas became aware that the old man had locked his eyes on him. All traces of the kindness that had been in them only moments before was gone.

"Look after her," Gildas said. "As she has done for you. And remember what we discussed."

"It was not much of a discussion, as I recall," Thomas said.

Seraina stared after Gildas and Oppid for a long while after they disappeared into the forest. Finally, she and Thomas began walking down the slope toward the village.

"I do not understand why Gildas refused to stay at Sutter's for even one night," Thomas said. "Surely a comfortable bed and a hot meal would do the old man some good. Is he in that much of a hurry?"

Seraina held out one hand and dragged it through the waist-high grass. It was late afternoon and Thomas was beginning to feel the autumn chill through his cloak, but Seraina did not seem to notice.

"Gildas does not like to be around people much. Even the smallest village unnerves him," Seraina said.

"He cares about you, though. How did you come to be raised by him?"

"He bought me," Seraina said.

"Bought you? Such as at a slave market?"

"You are one to talk," she said. "It was not like that. I was only a baby when Gildas found me. My parents were very poor and already had five children, so Gildas convinced them to give me up."

"Why did he choose you over one of the others?"

Seraina smiled. "Because I was special. Can you not see

that?" Her spirits seemed to be improving.

Thomas shrugged. "He may have been able to get two, or even three, of the other children for the same price as one *special* one."

Seraina slapped him on the arm. Thankfully, it was his uninjured one.

"We are a pair, you and me," Seraina said. "Each sold to the highest bidder. I wonder what our lives would be like if that had not happened…"

That was a question Thomas had never once asked himself. He remembered almost nothing about his life before the *Long March* to the port of Genoa, where he and the other Schwyzer children were loaded onto a ship bound for the Holy Lands.

Sometimes, late at night, he would catch a glimpse of a tall man cutting wood, or a woman with sandy hair, standing in a black earth garden and wiping her brow with the back of her arm. But they were fleeting images, just as likely to be based on dreams as reality.

Perhaps the only true memory he could claim of those early years, was that of a shivering boy trying to spread a small blanket over the half-frozen bodies of his dead parents. Since that was what he usually saw whenever he attempted to remember his parents, he eventually stopped trying altogether.

"My parents died when I was very young," Thomas said. He was not sure why he had said that.

"I know," Seraina said.

When he looked at her with confusion on his face, she added, "You talked out loud, and often, when you were stricken with the blood fever."

"Ah," he said.

"In fact, I think you talked more when you were at death's

feet than you do now."

"Perhaps my silent nature is the reason the Hospitallers paid more for me than Gildas did for you," Thomas said. He found himself smiling, and if the scar on the left side of his face tightened, he did not notice.

"Oh, ho! The fox bares his teeth," Seraina said. "Speaking of Gildas, what was it that you and he *discussed* when I was gone?" If anyone looked like a fox at that moment, it was Seraina.

Thomas shook his head and tried to keep his eyes locked on the thatched roof of Sutter's house in the distance.

"Was it about me?" Seraina asked, innocently. But her grin and the tilt of her head told Thomas she knew that it was.

✧ ✧ ✧

Seraina saw Sutter cutting wood behind the inn as she and Thomas approached across a field. He straightened up when he saw them coming and, after shielding his eyes from the sun to get a better look, shouted something toward the kitchen window. Within seconds, both Vreni and her daughter Mera ran out the back door.

Seraina left Thomas behind and ran to meet the two women with tearful embraces all the way around. By then Sutter was there, and even the gruff innkeeper wrapped his long arms around Seraina.

Mera had her crying under control by the time Thomas limped up, but one look at him and her pretty features began to waver. She ran at Thomas, as though it were a race to get to him before her tears exploded, and threw her arms around his neck. She got her head on his chest just in time.

Seraina looked on as Thomas held his arms out to the side for an uncomfortable moment, but then in small jerky movements, managed to put them around the girl and comfort her as best he could.

"I am so sorry Thomas," Mera said. "None of us deserved to have Pirmin taken from us, but you least of all."

Thomas said nothing, but Seraina was sure she saw his arms squeeze the girl a little tighter.

While Vreni and Mera disappeared upstairs to make up two rooms, Seraina and Thomas sat with Sutter at the small kitchen table, since it was the dinner hour and there were a few guests in the main room.

"You have been to Altdorf, then?" Sutter said to Seraina.

She nodded. "More men flock to Noll's fortress every day, from all corners of the Forest Regions," Seraina said. "If Leopold comes next year, he will be in for a surprise."

Sutter's mouth became hard. "That is good to hear. And what of Landenberg?"

Seraina feared he would ask about the Vogt of Unterwalden. "The Council will meet and decide his fate," she said.

He looked up at the ceiling for a moment and then lowered his voice to a whisper. "He should be hung."

Seraina could feel Sutter staring at her, but she could not be sure because her own eyes refused to leave her fingers. "I know how you feel, and if it is any consolation, Noll punished the man. I saw his injuries."

"That will not stop him from coming right back here and terrorizing us all over again." He paused. "I have given this some thought. I am going to join the Confederate Army."

Seraina could not believe what she was hearing, but it was Thomas who responded first.

"No, that is a very poor decision. Look around you, Sutter. You have a business, a family, and both need you more than any band of Melchthal's. If you go to Altdorf, you throw all of this away."

"I believe in what Noll is doing," Sutter said.

"War is for young men," Thomas said.

"You serve this cause better by staying alive," Seraina said. "Your family needs you."

Sutter closed his eyes and massaged his temples with one hand. "You are both right. I am not thinking straight these days." A dry laugh forced itself from his chest. "I am just a tired, old innkeeper."

Seraina could tell Sutter was lying by the way he laughed. He was telling them what they wanted to hear. Thomas seemed to sense it as well, for in a rare show of affection, he reached over the table and put his hand on Sutter's shoulder.

"Do what is best for your family. You will never regret that," Thomas said.

"What will you do?" Sutter asked.

As Seraina waited for Thomas's response, bits of her recent vision flashed through her mind.

"I have not given it much thought," Thomas said, leaning back slowly in his chair.

"You could come stay with us. We need an extra set of hands around the inn."

Thomas smiled, but there was more sadness about it than joy. He looked around the kitchen.

"Thank you, Sutter. I would like that," he said. "But I think I had better ask Pirmin first. He was always rather protective over this place."

While Sutter chuckled at the joke, Seraina looked into Thomas's dark, almost black, eyes and trembled at what she saw.

CHAPTER 7

THE ARCHBISHOP'S MESSENGER walked his horse through the gates of High-town just after midnight. A bank of clouds had moved in an hour before, and the evening air was muggy. When the rain finally broke loose, it came in the form of a mist so fine and light he did not bother putting up the hood of his cloak.

He kept his horse to a walk as he passed through Low-town. The sound of a cantering horse in the dead of night made people nervous and was sure to draw attention. But once he had navigated the maze of cobbled alleys and streets, and the last group of houses lay behind him, the messenger dug his heels into his horse's side and urged her into a gallop.

The horse's shod hooves hit the bridge over the Salzach a minute later, and the sound echoed off the trees and drowned out the noise of water rushing below. The rider did not let up on the reins. Time was more important than stealth now. He knew he was far enough out of the city that no one would hear.

But he was wrong.

After the end of the bridge the road banked to the left and narrowed. With the cloud cover, and the drizzling rain, he had no hope of seeing the black-dyed rope stretched taut in his path. It caught him high in the chest and snapped his head back to bounce off his horse's flank. He rolled backward off his mount and landed hard in the middle of the road. It took several moments before he could breathe, never mind push himself up to his hands and knees. His head cleared enough to realize what had happened and he drew his sword at the same time as he staggered to his feet.

"Take your time," a rough voice said. "Neither one of us is in a hurry now."

A man, huge as the night was dark, stood on the road a few feet away. His sword was drawn, but rested point down in the road. His hands were folded over one another on the hilt of, what would be for most men, a two-handed sword.

The messenger pointed his blade at the figure. He glanced around warily. Emboldened when he saw no others, he at last found his voice.

"Who are you to waylay a messenger of the Prince-Archbishop?"

"At this point, it no longer matters."

The Archbishop's man squinted his eyes and took a step sideways. "I know you", he said. "You are Leopold's man. What is the meaning of this?"

Klaus grunted, and lifted his sword. "You sound plenty rested enough now," he said.

The messenger's eyes widened. "You would raise swords against an official representative of a Prince of the Empire?"

"No. I just mean to kill one."

Klaus shuffled forward and aimed a slow thrust at the man's midsection. The messenger was surprised by the attack, but he was light on his feet and managed to step back and block. Klaus thrust again, another cumbersome stroke, and this time, encouraged by his opponent's lack of speed, the messenger countered with a slash at Klaus's throat.

Klaus's sword came alive. It deflected the blow downward and then Klaus whipped the flat of his blade against the man's leg and head so fast the pain registered in both places simultaneously. He cried out and fell to one knee. Klaus grabbed the wrist of the man's sword-arm in one of his own massive hands, and squeezed until the messenger's fingers went numb and the blade fell to the road. Klaus elbowed him in the face, and he fell over with the criss-cross pattern of chainmail covering both eyes and a freshly broken nose.

Klaus leaned over, took up the man's sword and threw it as far into the bush as he could. He sheathed his own weapon, grabbed the messenger by his long hair, and dragged the half-unconscious body into the woods. He slowed to pick up a shovel leaning against a tree, and then continued with his prize deeper into the black forest.

When he felt they were far enough from the road, Klaus let go of the man. His head bounced off a root and he groaned. Klaus kicked the messenger's feet.

"Wake up," he said.

Only a fool would throw a body into a river. They have a tendency to bloat, rise up to the surface, bounce along on currents, and eventually show up in a fisherman's net, or get mangled in some miller's wheel. Careful men preferred holes. So long as they were deep enough to keep the meat from prying wolves, holes were always a better alternative than water.

Looking after Duke Leopold had made Klaus a careful man. And sometimes, a lazy man. Digging holes was hard work, and Klaus was no longer a young man.

Klaus kicked the messenger's feet until his eyelids flickered open. He threw the shovel on the ground and its sharp tip broke the earth, spilling soil over his face. The man turned his head and spit dirt from his mouth. His eyes were white with fear as he looked up at the giant above him.

"Dig," Klaus said.

✧   ✧   ✧

The sound began as a *pitter*, like the first few drops of rain hitting an oiled cloak. Rhythmic, almost comforting, it did not penetrate far enough into Leopold's sleep to wake him. But the pitter grew into a thump, followed by two more, and then a series of bangs. Finally, a frantic whisper cut through the heavy door and reached Leopold's ears.

"Dawn approaches, my lord. You said to wake you well before. Do you hear me?"

The voice was coarse and gruff. Completely unsuited to whispering.

Klaus! What time was it?

Leopold's eyes snapped open. He threw back the heavy down quilt and tried to stand, but his foot caught in the blanket. He crashed onto the floor. His head ached and his tongue felt like the wings of a giant moth. He cursed as he scrambled about on the cold flagstones, thankful that he had had the foresight to sleep fully clothed. He pushed himself up and swayed unsteadily until his head cleared.

By the blood of Mary, I hate mornings.

The banging started anew.

"Stop it!" Leopold pulled open the door and Klaus took a step back. "I am up. No need to wake the entire castle."

"You said to wake you before first light. No matter what," Klaus said.

"Do I look like I am sleeping?"

"I have seen dead men look more awake," Klaus said, as Leopold scrubbed his face with the palm of one hand.

"You have somewhere to be," Leopold said and slammed the door shut.

Leopold watched the Archbishop from an alcove in the keep's outer wall. He was right on time for his morning ritual of walking the entire length of his fortress wall. As the autumn sun crested the surrounding peaks, it began to bathe parts of the city in a warm glow. From this vantage point, the Archbishop could see almost every single household in his city state.

Leopold rolled his eyes as the Archbishop stopped and stared out over the wall. Seeing his lands and subjects spread out before his feet like that must feed the man's already bulging sense of self-worth, he thought. He took a breath and stepped out from his hiding spot.

"Salzburg has indeed flourished under your rule," Leopold said, strolling forward casually to join the Archbishop.

He twisted his head at the sound of Leopold's voice and the bulk of his body followed later, as though they belonged to different people. His eyes narrowed and his tongue flicked his lips. Extreme annoyance twisted his features for only the briefest of moments before it disappeared, but not before Leopold could notice.

What is the matter, my Archbishop? Did I interrupt your daily moment of solitude?

"I hope I am not intruding, Archbishop."

"Of course not. You surprised me is all. I did not take you for an early riser, Duke Leopold."

Leopold put his elbows on the wall and gazed out over the landscape. He let out a breath and the cool morning air turned it to vapor.

"Oh, I do so enjoy a morning walk. It clears one's mind and presents previously unimagined possibilities." Leopold's puffy eyes squinted against the brightness of dawn. "Salzburg truly is a beautiful city. I must make the time to visit more often."

"You are welcome here whenever you wish, Lord Leopold. Your father was a great friend to me and it is my hope that our friendship will live on in our own relations."

You hated my father. Perhaps even as much as I did.

"Why thank you. I do always enjoy the time we spend together. And I apologize for not calling upon you the last time I was in Salzburg."

The archbishop blinked. "You were in the city recently? I wish I had known."

I am sure you do.

"I meant to come up to the castle, but my business confined me to Low-town, and before I knew it, I had to leave again for Habsburg. I am sure you understand. Men in positions such as ours have so many demands placed upon our short time here on this earth."

"And some men's lives are cut shorter than they would like," the Archbishop said.

Some live far too long.

Leopold laughed. "All men's lives are shorter than they would like. Young, or old, it does not matter."

"I trust your business went well?"

Leopold stopped smiling and put on his best disinterested look. "Business, archbishop?"

"In Low-town. You claimed you were there on some sort of *mercantile* endeavor." When he mentioned the merchant class, the bishop's face soured like he had drunk week-old milk.

Leopold chuckled. "A slip of the tongue. I was unclear. When I said business, I really meant nothing of the sort. It was mercy that brought me to Salzburg that day. A weakness of mine, some say. You see, I have a soft spot for widows. Especially ones with children to care for."

The archbishop said nothing. The skin at his neck turned a mottled shade of red and gray.

Leopold patted his chest while he gazed out over the wall at the city below.

"Ah, here it is." He removed a cylindrical object from a pocket beneath his vest. He carefully unwrapped it from a short length of yellow silk and held it up for the Archbishop to inspect.

"Have you seen one of these looking glasses?"

The Archbishop nodded. "I have. The church still debates the godliness of these instruments. I must say, it saddens me to see one in your hand."

Leopold slid the looking glass open to its full length. "It is only a matter of time before the Pope himself has his very own."

Leopold stepped near the wall and held the scope up to one eye. He looked toward the snow-capped peaks in the distance and then slowly lowered it until it passed over the Salzach River. He scanned the three-story noble houses of Low-town until he found what he was looking for.

"Very useful tool," he said. "Oh, look. Is that… why, yes it is! The red lion of Habsburg held by my very own flag bearer. Incredible."

He pulled the looking glass away from his eye and held it out to the Archbishop.

"You really must see this."

When the Archbishop made no move to take the scope Leopold said, "Do not worry. This one was made in Strassburg, by German craftsmen. It is not an original from the

Mohammedans' land. No infidel hands have touched it, I assure you."

The Archbishop took a half step back. "I would rather—"

Leopold thrust out the looking glass and pressed it against the Archbishop's chest.

"I insist," he said.

The Archbishop's hands shook as he held the glass up to his eye. For all his resistance to the idea of the instrument, he seemed quite familiar with its use.

"Did you really think you could keep your whore and her five children a secret?"

The Archbishop said nothing. He kept the glass pressed against his eye.

What part of the scene below holds your attention so? Is it the sight of my soldiers standing in your secret mistress's courtyard? The woman herself, kneeling, in tears? Or is it her children being loaded into a carriage by armed Habsburg men? These clerics can be so hard to read at times.

"How old was the whore when she bore your first bastard? Eleven? Twelve, perhaps? Surely not thirteen. What a hag she must have been."

The Archbishop whirled on Leopold. He threw the looking glass to the ground and the lenses shattered.

"She is no whore," he said. A vein throbbed at his temple and his skin flushed with rage.

Leopold took a step back and held up his hands. "No? Well, perhaps I am wrong. Maybe we should ask the Pope to be the judge of what she is or is not."

The Archbishop's face paled instantly. But to his credit, his voice was steady and in control when he spoke.

"What is it that you want, Leopold?"

"Two thousand infantry, a thousand knights, and five

hundred gold. To provide for the upkeep of your men while in my care."

"Their upkeep would not cost half that," the Archbishop said.

Leopold shrugged. "I treat my men better than you, I suppose. And one more thing. I should think a public holy blessing would not be too much to ask."

"What of the woman?"

"She may remain in Salzburg, in that lovely house you had built for her. But the children will come to live in Habsburg for a time, as my wards. Their mother being a poor widow and all."

The Archbishop turned away and stared down once more at the city. In a few short moments his body had experienced a full gamut of emotions. They had taken their toll, and now he just looked like a tired old man. Even his flowing red robes could not hide that fact. Leopold put his hands on the wall and, like the Archbishop, gazed out over the city.

The sun was at full light. Soon the city would come alive.

"What a beautiful day. I do so love mornings," Leopold said.

CHAPTER 8

ALTDORF'S SMALL, STONE CHURCH, situated on top of a hillock at the eastern edge of town, was a squat, gray structure seemingly as old as the hills themselves. Thomas stepped into the shadow of the cross erected on its roof and walked around to the back of the building.

Most people hated cemeteries, but Thomas had always found them comforting. As a child, whenever he felt the need to be alone, he would leave the stench of the city behind and run to the cemetery outside Acre's gates. Later, as a young man in Cypress, he would spend hours walking amongst the graves, trying to read their inscriptions. Of course he felt closer to God when he set foot on holy ground, but, he doubted that was the only reason for the attraction. He suspected it had more to do with escaping the world of men, even if it was for only a short time.

Today, however, his steps were heavy, and not just because of his injuries. He avoided looking too closely at the crosses until he was surrounded by them. When he did finally look up, wondering where he would find Pirmin's grave, he saw a young boy and a dog. The boy sat on the ground next to a mound of dirt, blacker than the other ones nearby, and much larger. He looked up at the same time Thomas saw him. He jumped to his feet, gave his backside a quick brush with his hand, and ran away toward the far gate.

Thomas paid the boy no mind, for his full attention was captured by the dog. It was Pirmin's young pup. He tried to remember the dog's name, but the boy was quicker.

"Vex! C'mon boy!"

The dog stopped sniffing the ground and bounded after the boy without any hesitation. The boy gave Thomas a scowl and then both he and the dog disappeared through a gap in the fence.

Thomas limped to the fresh grave. *If that is indeed Pirmin's grave and the street rat has defiled it in any way, I will make him sorry....*

Sure enough, as he got nearer, Thomas saw that the boy had left something behind near the head of the grave. An old, chipped, clay pitcher stood on the ground. Thomas picked it up and liquid sloshed inside. He smelled it.

Wine. Cheap wine.

A wet bit of dirt in the middle of Pirmin's grave told Thomas the full story. The boy had brought Pirmin wine, and then shared a drink with him. Thomas shook his head in amazement. Even in death, Pirmin had more friends than most. Thomas suddenly regretted thinking the worst of the ragged child.

The cross marking Pirmin's grave was thin, frail, and unassuming. It was so unlike the man and his life that it brought a sad smile to Thomas's face. He could almost feel Pirmin's giant hand patting him on the head like when they were children.

"Thomi, Thomi. So this is where you will dump me. Marked with nothing more than a couple of twigs, for the rest of eternity. When did I ever piss in your oats?"

Thomas gazed out over the rolling hills. With the small church at his back, the elevated grounds provided an idyllic view that stretched for miles down the mountain-lined valley.

"Easy now," Thomas said out loud. "This is a fine spot. You have your own cherry tree for shade. And you will have many visitors, for this rise will give them far more interesting things to look at than just your horse-sized pile of dirt."

"Only you could make being dead sound not so bad. But you better do something about that cross. I want a proper headstone. One with letters saying my name and all the great deeds I did over my life."

Thomas looked at the two uneven sticks lashed together. The crosspiece drooped so much the cross looked more like an 'X'.

Thomas nodded slowly. "I will write the words myself," he said.

He stood for a long time, staring at the grave.

When he started to imagine he could see Pirmin's outline beneath the mound of dark earth he closed his eyes and admitted it was time. He scooped up a handful of soil and bowed his head to pray for the soul of his friend. When he was done, Thomas released the soil from his stiffened fist and watched as the wind carried it the length of Pirmin's final resting spot.

When Thomas turned back to the church, he saw Noll standing in the shade of one of its walls. He leaned against the stone, unmoving, as though he had been there a long time. When he pushed away and started walking, Thomas could see he held a long staff in one hand. As he closed the distance, Thomas realized it was not a staff after all, but rather, Pirmin's great ax.

Noll held out the ax to Thomas and he took it in both

hands. At over eight feet in length, it appeared cumbersome and unwieldy. But Urs had designed the handle and weighted it perfectly to serve as a counter-balance to the heavy, flanged ax head. He had also cut a small cross from the head's center to make it lighter. Urs had created a number of shafts for Pirmin over the years, with each new version an improvement over its predecessor, but he had never managed to come up with a design superior to the current steel tube version.

Thomas gripped it with both hands, squinting his eyes against the sun's glare as it danced from the finely honed cutting edge to the pick-like hook extending from its opposite side like a giant finger. A digit Thomas had seen Pirmin use to flick many a man from the back of a horse or off a battlement's wall.

"I found it in the jail's armory," Noll said. "Thought you might want it."

Thomas shifted his grip and powerful emotions swept forward as an old memory of Pirmin overtook him. Dressed in his full red battle kit, Pirmin stood amongst several other Hospitallers as a few Genoese crossbowmen, their bolts spent, retreated behind the line of the Knights of Saint John. The Hospitallers braced themselves for the enemy's charge. Pirmin held his ax horizontal to the ground with both hands. He gave the shaft a quick roll, making the ax head flip toward heaven, for the briefest moment, before it descended back down to point at Hell. It was Pirmin's ritual salute to the Two Powers That Be, and he always followed it with an unabashed grin in Thomas's direction. Like it was a jest only Thomas could appreciate.

The image of Pirmin's face faded and Thomas found himself staring at his hands as they clutched the cold steel shaft.

"We are glad to see you alive, ferryman. For some time we

feared the worst," Noll said. He cleared his throat before continuing. "Seraina told me what you did for her. I am in your debt for that."

With effort, Thomas pulled his eyes from Pirmin's ax and looked at Noll. "No one owes me anything," he said.

Noll stepped around Thomas to stand in front of Pirmin's grave. "I know I only met him a short time ago, but Pirmin was one of the best men I have ever known." He turned and looked down the valley. "I chose this spot for him, but I will understand if you want him moved."

Thomas studied Noll's face. The young man had aged ten years since he had seen him last. His chiseled features were overgrown with stubble and haunted by the shadows and creases of responsibility. He had finally gotten his war, and if he was anything like most people, it was not what he had envisioned.

"It is a fine spot," Thomas said. "Pirmin would complain, of course, but I believe he would be happy with it."

Noll turned to Thomas, but did not meet his eyes.

"I was there when they took him," Noll said.

"I know."

"Hiding in the woods like a frightened hare."

"You already told me that."

"I watched Habsburg soldiers take him to the ground and beat him without mercy. He fought back, and it took forever. I had all the time in the world to act, to help him, but instead I watched like a child seated on the ground in front of a puppetry troop."

Thomas said nothing.

"If I had given myself up—".

"You would now both be dead," Thomas said. He stood the great ax upright and drove its butt-end against the ground.

"Most men would have done the same as you."

Noll shook his head. "Not Pirmin. He would have waded into the midst of an army to save a friend."

"Pirmin was not most men. Do not compare yourself to him. Ask forgiveness from God, if that is what you seek. But do not look for it from me."

Noll turned away once again to stare at some far point down the valley. Thomas bit back the urge to say more. He was not one to waste words. In his experience, words never changed a man's intentions, stopped wars, or brought friends back from the dead. Perhaps Noll felt the same, for he continued to stare at that far-off point, as though Thomas was no longer beside him.

"What will you do now?" Thomas asked, finally.

Noll's blue eyes came alive when he looked at Thomas, but not in a warm, inviting way. They were the color of a cold mountain stream running over a bed of rocks, which, near the surface, were polished smooth. Those in the dark swirling waters below, however, were jagged and dark.

"I mean to finish what we started. The Habsburgs will attempt to take back their fortress, but we will see them broken against their own walls."

"I trust you have the men to do this," Thomas said.

"I will have. When the time comes."

Thomas doubted that, and he could tell by Noll's voice he was not fully convinced himself. Thomas had seen the walls of the Altdorf fortress and knew how many men it would take to man them against a siege.

But what did it matter?

"Very well," Thomas said. "Then I will stand on your walls and fight against Leopold's men."

Noll blinked. His mouth opened but no words came out at

first.

"We would welcome your sword, Thomas. But I must admit I am surprised you would fight for me."

Thomas shook his head. "Not for you. I said I would stand on your walls, but I do not fight for you. It is best we get that in the open."

Thomas watched Noll's teeth clench and a tremor run the length of his jaw. He held his tongue for some time before he spoke.

"Very well. No matter the reason, I accept your offer," Noll said.

What choice do you have? You are in the deepest pit of your life, and you know that the only way out is to climb upon the backs of many a dead man.

Noll was brave, Thomas admitted. There was no denying that. But he was also young and rash, and had yet to experience the darkness of a bottomless pit.

"While I remember," Noll said, as he turned to go. "There is a merchant in town that has been asking after you."

"I know no merchants."

Noll shrugged. "Said he came from Zug and would be staying at the Altdorf inn should I see you. Whether you meet with him or not, is no concern to me. The fool tried to sell me spices, of all things. What use do I have of spices?"

Spices?

Noll left Thomas standing in the cemetery, leaning on Pirmin's giant ax. Thomas decided to pay his respects to Pirmin once more, and then, when he was ready, he would go to the inn to meet Maximilian.

A sadness came over him as he thought about how much Pirmin would have wanted to join them.

✧ ✧ ✧

The Altdorf inn was filled to capacity when Thomas arrived that evening. With Noll's army attracting so many men and women from the neighboring villages and farms, the innkeeper and his staff were wearing ruts in the floor trying to keep up with food and drink orders. Thomas stood inside the door and scanned the twenty or so tables crammed into the low-ceilinged room. Smoke hung trapped between ceiling beams, and the smell of both sweat and old ale made his lip curl. He found himself wishing for the spotless oasis of order that was Sutter's place in Schwyz. He and Vreni knew how to run a traveler's house.

"Cap'n, over here."

Ruedi had his arm raised a half dozen tables away. A stocky form sitting across from him twisted on his bench and looked over his shoulder. Max, his neatly trimmed beard grayer than Thomas remembered, waved and his mouth spread into a grin. As Thomas weaved his way over to the two men, he realized that a woman also sat with them.

Max stood and grabbed Thomas in a rough embrace. "There he is! Been looking all over for you," Max said. "Some said you were dead. Others, you were in prison. One said you got yourself a woman and moved away when they burned your ferry," Max said. He looked at Thomas sideways as they sat down. "Was pretty sure that fellow was spinning a tale, though."

"You look good Max," Thomas said. "Judging by your clothes, you managed to set up a little shop in Zug after all?"

"Little shop? Look at him," Ruedi said. "Another few years and Max will own that town. I hear he has so much extra coin he makes loans to the nobles."

Max shook his head. "Now, I would not say that. Usury is a sin after all."

"It is at that," Thomas said.

"You mean you would not admit to it," Ruedi said.

"My money is made from pepper, believe it or not. I thought turmeric would have been my future, but it seems the noble households cannot get enough of plain black pepper. Apparently, nothing hides the flavor of rotting meat better—"

Ruedi cut him off by introducing Thomas to the woman sitting beside him.

"This here is my sister, Margrit Burkhalter. That damn Norseman knew what he was talking about."

Perhaps five years younger than Ruedi, she had dark hair and gray eyes.

Thomas bowed his head. *Burkhalter... was that Ruedi's last name?* Thomas realized he had no idea what his true name was. Ruedi *Schwyzer* was all he had ever known him as. And the same went for Max. They were all *Schwyzers*.

"Pleasure to meet you, Captain," Margrit said. "These two boys have been talking non-stop about you and your friend Pirmin. Enough to make a lady blush. If one happened to overhear, that is." She was a handsome woman, and she looked Thomas straight in the eyes when she spoke. He had no doubt Pirmin would have found her attractive.

Max and Ruedi fidgeted when she mentioned Pirmin's name and she caught their sidelong glances to one another.

"What," she said. "A friend leaves this world and suddenly you have to stop talking about him? You think he would like that?"

Max grinned. "No, he most assuredly would not."

"Well then," Margrit said. "I look forward to hearing more stories about the man. But another time. Got to get home to the family. Some people may be able to waste their day with their head in a mead barrel, but I am not one of those."

So Burkhalter was most probably her husband's name. Maybe someday Thomas would ask Ruedi what his real name was. But then again, maybe not.

Once Margrit had left, Thomas managed to flag down one of the inn's women. Tired and bored, she listened to Thomas while juggling a tray in one hand and three pitchers in the other. He asked her to bring him wine and whatever food the kitchen was serving that night.

With Margrit gone, the three men sat in silence for a moment, not quite sure where to begin. Max was the first to speak.

"Glad to see you made it out of that mess, Thomas. Ruedi told me what Gissler done." He shook his head. "Never would have believed it."

"And I would be in a prison cell in the Aargau if it were not for Ruedi," Thomas said.

"I doubt that," Ruedi said. He turned away and examined something crawling up the wall.

"You will be glad to hear I still have your Genoese war bow," Thomas said.

This got Ruedi's attention and he turned to Thomas. "Well, do you now," he said, twirling one of the braided ends of his forked beard between his fingers. "Did not expect to see that one again, to be honest."

"What are your plans, Thomas?" Max asked.

Thomas shrugged, but said nothing.

"People are scared in Zug," Max said. "The Habsburgs have tripled the soldiers in town and they been building barracks and supply houses."

"Is that why you came?" Thomas asked. "To warn us that the Habsburgs are going to invade? That is old news around here I am afraid."

"I been up to the fortress and I saw what Melchthal and Stauffacher are doing up there." Max shook his head. He leaned over the table and lowered his voice. "They have no idea what is coming for them, Thomas. Zug is being turned into a base camp for a real army. Judging from the structures so far, I would say upwards of eight or nine thousand men."

Ruedi also leaned in. "I asked Max to help me get Margrit and her family out of Altdorf. You should come with us."

As soon as he heard Ruedi say he intended to leave Altdorf, Thomas let out a breath. Tension slipped away from his shoulders and he reached a hand behind his head to rub his neck. The moment he first heard Max was in Altdorf, a gnawing fear had begun to fester inside him. He was worried Max and Ruedi had decided to join Noll's army and was relieved that they had made more sensible plans.

"Travel on the roads is restricted, these days. Even to merchants," Max said. "But I have made arrangements to get a small group of people safely to Berne. We have room for another three or four people if there is anyone you would like to bring along."

Before Thomas could answer, the inn woman dropped three cups of mead on the table and a bowl of something that could have been brown porridge, with chunks of black meat in it.

"Armin says he is too busy to water down a new cask of wine right now. So mead is all we got," she said.

"That will do," Thomas said, grateful for the interruption.

She turned and was about to leave, but Thomas touched her arm. She spun on him and all three men swayed back on their bench seats.

Thomas pointed at the bowl of food. "What is this?"

She leaned over and peered at it like she was seeing it for

the first time. "Porridge. With meat. What do you think it is?"

Thomas nodded. That was good enough for him. The woman leaned her wooden tray on one hip and stared at Thomas.

"I was there, you know. The day you bled those Habsburg boys up on the hill." She nodded in the direction of the Altdorf fortress. "Some people talk and say how you best not have done that. How we will all pay for what you did. But I was there, and I seen how you tried to help Seraina. She pulled out my first baby, you know." Her voice lost its calloused edge for just a moment. "You did a good thing that day."

A waving customer caught her eye. "Finish what you got, first!" she shouted across the room. She started walking away, but after a few steps she called back over one shoulder, "Just wanted you to know why you got extra meat. But do not expect it every night."

Max wisely waited until she was out of earshot before he laughed. "Now that is a woman," he said. "But I am afraid she would chew a man like me up and spit me out like so much gristle." He scratched his beard with one hand. "But Margrit on the other hand, now she might be more my taste. Just how good does she get along with her husband these days, Ruedi?"

Ruedi took a sip of his mead. "I been working on a new crossbow bolt," he said, ignoring Max and looking only at Thomas. "It has two, side-by-side, rusty broadheads on its tip. I call it the *plum-picker*."

"Have you tried it out yet?" Thomas asked.

Ruedi shook his head. "Just waiting for the right time."

CHAPTER 9

ENCIRCLING THE FOUR VENETIANS, nearly five hundred men sat on the ground. They were silent and attentive, perhaps some of them nervous, for none of them knew what to expect from a training session lead by the flamboyant outsiders. It was a cloudless, late autumn morning, and though the ground frost had retreated under the morning sun, the air still had the bite of winter to it.

Thomas sat on a stack of stone blocks at the sunniest end of the courtyard, far away from the center ring. He pulled his cloak tighter over his shoulders, and then abruptly changed his mind and took it off. He folded it several thicknesses deep and sat on it.

How did they do it?

He shook his head at all the men lounging about on the half-frozen ground, many wearing thin, sleeveless shirts, and watched the man called Giovanni Pomponio put on a display of swordsmanship. Thomas had lived with the men of the valleys and mountains for almost a year, and though they kept their feelings to themselves for the most part, Thomas felt he could often read them now. A wince here, a shake of a head there, the complete silence in the square; these were all indicators of a crowd in awe.

Today was the official start of training for the "Confederate Army of Free Men" as Noll had officially named his volunteers. The local judge named Walter Furst, and old Werner Stauffacher of Schwyz, known more for being the husband of Gertrude of Iberg than for any particular doings of his own, had opposed the idea. They wanted to simply call the army the "Eidgenossen", an old way of referring to those who had sworn *The Oath*.

Thomas had learned in the last few days, that the oath they referred to was some written pact made twenty-five years previously between the people of Uri, Schwyz, and Unterwalden. Each member community swore to uphold their ancient laws and to come to the aid of one another if they were threatened by an outside force.

Thomas suspected that they had envisioned that threat would more likely be from bandits, or some minor lord looking to take advantage of unprotected peasants. But Noll had pulled out the original document and had inflamed the passions of the locals by claiming *The Oath* may have been drawn up before his time, but there was no doubt it was created for just such a moment as today. Now, he said, was their one chance to throw off the yoke of their Austrian overlords, and with the support of Walter Furst and Werner Stauffacher, the three communities rallied to his words. Word spread quickly, and men began to trickle in to Altdorf, and the *Confederate Army of Free Men* was born.

An appreciative murmur shot through the crowd. Pomponio had just demonstrated a disarming technique on one of his men, and now basked in the crowd's attention.

The Venetian was a man of excess. He wore a red vest over a cream-colored blouse of silk, and breeches that fit so well, Thomas had no doubt they must have been tailored. But, as grand as his clothes looked, especially compared to the simple farmers and foresters seated before him, Thomas noted the fabric was thin in places and the colors faded from too many washings. Though he was far from an expert in fashion, Thomas had been around enough nobles and high-born merchants to recognize the outdated styles of yesteryear. However, when looking at the Venetian, most people would never notice these things, for they would inevitably find their eyes drawn in by Pomponio's outrageous hat.

It was a blue, wide-brimmed piece that could have been cut from half the felt. With several brightly dyed feathers thrust through its green and turquoise hat-band, it flopped around like a living thing, yet somehow managed to remain on his head while he lunged, parried, laughed, and mocked his opponent.

Pomponio dismissed his current adversary and beckoned to another one of his men, a dark-haired, younger man with a smooth complexion and wide shoulders set atop a narrow waist encircled with a purple sash. His long, oiled hair was pulled back from his face and gathered behind his head with a length of white lace.

"Salvatore. Lend us your strength for a moment if you would."

Salvatore took his mark across from Pomponio and raised his sword in front of his face in a salute.

Pomponio raised his own long, narrow blade. It was a fencer's weapon, with a basket guard that served to protect his hand.

"Attack," he said.

Salvatore immediately bellowed out a loud war cry, which induced flinches from the first few rows of onlookers, and then he thrust straight ahead at Pomponio's mid-section. Pomponio stepped forward and met the attack with his own hair-raising yell, and smashed the young man's sword away with a powerful, straight-on block. Then, he drove Salvatore back the way he had come with a strong series of thrusts and attacks. The young man back-pedaled furiously, parrying as best he could, until he stumbled under the assault and fell to his back.

Pomponio put a foot on the man's chest and gently rested the tip of his sword under his chin. He looked into the crowd. "The man is dead, no?"

The comment produced some chuckles from the crowd. They were beginning to warm up to the Venetian.

"Although my technique was effective, it was ugly. Very ugly." Pomponio stepped away from his opponent. He leaned over and placed his hands on his knees to catch his breath. "You see how tired I am? You see what ugly technique can do to a man? If I must fight like this all day, like the common soldier is taught, I am soon exhausted." He removed his hat and wiped his forehead with the sleeve of one arm. "Come evening, even if I survive the day, my *bella* waiting for me at home, she will be very disappointed, no?"

The laughter came much easier from the villagers now.

"If a man practices swordplay solely with the intention of besting an opponent, that man is missing the point. A dancer must train hard to make his craft appear effortless. Should it not also be so with a master swordsman?"

He smoothed one of the feathers from his hat and then carefully placed it on the ground behind him. "Seeing is believing. Let us try."

Without being asked, Salvatore bounced up to his feet and slashed the air with his sword. The other three Venetians drew their own weapons and spread out.

"We have you now, you Venetian fop," Salvatore said. His

voice rang out clearly, easily carrying to every set of ears in the courtyard. A few men laughed, some only smiled, but all sat up a little straighter to get a better view.

Pomponio waved his sword arm in a graceful circle and carried the motion through into a bow. Then he straightened up, and with another arc of his sword, settled into a relaxed, upright fencing stance.

"Very well," he said. "Please, attack."

As one, the four men screamed and charged Pomponio. He deflected the nearest man's sword and slid behind him, while ducking under another's wild swing. He reached out with the flat of his blade and tapped the first man on the back of his head.

"Dead!" he shouted. The man cursed, gave a quick bow, and retreated out of the circle where he sat cross-legged on the ground. He rested his chin in both hands, looking more than a little dejected.

The others continued to come at Pomponio with powerful-looking attacks, but the swordsman weaved and spun about them, deflecting blows only when absolutely necessary. He grinned and laughed and twirled like the only man present at a ball of princesses.

"Dead!" he said to another, who groaned and backed out of the fray.

He parried an attack, and touched the man's heart with his slender blade.

"Dead!"

Only Salvatore remained. The anchor-shouldered man charged, and Pomponio slipped to the side. He whacked the man on his buttocks with the flat of his blade, and Salvatore jumped and let out a squeal.

"Cut! But, not dead," Pomponio said, grinning and shaking his head. Salvatore roared and raised his sword over his head. He brought it crashing down toward Pomponio's head, but when the blow fell it struck only hard dirt. Pomponio stood to the side of Salvatore with the tip of his blade touching his neck.

"Dead," he said. "Oh, so very dead, no?"

One villager had become so engrossed with the battle that when Pomponio dispatched the last man, he could no longer contain himself. He shouted and began clapping. Others also forgot all sense of inhibition, and they too let out a few whistles. The mood spread like wildfire and within seconds the entire crowd was caught up in cheers for the Venetians.

Pomponio took his bows and then held up his arms for silence.

"This is the Pomponio way. My friends and I will teach you my methods, and in a few short months each and every man here will be the equal of five Austrians!"

There were some doubtful looks exchanged throughout the crowd, mostly amongst the older faces, but they were by far the minority. To the young men of Altdorf and Schwyz, the flamboyant Venetian represented hope.

"So today, my students, your first exercise is to go into the forest and find for yourself a training sword. This is no mindless task. Put careful thought into its selection, and treat it as you would your best friend. We meet back here the day after tomorrow to begin training in earnest."

Thomas had seen enough. He pushed himself to his feet, picked up his cloak off the rock, and almost walked straight into Seraina. He hopped to one side to avoid hitting her and put too much weight on his still healing leg. He grimaced and Seraina reached out to steady him.

"Oh, I am sorry Thomas. I do have a habit of startling

you," she said.

"It is my own fault," Thomas said. He stood up straight and tried his best to ignore the tremors of pain running through his thigh.

"I could start wearing a bell, I suppose," Seraina said.

"I would not oppose that. At least until my injuries have fully healed," Thomas said. The truth was, he was recovering amazingly fast. Whether it was thanks to Seraina's skill, or simply God's Will, he could not be sure.

"Well? What are your thoughts?" Seraina asked.

"I... think you saved my life," Thomas said. "In fact, I am sure of it."

Seraina cocked her head and gave him a puzzled look. "Not about that," she said, and nodded toward the center of the courtyard. Pomponio and his men stood talking with Noll. The villagers were filtering out of the courtyard since there would be no more training for the day.

"I wish to know what your impressions are of the men Noll hired to train his army."

Thomas shrugged. "I think this Giovanni Pomponio puts on a good show."

"He does at that," Seraina said. She stared at Noll and the Venetians. "But I wonder if he is truly capable of teaching farmers and goatherds how to use a sword."

Is anyone?

Thomas kept the thought to himself and looked at the sky. Thick clouds were gathering, blowing in over the Alps, where an hour before there had been nothing but blue.

✧　✧　✧

"The day after tomorrow? What is wrong with tomorrow? Or even this afternoon for that matter," Noll said. The Venetians had been in Altdorf for six days, and they had yet to hold a single training session for Noll's army. But they had not missed a single night of drinking at the Altdorf inn, compliments, of course, from the Confederate Army of Free Men.

Army.

The word still sounded strange to Noll's ears, even when spoken in only his inner voice.

Pomponio sighted down the length of his sword, looking for nicks. "One must learn to conquer haste, Master Melchthal, lest it conquers you, no? That is the Pomponio way."

Noll crossed his arms. "What about not keeping your side of a bargain? Is that also the Pomponio way?"

Salvatore heard Noll's comment and made to step forward, but Pomponio put his hand on the taller man's broad chest.

"Easy now, my friend. If you are unsatisfied with my methods, I give you back your gold. We return to Venice and I shall go back to teaching at my famous school, where I have students from the families of nobles and kings begging me to impart even a small piece of my fighting style. It is no problem."

"Just how much time do you think we have? The Austrians will be here next summer and our only hope is to create an army from nothing," Noll said.

Pomponio nodded and placed his hand on Noll's shoulder. "I hear what you say. And it can be done. But we must mold these villagers of yours into fighting men, and to do that we must treat them like iron. We heat them, little by little. Then pound out their imperfections, and then we heat them some more. Only when they are ready, do we dare thrust them into water. It is a process that cannot be rushed, no?"

Noll looked into Pomponio's eyes. "The day after tomorrow then. But no later."

Pomponio smiled. "You carry too many worries for one so young. Let us carry some of them for you."

Noll spun and walked away.

CHAPTER 10

TWO OF NOLL'S burliest men dragged the shackled and weakened form of Berenger Von Landenberg from his prison cell out into the frigid courtyard. When they let go of his arms, he groaned and dropped to his knees. He squinted against the direct sunlight and attempted to shield his eyes with his manacled hands.

Walter Furst, Werner Stauffacher, and his wife, Gertrude of Iberg sat at a simple table in front of him. To their right stood Noll, shaking his head. Seraina leaned against a boulder in the background holding the boy Mathias on her lap. She cringed when the men brought out Landenberg. Noll recognized the pity in her eyes, but he could not understand it. Landenberg was a monster, and the world would be a better place without him.

"Stand up," Noll said.

Landenberg blinked and turned his head in Noll's direction, but did not make any attempt to push himself to his feet. Noll nodded to his two men. "Make him stand," he said.

They each grabbed an arm and lifted the overweight Vogt unceremoniously to his feet, as if he weighed no more than a child. Landenberg's legs shook, but before he could collapse, his captors steadied him.

Walter Furst, the once Habsburg appointed Justice of Uri, cleared his throat. Today, he did not wear his black cloak of office. All three of them seated behind the table were dressed in the normal, loose-fitting garb of peasants who worked the land.

"Sir Berenger Von Landenberg, we the Council of the Eidgenossen, find you guilty of all charges. Do you have anything to say before we pass sentence?"

Fueled by his hatred of Noll, the Vogt summoned up a small burst of energy, enough to spit in the young man's direction. Noll did not bother moving, for the small ball of phlegm stopped far short of his boots.

"Missed again," he said.

"Your time will come! All of you, your time is near. Heed my words you godless, peasant gecks! Soon this place will be thick with soldiers cutting off your heads and having their way with your rotting corpses."

Landenberg had to break off his mad sputtering due to a series of coughs. Red-faced, and exhausted by his brief tirade, his chest heaved as he glared at the three people seated in front of him.

Noll too looked to the table. "Anyone wish to recast their vote? I still stand behind a hanging."

Furst shook his head. "That is in Landenberg's hands now."

Landenberg's eyes widened. Apparently, the thought that he might be executed had not yet entered his thick skull. "You cannot hang me. It is not within your rights!"

Gertrude spoke up. "As of this moment, we have every right. For we have decided that we will no longer be subject to the laws of the Holy Roman Empire. Or the Habsburgs. We, this council, will be the final stage of justice for all of Schwyz,

Uri, and Unterwalden and will recognize the authority of no other court. Now, do not speak again unless you have our leave."

Landenberg looked from face to face, his skin was suddenly pale.

"What Gertrude says is true," Furst said. "However, we are determined that this court will not be unjust. Therefore, today you will be presented with two choices."

Noll rolled his eyes. *Who ever heard of giving criminals choices?*

"The first choice, is a quick and painless hanging. Someone will pull on your legs to ensure that it is so," Furst said, almost cheerfully.

Landenberg's mouth twitched. "What is the second choice?" he asked.

Stauffacher spoke up. "You will swear the *Urphede*."

"What is that?" Landenberg said.

"You must swear an oath that you will never return to these lands upon pain of death."

"And what happens to me if I take the oath?" Landenberg asked.

"You will be allowed to go anywhere you like, so long as you never set foot in Uri, Schwyz, or Unterwalden ever again. If you do, your life will be forfeit."

Noll could not help himself. "Does not a simple hanging sound so much better?"

When Landenberg spoke, he could not get the words out fast enough. "I swear to never return. I choose the oath! I swear it," Landenberg said.

"Of course you do," Noll said. He addressed his next words to the council. "And I swear to see Sir Berenger Von Landenberg delivered safely to Habsburg Castle."

"Noll, I do not think we can allow that," Furst said.

"He is my prisoner. My responsibility. That is the *least* the Council should allow."

"He has a point," Gertrude said. "Someone must escort the Vogt off our lands, and who better for the task than Noll Melchthal? No one knows better than he where our lands begin and where they end."

"You might as well hang me now as allow this highwayman to slit my throat on the road to Habsburg!" Landenberg said.

Furst glanced over at Gertrude and Stauffacher. Something passed between them and then he turned back to Noll. "Do you swear you will do all in your power to deliver him unharmed?"

"Define *unharmed*," Noll said.

"Alive, then," Gertrude said.

"That I can do. I swear it on my father's good name."

"A father you have not visited in years," Stauffacher said.

"How does that concern you?" Noll said.

"Henri is a friend. A blind friend who spends far too many evenings alone," Stauffacher said. "I know for a fact that he would more than welcome a visit from his wayward son."

"You know less than you think," Noll said.

"The whole lot of you are mad!" Landenberg shouted.

"Gag him," Gertrude said. "He has had his say."

The two men complied and within seconds Landenberg's shouts were reduced to muffles.

Noll called Mathias and the boy bolted over to him. "Pack me some food and water for the road."

"Will you need horses?" the boy asked.

"No. I will go on foot. It will be safer that way." He glanced over at Landenberg. "But our fat friend will never make it. So get me the most ornery, skittish mule you can find."

Mathias grinned and saluted. He was off running before anyone could say another word.

Noll took no chances. He pushed deep into the forests and traveled only on seldom-used game trails. If he had been alone, he would have stayed closer to the main roads, but with Landenberg draped over the mule, grunting at every jostle, he could not risk being heard by one of the frequent Habsburg patrols. Noll was well aware of how human sounds had a peculiar way of echoing through the trees and off of boulders, and carried much further than most people realized.

He kept Landenberg gagged for the entire two-day trip. He had sworn to deliver him alive, after all, and he was not sure he would be able to keep his word if the man were allowed to speak. He had tied Landenberg on his stomach, with his face hanging over the mule's backside. So long as Landenberg had the strength, he could keep his head up and mostly avoid the mule's swishing tail. But, once his neck muscles gave out, his head bounced in and out of dark places, competing with the flies.

Noll kept up a constant stream of chatter to make up for the Vogt's relative silence. He spoke of all the times he had raided Landenberg's camps, the tricks he had played on his men, the various occasions when Landenberg had almost captured him, but always failed.

"Who would have thought it?" Noll asked. "That day you had my father's eyes cut out, that a few short years later you and I would enjoy a stroll through these woods together. As traveling companions…" He gave his head a shake.

One of the mule's hooves slid off a moss-covered rock and he stumbled. Landenberg's head smacked against the animal's flank several times before the mule regained its footing.

"Yes, it will sadden me greatly to have to part. But I suspect the mule will be happy enough to get your head out of its arse."

✧ ✧ ✧

"My lord…"

Leopold looked up from his soup to his wife seated across from him. Three servants stood nearby but, in the manner of all good servants, were almost invisible. In fact, the best members of Leopold's staff were people whose names he did not even know. They were the best of the best, yet relegated to a life of obscurity.

He set his spoon down. One of the older men stepped forward and removed it.

"Yes, my dear?" He looked up, but Catherine's eyes still unnerved him. They were simply too far apart, and he found it impossible to share prolonged eye contact with her. He glanced away, under the pretense of reaching for his serviette.

Somehow, a clean spoon had appeared on the table.

Remarkable. Which one of you was it?

"My lord. I am with child."

Leopold realized that, with the proper incentive, he actually could look his wife in the eyes. Albeit one at a time, and with a slight head twist.

"Why, that is wonderful," he said. "Have you spoken with my physicians?"

"Of course, my lord. And they insisted I be the one to tell you."

Leopold made a mental note to have a little talk with them both. He hated surprises. Even good ones.

He picked up his new spoon and dipped it into his soup. But he did not put it into his mouth. Instead, he dropped it once again on the table, making a small splatter.

"And have you had the child divined?"

Catherine's head bobbed. A curt, enthusiastic motion. But nothing more. Apparently, she would have him drag it out of her.

"And… what do they think it is?"

The spoon was gone, but the splatter remained. He caught the older servant in the act of placing a fresh spoon beside the bowl. As he put the utensil down with one hand, the other wiped up the small splatter with a square of cloth concealed in the palm of his hand. Leopold had almost missed it.

"A boy, my lord."

"Fantastic!" Leopold said, slapping his palm onto the table.

Catherine's eyes widened, but not even one of the servants so much as blinked.

"I must admit, that is how I felt when they told me as well, my lord."

"This is cause for celebration," Leopold said. He waved to the servants. "Get rid of this broth. Bring us some meat!"

"You seem pleased," Catherine said.

"Of course I am. This is a special day. My first child," Leopold said.

Catherine nodded. "I am glad to see you happy, my lord. For some women, that in itself would be enough."

Uh-oh. Something is coming….

Leopold glanced down for a spoon to stick into his soup, but remembered he had just had them both taken away. He shot an angry glare at the nearest servant.

"I have tried to make you happy, my lord, in the short time we have been married. Do you think I have been a good wife?"

No soup, no spoon. Where is that meat?

"Of course. There is no man more fortunate in all of Austria," he said.

Catherine paused, and sat up straight in her chair. "I am not content. I wish to do more. For both the House of Habsburg and the Duchy of Savoy. My father always told me I had a keen sense for politics, better than any of his sons. He did not raise me to be a royal nursemaid."

She punctuated her outburst with a curt nod, and stared straight ahead at Leopold.

If Leopold had had a spoon in his hand at that very moment, he definitely would have dropped it.

Well, well, well. What have we here?

He leaned back in his chair and looked at Catherine, carefully, wondering how he had missed this side of her.

"And what exactly is it that you can do?" he asked.

She did not avert her gaze, and surprisingly, this time Leopold found himself in no hurry to look away.

"Many things. If you would but share with me some of the problems you encounter in your role as Duke of Styria and Further Austria, I am sure I could be of some help. You try to do too much yourself, but you are only one man, after all."

"Very well. I need money."

"Money?" she said it like it was a subject she had never given much thought.

"Yes. You know. Gold, silver, bronze. I would not even turn away copper at this point, although, if you can manage it, some nice florins or gold bezant would be preferable."

"And what need do you have for all this?" Catherine asked.

Leopold laughed. "Have you not noticed the new barracks being erected in the woods? Come spring I expect to have thousands more mouths to feed. Of course they are mostly infantry, so it will not take much. But, by summer, the

Archbishop's knights will arrive. Knights, and their equipment, make short work of any man's coffers."

"But it is the Archbishop's responsibility to maintain his knights and provide funds for them while in the service of the Crown, is it not? And I saw the chest you brought back from Salzburg."

"Oh, yes. That chest. Well, it only looked big," Leopold said. He may as well have thrown it in the Salzach river for all the good it did him.

"I see," Catherine said. She looked at her hands, her slender fingers twisted about one another like a bird's nest. She raised her head. "I believe I can help. Give me some time."

Leopold almost laughed, but a part of him believed her. Or wanted to believe her.

"That would be lovely," he said.

"In the meantime," Catherine began, "In light of recent developments, I trust that you will no longer see a need to send your gorilla to our bed? I fear the posts have weakened, and I am not sure they can withstand his weight any longer."

"Of course. I will tell him to cease his visits immediately."

Leopold smelled the meat before he saw it. Steaming beneath his nose was a generous portion of braised lamb, served atop a freshly baked trencher made with white flour. He saw the black specks, and a grin spread across his face. It was the latest culinary craze, and like most people who could afford it, Leopold could not get enough.

Pepper, lots and lots of pepper.

✧ ✧ ✧

Evading Habsburg patrols lengthened the journey far more than Noll had anticipated. It took them the better part of four days to reach the Kussnacht, and another hour of traveling after dark before they finally heard the sounds of Habsburg Castle. Minutes later, light from torches on the outer walls peeked through the trees. Noll tied the mule to a bush and checked to ensure Landenberg's gag was still in place. The Vogt's eyes were closed from exhaustion, but he was still very much alive. He did not even wake when Noll slapped his face to crush a mosquito.

Seeing the man helpless before him, a man that only a few short years ago Noll had sworn to kill if given the opportunity, was not as satisfying as Noll had always dreamed it would be. He knew he should slit the Vogt's throat now and be done with him. If their roles had been reversed, Noll was sure that Landenberg would have executed him without a second thought.

Damn the council.

But he could not bring himself to do it. The last few years had not only been about bringing justice to the man who had maimed his father. They had been about fighting the system that had condoned it. And that system would still exist even if Landenberg was no longer part of this world.

Noll turned toward the castle and slid off into the woods to get a closer look. After climbing a short distance through the brush, he could make out the front gate. Several guards milled about.

Perched on top a hill, Noll imagined that the multi-floored keep within its walls commanded an impressive view of the surrounding farmlands, but overall, the castle itself was nothing extravagant. Its original design had been one of function rather than form. The road leading up to its main gate was steep and straight. At one time, there would have been no trees on either side of the road, but over the last few hundred years the castle's owners had grown lax with their defenses. Forests had reclaimed large parts of what had once been killing fields.

The castle was no fortress. But it did not need to be one, for who in their right mind would dare attack the hereditary home of the Habsburgs? Noll had never heard of anyone ever laying siege to the castle. Which could have been because of the political strength of its owners, but just as likely due to its remote location and the relatively poor lands surrounding it. In other words, no one wanted it.

As he crept closer through the woods, Noll allowed himself to fantasize about marching his own army up the road and storming the front gate. The thought of taking Habsburg Castle put a smile on his face and he covered his mouth with one hand, on the off chance that the white of his teeth reflecting torchlight might give him away.

Even if it were possible, he quickly dismissed the thought. What would he do once he had it? The place would be completely indefensible. *But what a blow it would be to Leopold!*

It was less than an hour past full dark, so there was still plenty of activity near the front gate. Workers were leaving for the day. Some carried axes and shovels, others lead oxen hitched to empty wagons. A dozen soldiers, with the red lion of Habsburg emblazoned on the chests of their tunics, marched forth and relieved the current guards spread along the wall near the front gate.

Noll became aware of an excessive amount of noise and light coming from within the outer walls. Curious, he moved away from the main gate and found a tall oak tree not far from one of the side walls. He climbed, moving slowly in the darkness, and after several minutes he turned his attention back to the castle. There, suspended high off the ground with his arms hooked around two branches, he had a view of the courtyard all the way up to the front steps of the inner keep.

What he saw made him want to jump down from his perch and run. The only thing that stopped him was he had no idea where he would go.

He counted a full score of new buildings in various states of completion. Most were long, rectangular structures that Noll knew only too well, for he had seen them in every Habsburg-controlled town he had ever visited.

They were soldier barracks.

Hundreds of tents surrounded these incomplete buildings, and armored men milled around cooking fires that lit the grounds like it was a full moon night. Noll had never seen so many soldiers in a single location. His mouth went dry and images of his own minuscule army of farmers, boys, and old men slapping one another with wooden swords, mocked him.

As soldiers wandered in and out of the light, Noll identified the red lion of Habsburg on many a chest, but far more bore the black eagle of the Holy Roman Empire. Even though his brother was embroiled in war against Louis the Bavarian, Leopold had still managed to call in Empire forces.

Noll felt the beginnings of panic set in.

The panic became a wave of vertigo and the dark night became darker still. He hugged the tree until it passed and he could see clearly once again. He took a deep breath and gazed out over the multitude of fires.

Perched in his fragile hiding spot, the reality of the situation overcame him. Did he think he was in a struggle against only Habsburg tyranny? Had he not considered Leopold would use all the resources he could muster, including those of the vast Holy Roman Empire?

Noll had assumed the German princes would be too preoccupied with the war for the crown. They would have enough problems of their own and would not pay any attention to a small uprising in a remote alpine town.

He tried to tell himself that. But he realized the truth was he had given the matter very little thought before attacking the Altdorf fortress. He had been driven with a righteous anger. Anger at what Leopold had done to Pirmin and what he was about to do to Seraina. He did not give a moment's thought to how his actions would affect the people of Altdorf.

He had simply acted without thinking. Just as he had when he smashed the fingers of Landenberg's tax collector. That day had cost his father his sight. What would the people of Altdorf have to pay for his latest rash act?

Noll made the hazardous climb back down and then crept his way from shadow to shadow back to Landenberg's tethered mule. He led the beast and its semi-conscious cargo to a spot on the road that could not be seen from the castle. Without a single wisecracking comment to Landenberg, he slapped the mule and sent him trotting toward the front gate.

✧ ✧ ✧

"Please forgive the intrusion my lord," the oldest servant said. He acknowledged Catherine at the other end of the table with a deep bow. "My lady."

"What is it?" Leopold said, putting down his eating knife.

"A disturbance, my lord."

"I could tell you as much," Leopold said.

"At the front gate, my lord."

"Does it warrant interrupting my evening meal?" Leopold asked the question but he already knew what the man's answer would be. He was an impeccable servant and would not dare bother his lord and lady with something mundane.

"I believe so, my lord."

Leopold glared at the man, and although he avoided Leopold's eyes with his own, he continued to stare straight ahead without flinching. Leopold stuck his knife into the table and left it there, quivering.

"And I believe you," Leopold said. Then he turned to his wife. "Excuse me, my dear. I will not be long."

He stood and Lady Catherine also put down her utensils and pushed away from the table. "I shall accompany you," she said.

Leopold was about to protest, but remembering their earlier conversation stopped himself.

"Very well."

He walked around to Catherine and offered his arm.

"Shall we?"

✧   ✧   ✧

Hunched over in the darkness, less than fifty paces from the main gate, Noll regretted asking Matthias to bring him the jitteriest mule he could find. The animal had trotted up to the gate well enough, but when the guards approached with their torches, he spooked and would not allow anyone to get near. The soldiers called out others, and they came brandishing more torches, which only made things worse. Soon a dozen men chased the mule back and forth in front of the gate, and the animal became so frantic he began snapping at hands as they reached for him.

There was movement at the gate again as soldiers stepped out of the way. They lined up, forming ranks, and Noll was surprised to see Duke Leopold himself stroll forward. He stood with his hands on his hips and watched as the wide-eyed mule charged between the soldiers, evading all attempts at capture.

Leopold shouted something to a huge, gray-bearded man at his side, who snatched a spear from the hands of a surprised guard and stepped forward. When the panicked animal next came toward him, he thrust twelve inches of tempered steel behind his foreleg, puncturing his lung but missing his heart. The mule let out a sound that began as a horse's high-pitched whinny but died off in a breathless donkey's bray. He bounded away from his attacker and walked stubbornly for twenty seconds with the spear's butt-end dragging on the ground, and Sir Berenger Von Landenberg still tied to his back. Then the mule stumbled and his front legs began to give out.

Noll closed his eyes as the animal let out a last strangled cry and crumpled to the ground.

"Arnold Melchthal!"

Noll's heart pounded in his ears. He looked up to see Leopold striding directly at him. It took every last bit of self-control Noll possessed to resist the temptation to flee. He knew an animal flushed from cover was as good as dead.

"Or is it Thomas Schwyzer? Perhaps both of you hide within earshot?"

Leopold stopped walking and his head slowly turned as he scanned the dark woods.

Noll reminded himself to breathe. Silently.

When Leopold next spoke he looked into a section of forest fifty yards up the road from Noll's actual location, which was now less than ten paces from the Duke.

"No, I doubt very much the Hospitaller is here," Leopold said, shaking his head.

If only I had a crossbow.

"It is just you, *Noll*. That is what your friends call you, is it not?"

Noll fixed his eyes on the dead mule, for he did not want

to look directly at Leopold. It was a hunter's trick that every old-timer swore by: you can only get close to your prey if you avoid looking at it directly. Prey knows when it is being watched.

But who, in this instance, was the prey?

At that moment, staring at the dead mule, Noll did not feel like a hunter. He shook his head in disgust. His idea of a joke had cost the animal its life.

More soldiers flowed out of the gates. Their yellow tunics bearing the black eagle seemed to light up the road. These were the hardened fighting men of the Empire; professional killers that knew no other trade. They were not part-time farmers or millers patched together to form a militia.

"I know why you hide," Leopold said. "I do not fault you for it. It took a brave man to come here tonight."

Leopold turned away from Noll and began walking to the gate as soldiers hurried to his side. Before they reached him, he turned back one last time.

"I will see you soon. Enjoy the night, Arnold."

Leopold disappeared amongst a sea of torches. Seconds later he was back inside the walls.

Noll sat shivering in the dark for a long time before he dared to move. He did not feel like a brave man.

CHAPTER 11

SERAINA WATCHED NOLL pace circles around the only tree within the walls of the Altdorf fortress. The last of the day's sun had fled, leaving the two of them shivering in the pre-darkness of night.

"You were right," Noll said. "I admit it. The Venetians have no interests but their own at heart."

Seraina did not answer. What could she say that would not agitate Noll further? He had been stewing and miserable ever since he returned from delivering Landenberg to Habsburg Castle.

She put the hood of her cloak up and tested the air with her breath. It was cool, but no mist formed.

"Perhaps we should go in," she said.

Noll stopped pacing and leaned against the tree.

"I would rather not. I spend too much of my time inside as it is," he said. "The place feels like a crypt."

Seraina knew exactly what he meant. She too could not shake the ill feelings she held for the Altdorf fortress. And it was not just because of her vision. The massive stone structure, with its high walls meant to hold out the world, was a constant reminder of how her people had been subjugated by outsiders for centuries. It began with invading Germanic tribes from the north, then the Romans from the south. And now, the Habsburgs, on behalf of the Holy Roman Empire.

"The men like the Venetians well enough," she said. "I watched several training sessions while you were gone, and they seem to be learning."

"I am sure they work hard enough. I have no qualms about that. But most of them have yet to touch a real sword. Pomponio has them tapping at each other with sticks all day long. At some point I have to see them properly armed."

"Was there nothing in the armory?"

"A few blades. Some spears. But no more than a hundred in all," Noll said. He leaned his head back against the tree and looked up into its almost leafless branches.

A sadness tore at Seraina as she looked at Noll. He did not know it, but he had much of the Old Blood in his veins, and the way he naturally sought comfort by pressing himself against the tree proved it. Seraina had done the very same thing herself many times as a little girl. Gildas would often find her sitting in the shadow of one giant oak in particular, picking at clover. Somehow, he always knew where to find her, and what to say to ease her troubles.

Seraina stepped in and took Noll's hand. At her touch, Noll looked up and, for the briefest instant, the creases on his forehead and around his eyes smoothed over. Seraina saw the same handsome, self-confident, young man who had startled her six years ago by swaggering out of the woods into her camp; his presence unannounced by neither the wind nor the rustles of the trees. He was a child of the Weave, and Seraina had recognized him immediately.

She made it her purpose to protect him, then, and to guide him along the complicated paths the Great Weave had in store. And that was why, as she watched his face harden once again, and dark worries cloud his eyes, she could not help feeling responsible for his pain.

He had been the cocky son of a well-to-do farmer, a freeman, when she had first met him. For the first time, she wondered where Noll would be now if she had not come along. Would he have struck Landenberg's collector when he tried to take the family's ox? She thought back and tried to remember what she may have said that would have prodded him into action on that fateful day. She could think of nothing. And everything.

"Seraina…" Noll said.

She looked up and realized Noll had moved closer. Very close. He took her hand off his arm, eased her toward him, and before she knew it, he was kissing her.

It was a strong kiss. Not forceful in any way, but it was the action of a man who knew what he wanted and was not afraid to let anyone know. Seraina felt her lips, and her body, respond.

She opened her eyes. *When had she shut them?* She let go of his strong hands and forced her arms between their bodies.

"Noll, no… I cannot," she said, leaning away.

He wore a half-grin. The old Noll had returned. "You just did," he said.

He made no move to back away and his blue eyes were as warm as Seraina had ever seen them. She stepped back, creating some space to breathe.

Seraina shook her head. When she spoke her voice was firm. "I have told you before that we can never be together. Not like this."

The moment was gone, if there had ever truly been one, and Noll sensed it. He threw up his hands.

"Why not?" he asked. "And do not tell me it is because I

am this *Catalyst* you are so fond of preaching about. I am not sure I even know what the word means! There is no mystical hand guiding my actions. I do what I think is right—nothing more."

"That is precisely what makes you special," Seraina said. "For very few people have the courage to do what they know is right. It is not important for you to understand what being a Catalyst means. It is enough that you are."

"I am a man. *That* should be enough." He slid down the tree and sat on its roots. "What exactly is it that you want from me? If anything." He looked up at her. "You drive me mad. Do you know that? I look into your eyes and I have no idea what you are thinking. It is like gazing into the green waters of a bottomless lake."

His words stirred a memory in Seraina. The recent conversation she and Gildas had had when he left her and Thomas.

"*...and so was I. Happier than at any other moment in my long years. And when I look at you now, it gladdens me to see that green lake reflected so clearly in your eyes. Somehow, you have preserved the same wonder and innocence as back then, but like those waters, I see the strength of steel as well.*"

Her breath stopped.

Noll sensed something, for his eyes narrowed. "What is it?" he asked.

"I see the strength of steel as well!" she said.

Noll cocked his head. "What are you talking about? When you say things like that I—"

Seraina cut him off. "Noll! Stop talking and listen to me. I think I know where we can get swords for the men! I cannot believe I did not see it until now."

Noll crossed his arms. "You do know how to change a

topic. I will give you that," he said.

✧ ✧ ✧

Thomas had leaned a few cut saplings against the warm outside wall of the forge to construct a simple roof over his head. The open-ended shelter was not high enough for him to stand in, but it provided more than enough space to spread his bedroll. As long as someone kept the forge burning, it would serve Thomas all winter. If it became colder, all he needed to do was close off the ends with skins to retain more of the forge's heat.

Thomas lay under his blankets and looked up at the patchwork roof. It was dark, but flickering torches nearby allowed him to see enough to make him cringe at the shoddy workmanship. A child could have built a similar structure. Perhaps he should have tried to make it more elaborate.

Of course, why would I bother?

It could have been a good permanent home… for someone. But as far as Thomas was concerned, it need only last until the Austrians came. After that, he did not care who took over the space.

"You have made quite the cocoon for yourself, ferryman."

Thomas jumped at the sound of Noll's voice. Every muscle in his body seemed to contract and lift him a hand's width off the ground.

Damn him. The man treads on cat paws.

"Sorry. Did not mean to startle you."

"Was just falling asleep, is all," Thomas said, his pulse beating out of control.

He sat up and looked over his shoulder to see Noll crouched outside the lean-to. Torchlight glowed behind him, basking Noll's face in shadow. He picked at a stone on the ground and tossed it away, then plopped down to sit cross-legged. Thomas could not tell where he was looking, but he had a feeling it was the ground.

Trapped, Thomas thought. He prayed the man had not come to ask forgiveness again for what happened to Pirmin. He turned around and pulled himself out of his warm blankets to sit facing Noll. The cool autumn air soon had him reconsider. He pulled a blanket over his shoulders.

"Something on your mind?" Thomas did not want to ask, but the sooner Noll said his piece, the sooner he could go back to his bedroll.

"Seraina," Noll said.

That was not the answer Thomas had expected.

"What about her?"

"She has to go on a journey. It will take a couple days and I would ask you to go with her. To look after her."

"She has done well enough until now, without me looking after her. Or anyone, I suspect."

"Just the same," Noll said, scratching at the dirt with one hand. "Will you do it?"

Of course he would, Thomas thought. But he hesitated with his response. It was not like Noll to ask a favor of someone like this.

"Why not go with her yourself?"

"Because she wants you," Noll said.

"I spoke with her today and she mentioned nothing of—"

"Damn it, Thomas. You do not make this easy. Will you do it or not?"

Thomas nodded. There was nothing he would not do for her. Even if she had not saved his life. Thomas realized that Noll probably could not see him nod in the darkness.

"You know I will," he said. "Anything else?"

"I want you to take command of the Army of Free Men."

If Thomas was surprised at Noll's first request, he was doubly so at this last one. He did not answer for a long time, and the two men sat in the darkness with silence hanging between them. A few scattered bits of conversation from nearby cooking fires drifted up to them, but the words were gibberish whispers by the time they reached Thomas and Noll.

"I cannot," Thomas finally said. He found his hand holding a pebble he could not remember plucking off the ground.

"You mean you will not," Noll said. There was a bitterness to his voice but Thomas did not feel that it was meant for him.

"They would never follow me."

"They would if you were backed by Furst, Stauffacher, Gertrude, and myself."

Thomas shook his head. "You are the reason they are all here, Noll. They follow you. I think the fools have come to believe in your cause more strongly than you do."

"Be careful, ferryman. No one believes we would be better off out from under the Habsburgs than I do."

"Then why this sudden back-stepping? Why give up control of your own army?"

"Because if I lead them into battle, not one of them will live through it! There. Is that what you wanted to hear?"

Thomas remained silent. What could he say? For perhaps the first time, he completely agreed with Noll Melchthal.

Noll took a deep breath and when he spoke again his voice was quiet and under control.

"I have been to Habsburg," he said. "I saw the army Leopold is building and I counted at least three thousand men. Hardened soldiers. Not a farmer among them, I suspect."

"It is early," Thomas said. "The ranks could swell to triple that just before they march."

Noll became quiet and Thomas regretted saying what he had. But it was the truth. Leopold would gather a few infantry about him now as a precautionary measure, but horses would be too expensive to keep all winter. His knights would flock to his banner at the last moment. If the sight of simple infantry had unnerved Noll, what would he think when faced with fully armored knights mounted atop steel-clad war horses?

"I am in this to the end," Noll said. "One way or another I will make a stand. And I will do everything in my power to give the men and women who side with me a fighting chance. Even if that means relinquishing control of my army. I am wise enough to know when I need help."

"And foolish enough to ask me for it," Thomas said.

"There is no one else," Noll said. "You are the only one."

"And what would you expect of me?" Thomas said. He felt his heart quickening and his face flush. "I do not have God's ear any more than the next man, and the truth is, without His help we will not hold Altdorf. It does not matter who leads the defenses. You saw Leopold's army yourself. He has the finest fighting men in Christendom at his disposal. What do we have? A partially built fortress with not half enough men to defend its walls."

"You speak as though the battle has already been fought. If you feel our cause to be such folly, why do you stay?"

"I do not have to explain my actions to you or any other man," Thomas said.

Noll stood and brushed off his breeches. "No, ferryman, you do not. But do not expect any special treatment if you intend to stay on as part of the Army of Free Men."

Thomas turned his back on Noll and began to slide under his blankets. "I have asked for nothing so far, and I do not expect that to change," he said.

Noll grunted and turned to leave, but whirled around at the last moment. "And do not discount your countrymen so easily. We are more resilient than you know."

He tried to leave again, but after only a step, he stopped and leveled a finger at Thomas. "And one more thing! If you hurt Seraina, I swear I will come and kill you in your sleep."

Thomas blinked and sat upright. *Why in God's name would I hurt Seraina?*

Noll appeared to stomp away in the darkness after that, but try as he might, Thomas could not hear a single footfall. He rolled himself up in his blankets and pressed his back against the heated wall of the forge.

He was warm and comfortable, yet sleep was a long time coming.

CHAPTER 12

THOMAS AND SERAINA took the main road north to Brunnen, and when they came to the site of Thomas's ferry, they stopped to rest. Thomas's tent still stood, and when he poked his head inside he was surprised to see his belongings still there. That is, the few things that he had salvaged from the burned out remains of his cabin.

He changed into a fresh tunic and strapped on his belt knife. He also added another blanket to the bedroll he carried slung over one shoulder. The days were still comfortable enough, but the nights were not getting any warmer.

When he ducked back out of the tent, Seraina had covered a boulder with a cloth and spread out some cheese and black bread.

"You had best eat something," she said. "Soon we should stay off the road as much as possible, so you will need your strength."

Thomas spoke little during the simple meal, and when they were done, he stood, eager to be away. His eyes settled on the nearby woods for a moment. There were memories here: a forest missing four score of trees, cut, limbed, and peeled by Pirmin and himself. The work had taken them all spring and part of the summer.

"You can come back here," Seraina said, mistaking his pause as a sign of him not wanting to leave. "You can rebuild the ferry. The people of Schwyz would gladly help." She spoke quickly, her words full of hope.

A ferry. It had been a childish dream, nothing more.

"Altdorf is not your fight, Thomas, and Noll has more than enough men. After we get the swords for them, you can come back here. Rebuild. The people will need a ferryman."

He looked at the yellowed end of a cut stump. He saw Pirmin laughing, as the tree that used to be there fell in the opposite direction Thomas had intended, and crushed their cooking pots.

"We shall see," Thomas said.

Seraina started, and looked to the road. Thomas followed her eyes and saw what she was looking at: two people walked toward them. After a moment, Seraina relaxed and waved.

"It is Sutter and... Mera, I think," Seraina said, shielding her eyes against the sun.

The innkeeper and his daughter joined them for their simple meal. But Thomas had lost what little appetite he had. He kept staring at the heavy packs Sutter and Mera carried.

"Where are you headed?" Thomas asked.

Sutter glanced out over the lake. It was Mera who answered.

"We are on our way to Altdorf. Father has decided to join Noll's army and I insisted on going too. Someone has to feed them all." She gave her father a stern look.

Thomas and Seraina looked at one another. "This is the very thing you said you would not do," Thomas said.

"You are right that Noll could use your help," Seraina said, directing her words at Mera. "But Altdorf will be a very dangerous place to be when the Austrians come. No one will be safe."

Thomas sensed she was trying to keep her voice calm. Something that he should do as well, but he could not.

"Turn around right now and go back to your inn, Sutter. Altdorf is no place for you. And definitely no place for a father to allow his daughter to go," Thomas said.

Sutter glared at Thomas. "You think I do not know that? You have no right to tell me how to protect my own family. Once Leopold has an army in Altdorf, do you really think he will leave Schwyz alone and unscathed?"

"And you think Noll's army can stop him? You are a fool," Thomas said.

"My father is no fool!" Mera said. "He believes in Noll and his cause. As do I."

Sutter put his hand on his daughter's shoulder.

"But what about Vreni? Who is helping her look after the inn?" Seraina said.

Sutter grunted. "What inn? It is no more than a large house that eats firewood these days. Leopold has all but shut down the roads to simple travelers, and he has put out the word that merchants are to bypass Schwyz. Vreni is staying at her cousin's farm."

"Then you should both join her there," Thomas said.

Sutter stood. "Come Mera. It is time to be on our way."

"I am sorry I yelled at you, Thomas," Mera said. "But if we do not help Noll, who will? He needs us."

Thomas stared after them as they left.

Seraina touched his arm. "Do not worry. I will talk to them both when we get back. We still have time to convince them to leave Altdorf."

Thomas did not hear her. He was thinking about what Sutter had said, how he thought Leopold would march his army on Schwyz once he had taken back the Altdorf fortress. Thomas knew Sutter was wrong. Leopold would not do that.

He would go through Schwyz first. And it would burn.

Thomas and Seraina walked in silence. They left the road and entered the forest, passing an ancient mound of moss-coated stones only a few steps from the modern path. The remains of an old wall, or structure, built by a people whose time had long since passed. A few minutes later, they came upon a similar pile of rubble, and then a half hour later, another.

"Are we on some kind of an old roadway?" Thomas asked.

Seraina nodded, but kept walking, weaving her way unerringly through the trees and clumps of underbrush.

"People think the Romans brought us roads and civilization," she said. "Yet our Celtic warriors were feared for the use of their one-horse war carts. You tell me, how could we have horse-drawn carts with no roads? They may not have been as straight, or hard-packed as the Romans built them, but they worked well enough."

"Those stones, then, they were walls," Thomas said.

"Yes. Built to keep the Romans out of our lands," Seraina said. "Unfortunately, they did not work."

Against a vastly superior force, walls rarely did, Thomas thought. They only postponed the inevitable.

They passed another mound and a chill went through him as he imagined what it would have been like standing behind that barricade as legions of Roman soldiers, perhaps the most fearsome fighting force in history, came marching toward them. The legionnaires were career soldiers, disciplined and drilled better than any army before them. Their javelins would have come first. Then an unstoppable red wall of interlocked shields, their short, wide-bladed swords thrusting straight ahead at anything that came in front of them. It would have been a spectacular sight.

He crossed himself and whispered a quick prayer for the dead.

The Celts never had a chance.

They slept along a remote stretch of the Great Lake's shoreline that night and set out again at dawn. It was a dazzling, blue-sky day and the sun reflecting off the lake had even Thomas removing his cloak after only an hour of walking. Seraina became quieter as the morning wore on, and she stopped several times to gaze into the woods or look out over the lake. Thomas did not interrupt her periods of silence, for he could tell by the occasional smile, or shake of her head, that these were personal moments for Seraina. Memories of a simpler time, perhaps.

Eventually, in early afternoon, they came to a small tree-lined bay with a clear view across one arm of the water to a rugged line of white peaks that seemed to float on the very lake itself. Seraina dropped her pack on the pebbled beach. Then, without a word, waded in without removing her sandals. She stood with her hands on her hips and stared out over the emerald lake, oblivious to how the water lapped at the hem of her dress. As her auburn hair played in the breeze, and the sun danced off the mountains, water, and Seraina all in equal measure, Thomas sat where he stood, unable, or unwilling, to take his eyes off the scene in front of him.

And then she began to take off her dress.

"Uh…," he had no words in mind, but thought he should at least try to make some noise in case she had forgotten he was there.

She turned and stepped back onto the beach, slipping one arm out of her dress and revealing one creamy, lightly freckled shoulder and the strap of her undergarment.

"This is it! I am sure of it, Thomas!"

Her green eyes flashed in the sunlight and the brilliance of them, combined with the shimmering lake behind her, made Thomas's mouth go dry. She laughed, shrugged her other shoulder free and undid her belt. She stepped out of her dress and kicked it high up onto the shore.

Like a siren in some old sailor's tale, she beckoned to Thomas from the water's edge wearing nothing but a thin, white shift that the sun's rays transformed into pure gossamer. The image was soon shattered, however, when she ran into the water and began splashing around, screaming and cursing at the coolness of it. She let out another yelp, took a big mouthful of air, and plunged beneath the surface.

The world went silent.

Seconds, shaped like minutes, passed, and Thomas felt the dryness of his mouth spread to his throat. He stood up and covered his eyes against the sun's glare.

As he took a step toward the water, Seraina bounced up a short distance away, her hair was slick against her head and her mouth opened wide as she took in a deep breath. The water was only waist deep, and the fabric of her shift was plastered tightly to the contours of her body. While that image alone would have been enough to fully occupy any man's mind, Thomas found his gaze drifting to what Seraina held in her hand high above her head: a very long, and very old, sword.

With an enthusiastic shout, Seraina lobbed the sword with both hands toward Thomas, and disappeared under the water again.

By God, Mary, and all the angels in Heaven, what is going on?

He managed to move his foot aside just in time as the sword clattered up the beach to where he stood. He looked down. It was a sword, all right. Ancient, and covered with a good deal of rust, but it was a sword.

He looked up as another shout came from Seraina, and another sword spun through the air toward him. This one did not have near as much rust on it. In fact, it looked like someone had just drawn it from a well-oiled scabbard.

By the time the third sword hit the beach, Thomas had his shirt off and was unlacing his breeches. Seconds later, he was screaming as the cold water took his breath away.

Seraina laughed and splashed her way toward him.

"We found them!"

With a shriek of pure joy, she grabbed his hand and pulled him after her through the frigid water.

When they were done, the beach was filled with swords, like pieces of driftwood strewn about after a storm. Thomas was blue when he came out of the water, and his fingers could not work flint and steel, so Seraina had built a small, sheltered fire amongst the trees. Thomas had put his clothes back on and gave Seraina his blanket, which she wrapped about herself while her own clothes dried next to the fire. By the time darkness set in, they had finished a quick meal of melted cheese on toasted bread with berry jam.

Seraina was still high from the afternoon's events and she talked non-stop.

"How did they get here?" Thomas asked, when he could get a word in.

"I cannot say for sure, but Gildas used to tell me stories of how some people would collect them after battles and hide them. Some tribes burned their dead, and they would often throw a warrior's sword in a lake or river, as a way to maintain balance. And by not destroying the sword, it would be waiting for him to reclaim when he was reborn."

"But how is it that they are in such good condition? The first few were quite rusty, but most of the others need only a slight filing and their edges honed."

"It is the silt in this particular part of the lake," Seraina said. "If they are buried under even a thin layer, it will protect them for centuries."

Thomas stood and put two pieces of wood on the fire. He was still cold and would have given anything for a drink of Max's kirsch.

"The question is, how do we get all of these back to Altdorf?" Seraina asked.

"I have given that some thought. How far are we from the Kussnacht? Specifically, the shoreline at the bottom of the road where I found you and Gissler?"

Seraina's face darkened for a moment. The memory of being held prisoner in a cage wagon bound for a session with Leopold's inquisitors would do that to anyone, Thomas thought.

But then she looked up. Her eyes widened, the whites of them clearly visible in the firelight.

"You think the boat is still there?"

"How did you know I had the use of a boat?" Thomas did not recall telling her how he had overcome Leopold's guards, with Ruedi's help, and stolen the small sail boat.

"How else could you have gotten to me so fast? Surely they would have found it by now. Unless you took the time to hide it."

"I was in something of a rush, so no, I did not conceal it very well. But I had some good speed when I ran it aground. It is a little further in the trees than one would normally expect to find a boat." *Some very good speed. Ungodly even.*

Seraina smiled, like she had heard Thomas's thought.

"We can hide the swords here, and try to find the boat tomorrow," she said. "Then, you can put me and the swords ashore near Altdorf and you can take the boat back to your dock. It will be your new ferry." She said it all matter-of-factly, like it was the most obvious of plans and had already been decided.

Well, it had not been decided by everyone.

"I mean to be in Altdorf when Leopold comes," Thomas said. "I think you know that."

Seraina turned her head and stared at the fire. "You cannot," she said.

I cannot?

Thomas felt a laugh building inside. But it was a cruel, mocking thing and he refused to let it escape. "And why not? You heard Mera. Noll needs every sword he can gather." *And even then….*

Seraina turned on him. "Because you cannot!"

She turned to stare at the fire once again and spoke to the flames. "I have seen something. Something terrible, and I do not pretend to understand it. But I believe if you are in Altdorf when the Austrians come, you will die, Thomas."

"A lot of people will die. We are beyond that now," Thomas said.

She pulled her knees up to her chin and looked over them at Thomas. "I know what you are doing," she said. "You have given up, and this is your way of taking your own life."

"That is a sin," Thomas said. "And a ridiculous thought."

"Is it? So you feel Noll's army has nothing to fear. The Austrians will crash against the Altdorf fortress and be thrown back like drops of rain from oiled leather. Is that what you think, Thomas?"

The dark laugh that he had so far kept in check, finally crawled out of his throat. "We will be slaughtered to a man! Leopold will reclaim his precious fortress and take up where he left off. Nothing will have changed. That is what *I* have seen."

Thomas stood and began feeding pieces of wood into the fire. He refused to look at Seraina, so it came as a surprise when he felt her hand on his arm. She moved her head so he was forced to look at her.

"No. That is not what the Weave has in store for us. You must believe me—that much I have seen and I know to be true." Her voice cracked. "It is you, Thomas. You that I fear for. Please, I beg you. You have everything to lose by being part of this."

Thomas gripped a stick of wood so tightly his forearm muscles cramped, but he could not let go. He tried to turn away but her small hand found the left side of his face and pulled him back to look at her. Somehow, the heat of her hand penetrated even through the childhood scar.

"Promise me," she said. "No, you must swear. Swear to your God, that you will not stand upon the walls of the Altdorf fortress."

As he watched her defiantly blink away the tears threatening the corners of her eyes, he knew then that she could have asked him for anything, and he would have given it to her. An image of Sutter and Mera came to him. They would be in Altdorf now, or close to it. Along with hundreds of other people Thomas did not know the names of, but people he had come to recognize all the same. Like the woman in the inn who had given him extra 'meat' in his porridge. When the Austrians finally did come, the lives of these people would be irrevocably changed for the worse. And that was the best case scenario.

He knew it was madness, but he would have to accept Noll's offer.

"I swear…" he said.

Seraina let out a breath and a soft sigh at the same time, and while the sigh was still on her lips, she pulled Thomas's face down to hers and kissed him. Thomas flinched at first, but the kiss lingered. Thomas had never known anything so soft in all his life. The wood in his hand dropped to the ground, and not knowing what else to do with them, he put his fingers to the side of her face.

Seraina pulled away from the kiss and smiled at Thomas, perhaps to suppress a laugh. She took his hand from her cheek and guided it slowly down the side of her body, all the way to the small of her back. Even though she had the thick wool blanket wrapped around her, the sensation of his hand sliding down over her ribs, skimming the side swell of her breast, and settling at the hollow of her lower back, filled Thomas with an urgent need to feel her pressed along the entire length of his body. He encircled her with both arms and pulled her in tight. Their lips found each other again.

Thomas opened his eyes. She had misunderstood him. His oath was not what she thought. He placed his hands on Seraina's shoulders and gently broke the embrace. She stepped back, a puzzled look on her face.

"I did not swear to you because I wanted to… well… this—,"

Seraina cut him off by reaching out and putting her hand to his lips.

"Oh, Thomas. How could a man who has seen so much of this world, have experienced so little?"

She took Thomas's hand and kissed it. The combination of the moistness of her lips and the cool night air set his palm on fire. She stepped back and, with a smooth roll of her shoulders, let the blanket slide off and fall to the ground. The firelight flickered across her nude body, turning her skin the same auburn shade as her hair for a split second, before plunging it back into shadows.

"Tonight, I think it is time to change that," she said.

He had been searching for a way to tell her he had decided to accept Noll's request to assume command of the confederate army. But when Seraina stepped in and kissed his neck, and he felt the warmth of her bare skin against him, all such thoughts fled from his mind, and he made no effort to reclaim them.

He was, after all, merely a servant of life.

CHAPTER 13

SERAINA AND THOMAS crouched in the thickets and watched as three Habsburg soldiers sat in the sun pulling at pieces of dried meat for their midday meal. A small, single-masted boat bobbed a few yards offshore. Its sail was down and a long bow line tied to a nearby tree was the only thing stopping it from drifting away. Looking at the amount of ash burnt in the campfire pit, Seraina felt they could not have been here for more than one, perhaps two, nights.

If the boat had been grounded high up on the shore, as Thomas had said, then it were these soldiers who had slid it back into the water. If only she and Thomas had come a day or two earlier, Seraina thought, the boat would now be theirs.

She turned to tell Thomas to crawl back through the brush, but he was already standing. He turned his belt around so the long dagger was at his back. She whispered his name and he looked up. He put his finger to his lips, and then motioned for her to stay put. Before Seraina could stop him, he began walking noisily toward the soldiers. Trees bent and slapped at him, while twigs snapped under his boots.

Just when she was sure things could not get worse, she heard Thomas call out, startling more than one bird out of its nest.

"Hello at the camp!"

Seraina winced and dropped to her belly. She had been about to tell Thomas that they did not need the boat. They would find another way to transport the swords.

No one needed to die.

"Have you got a spare bit of that for a fellow traveler?" Thomas said, pointing at the dried meat in their hands.

There was a pause. Then one of the men answered. "Sorry, friend. This is the Duke's food and we have no right to give it to every beggar that comes along."

Seraina inched forward on her elbows until she had a clear view. The three soldiers all stood. Two were focused on Thomas, but the other had his hand on the handle of a dagger tucked into his sword belt. He was older, more experienced if not higher in rank, and he swept the forest on all sides with a suspicious gaze. Seraina held her breath when he looked right at her. But, after only a second, his eyes moved on, and he remained ignorant of her trembling only a few strides away. She mouthed a silent thank you to the trees for protecting her yet again.

Thomas stood in front of the men now; the dagger hanging off the back of his belt clearly visible to Seraina but hidden from the soldiers.

"Please, me lords. I would not ask, but I have been out here lost coming on three days now. With nothing but bark to fight the rumbling in my belly."

"Why are you here?" one of the two younger soldiers asked.

Thomas swayed on his feet. "Looking for a goat that run off. Please, just a strip of that meat and I will be on my way." He shuffled closer.

"You do not look like a goat herder to me. Now, get back,

or you will have more than a rumbling belly to worry over."

The soldier stepped forward and raised his hand. Thomas hunched over and put one arm up in a feeble attempt to ward off the man's blow. Whether or not the soldier actually intended to strike Thomas was something Seraina would never know, for the man suddenly screamed out in pain. He remained rooted in place while his piercing cry shattered the forest stillness. Seraina finally understood the reason for his lack of movement: a dagger was sunk up to its handle in the soldier's foot. Thomas had slammed his weapon clean through the man's boot. The steel blade had pierced the top of his foot and exited through the leather sole, staking him to the ground. Thick blood crept over the dirty leather, making it glisten.

The older soldier began drawing his long dagger but, before he could get it all the way across his body, Thomas stepped in and, using both his hands, redirected the deadly tip into the man's mouth. It slid in at an angle, piercing the man's soft palate and continuing up through the base of his brain. He died instantly, but his legs kept him standing for a few seconds longer, until the blood drained out of them and he collapsed like a rotten tree.

Seeing the steel go into the man's mouth brought images into Seraina's mind she had hoped to forget. She watched, frozen in place, like the trees were pressing her to the ground. Thomas bent over and tore his dagger out of the screaming soldier's foot, and then the woods went quiet when Thomas stood and slashed the man's throat.

Blood splashed across the third soldier's clean-shaven face, making him close his eyes. He was young. Much younger than the other two. He stumbled back, and then tripped over nothing but fear. He fell to his back, but quickly flipped over and began to scramble away on his hands and knees.

Seraina remembered her vision of Thomas in a tunic dripping with red, and as she watched him walk behind the young man trying to crawl to safety, she found the strength to push herself up off the ground.

"Thomas, no!"

She shrugged off the trees' attempts to hold her back, and threw herself at Thomas as he wrapped one hand in the man's hair and pulled his head back, stretching the softness of his throat toward the sun.

"Thomas…" She folded herself around Thomas's dagger arm and called out his name again, but softer this time.

He looked at her. His eyes were cold and distant at first, but they began to soften the harder Seraina squeezed his arm.

"You cannot kill him," she said.

His eyes narrowed and blinked, like she had told him something truly ridiculous.

"I must," he said. "There is a checkpoint fifteen minutes from here. He will bring a dozen men before we are even half loaded."

Seraina looked at the young soldier. Thomas still held him with one strong hand twisted in his hair. The boy was less than twenty, and the way his chest heaved with deep, frenzied breaths, reminded Seraina of a wounded deer who knew the hunter would be along soon enough.

"There is rope on the boat. We could tie him," Seraina said.

Thomas scowled. "We may need that rope. And even if we did not, we owe his kind no mercy. Not after what they did. And what they stand to do."

Seraina stepped forward. "There is another way."

"You do not know his kind like I do," Thomas said, shaking his head.

She let go of Thomas's arm, slowly. "Trust me," she said.

He stared at her for a long time but, eventually, he relinquished his grip on the boy's hair and stepped back.

A boulder at the soldier's back was the only thing that stopped him from scrambling away. He pressed himself against the stone and looked from face to face, then pleaded in a rattled voice. "I swear I will not utter a word of what I saw. If you let me go, I swear it."

Seraina saw the dagger in Thomas's hand twitch, so she stepped between the two men before it was too late. She crouched in front of the soldier at eye level.

"Do I have your word you will stay exactly where you are? To not move until someone comes looking for you?"

"I swear. On the Virgin Mother, I swear it."

"He lies," Thomas said, moving forward.

Seraina stopped him with a glare. "Trust me," she said.

She reached down and gripped the boy's lower leg with both her hands. He tried to pull it away, but she tightened her hold.

"You too must trust me," she said. "If you wish to live."

The boy looked at Thomas, hovering close behind Seraina, and at the naked blade he held, and went very still. He nodded.

Seraina probed above his ankle with her fingers. She slid one hand along the larger bone of his lower leg; the mother bone. Beside it was the child bone, which was slender, and much smaller. Together they nurtured one another and were capable of supporting a great deal of weight.

With a deft twist of her hand, Seraina stretched the bottom of the mother bone away from its base. The young soldier yelped and pulled his foot away.

"What are you doing to me, witch?"

Saving your life. And ours.

Seraina stood. "You are fine. But do not try to stand for at least twelve hours. The mother bone will need time to re-align herself."

He eyed her while he flexed his toes and rolled his ankle. Seraina knew he felt no pain. He had only been surprised by the odd sensation of Seraina shifting his mother bone.

She turned to Thomas. "We can go now."

He stared at her and made no move to sheath his knife.

"Trust me, Thomas."

"You keep saying that," he said.

"And I will continue saying it until I see by your eyes that you do." Seraina pointed to the boat. "Prepare for cast-off, ferryman."

Thomas shook his head, but he returned his blade to his belt.

"*You* are the ferryman?" the boy said. His eyes went wide. "The outlaw that attacked the Duke and shot his man?"

Thomas gave no response, but kept one eye on the soldier while he untied the boat's bow line and pulled it closer to the shore.

Seraina picked up a water skin and placed it next to the boy. "Remember. Do not attempt to stand until this time tomorrow."

They pushed out into the lake and Thomas busied himself with setting the sail. Soon, the trees on the shore obscured their view of the soldiers' camp, but they were still near enough to hear the boy's pain-choked scream.

Fool, fool, fool. I warned him.

Thomas jerked his head up at the sound.

"What happened?" he asked.

Seraina shook her head sadly. The foolish boy had tried to stand. But with his mother bone pulled out of line, only the child was left to support the boy's entire body. It would have snapped in half with even a fraction of that weight.

"I told him to trust me," she said.

CHAPTER 14

THOMAS AND NOLL sat at a table near the inn's entrance. They leaned their backs against the wall, with untouched mugs of mead before them, and waited for Pomponio.

"When he comes, I will do the talking," Noll said.

Thomas nodded. He would not have it any other way. He had no desire to exchange words with the likes of Pomponio. Thomas looked around the tap room. It was more crowded than he would have liked. The evening rush had just begun, and three women and a man ferried drinks and trays of simple food between the kitchen and tables.

Noll's knee bounced non-stop and every time the door opened he looked up. Thomas rested his hands around his clay mug and stared at it. Inside was a plum mead, and it had a reddish tint that reminded him of Seraina's hair at dusk. Mind you, since their return from retrieving the swords, almost everything Thomas looked at reminded him of Seraina. He looked at the mead again, and this time was tormented with the memory of how her naked body had glowed under the soft light of their campfire.

He was about to take a sip when the door opened. Noll's knee stopped bouncing. A second later the shadow of

Pomponio's ridiculous hat fell over Thomas's mug. As the shadow grew, Thomas's annoyance grew into an irrational anger, and he was surprised to find himself gripping the mug tight enough to turn his fingertips white.

"Master Melchthal," Pomponio said in a booming voice. His Venetian accent stood out, and several sets of eyes from neighboring tables looked their way. He stood for a moment, allowing curious onlookers to get their fill, and then sat down across from Noll. He was accompanied by all four of his fellow Venetians, and once Pomponio had settled himself, they also took up spots across from Thomas and Noll.

Thomas looked up to find Salvatore's broad shoulders at eye level. The man plunked his elbows on the table and began cleaning his fingernails with a long dagger, studiously oblivious to all around him.

Pomponio held up a hand to get a server's attention, but Noll stopped him before he could shout his order.

"Any drink will be coming from your own purse tonight," Noll said.

Pomponio lowered his arm slowly. He turned to Noll. "That was not our agreement," he said.

"That agreement is no longer in effect," Noll said. "In fact, consider it terminated. Your services are no longer required. You and your men have until tomorrow morning to gather your belongings and leave Altdorf."

The Venetians did not look the least bit surprised at Noll's words. Pomponio smiled and shook his head sadly.

"Master Melchthal," he said. "Your men are just now beginning to learn the fundamentals of the sword. If we leave, all their training will have been for nothing. Next summer, when the Austrians come, they will make very short work of your… *army*."

Noll stared at him. "They will be ready," he said.

Pomponio leaned back and put his hands behind his neck. "So you say. But tell me, who will train them? You?" The disdain in his voice matched the contempt in his smile, and Thomas found himself crushing his mug once again. But if the Venetian's attitude bothered Noll, he did not show it.

"No. He will," he said, nodding toward Thomas.

Both Pomponio and Salvatore looked at Thomas like he had just snatched the last piece of meat from a communal trencher. Salvatore stopped fussing with his dagger, and with a slow, deliberate motion he placed it on the table in front of him, between himself and Thomas.

"Are you sure that is wise?" Pomponio said to Noll while staring at Thomas's face. "This man is obviously a soldier. Perhaps even a decent one. Although, not good enough to avoid at least one man's steel, no?"

All the Venetians got a chuckle out of that. While they laughed Thomas lifted his mug to his lips and took a long drink. The mead no longer had the dark auburn hue of Seraina's hair. The liquid appeared much redder now.

Pomponio dismissed Thomas with his eyes and turned back to Noll. "But a common soldier is no replacement for a sword master from the most famous school in Venezia. You do your men a disservice if you choose him over us, Master Melchthal. I fear you will regret it."

Noll cast a sidelong glance at Thomas. "You may be right. But all the same, I want you gone by morning."

Pomponio let out an exaggerated breath. "Very well. You negotiate strong, my friend. Tell me what you are paying this mercenary and we will work for merely double his fee, though we are ten times the talent. A better bargain—"

"Thomas! By God I never figured to find you in the first

tavern I stuck my head in, but here you are!"

A small, wiry man, dressed smartly in a blue and red vest, walked toward the table. The sword swinging at his side seemed to be too long for him, but somehow it never dragged on the ground or impeded his movement. His hair was pulled back neatly from his face and glistened with oil. Hoop earrings dangled from each ear and his clean-shaven face beamed as he shouted in Thomas's direction.

Thomas blinked.

Anton? Where had he come from?

Thomas had been so preoccupied with the Venetians he had failed to see Anton come in the front door.

"Thought for sure I would have to spend the better part of a day tracking you down," Anton said. He gave a quick nod to Noll and the Venetians and then stepped over the bench and squeezed himself in between Pomponio and Salvatore. A normal-sized man could never have accomplished the feat, but Anton was much smaller than average.

"Planned on coming in here for a quick drink, or three, and see if anyone knew you. But by the Grace of Mary, who is the first person I set eyes on?" He looked around the table and grinned, then slapped his hands down flat. "Well, I have accomplished more today than I thought to, so let us get some drinks. You lot look like you could use one as well."

"Hello Anton," Thomas said, knowing full well he would just keep on rambling if Thomas did not say something. He fought back a smile at how comical his friend looked squeezed between the two scowling Venetians.

Pomponio's scowl turned into a laugh, albeit one with very little true humor behind it. "Is this another of our replacements? One of the wandering folk is it?"

Anton smiled at first, but then Salvatore said, "She smells

good enough to eat."

"What is that scent?" Pomponio asked. "Something from your sister's caravan?"

"Orange blossoms," Anton said quietly. He no longer smiled and Thomas could see his eyes beginning to hood over.

"Of course it is," Pomponio said. He turned to Noll. "Really, Master Melch—"

Anton drew back his arm and elbowed Pomponio in the side of the head. He jumped up off the bench and stood calmly by with one hand resting on the handle of the sword at his belt.

"Not sure if you was insulting me on purpose, or not, but thought that would be the fastest way to find out," Anton said.

Everyone at the table froze. Pomponio, with his eyes clenched tight, gave his head a few shakes and rubbed his temple. Then, he slowly pushed himself to his feet. "This gnat has a sting, no?"

Salvatore and the other Venetians relaxed as Pomponio took up a position across from Anton. Salvatore licked his lips. He pointed at Thomas.

"No one moves," he said.

He inched his hand close to his dagger laying on the table, and turned sideways on his bench so he could see Pomponio, as well as keep one eye on Thomas and Noll.

Pomponio faced Anton and slid his narrow-bladed sword out of its scabbard. There was a shout from a nearby table and people fell over themselves to give the two men some room.

"Before I teach you today's lesson, I would have your name," Pomponio said.

"Aye, you would," Anton said. "If I was of a mind to give it to you."

Pomponio grinned. "Well, my rude gypsy friend, let me

introduce *myself*. I am Giovanni—"

Gissler was the fastest man with a blade Thomas had ever seen. But no one was quicker than Anton when it came to moving unarmed. One moment he was standing relaxed with his hand resting on his sword handle, and the next he seemed to materialize beside Pomponio. Perhaps, because Anton had never drawn his weapon, Pomponio's mind had failed to recognize him as a threat. Or, maybe Anton was simply too quick. Whatever the reason, Pomponio had a puzzled look on his face when Anton seized his wrist, forced the point of his sword against the wooden floor, and then stomped on it. The thin blade snapped like second-year kindling. Anton then twisted Pomponio's wrist back against itself and there was another snap, followed by a scream as Pomponio dropped to his knees.

"Do not much care what your name is," Anton said, and then brought his knee up into Pomponio's face.

Strange, Thomas thought, how a man's screams never reveal even a hint of his accent. Pain sounded the same in any language.

Salvatore's hand snaked out for his knife. It fumbled blindly, once, twice, before he tore his eyes away from Anton kicking Pomponio on the ground. He turned just in time to see Thomas drive Salvatore's own dagger into the back of his hand, pinning it against the table. His screams became the new loudest sound in the tavern.

Keeping one hand on the dagger handle, Thomas leaned over and grabbed a handful of Salvatore's thick hair. He slammed the man's head into the table and then pressed his cheek into the hard surface so that he could see his hand skewered in place. Like lava, blood seeped out of the wound and ran down the sides of Salvatore's hand. And when

Thomas leaned the blade to one side, it very well could have been lava seeping into his flesh the way Salvatore screamed.

Thomas allowed the blade to stand up straight, and Salvatore quieted down. His eyes were still clenched shut, however, and tears streamed down his cheeks.

"Do not move," Thomas said. He spoke to Salvatore, but he fixed his eyes on the other two Venetians who were still seated across from Noll.

"I think he means you two," Noll said. Their eyes looked at their master being pummeled on the floor, across at Thomas resting his hand on Salvatore's bloody dagger, and then at one another. As one they held up their hands to show they were unarmed and intended to stay that way.

Noll eased himself away from the table and walked to where Anton had just delivered one last knee into the moaning form of Pomponio. Rivers of blood ran from his nose, one corner of his mouth, and from cuts around his eyes. One side of his face was purple and had already puffed up to almost twice its original size.

Noll drew his own sword and put it against the Venetian's throat. Pomponio moaned.

"Dead," Noll said. "Oh so very dead, no?"

✧   ✧   ✧

Noll decided to keep the Venetians' horses in exchange for an open clapboard wagon pulled by two nags. While Thomas, Anton, and a dozen of Noll's men stood nearby, Pomponio's men loaded him and a still-groaning Salvatore into the back. Noll tossed Pomponio's hat into the back of the wagon and it hit Pomponio in the face. He grimaced as he was was forced to move his broken wrist, which he held tightly against his chest.

"I will have men following you with crossbows. If you stop

before the top of the pass, I have ordered them to shoot," Noll said.

Pomponio's face was beginning to bruise over and swell from Anton's beating. He mumbled at Noll through his stiffened jaw.

"The Austrians will see you get what you deserve. Come summer, I will be drinking to your demise, young Melchthal."

Noll cut him off by slapping one of the horses. The wagon lurched into motion and both Salvatore and Pomponio grunted in pain. They watched in silence as the slow moving wagon crawled up the road, headed toward Saint Gotthard's Pass.

Before it disappeared from sight, Noll turned to Thomas.

"We should discuss the training regimen. The next session was scheduled for the day after tomorrow by Pomponio. Unfortunately, the men have already been told, so we will have to stick with that. Too bad."

Thomas nodded. Noll was about to hear something else he would not like.

"On that day, we will need to make a list with every man's name on it. And they will have to mark it. If any man misses training he will be punished. And I want to know exactly how many men we have and what weapons or armor they bring with them."

"Fair enough," Noll said. "Then what?"

"We will divide the men into units. Half will participate in martial training and the other half will work on constructing the defenses," Thomas said. "They will switch every two days."

"That is a sound plan. The men will learn better in smaller groups. Tell me what sort of structures we will be working on so I can line up tradesmen and tools."

"The fortress wall," Thomas said.

"It is finished already," Noll said. "You want to add to it?"

"We must tear it down."

Noll laughed. "What? And rebuild it thicker? Higher?"

"No. Just tear it down. But try not to damage the materials too badly. We may need them."

Thomas began walking away.

Noll was no longer laughing. "You jest."

Thomas stopped and shook his head. "We have no hope of defending that structure. No sense leaving it standing for the Austrians to use against us in the future."

"Are you mad? It is a fortress! The only one we have, I might add. It represents the greatest victory we have ever made over the Habsburgs."

"The only one, actually," Thomas said.

"I refuse to give it up. I will find the men to defend its walls."

Thomas stepped in close. He kept his voice low so no one could overhear.

"Not with ten thousand men could you do that. And you have what, five hundred?"

One end of Noll's mouth lifted in a sneer, so Thomas continued.

"You know nothing of siege warfare. The Austrians would surround the fortress, cut off your food supply, bribe someone to poison your well, and wait. For months. Years even. Half your men starve, most of the others are so weakened with gut-rot they cannot even keep down dry bread, if they can get any. Eventually, you turn on one another. Begin eating your dead. In the end, you throw open the gates and beg Leopold to save you from your own men."

Noll pushed Thomas away. He ground his teeth and stared at the Hospitaller, but eventually, what Thomas said found its way through his anger.

"It is the only stronghold we have," Noll repeated.

Thomas held up his hands. "Then you defend its walls. But I warn you, it is a death trap. You swore you would not question me. That I could run this army how I saw fit. If you have had a change of heart, I would know it now."

After a long moment Noll gave a curt nod.

"Very well. We will tear it down. But know this. I would slit my own throat before I would beg anything from Leopold of Habsburg."

Thomas let out a sigh. "I have seen stronger men than you fight over the boiled knuckles of a fallen comrade. Do not be so quick to preach of your convictions."

"Preach? Look who rants on about the end of the whole world like some crazy monk!"

Not the end of the whole world. Just ours.

Thomas was about to say more, but he noticed Noll's eyes were focused on something behind Thomas.

"Uh, oh. Here comes Seraina," he said. "And she does not look happy."

Thomas turned just in time to get her finger jabbed into his chest.

"I thought at least one man of god could be beyond lies!" she said.

She jabbed him again. "You swore to me Thomas. I should have known better than to trust the word of any man. Especially one brought up by the Church. And you," she turned and withered Noll with a furious glare.

"Me? What have I done?" Noll said.

"How could you ask him to lead the defenses? You know what I saw. You know what will happen to him if he stays in Altdorf!"

Her voice verged on hysteria. Thomas sensed she was about to run off, so he grabbed her arms and turned her toward him. "Seraina, listen to me. I did not lie."

"You did." She struggled in his grip and refused to meet his eyes.

"I promised I would not stand upon the walls of the Altdorf fortress when the Austrians attack. And that is a promise I intend to keep."

Seraina wiped at her cheek. She looked at Thomas, her eyes red-rimmed slits.

"How can I believe you?" she asked.

"Oh, you can believe him," Noll said, shaking his head like he could still not believe it himself. "For in a few weeks time those walls will be nothing but rubble."

She looked from man to man. "What do you mean? And do not bandy your words any more than you already have."

"We will leave the keep itself standing over the winter, so the men have shelter, but I intend to see that fortress destroyed," Thomas said. "Before it destroys us."

"But how will we defend ourselves?" Seraina asked.

"Now there is a fair question," Noll said.

"We will rebuild the line of ancient forts we passed on our journey together."

Seraina blinked and her mouth opened but no words came forth.

"You mean the overgrown rubble piles to the north of Schwyz?" Noll said.

Thomas nodded.

Noll turned a full circle and threw up his hands. "Now I know you have lost your mind! Those are ant hills and fox dens. They have not been *forts*, by any stretch of the word, for centuries."

"They will be once we relocate the stones and timbers from Altdorf."

"But how will a few hastily built forts be more effective than an already completed fortress?" Seraina asked.

Thomas drew his dagger, flipped it over in his hand, and crouched low to the ground. Using the handle, not the blade, he began drawing in the dirt.

"Leopold will come from the north and most probably take the town of Schwyz. From there he can resupply and march on to Altdorf. If we construct a series of stone barricades and wooden palisades above and to the west of Schwyz, we can fight a retreating battle from one wall to the next."

As he drew more lines and X's, his dagger handle picked up speed, as did his words. He took a breath to slow himself down. "If we stagger them properly, we will always be able to attack him from two sides and never allow either his cavalry or infantry to achieve proper formations. We could never hope to face the Habsburg army head on. Outflanking them at every turn is our only hope." He stabbed one last time at the ground and looked up.

Noll and Seraina's eyes were wide and they glanced at one another. Seraina smiled.

"I have no idea what you just said, ferryman, but you do draw a pretty picture," Noll said.

CHAPTER 15

AS THE MEN filtered into the courtyard, Thomas saw the puzzled glances, darting eyes, and hushed voices questioning one another about the whereabouts of the Venetians. They knew something had changed. As those few, who had been at the inn two nights before, eagerly shared what they had seen, the noise of conversation began to rise.

Thomas wondered just how far the story had strayed from the truth. Judging from some of the wide-eyed glances he and Anton were getting from men, he suspected a fair ways.

Noll picked up a horn and blew a lingering note that brought silence to the crowd.

"The Venetians are gone," he said. "They should have never been here in the first place. And that is my fault. I should have known better than to put my faith in outsiders. From this moment on, the ferryman will command this army and see to its training. Now, those who are still with us, line up and be counted."

No one cheered, or applauded, at the news, but not a single man left the courtyard. And throughout the day, at one time or another, Thomas would receive a back-slap or a 'well-done' nod from nearly every one of the five hundred men present, starting with a certain innkeeper from Schwyz.

The day wore on as Thomas, Noll, and Anton sat on a log with a never-ending line of men stretched out before them. With quill in hand, Thomas leaned over a sawed-off log end that served as a desk. Each man shuffled forward, stated his name, and answered any questions he was asked. Then Thomas would scratch his name onto one of several yellowed sheets of parchment that Furst had provided.

"Name?"

"Marti Rubin."

Thomas looked up at the young man. He had red hair and his fair skin was tanned and heavily freckled from spending a great deal of time outside. Thomas was sure he had already seen him today.

"Were you not already here?"

"No, sir."

Noll chuckled. "That was his brother. Marti and Sepp are twins."

Thomas shuffled through the parchment pages until he found the one with Sepp Rubin's name on it. Each page represented a unit that would train, build, and fight alongside one another. Many years ago he had learned that it was best to avoid having brothers on the same squad, but to never separate twins. They had an eerie way of reading one another's thoughts and did wonders for a group's cohesiveness.

He wrote Marti's name beside his brother's, then re-dipped his quill and held it out to the young man.

"Make your mark," he said.

Marti took the feather in his fist and stared at what Thomas had just written. "How do I know that is my name?"

"It is yours," Noll said. "And right next to it is your brother's."

Marti screwed up his face as he examined them side by

side. His face lit up and a self-satisfied grin took over his freckled features. "Mine is prettier," he said.

"Because you are the better looking one," Noll said. "Now scratch your mark and move on. We have two hundred more to go this afternoon. Next!"

A young boy appeared. He looked hauntingly familiar to Thomas, but he could not quite place him, until he saw Vex, Pirmin's dog, beside him. The boy was the one he had seen at Pirmin's grave.

"Who are you signing up Matthias, you or the dog?" Noll asked.

"Who do you think?"

"Well, do not look at me. It is Thomas that you have to plead with," Noll said.

The boy, who was not older than eight or nine, turned to Thomas. "I want to sign up," he said.

"How old are you boy?" Thomas asked.

"Fourteen," he said.

Thomas narrowed his eyes. "Does this look like an army of liars to you?"

Matthias glanced over at Noll. "Could be," he said.

Noll laughed. "You will have your hands full if you take on this one," he said to Thomas.

"Why do you want to join this army?" Thomas asked.

"I am going to kill Duke Leopold."

Thomas could not keep the hint of a grin from taking over his face. Noll chuckled. Matthias looked back and forth between the two men. "I mean it! I do not care if you let me into your army or not. I am going to stick my sword in his neck and watch him bleed to death!"

The anger behind his words wiped the smiles from both men's faces and made them sit up straight.

"Why would you want to do that?" Thomas asked.

"He deserves it. He killed my friend."

"What was your friend's name?"

"Pirmin," Matthias said.

Even though he knew what the boy was going to say, it still took a few seconds before Thomas spoke.

"Leopold has killed a lot of people's friends," Thomas said. "But you are too young to be thinking of killing men."

"Yeah, I thought you would say something like that. Come on Vex."

As the boy turned away, Thomas said, "Can you ride?"

Matthias turned back and his distrusting eyes fixed on Thomas. "No," he said. "Well, I sat on an ox a few times."

"You will have to learn, then. I need a runner. Someone to deliver messages for me. Until you are able to ride, you will have to do it on foot. Can you run?"

His face lit up, the distrust in his eyes fell away, and he looked just like any normal eight-year old should. He pointed at Noll. "Almost as fast as him!"

"That will have to do," Thomas said. He looked around and saw Ruedi standing not far away oiling his crossbow. "See that man over there with the forked beard? Go ask him to teach you how to ride. But ask nice. If you do not, he may shoot you."

The boy nodded and hooked one arm around Vex's neck. "Come on, boy."

"And one more thing, Matthias. A good soldier never lies to his captain. A poor one often does. You choose which one you want to be."

Thomas could see the boy thinking as he led the dog away. That was a good thing. He had been forced to grow up too fast, but then again, so had Thomas.

The next man stepped up and placed his hand on Thomas's makeshift desk.

"Touching," he said. He was missing the top half of most of his fingers. In his late twenties, the man had thick arms but long, sleek legs that looked like they could carry him for days without any rest. His eyes were hard and restless.

Thomas recognized him immediately. He was the brigand leader of the band that had tried to ambush him and his men near the Gotthard those many months ago. The memory of that time was so far away from his life now, it seemed to belong to another man. He glanced at Anton. He too was eying the man curiously.

"Hello Erich," Noll said, his tone flat.

The man's eyes jumped from Thomas to Noll. He nodded and gave Noll an imaginary tip of the hat with his stumpy right hand. "Nice to see you Noll."

"Better here than on the road," Noll said. "What brings you to Altdorf?"

"The lack of soldiers," Erich said.

"Must be quite the experience for you. Being able to walk into a town without a Habsburg man trying to take your head."

Erich shrugged. "It might be something a man could get used to. But I do not need to tell you that."

"What do you want, Erich?"

He stared at Noll and his chest rose and fell. "A place for me and my men in your army."

Noll leaned back on his log. "How many men are we talking about?"

"Twenty-seven."

"You realize what we are doing here? You know this is not just some warm place to spend the winter?"

Erich nodded slowly. "Like I said. A man could get used to being able to walk free in this town."

Thomas put his quill down and spoke up. "I am afraid we cannot accept your offer."

Noll looked at Thomas like he had just bitten the head off a chicken. "Uh, Thomas… maybe we should discuss this? Sure, Erich is an outlaw, but who can fault someone for that? He just offered us twenty-seven men."

"Twenty-eight, including me. And this." Erich pulled a leather-bound manuscript out of a sack at his feet and dropped it on top of Thomas's pile of parchment.

Thomas struggled to keep the surprise from his eyes, but as soon as he saw the title, he recognized the book. It was Duke Leopold's *Malleus Maleficarum. The Hammer of Witches.*

"Where did you get this?"

"Found it a while back in a cage wagon in the Kussnacht. Along with the corpse of a man both you and I know only too well."

He held up his shortened fingers and ran his palm over their blunt ends. He directed his next words to Anton. "You did a fine job firing these. Healed up real nice. I suppose I should thank you for that."

Anton shrugged. "I have done better work. But I usually reserve that for people who do not try to kill me first."

Erich looked back to Thomas. "What do you say? I have some skilled men in my band."

"And that is one of the reasons I must say no."

Noll held his head with both hands. "Thomas, I can vouch for this man. As far as I know, he has never preyed on our people. His targets have always been rich merchants or travelers from far away lands."

"And me and my men," Thomas said. "I am sorry, but I

cannot take the chance. His kind are easily bought and I will not expose our army to that risk."

Thomas pushed Leopold's manuscript back toward Erich. "I commend you for the change you are trying to make. And even though I suspect your intentions may be true, I regret I cannot allow you a place amongst my men."

Erich looked down at the book, his face pinched. These were obviously not the words he had expected to hear. "You let that waif join, but refuse skilled men?" He pointed and sneered at the manuscript. "Keep it. Put it toward the cause. You are going to need all the help you can get."

He spun on his heel. "Out of my way," he said as he pushed through the men behind him.

Noll said something to Thomas as Erich walked away, but Thomas heard nothing. His eyes, as well as his thoughts, were fixated on the book in front of him. He ran his fingers over the fine leather cover.

Malleus Maleficarum.

Leopold's choice of Latin made Thomas's hand curl into a fist and an image of Seraina being forced into a cage wagon flashed before his eyes. *Maleficarum* was the feminine form of witch, so the title presupposed that all witches were women. Otherwise, he should have used *maleficorum*, which could mean either a male witch or a female witch. Was it a simple Latin mistake on Leopold's part? From what he knew of the man, Thomas doubted it.

Thomas was still staring at Leopold's manuscript when the next man in line dropped a scabbarded sword on top of it. Scowling, Thomas looked up and saw nothing but forearms. He knew the man before he even saw his face or heard his rough, guttural voice.

"Add me to your list, you distrusting bastard, and make

whatever mark you want next to it."

Thomas shielded his eyes against the midday sun. He was afraid this would happen.

"Hello Urs. I see you got yourself a new blade."

"That one is yours. I made it with your awkward form in mind."

Thomas raised his eyebrow at that and picked up the short sword. He freed it from its scabbard with one quick motion. The sun glinted off it so fiercely Thomas had to squint. It was a straight, double-bladed weapon that reminded Thomas of an ancient Roman gladius. But the cross-section of its blade was shaped like a diamond. It was thick near the simple curved crosspiece, but it tapered to a deadly point.

"An in-fighter's weapon," Urs said. "The four-sided design makes it stronger than anything I have come up with yet. It separates chainmail like a straw mat and will punch a hole through plate if given the proper encouragement."

Thomas took hold of the honey-colored wooden grip and sighted down the finely honed blade. Urs was not one to exaggerate. If he said it could pierce plate armor, Thomas believed him.

"This is an interesting piece," Thomas said.

"I call it a *baselard*. Seeing as that is where I made it."

A blade from Basel. Urs had never been one for fancy names or frills in the weapons he designed. He was far too practical.

Thomas slowly guided the sword back into its scabbard. As good as it was to see his old friend, this was the last place he wanted him to be.

"This is not your fight," Thomas said. "But Max and Ruedi could use your help getting Ruedi's sister and family out of Altdorf. You should seek them out."

Urs shook his head. "Blood and ashes, Thomas. Who do you think told me you were putting together a rebel army in the first place? And they said I was to tell you to put their names on one of your lists, as well. Seems Ruedi's sister is refusing to leave her farm. They would have come themselves, but they know what kind of a bastard you can become once training starts, so they decided to spend their last free afternoon drinking."

He tapped his foot and pointed at the pile of parchment in front of Thomas. "And I mean to join them, just as soon as I see your quill finish scratching. So get on with it, would you?"

CHAPTER 16

IT HAD SNOWED in the early hours of the morning. A light skiff covered the still frozen ground, but with hundreds of men churning it up, Thomas knew it would be a field of mud before the end of the day.

He watched the men come through the gates in groups of five or ten with their training swords in hand; fathers, sons, brothers, friends, and more than a few wives and mothers leading the way with packs of provisions to see the men through the day. One minute the courtyard was empty, the next filled to overflowing. Was it his imagination, or were many of them newcomers, men not yet on any of his lists?

They took up places on the ground, forming a semi-circle around the center of the yard, in front of Thomas and Noll. Behind the two men stood Ruedi, Max, Urs, and Anton.

The murmurs of the group began to grow louder, until Thomas stepped forward and held up his hand. He waited patiently for silence. He looked out over the crowd and felt curious eyes on him and his men. He saw many grin and sit back, exchanging nods with their neighbors. They expected a show, like the Venetians had put on.

And they will get one. But no one will be smiling at the end of this day.

Thomas scanned all those seated, looking for one man in particular. He found him almost instantly, for he was not hard to pick out: Gruber, Hans Gruber. The young giant from the Fall Festival that Pirmin had wrestled in the Schwingen finals. He had become a hero that day by defeating Pirmin with a skilfully executed hip throw.

Thomas called him up. The men around Gruber slapped the man on his broad back as he stood and made his way to the front.

"Today will be devoted to bare-handed training," Thomas said.

Gruber removed his vest and rolled his massive shoulders. Thomas met the man, well aware that he must look like a sapling growing next to a giant cedar.

"What do you want me to do, Thomas?"

"You will fight one of my men," Thomas said.

Gruber nodded. "All right."

The first row of spectators had overheard, and Thomas could feel them vibrate with anticipation. He looked to his men, and nodded to Max. The gray-bearded man took a drink of water, removed his sword belt, and began to walk toward Gruber.

Thomas caught Gruber's eye, and as he backed away from the man, he said, "What you do here today will save lives."

Gruber's brows knit together as he began to puzzle out Thomas's words, but he did not get very far, for without warning, a loud scream erupted from Max and he charged the bigger man. Gruber's eyes went wide and he backpedaled, but Max lunged forward and struck him in the soft hollow beneath his sternum. Gruber tried to cover up but Max shuffled forward, yelling and hitting him in the face and body.

Gruber realized he was having difficulty breathing and his

body tensed as he struggled for air. Panic overtook him. Max smashed his nose with the palm of his hand and wrapped the other in his hair. He bent the big man in half and delivered a series of forearm strikes to the back of his head, shouting with every blow. By the time Max brought his knee up into the young man's face, knocking him to the ground, many in the crowd had averted their gaze or closed their eyes to shut out the bloody spectacle.

Gruber hit the ground and a sickly wheeze came from his mouth as his body struggled to get air. Max jumped on top of him and straddled his chest. He rained down more blows until Gruber's thick, flailing arms gave up trying to protect his head and fell limp to the ground.

"Enough," Thomas said.

Max pushed himself off the still form of Gruber and wiped the blood off his hands onto his breeches. He turned his back on the young man and walked slowly over to stand with the others.

Sutter and another man hurried over to where Gruber lay curled up in a ball.

Sutter put one hand on the young man's shoulder and his head snapped up to look at Thomas. "There was no need to hurt this boy," he said.

"There was every need!" Thomas shouted, and all eyes fell on him.

"Look at him," Thomas said, pointing to Gruber. The man lay on his side, shaking. Soft whimpers came from somewhere beneath the huge arms still covering his head.

"He froze. His body shut down. To be *paralyzed with fear* is not just a saying. It is God's way of sparing us pain when we are about to die. When a lion begins eating you alive, there comes a point when you no longer feel the agony of crunching bones. Your breathing slows, your muscles no longer respond to your commands, and pain is nonexistent. God is merciful. When we are convinced we are about to die, God shuts down our minds and our bodies, so that our passage from this life can be eased."

Thomas drew his new short sword and pointed it at the crowd.

"The first time you meet a fully armored knight in battle, a man trained from birth to kill, you will wish he were just a lion. Your lungs will stop working, and you will freeze. Your muscles will betray you, your mouth will go dry, your sense of smell will play tricks. *But*, if you can manage to stay alive for a few seconds, and remember to breathe, God will know you want to live and he will give you back your body."

As he spoke he bent down and helped Sutter lift Gruber to his feet. The young man's face was swollen and bloodied, but he stood without difficulty. He dabbed at his red-rimmed eyes quickly with the back of his sleeve and looked at his feet as he straightened his clothing.

"There is no shame in being paralyzed with fear, for we all have felt it at one time or another. But we must learn to recognize it when it happens, and realize it is merely God's test."

"Today, you will fight your friends and brothers as if your life depended on it. Your goal is to paralyze the man across from you, and if I see any man holding back," Thomas pointed at Max, Ruedi, Urs, and Anton, "his next opponent will be one of my men. We will devote a portion of every day to this exercise until every single one of you has experienced this fear and pushed his way through it."

Thomas re-sheathed his sword. The crowd was silent. Men averted their eyes from Thomas's stare and glanced at each other nervously.

"Today," Thomas said. "I will teach you how to breathe. Tomorrow you will begin training with naked steel. Take your wooden swords home tonight and burn them. You will not be using them again."

⋄ ⋄ ⋄

Seraina stepped over the raised threshold into the keep's kitchen where a score of women and a few younger children were working hard to keep everyone fed.

"Seraina!" Mera called out to her from across a large cauldron of soup, its vapors rising up and mixing with the steam from many other pots to contribute to the mugginess of the warm room. She ran over and grabbed Seraina's hands. Her face was flushed.

"Where does the tally stand now?"

Seraina had been helping Mera and the other women in the kitchen most of the week, but she was so excited she found it impossible to stay indoors for more than an hour at a time. She kept making trips outside to check on how the training was going and to see how many new faces she could spot. She pestered Thomas constantly with questions about his lists.

"Another hundred and fifty have come from Schwyz so far this week," Seraina said. She could not keep her voice from rising. "Thomas says they are past seven hundred men now!"

Mera bounced once and gave Seraina a quick hug. "Noll was right to ask help from Thomas. People trust him and after he stood up to the Habsburgs last fall, there is no one in the valleys who does not know his name. Many more will come. I am sure this is just the beginning."

Despite her earlier doubts, Seraina had to admit that Noll had made the right decision to hand control of the army over to Thomas. Seraina was proud of Noll, for it must have been a hard thing for him to relinquish control like that. But that is what Catalysts did. They made the difficult choices, the ones no one else had the courage, or insight, to make. They were, after all, the agents of change.

Seraina smiled and allowed herself to get caught up in Mera's enthusiasm. Seven hundred men did not make an army, but it was a start. A very good start.

CHAPTER 17

ABBOT LUDOVICUS SAT in the library of the Einsiedeln monastery. The large space was cold, for it had no hearth and the stone walls did little to keep the winter chill outside. He did not particularly like working in the library. But its three arched windows, with glass of such good quality they were almost clear enough to see through, provided the best light of any room in the monastery.

Beside the Abbot, on the same table, three monks labored silently copying texts. Two of the men's fingers were stained completely black. But one of the three, a younger man whose eyesight had not yet deteriorated, held a half dozen delicate brushes in one multicolored fist. He hunched over his work protectively, like someone trying to start a fire on a windy day. He dipped his brush in a vial of red ink and with almost imperceptible movements, added color to one of a hundred regal-looking characters squeezed into the margins surrounding a page of flowing script. Watching the illustrator at work stiffened Ludovicus's neck and he returned his focus to the ledgers in front of him. Horse revenues were the highest he had ever seen this year, but ale sales were low. Suspiciously low. He would have to talk to the brothers about that.

The timber door squealed on its hinges and a monk entered the room. He stood beside the Abbot and waited to be acknowledged. Ludovicus finished adding the numbers he was working on and then did another calculation before he set down his quill.

"Yes?"

The monk cleared his throat. "There is a Schwyzer at the gate demanding to see you."

"Demanding?" Ludovicus turned back to his ledger and picked up his writing feather. "Send him away. I do not have time."

The monk hesitated. "It is the Hospitaller. The one who brought in the black."

This got the Abbot's attention and he placed the quill back down. With a groan he pushed himself to a standing position, being careful not to jostle the table.

"Tell him I will see him," he said. "Once I have finished lunch."

The Hospitaller was sitting on the snow-covered ground outside the main gate when Ludovicus emerged an hour later. He did not stand when the Abbot approached.

"Nice to see you again, my son. Thomas, was it not?"

"I want to buy him back," Thomas said.

"Who would you like to buy back?"

"My horse."

"Ah, yes of course. Forgive me. My mind gets addled easily these days. Now, which horse was yours again?"

"You know well enough. His name is Anid."

The Abbot nodded after a moment. "Yes, I remember now. The Egyptian with the infidel name. We call him simply 'the black' these days. But I am afraid he is not for sale."

Thomas lifted a bag he held on his lap. "This will change your mind."

Ludovicus grinned and shook his head, the flesh below his chin swaying with the movement. "Perhaps. If it is filled with gold florins."

He could tell it was not filled with gold simply by the ease with which Thomas lifted it. Thomas lowered the bag back into his lap and undid the length of rope securing it shut. He reached in his hand and pulled a manuscript halfway out.

Ludovicus laughed. "I know to someone like you a book must seem a true treasure. But I have an entire library filled with those."

"Not like this one," Thomas said. He pulled the bag down some more. "Read the title."

Ludovicus stepped closer and put his hands on his knees to lend some support as he bent over. He began reading aloud.

"Malleus Malefic…" his words died out and his eyes widened. *By the Devil's breath, it was Duke Leopold's missing manuscript!* And it was no forgery. He would recognize Bernard's bold script anywhere.

"Let me see that," Ludovicus said reaching for the book.

Thomas pulled it away and closed the sack around it once again. "You bring Anid out and we will talk."

Ludovicus smiled. That book was worth ten infidel stallions. The Schwyzer was about to receive another lesson in the fine art of commerce, although the Abbot doubted it would make him any wiser. For, like most peasants, the ferryman most likely lacked the capacity to truly learn anything.

They exchanged sack for reins simultaneously, watching one another like stray cats who had accidentally wandered too close. Ludovicus clutched the bag with Leopold's tome in it to his chest, while he watched Thomas step up to the horse and whisper something in his ear. As he patted the stallion's neck with one hand his gaze got caught on the animal's saddle.

"That is not my saddle," Thomas said.

"Our agreement was for a certain horse. I recall no mention of a particular saddle."

A knife appeared in the Hospitaller's hand and Ludovicus took an instinctual step back.

"This one is too long for an Egyptian's back," Thomas said. He carefully sliced through the leather straps holding the saddle in place and let it and the under-blanket slide to the ground. "You can keep it."

"Very well," Ludovicus said. *This deal kept getting better by the moment.* "I must say, I will be sorry to see him go. He is a magnificent animal. Does the heathen name you gave him hold any special meaning?"

Thomas raked his fingers through the black's mane to pull out a tangle. He grabbed a handful of hair and swung himself up onto Anid's back in one easy motion. He looked down at the Abbot.

"It means 'stubborn'."

"How fitting," Ludovicus said.

Abbot Ludovicus eased open one of the library doors with care. He did not particularly care about disturbing the monks working within, but he did want to avoid having them pester him with questions about how he managed to acquire Leopold's manuscript.

He slid into the room with the bag containing the book clutched beneath one armpit. He wound his way through shelves lined with books and scrolls until he came to a pedestal desk situated in the farthest corner of the library. His hands shaking, he reached into the bag.

What to do, what to do? Sell it back to Leopold outright? That could indeed prove lucrative, *if* Leopold ever paid him. No, it would be safer to approach the Duke and mention he knew someone who had a knack for acquiring lost objects... for a price of course. Playing the third party in this scenario would be much safer. Even being the Abbot of Einsiedeln would not count for much if Leopold got it in his mind that Ludovicus was in possession of something he wanted.

Ludovicus withdrew the manuscript and placed it on the stand before him. Biting his lip, he undid the buckles and flipped open *The Hammer of Witches*.

"No..." He shook his head in disbelief.

The interior parchment had been torn out and replaced with wads of sack cloth.

He scattered the worthless rags to the floor as he dug through them looking for even one page of text. But there was none. He reached the end cover and threw the last bit of stuffing against the wall in a silent fit of rage. He grasped the podium with both hands and ground his teeth together to keep from crying out. He stood like that until his temples throbbed and his jaw muscles ached.

Finally, he opened his cramped fingers and released the podium. He eased the cover of the manuscript shut and refastened its buckles. After a quick look around to make sure no one was near, he climbed a step-stool and shoved the book into the middle of a great wall of manuscripts and scrolls dusty with neglect.

Then he left the library, and this time, he slammed the doors on his way out.

✧ ✧ ✧

As Seraina walked across the courtyard in the darkness to the forge building, snow fell on her in swirling, dry flakes. She had put away her dress for the season, and now wore breeches, lined with rabbit fur, and tucked into high-cut boots that hugged her calves like a second skin. She wore a similar looking fur-lined vest over her white shirt and draped over everything was her simple, greenish-brown cloak. Even though her hood was up, snow worked its way under and melted on her eyelashes, making her squint. She could have easily wiped the moisture away, but her mind was on other things.

The Weave was quiet. Seraina had not even heard a whispering from the wind, never mind a full vision, since she and Thomas had brought back the ancient swords.

Had she made a mistake? Perhaps the swords of her ancestors were not meant to be used for Noll's cause. But the Weave had led her directly to them. It had been so easy and felt so right at the time. Now, she had her doubts.

As she approached Thomas's lean-to she noticed the heavy end-flap was opened part way and a thin tendril of smoke escaped into the night sky. Thomas did not usually have a fire inside, for the forge furnace was always burning and provided more than enough heat through the common wall. But tonight it would be especially warm.

Thinking of the comfortable shelter, with Thomas waiting inside, drove Seraina's self-doubts to the back of her mind. Since returning from their journey together, she had spent most nights there with Thomas. During the day, they went about their respective activities: he training Noll's army, she applying salves and setting bones. Thomas broke the men down and Seraina stood them back up.

It had bothered Seraina at first, seeing her people hurt so often, but when she realized that Thomas felt just as badly, and was only doing everything he could to prepare them, she grew to accept their delicate balancing act. And when she spent each night in Thomas's arms, it felt so perfect, she was sure they were both doing exactly what the Weave had intended.

Seraina had never spent so much time in one man's bed. Sometimes, when she found herself longing for nightfall and wishing the hours of the day away, she wondered if she was falling in love. It was possible, she thought. But she could not be sure, for that was one path she had never traveled.

Seraina removed her cloak and shook off the snow before pushing the flap aside and crawling into the lean-to. Thomas sat at the far end feeding a small fire. He glanced up and smiled nervously for a second, before reaching down and pulling a piece of parchment off a stack beside him. He tossed it into the flames.

"What are you burning?" Seraina asked as she crawled over their bed of fresh spruce boughs and wool blankets.

Thomas held the edge of another page to the flame and watched it catch. "Lies and half-truths," he said.

"Did you write them?"

"No," Thomas said. There was a harsh edge to his voice.

She squinted at the markings on one of the pages. They were meaningless to her and she wondered why anyone would bother with written words when so few could decipher them.

"Then how do you know they are lies?"

Thomas looked at Seraina and his dark eyes softened.

"I just know," he said.

He reached out to touch Seraina's cool cheek and she leaned into the warmth of his hand. He kissed her on the lips and then she slid in close and rested her head on his shoulder. She watched in silence as he resumed feeding sheets of parchment into the fire.

✧　✧　✧

Thomas stomped across the snow-covered courtyard to where Urs and Maximilian were talking in raised voices. A crew led by Sutter was cutting down the circle of tall flag poles nearby for firewood to heat the keep. They had all but stopped working, distracted by what looked like a disagreement on its way to becoming a full-blown argument.

As Thomas approached he heard bits of a conversation that would not be good for morale if the men overheard.

"…shields will keep them alive," Max said.

"They cannot stop dropping their blades as it is. And you want to give them even more to think about?"

"Keep your voices down," Thomas said. "The men are looking."

Urs crossed his arms and grunted. "I will if you can talk some sense into Max."

Thomas took a second to glance over his shoulder at Sutter and his work party. They saw him looking and made a show of picking up their tools and resuming their respective tasks.

"Now, what is the issue here?"

"Max wants to equip the men with shields," Urs said.

"We do not have any shields," Thomas said. "So that is not likely to happen."

"Then we had bloody well better make some, Thomas," Max said, his voice once again escalating. "Or we are going to have a mess of dead farmers on our hands!"

Thomas gave him a moment to calm down. "Out with it. What is on your mind?"

Max paced a quick circle in front of Urs and Thomas and then stopped inches from them. He kept his voice low. "I cannot teach these heavy-handed farm boys and old men how to use a sword. If we had ten years, maybe then we could get half of them to a competent level. But not in a few months. We are wasting our time here."

Thomas looked to Urs. "Do you feel the same way?"

Urs still had his massive forearms crossed over his chest. He looked off to the side.

"It might help if they had the same length and type of blades. We have piercers practicing slashing techniques and men with single-edged weapons learning back-cuts. There is no consistency, and we simply do not have the time."

They were both right. Thomas had known from the beginning that it would take a miracle to make an effective army out of farmers and shepherds. No matter how hard they worked.

He looked over and caught Sutter staring at him. The innkeeper turned quickly away and resumed chopping at the thick flag pole that a short time ago had displayed the Habsburg pennant. These men of the forests were a sturdy lot, and they had heart. But they would be up against professional soldiers, and even worse, knights. Men who had been swinging swords since childhood, their bodies growing to accommodate the blade. Armor and weapons would become such a natural part of them that they would limp and feel less than whole when unarmed.

You cannot teach a man something in a few months that another has spent his entire life learning.

Sutter stepped back from the tall pole and said something to the Rubin twins who were sawing another log into firewood on the ground nearby. They put down the two-man saw and walked to stand behind Sutter, then Sutter reached out with his hand and gave his pole a gentle touch. Nothing happened at first, but then it began to slowly fall, picking up speed as it went. It bounced once and shook the ground when its full length hit. One of the twins picked up his own ax and began chopping at another pole.

"Axes…" Thomas said. *How much time had he wasted?*

Urs and Max had started arguing with each other again and had not heard him. Thomas left the two men and walked quickly over to the forge. He retrieved Pirmin's blanket-wrapped ax and carried it over to Sutter's work party. With Sutter and the twins looking at him with curiosity, he unwrapped Pirmin's ax.

"What are you going to do with that?" Sutter asked.

"Not me," Thomas said. He tossed it to Sutter, who caught it deftly in one hand. Thomas pointed to a fresh pole, thicker around than a man's waist. "Cut it down."

Sutter shrugged. "I can try. But the length of this handle is going to make it a tad awkward."

Max and Urs came up behind Thomas. "Are you thinking what I think you are?" Max asked.

Thomas did not answer, but his pulse quickened as he watched Sutter step back from the pole and line up his distance. He set his feet and swung.

The ax head went past the pole and the shaft clanged against the wood. The vibrations tore the ax out of Sutter's hands and it fell to the ground. Sutter shook the sting out of his hands and cursed.

Urs and the twins laughed.

"It was a nice idea," Max said, touching Thomas's shoulder.

Thomas held up his hand and pointed at Sutter. The innkeeper had already retrieved the ax and was readjusting his feet.

He swung.

The blade hit the pole with a *whump* that Thomas felt deep in his stomach. He swung again and Thomas felt the force of the blow in his entire body this time. A thick wedge of wood spun off into the air. Sutter kept swinging. He settled into a rhythm, his movements were fluid, graceful, and appeared effortless. Less than a minute later he pushed the pole over.

Thomas had spent all of last summer cutting down trees for his ferry, and he knew it would have taken him five times as long. And he would have been winded, probably exhausted. But Sutter's mouth was not even open. He was about to lay into the next pole when one of the twins convinced him to let him have a go. The result was similar. After a couple of swings to get the new distance figured out, the young man seemed to be finished in seconds.

Urs and Max looked at Thomas with wide eyes and their open mouths slowly turned into grins.

"Not bad for an innkeeper," Thomas said.

Urs picked up one of the men's axes laying on the ground. He fingered the head of the ax and held it up to his right eye. "This is good steel," he said. "Who sharpened this blade?"

The twin holding Pirmin's ax replied. "I did, of course. Who else is gonna sharpen my ax for me?"

"Not me, that is for sure," his brother said.

"What do you think Urs?" Thomas asked.

He nodded. "They can use their own heads. All we have to do is fashion handles. They will have to be wood, though. Do not have the time or material to make them out of steel like Pirmin's."

"If we melt down all the old swords, can you make spikes for the ends? Or maybe hooks?" Max asked.

"You know the answer to that," Urs said. "And by the way, you still owe me for shaping the sword that *you* carry."

"Well, you better make damn sure nothing happens to me, then," Max said.

The two men continued their casual bickering, but Thomas no longer heard them. He was too focused on Pirmin's ax.

CHAPTER 18

IT HAD BEEN a mild winter, or so everyone kept telling Thomas. But to a man brought up in the scorching sun of the Levant, he thought he would never be warm again. The long winter months had been almost unbearable, and Seraina often joked that he would have perished if she had not taken it upon herself to keep him warm. Although she said it in fun, he suspected it was closer to the truth than she knew.

When the season ended, and the snows receded, he felt reborn. Now that it was spring, he had planned to redirect all efforts from military training to working on the defenses. One cloudless spring morning he made his way to the training ground and was surprised to find it deserted. Puzzled, Thomas sat down, wondering where everyone was. A half hour later Noll walked up with a bucket in hand on his way to the well.

"Morning, ferryman. What are you doing here?"

"What do you think? Where is everyone?"

Noll scratched his head. "What do you mean?"

Thomas waved his arm over the empty training yard. "The men. Did we give them a church day?"

Noll laughed. "You really do not know? I thought we talked about this."

"About what?"

"Planting season. We agreed that we had to allow the men to return to their homes to get their crops in the ground."

"Oh." Thomas did recall something about that a couple months ago.

"Everybody has got to eat," Noll said.

"Well, how many days before they come back?"

"Days? We will be lucky to see any of them for at least a month."

"A month? Leopold could be here in a month!"

Noll shook his head. "No, he will not risk marching an army over passes still wet from the winter thaw. I suspect it will be past midsummer before we have to worry about any Austrians crossing our borders."

An entire month of training lost. This did not bode well, Thomas thought. Last week he had introduced the men to the fighting formations he had decided would serve them best. A variation of a Greek phalanx. He had divided his army into groups of one hundred men and arranged them in squares ten men wide by ten men deep. With their long-handled axes, or halberds as Urs called the new weapons, held before them, the square would prove difficult for cavalry to approach and with training, maneuverable enough to make them almost impossible to outflank.

At least that was his hope. The men had taken to the new squares well enough, but they were still too sluggish when they had to move and reform. It would require many weeks of drilling yet before they could be called proficient.

"What about their families? Perhaps the women and children could see to the farms," Thomas said.

Noll's face went dark. "And just who do you think has been feeding our army, and us, I might add, all winter? You really know nothing about the life of a farming family, do you ferryman? It is thanks to the men's wives and mothers that we have any army at all to train. It is they who have shouldered many times their regular burden so that their husbands and sons can escape farm work for a few hours every day, in the hope that their men learn enough to keep them alive."

Thomas felt suddenly foolish for making the suggestion. "And what about work on the palisades?" he asked.

Noll shrugged. "The roads are still too wet to move the material we salvaged from the fortress. We will not lose any time there."

Thomas knew Noll was right, although, he still could not help thinking they were losing valuable time. But what else could he do? If he did not allow the men to tend to their animals and get their crops planted, the Austrians would be the least of their worries.

"Very well. I need you to get word to the men then. We cannot allow them to forget everything they have learned thus far, so make sure that not one among them uses a short-handled ax for anything. If the job requires an ax, they must use their halberds. Can you do that?"

"Easy enough. Of course that might mean they will be gone for a month and a half then," Noll said, his cocky half-smile turning up the corners of his mouth.

"You look like you are happy about all this," Thomas said. "Or are you just pretending because you know how much it bothers me to sit idle?"

"I would be lying if I said I was not looking forward to a month's break from your miserable drills. But I, for one, do not plan on sitting idle," Noll said.

Thomas's eyes narrowed. He did not ask for any more information, but Noll offered it freely.

"I will go to Schwyz and help out Sutter around the inn for

a while," Noll said. That same half-smile found its way to his face again.

"You mean you aim to help out Mera," Thomas said, crossing his arms. He was not the only one who had noticed Noll and Mera spending a suspicious amount of time together over the winter.

Noll let out a nervous chuckle and looked away. It was the first time Thomas had ever seen him display even a hint of embarrassment.

Noll recovered quickly though, and held up the bucket in his hand. "Sorry, much as I would like to, I cannot stand around all day chatting. Chores to do, and all." He gave Thomas a crisp salute. "See you in a month, Captain."

As Noll walked away, Thomas shouted at his back. "You just tell Sutter that if he decides to chop off your head he has to do it with his long-handled ax."

Noll waved his bucket-holding hand but did not look back. Thomas thought it may well have been the first time he had gotten in the last word with young Arnold Melchthal.

When Thomas arrived back at his lean-to, Seraina was just coming out. Her traveling cloak was fastened about her shoulders and she wore a pack on her back.

"Going somewhere?" he asked.

Seraina offered up a weak smile. "I will be gone for a few days. I was just on my way to say goodbye."

"Would you like company? It seems I have lost most of my army for the next month and suddenly find myself with a lot of time on my hands."

Seraina shook her head quickly. Too quickly, it seemed to Thomas. "No, you should stay here and help Urs finish crafting the rest of the halberds. I will only be gone a few days."

Now Thomas was sure something was wrong. When Seraina first heard about his plan to melt down the swords of her ancestors, she was furious and had threatened to throw them all back in the lake. It had taken Thomas a long time to explain how the swords were not being destroyed, but just reshaped into weapons the men could actually use. After a while, she had accepted his explanation, but was never truly happy about it.

Thomas looked at her, but she avoided his eyes and busied herself adjusting the strap on her pack.

"Seraina."

"Hmm?" She leaned down and retied one of the laces on her boot.

"Look at me. Please."

Her hands stopped moving and she slowly straightened up. She lifted her head. Her green eyes lacked their usual brilliance, and the skin around them was puffy from recent tears.

"I have to go," she said.

"Is it because of your visions?"

She nodded. The movement of her head almost imperceptible. "I cannot remember ever having gone so long without one."

"I wish I could fully understand why they mean so much to you," Thomas said.

She shrugged. "They are as much a part of me as any of my other senses. And without them, I feel like I have hidden a piece of myself, but I cannot remember where."

"Perhaps it is a good omen that you have not had any all winter."

Seraina looked at him and her face turned pale. She shook her head. "No, Thomas. To lose one's sense of the Weave is most definitely not a good sign."

"And how will running away help solve any of this?"

Seraina was quiet for a moment, like she was considering her next words carefully. She placed her hand on Thomas's arm.

"I know this is difficult for you, but please try to understand. Never before have I spent so much time in one place, with so many people I truly care about. I think their voices have played a part in drowning out my visions. If, for a time, I could put some distance—"

Thomas felt a lump form in his throat. "You mean me. I am the cause."

She shook her head and Thomas saw regret flicker behind her eyes. "No, that is not what I meant. Not at all."

"Then stay here. With me."

Thomas held his breath and waited for her answer. But Seraina was not the only one who could see things, and he knew what she would say before the words passed her lips.

"I cannot," she said.

◆ ◆ ◆

Seraina walked all day, setting a furious pace that left her exhausted with the approach of dusk. She built a fire near a small chattering stream and brewed a pot of tea to have with her evening meal. Later, she spread her bedroll in a clearing filled with lillies of the valley. She lay there for some time breathing in the sweet smell of the bell-shaped flowers and listening to the sounds of the forest before sleep came for her.

And with it, finally, a glimpse into the patterns of the Weave.

A mist came and went, leaving her standing in a lightly treed forest. The ground was flat, with warm summer sunlight breaking through the canopy of leaves far overhead. The soil smelled of midsummer, and the leaves rustling against one another in the wind were thick and green. And nestled amongst the sound of wind and leaves, were children's voices.

Screeching with glee, a small boy burst out of a thicket and ran toward Seraina. He had light brown hair and eyes so dark they could have been black. He was no older than four, but his legs seemed long, his little feet uncannily sure-footed as he tottered along the forest floor. A few steps behind, came a girl a couple years older laughing herself breathless. As she ran, her long, light-colored hair flashed in the dappled sunlight and she looked toward Seraina with emerald eyes.

Seraina's heart ached and she felt a cross between pure joy and pride bubble within as she stared at the children running toward her. And then she saw Thomas, and her heart lurched once more. He was older, his hair more gray than brown, but his face was somehow younger, and unlined. The years even seemed to have faded his scar. As he chased the children, *his* children, he wore a smile so beautiful, so filled with happiness, Seraina wanted to cry.

With her vision beginning to cloud with tears, Seraina knelt down and opened her arms to the children. The boy ran past without even glancing at her. The girl too passed her by, but unlike her brother, she gave Seraina a curious look that seemed to ask *Who are you?*

Seraina realized then that the girl's eyes were not emerald green, but a deep blue.

Confused, Seraina whirled in time to see the children jump into the arms of a woman Seraina had never seen before. She was blonde-haired and beautiful. Thomas joined them a second later, and encircled them all in a hug. The children shrieked, Thomas laughed, and the woman smiled.

Seraina had never seen Thomas look so happy. And she had never felt so much pain.

She turned away from the sight, but something forced her to look back. When she did, the woman and children were gone. Only Thomas remained.

He now wore a tunic that looked like it was knitted together from drops of blood. He stared at Seraina and his face creased over with anger. And then he spoke.

"You mean me. I am the cause."

Seraina sat upright in the darkness. The sound of her heart pounding in her ears drowned out the stream and the surrounding forest. She took in a long, deep, shuddering breath.

It was Thomas.

It had always been him. He was the one around which all others pivoted.

He was the Catalyst.

The Weave was reforming around his actions, his decisions. Not Noll's. The changes in the Weave all began when Thomas arrived. Seraina had misread the signs.

Noll *was* special—he was an *Adept*. That is what Seraina had sensed. He could have been a druid, with the proper training, but he was discovered too late in life. However, he was no Catalyst.

How could I have been so blind?

Noll had been locked in a back-and-forth struggle against the Habsburgs for years, with no one able to gain the upper hand. Then Thomas appeared, and within the short span of less than a year, they had driven the Austrians out of Altdorf, seized control of their fortress, and raised an army. When Noll was in charge, men had trickled in to join his cause, but the moment Thomas took control of the Confederate forces, men flocked to his banner. Just as Vercingetorix had united the tribes against the invading armies of Julius Caesar over thirteen hundred years ago. Vercingetorix had seemingly come out of nowhere to terrorize the Roman forces. So too had Thomas.

Though much smaller in scale, the timing was right; the parallels unmistakable. The Weave had returned to them a wayward son of the Helvetii destined to unite the people against an unjust foreign occupation.

Looking back it all made perfect sense. But Seraina had become too close to see it. She had become blind to the Weave's pattern because she stood in its center and was unable to view it in its entirety. She had done the one thing an Eye of the Weave must never do: she had fallen in love with the very Catalyst she had been put in this world to guide. Even worse, she had allowed him to fall in love with her, thereby putting the future of all her people at risk.

Who knew what choices Thomas would make for her alone, with no thought toward the greater pattern? His concern for her would make him deaf to the subtle calls of the Weave and he could miss his one chance to lead his people successfully through a period of great change. Perhaps he already had. Seraina could not know for sure.

Seraina had gained a lover. But in doing so, she may have robbed the Helvetii of their last chance for survival.

Vercingetorix.

Seraina tried to put the name out of her mind, but she could not. Some say it was the Druids who had failed him, as well. After a series of brilliant victories against the Romans, he was ultimately defeated and imprisoned by Caesar. For five long years he was kept in chains and tortured. Once he had been reduced to an empty husk of a man, the greatest general the Celts had ever known was paraded through the streets of Rome and then slowly strangled.

Seraina hugged her knees and dropped her forehead to her arms. The lillies of the valley flooded her nostrils; so wonderful to smell, but deadly poisonous if eaten.

By Ardwynna's Grace, what have I done?

CHAPTER 19

FRANCO ROEMER ATTEMPTED to blink away the sweat in his eyes but only succeeded in making them burn. His arms were stretched back over his head and his fingers clutched a net stuffed with hay. His farm was located near Landeck, a small Austrian village located on a lush valley floor and squeezed between scenic mountain ranges.

The load was not heavy, balanced as it was over his broad shoulders, but it was awkward. The heat of the midday sun combined with the prickling spear-ends of the dry hay made for an uncomfortable task. But it was the last trip of the day. That thought brought a grin to his bearded face, and the knowledge that his wife was making meat pies for dinner added a bounce to his step.

His destination, a small hay shed on the other side of the road, was within sight. Franco tilted his head and did his best to wipe his brow on his shoulder without upsetting his load. He stepped over the ditch and stumbled onto the road, almost losing everything. He swayed back and forth, lurched forward a few steps, one back, and forward again, all the while talking to himself.

"Whoa now, easy does it. Hang onto her Roemer... there we go." Just when he thought he had it under control, the bottom half slid off his back and the entire thing slipped out of his fingers onto the road.

"*Merde!*"

He grinned at his sudden exclamation and shook his head. He was not French. But his wife was, and the use of her word told him something that he already knew. She was on his mind, and the sooner he got this task over and done with, the sooner he could be sitting at his table with her and the children.

He rolled his shoulders and rubbed the back of his neck with one hand while he looked down at the net of hay; its golden strands splayed across the road like a maiden's hair removed from the coif. He thought of what his wife would say and laughed out loud, thankful she had not been present to witness his clumsiness. When he had brought her back from Neuchatel six years ago, his family and neighbors had been delighted. To them, all born in the German-speaking Alps surrounding Landeck, she was a foreign exotic. They chatted about her like she was a countess from Paris, even though everyone knew she was merely the daughter of a dairy farmer a few valleys over.

Still, in many ways, she would always be considered an outsider in the close-knit community of Landeck. Franco knew it was sometimes difficult for her, but she was a resilient woman who knew how to stand up for herself. Although the locals soon learned to fear her sharp tongue, Franco knew it could be just as sweet. They had three fine children together, and if Franco had his way he would soon make it four.

He knelt and began re-stuffing hay back into the net. A familiar tremor beneath his feet gave him pause, and he stopped to look up the road. Three horsemen, riding fast, rounded a bend in the road. He shaded his eyes.

Soldiers. The King's Eagles, no less.

Franco stood. As he considered diving off the road, one of the men pointed in his direction. It was too late. They had seen him.

Within seconds they pulled up in front of him, their horses slick with sweat. The animals snorted and their nostrils flared as they took advantage of the break in their pace to refill their lungs. Even before their sergeant spoke, Franco had a bad feeling come over him.

"You there. Tell me of the nearest stream, or trough, where we can water our animals."

Franco wiped his hands on his work-stained breeches. His damp tunic clung to his chest. He looked at the hardened, sour faces of each man in turn and decided he did not want any of them near his home. Or his family. He raised an arm and pointed down the road toward the town of Landeck.

"Landeck is only a few miles ahead," he said.

The sergeant's eyes narrowed. "Our animals are thirsty. Where do you get your water?"

Franco avoided the man's gaze and looked over the horses. They were tall, fine mounts. "They are thirsty, all right. But they will easily make it to the Inn River before they have need to drink. If you rested them, they would even make Salzburg if need be."

"Will they now?"

He nudged his horse forward, forcing Franco to take a step back. The soldier let go of his reins and allowed his horse to graze on the hay at its feet.

"Where is your home, man? These are the King's animals. They have more right to your land, and everything on it, than you do."

Franco made no attempt to answer. He kept his eyes down

and focused on the sergeant's horse as it tugged at a few strands of hay caught in the netting.

"I ask again. Where is your farm? And do not lie to me or I will come back and pull out your tongue. And cut that twine, damn you, so my animal can feed properly."

Franco looked up. "Cut it yourself," he said.

A silence settled over the men like a wet blanket. Franco thought even the horse stopped chewing. The sergeant looked at his two men and laughed, but it sounded more like he had a pheasant bone caught in his throat.

Staring at Franco, the sergeant slowly drew his sword. The sound of steel grating against a leather scabbard rang through the air. He let out a tired sigh, like a man who had exhausted all reasonable methods of communication, and leaned forward to place the flat of his blade against Franco's shoulder.

"Take your time and consider your next words carefully," he said.

Franco looked up. He nodded. "In my life, I have suffered many beatings from men better than you," he said. "Mind you, I was a child, then." His lips spread into a grin. "So, I do not expect to get one today."

The sergeant's horse sensed a change come over his master and he jerked his head up from the hay. The soldier pulled back his blade and swung its flat edge at Franco's head. It was a quick, lazy swing, but it was unchecked and had enough force behind it to shatter the bones in a man's face. If it connected.

Franco dropped to the ground on his back, watching as the blade fanned through the air above. The sergeant tried to halt his swing, but he could not prevent the flat of his blade from slapping his mount's neck. The startled horse whinnied in alarm and gave a buck in protest.

Keeping his eyes on the horse's iron-shod hooves, Franco rolled beneath the belly of the animal and came to his knees on the sergeant's opposite side. He knocked the soldier's foot out of its stirrup, stood up, and grabbed the man's tunic. In one fluid motion he pulled the man toward him, hopped high into the air, and swung his leg over the stallion's back to land just behind the saddle.

The sergeant let out a surprised howl as Franco's momentum pulled him half out of the saddle. A lesser horseman would have been on the ground already, but the sergeant was a Royal Eagle, and Franco knew these men could ride. The sergeant dropped his sword and grabbed a fistful of the horse's long mane as he hung off its side and fought to keep his one leg hooked over the saddle. His foot quested blindly for the stirrup so he could push himself back up.

Confused and uncertain about who exactly its master was, the horse began turning in tight circles. Franco changed that by giving him a hard, open-handed slap on its rump.

"Hyah!"

The horse broke into a gallop, leaving the other two soldiers staring wide-mouthed after their commanding officer as he hung onto the side of his mount like a gypsy stunt rider. But his screams and frantic scrambling soon dispelled that illusion and revealed his lack of the wandering folk's talent with horses. The man seated behind him, however, was another matter.

Franco reached over the struggling sergeant, who continued to hold on with only one leg draped over the saddle, and took hold of the reins with one hand. He spun the animal in a tight circle and the sergeant cursed as he slid further over the side.

Franco laughed. He could not help himself. He guided the

horse straight and slapped its rump again. It bolted ahead, and then Franco spun him again. As the sergeant's heel slid over the smooth leather of the saddle, Franco helped it along with a flick of his hand. The soldier's feet bounced once and then dragged on the ground, and his fingers gave up their grip on the horse's mane. He fell onto the road amidst a cloud of dust. Franco heard him cough once as he hit and then he began shouting.

"After him! He is stealing my horse!"

Franco hopped forward to sit in the saddle and kicked his horse into a gallop. He leaned low over the stallion's neck and stroked it as he raced down the road.

"He thinks I aim to steal you, old boy," he said into the horse's ear. It twitched at his breath. Franco reined in the horse and guided him with his knees to turn around.

"Steal you," Franco repeated, contempt heavy in his voice. He gave the stallion another pat on his muscular neck. "You are a good mount. Well-trained and strong." He pointed at the two riders coming toward them.

"The dun on the left fears you, my friend. Pay him no heed. But the black stallion thinks you are weak. Together we shall show him the truth." He gave him one last pat and sat up straight in the saddle.

"Hyah!"

The two soldiers shifted in their saddles when they saw Franco turn and begin galloping straight at them. They fumbled to draw their swords and kicked their own mounts into a full charge.

Franco leaned over his horse's neck and took up the slack in the reins. He guided his horse directly at the gap between the two oncoming animals, using pressure from his legs and hands to remind his stallion that Franco was the one in full control. He waited until the exact moment he could clearly see the features of the men's faces and then he wheeled his horse hard to the left, directly at the flank of the dun. The horse's eyes widened and he veered a step away from the charge, cutting off the large black and there was a moment of panic as both men fought to prevent their horses from colliding.

Franco shot past and immediately turned his mount. The soldiers, with their horses once more under control, spun to see Franco already bearing down on them. But it was too late for them to meet him with a charge of their own.

Franco pulled his leg over his horse's head to ride side-saddle a second before his horse rammed into the side of the black with its shoulder. Caught from the side and off balance, the black whinnied in fear as its long legs flipped out from under it and it fell onto its side. Fortunately, his rider had the presence of mind to throw himself clear just before the collision. But Franco could see the man had hit the ground hard and was showing no sign of movement.

The other soldier closed on Franco and stabbed at him with his sword. Franco slid down off his saddle to avoid the blow. Keeping his horse between him and his opponent, he ran a few steps beside it until he could pull himself back up into the saddle in safety. He turned his horse and charged the man's weak side. He was right handed and once inside the arc of his sword, the soldier's options were limited.

Franco caught the soldier's arm as he attempted a backhanded slash. He struck him in the face and then looped his arm over the man's elbow. Then, using both his arms in a scissors motion, he jerked the soldier's arm back into a painful shoulder lock. The Eagle screeched as Franco dragged him out of the saddle and threw him to the ground.

Franco lifted his leg over his horse's head and slid off the saddle. He picked up the man's sword and pressed it into the hollow of his throat. The King's messenger clutched his shoulder, his eyes wet with pain.

"Who are you?" he asked, grimacing.

Franco saw movement out of the corner of his eye, and he turned his head but kept the sword at the man's neck. The sergeant limped slowly toward them. His sword was in its scabbard and one hand seemed to be favoring the small of his back.

"Fool," he said. "Who do you think he is?"

He paused to work up a mouthful of phlegm, then spit it onto the road. Franco noticed it was tinted with blood. The sergeant looked at him and the muscles around one of his eyes twitched.

"This here is Franco Roemer. Commander of the Stormriders."

He glanced over to where the other soldier was trying to catch a fidgety black stallion.

"The very man we have been sent to find."

✧ ✧ ✧

Leopold leaned back in his chair and dropped the messenger's parchment onto his desk. Even though he was alone, he suppressed the smile he felt building behind his lips.

He had feared the worst when a King's Eagle rode into Habsburg less than an hour before. He had a premonition that his brother had been captured by Louis. Or worse. But this... he had not dared dream it was possible.

"Husband? Am I intruding?" Lady Catherine stood in the door, her hands wringing one another in front of her. She too was pleased with something, but she was not as adept as Leopold at hiding it.

"Never, my dear," Leopold said. "Come in, come in. But close the door behind you." He suddenly felt generous.

Her brow creased and she did as he asked. She took a seat across from him, folding her hands in her lap. "You look happy. As happy as I have ever seen you I dare say."

Leopold could no longer keep the grin from his face. "Can I not hide anything from you?"

"Not a thing," she said. "Now will you let me know what pleases you so, or shall I tell you my own news?"

Leopold was glad she was here. The news he had received was simply too good to keep to himself any longer.

"I have received word from my brother," he said.

Catherine's gloved hand flew to cover her mouth. She spoke through it. "Has he defeated the Bavarian already?"

"Better, my sweet. He is sending me the Sturmritter. He has commanded their captain, Franco Roemer, to gather his knights and ride to our aid as soon as possible."

"Wonderful!"

Leopold put his hands behind his head and looked at the carved ceiling.

"I did not think it possible with him being at war. But apparently he sent Roemer and his men home for a break to get some rest before a major offensive he is planning. He suggested I use them when I invade the forest regions as a way to provide the men with a little exercise."

"Your brother is wise. Men like those of the Stormriders are not well suited to leisure. Did you know I met Captain Roemer once?" There was open admiration in her voice.

"I did not know that," Leopold said. A pang of jealousy shot through him and it took a moment for him to recognize the strange sensation for what it was. "When exactly was that?"

"It was before he had been promoted to Captain. He

stayed with us for a half year and was swordmaster to my cousins…" Her voice trailed off and she had a far away look in her eyes.

"And what impression did he make?"

"Oh, a very good one," she said. "Sir Roemer is a true gentleman," she quickly added.

"He is a killer. And a very good one. There is no man more capable with a lance in all of Christendom. I hear he once skewered three men with a single charge. Spitted them all like pigs."

Catherine looked away and laced her fingers together. "Well, he was always a polite, well-mannered nobleman when I saw him," she said.

"He was the seventh child of a minor noble in Landeck. We would not even know the Roemer name if Franco had not distinguished himself so on the battlefield. Some say his family's blood is more gypsy than blue."

"That might explain his eyes," Catherine said, and then bit her lip when Leopold looked at her.

"You had some news as well?"

Catherine nodded, and her face lit up. "I too received a message today. From my father."

"Oh?"

Catherine glided over to the door and threw it open. She called out and a man wearing the livery of Savoy stepped through. He kept his eyes straight ahead and his chin up. He exuded the haughtiness Leopold had come to associate with his wife's duchy.

Today, however, Leopold hardly noticed, for his eyes were drawn to the large strongbox the servant carried. He placed it on Leopold's desk and lifted the lid. It was filled to overflowing with gold florins.

"My father has agreed to finance your campaign to take back the Gotthard Pass from those treacherous mountain people," Catherine said, her excitement creeping to a higher level with every word.

Leopold stared at the box. And then at Catherine. She beamed like an angel. He looked back at the gold to make sure he had not imagined any of it. What a miraculous turn of events. First, the Sturmritter were his to command. And now this.

He looked to the ceiling and searched for the right words to express his gratitude.

"You are wrong my dear," he finally said. "Your father has agreed to finance *our* campaign. Yours and mine."

The way her face glowed told Leopold he had found them.

CHAPTER 20

MIDSUMMER CAME AND WENT, and the Altdorf fortress was completely dismantled. Thomas moved his army's base to Schwyz in early fall, since the network of forts and palisade walls had been completed and permanently manned with lookouts for some time. He set up his tent and command center behind the walls of the largest one, which guarded the main road leading south from Austrian lands.

The Confederate army numbered some eleven hundred men, but Noll's resources told them Leopold had assembled over eight thousand. It was what Thomas had expected, but when Noll heard the news, he insisted on making the rounds personally to Zurich, Berne, and Lucerne to find out where the additional men were that they had promised. He had been gone more than a week, and Thomas found himself wishing he had not let him go. The Habsburgs controlled all the main roads now, and travel, even for someone like Noll, was exceptionally dangerous.

One day, while doing an inspection round of the forts, Thomas stopped by Sutter's inn. He knew the innkeeper himself would not be there, for he was on duty at the main palisade walls. But that did not bother him, for it was Sutter's daughter, Mera, that Thomas had come hoping to see.

She greeted him outside with a hug and ushered him through the back door into the kitchen. Before he could protest, a plate of cheese and thinly sliced meats appeared in front of him.

"Have you heard from Noll?" She asked.

Thomas shook his head. "Nothing yet. But I am sure he will be along any time now."

She forced a smile and nodded. "How is my father doing? Have you made a soldier out of him yet?"

"He has become quite the natural leader. The men have taken to calling him 'the Baron'."

Mera laughed. "That is the perfect name for him, I can tell you that much."

Her laughter died off when she noticed Thomas looking distractedly around the room.

"What is it, Thomas?"

He pushed up one of his shirtsleeves and then pulled it down again. "I was wondering... if you had seen, or heard from, Seraina, as of late."

"Oh, Thomas." A sad smile crossed her lips. "Not since you asked me last. Three weeks ago she stopped by for a few minutes to drop off some salves and ointments for the men, but I have not seen her since."

Thomas nodded, and studied the larder shelves.

"I am sure she will be back before you know it though. This is not the first time Seraina has disappeared. She just needs her time alone, on occasion."

Thomas looked at Mera and could tell by her eyes that she was just trying to be kind. She had no idea when, or if, Seraina would ever be back.

Thomas left Sutter's inn at dusk. He walked Anid around the farmers' fields and took the forest path that lead to the west road. As Anid stepped out of the woods onto the wider road, he whinnied and his ears perked up. Ten feet away, sitting on a rotten log with his chin in his hands, was Noll. He looked up and then slowly stood as Thomas approached. His boots and the hem of his cloak were covered in dried mud, and his normally clean-shaven face showed a growth of several days. There were dark circles under his eyes, and sweat stains covered his chest.

"I just came from the inn," Thomas said.

"I know. I saw your horse there." Noll's voice rasped as he spoke. "Any word on Seraina?"

Thomas shook his head.

"Why did you not come in? Mera has been worried about you."

"I have news, Thomas. Bad news. And it is not something I wish to burden Mera with."

Thomas slid down out of the saddle. He pulled out his water skin and tossed it to Noll.

"Drink some of that, first. I do not want you dying halfway through."

Noll tipped the skin to his lips with both hands. When the water flow began to slow down, he squeezed it with one hand, drank some more, and then sprayed his face off with the remainder. He lowered the depleted skin and looked at Thomas.

"They are not coming," he said.

"Which ones?"

"Zurich, Berne, Lucerne. All of them. None of them. Zurich and Berne I can understand. Leopold has no doubt made the guilds better offers. But Lucerne? They are right across the lake from us. We share the same waters! Yet they believe they can distance themselves from this? Are they mad?"

He shook his head and sat back down on the decaying log.

"There must be someone else," Thomas said.

Noll shook his head. "Even if there were, Leopold has all the roads and passes blockaded. No one can get through to us now. And it gets worse."

"How?"

"Have you heard of the Sturmritter?"

"I have," Thomas said.

"They just rode into Habsburg three days ago."

Both men went silent. Thomas had been hoping for another thousand men, for that would have nearly doubled their forces. Noll's news, however, did not come as a complete surprise. Stauffacher and Furst had been in negotiations for months now with the other cities. If they had truly intended to make a stand with Schwyz, Uri, and Unterwalden, they would have sent men by now.

Thomas reached into his saddlebag and pulled out some cheese Mera had wrapped in a piece of cloth for him. He carried it over and sat down next to Noll.

"The Sturmritter are men, just like the rest of us," Thomas said, handing the cheese over to Noll.

Noll nodded a 'thanks'. He unwrapped the cheese, stuffed a good portion of it into his mouth, and mumbled around it. "So where the hell is Leopold anyways? He should have been here last month. Why does he delay?"

Thomas shrugged. "Could be waiting for the final harvest to come in. That is what I would do."

"Well, most of it is in. The first snows could be here any day."

"Then I suppose it is time we made our final preparations," Thomas said. He patted Noll on the shoulder and stood back up. "See you at the wall."

"What, no offer to give me a ride?"

Thomas shook his head. "You are on your way to Sutter's. You and I both know that. If Leopold attacks before you get back, I promise to not let Matthias kill him before you show up."

"You are one mad ferryman, you know that?"

"I have had no ferry for a very long time, thanks in no small part to you. So why do you insist on calling me that?"

Noll grinned. "Because it makes you angry. And the angrier you get the better chance I think we have," Noll said.

CHAPTER 21

LEOPOLD HAD TO admit Bernard was skilled at much more than just the use of a quill. Sculpting also seemed to be no small part of his repertoire.

Leopold's war council gathered around the wide table built especially for the detailed clay landscape that Leopold's chief scribe had built. Bernard had been out of sorts ever since the manuscript under his care had been lost when Leopold and Gissler were ambushed by Thomas Schwyzer, so when his lord told him he needed a very detailed map of the areas from Zug to Schwyz, Bernard had thrown himself wholeheartedly into the project. The result was a precise model of the two towns, complete with little wooden houses and stables. The surrounding countryside was also recreated from sculptor's clay, painted in life-like colors and complete with forests, mountains, and rivers.

It was so realistic, Leopold had trouble keeping his captains focused on the battle plans. The Habsburg Fool delighted in touching lakes and trees and then would hold up his finger for the dozen or so men in the room to inspect. And beside him, Landenberg also seemed to be infatuated with the model. He kept trying to peer inside the small windows of the buildings of Zug.

"Landenberg? Did you hear what I said?"

The Vogt straightened up. "Yes, of course, my lord. We overnight in Zug and then assemble at dawn."

Captain Roemer spoke up. "And from there we march straight on to Schwyz?"

Leopold nodded. "Most of us. Count Henri?"

Henri of Hunenberg had been quiet all night, Leopold thought. *Perhaps he suspected something like this was coming.*

"Yes my lord?"

"I intend to take the fight to them on two fronts. You will take your men over this pass," Leopold traced a line with his stick over the landscape, "and attack this village in Obwalden. The rest of us will take Schwyz."

The Count's eyes clouded over and he crossed his arms. He kept his eyes locked on the model and said nothing.

"And remember. Ensure every one of your soldiers has enough collars and rope to secure at least three captives. If any man comes back with fewer than that, he will forfeit two months of his salarium. Is that understood?"

There was some murmuring at that, as to be expected, but Leopold did not care at this point.

"Good. Then, if there are no questions I propose we adjou—"

The Fool's hand shot into the air and waved back and forth inches from Leopold's nose. "My lord Duke! I have a thought!"

Some of the men chuckled, a few rolled their eyes. But Leopold was feeling especially magnanimous at the moment. This night had been a year in the making. *Why not end the evening on a ridiculous note for the sake of morale?*

"You have something to add?"

The Fool stood upright and decided that was not enough.

He hopped up onto a chair and turned a full circle, looking at every man in the room as he did so. There were more than a few smiles as the men tried to guess what the jester was up to.

"You have all given wise council tonight," the Fool began, his voice deep and solemn. "Very wise council indeed, on how to get into the lands of the mountain people. But my question is…"

He paused and turned a slow circle again on his chair, pointing at each man in turn.

"My question is… how do you intend to get out?"

The room was quiet for more than a few seconds, as men waited expectantly for more. But when it finally became clear that the Fool had nothing further to add, someone began laughing. Others soon joined in, and eventually everyone had at least a smile on his face.

Everyone except Count Henri of Hunenberg, and ironically, the Fool himself.

Leopold dismissed the marshals and lords and they wasted no time in retiring to their appointed rooms within Habsburg Castle. Within minutes, only Leopold and Klaus remained in the council room.

"You disapprove of my plan. I can see that. Admit it. Tell me what is on your mind, Klaus."

"You split our forces by sending Count Henri to attack from the Brunig Pass."

He paused, and would have been content to leave it at that, but Leopold waved for him to continue. So Klaus grunted, and pushed on. "He does not command many soldiers. I agree. But the ones he has are good fighting men, and well disciplined. He has got men that even fought against the heathen of Outremer. Next to the Sturmritter, they are our best soldiers. I would rather it be Henri's men at my back than those riffraff from Kyburg and Toggenburg."

Why Klaus, what an impassioned speech. For you. The last time I heard you string so many words together, I was seven, and you had just caught me sticking a handful of crushed glass under father's saddle blanket.

"Good. If even you, a man who has been at my side for my entire life, cannot see what I am up to then chances are no one else does either," Leopold said.

Klaus squinted and the flesh of his eyelids bunched up, making his eyeballs all but disappear. Leopold could not help thinking how it made him look like a newborn babe. Albeit, a large, hairy one with very little patience for fast-talking princes.

"You are right, of course," Leopold said. "Henri's men are excellent. It is Henri himself I find fault with. You see, I simply do not trust that he will do what I tell him. He has a perverse sense of honor and I think it could come to haunt him someday."

"If you keep sending everyone away you do not trust, your army is going to get very small, very fast," Klaus said.

Leopold chuckled. "Truer words were never spoken. Fortunately, we only need to keep this force together until the day after tomorrow."

"Yes, my lord. And I for one will not be sad to see it disband."

"Oh, come now, Klaus. Enjoy it while you can. Did you find a suitable gathering ground south of Zug?"

"Aye, my lord. A farmer's field, about an hour south of the town. From there we will be able to form up into ranks and march into Schwyz."

"Does this farmer know what we intend to use his land for?"

"Damn rights. My lord."

"Excellent," Leopold said.

"And I told him to not be hiding any of his cows either, because I counted them when I was there."

"You need not have done that," Leopold said.

"The men will be hungry. We may need them all," Klaus said.

"Yes, yes. I realize that. But what I mean is, we will never be at that farmer's field."

A grin spread across Leopold's thin lips. He waited for Klaus to speak, but the old soldier just stood there, his eyeballs retreating further and further into the back of his head.

"Do you know why we are not going to use that field?" Leopold asked.

"It was a ruse. You wanted a mouthy farmer to tell everyone that we would be there."

"Precisely."

"But we will not be there," Klaus said.

"You are much better at this than you look."

Leopold walked back to the clay model of the lands surrounding Schwyz. He pointed to the road running south from Zug all the way to the village of Schwyz.

"As far as the farmer knows, and I am sure far more people are aware of it by now, our army will spend the night in Zug. Then, early the next morning we set out for Schwyz. We stop at this cooperative peasant's farm, break our fast, check equipment, form up into ranks and then charge the Schwyzers' little mud walls they have erected to protect their precious lands. Correct?"

"That is… or… was the plan, my lord?" Leopold gave Klaus a moment. It was not that he thought him to be a stupid man. Far from it. Leopold had been witness to, and the benefactor of, some very well thought out plans that the old veteran had concocted entirely on his own. But he was a plodder, and like most plodders, did not handle change well.

When Leopold saw the light flicker in Klaus's eyes, he continued.

"When we leave Zug, we will not go south. We will go east until we reach the far side of Lake Aegeri. Then we turn south, and take the paths below Morgarten."

"Morgarten?"

Leopold nodded. "The Schwyzers have been busy little builders, stacking up their wooden palisades and mud walls. They have managed to create a meager line of defenses that stretches from the Great Lake all the way to the western shore of Lake Aegeri. But that is where it ends."

"Bah, we would only lose a few men taking those stick walls," Klaus said. He had seen some of them and was not impressed.

"But why lose any? For every Austrian knight that falls off his horse and dies, years from now, there will be some ragged child sitting on the mud floor of his hut, listening to his grandfather regale him with tales of how he killed an honest to god nobleman."

Klaus shrugged. He saw the sense in Leopold's plan, but clearly did not care what tales might be told after he was gone.

"But no one is to know any part of this plan until we are on the road and headed east out of Zug. Is that understood?"

"Yes, my lord."

It was simplicity in action, really. A scheme as old as violence itself. Make your opponent look somewhere and then run around behind him and slit his throat.

Leopold felt his eyes growing heavy. He sensed he would sleep well tonight.

He waited a full hour after he heard the men leave and the massive door slam shut. He had almost dozed off twice, but had kept from doing so by biting his cheek. The pain reminded him of what was at stake.

He knew he was granted certain liberties and privileges because of who he was, and who his allies were. But he was under no illusion that any of that would save him from Leopold's wrath. The Duke would not let all his preparation go to waste. If he knew someone other than his trusted Klaus had even an inkling as to what he planned, that man would not see another sunrise.

So, he breathed, and waited, and ordered his limbs to stop cramping. The cold from the flagstones pressing up against his back had stopped bothering him long ago. When he finally tested his muscles by rolling onto his side, blood seeped into all the unused parts of his body.

It burned. He gritted his teeth and welcomed the discomfort, for it meant he was alive. This too reminded him of what was at risk.

When he was ready, he flipped the skirting of the strategy table aside and rolled out from under it. In the darkness, he could still make out the shapes of clay mountains and hills upon the miniature landscape. One mound, in particular, stood out.

Morgarten.

As quietly as he could he walked to the door and, holding his breath, he eased it open enough to glimpse into the lighted hallway. Seeing no one, he slipped from the room.

The entire time, the bells on his shoes made not a sound.

Sir Henri of Hunenberg sat up in his bed. It was blacker than a pit of tar in his room, but he had no trouble wrapping his fingers around the dagger handle hanging off one bed post. He withdrew the blade silently and stared into the darkness.

A soft rapping came once again from the door.

Someone was... knocking? At this hour?

The tapping came again. This time it had a playful rhythm to it. Henri growled and threw back his blankets. He fumbled in the dark for his night robe. He tied it about his waist, thrust the dagger through his belt, and then made his way to the hearth. He blew a small flame back to life, enough to light a candle, and then went to the door. He unlatched it and eased it open partway, keeping his foot lodged firmly behind its corner. He had to hold his own candle up to see who was there, for the hallway was shrouded in darkness and his late night visitor carried no light of his own.

"You? I do not find this entertaining. What—"

The Habsburg Fool held his finger to his lips. His white painted face stood out in the flickering candlelight like that of a ghost. "Night is the best time to visit a Knight, my lord. May I come in?" His voice was little more than a whisper.

"What do you want?"

"Oh, I cannot tell you all of that." The little man leaned against the door jamb and traced curved outlines with his finger onto the heavy wooden door. "But I can tell you more than enough to make you happy you invited me into your room." He began humming quietly to himself, turning his attention back to the door and the finger artwork that only he could see.

Henri cursed, threw back the door, and beckoned the simple man inside.

CHAPTER 22

SERAINA STOOD AT the forest's edge, on the outskirts of Zug, and gazed out over a vast sea of soldiers erecting thousands of tents. Darkness was less than an hour away, so there was an urgency to their activities that gave the scene a frantic, disorganized appearance. She could have been standing right in their midst, instead of hidden in the shadows of a giant oak, and no one would have noticed her.

Above the shouts of men and the sounds of horses, far away, in the mountains above and to the south, she could hear the deep notes of alphorns as Noll's lookouts relayed messages from peak to peak. She wondered how long it would take for Thomas to hear the same notes she was listening to right now. How many horns would it take to pass on the alarm?

Seraina sensed something behind her. Relief and anger flowed through her, competing to see which would overcome the other.

"Hello Gildas."

Seraina did not turn around, but she heard the old druid exhale. After a moment he came to stand with her and share in the shadows of her tree. He wore a nondescript gray cloak, not his usual white one. It allowed him to blend into his surroundings more easily, Seraina thought, but it had not hidden him from her.

"There was a time when I could surprise you whenever I wished," Gildas said.

"And there was a time when I knew I could trust you to tell me the truth," Seraina said. She looked at her mentor, but he turned away from her and stared at the army setting up camp in the distance.

"Tell me you did not know Thomas was the Catalyst," Seraina said. She had meant it to come out sharp and scolding, but instead, to her ears, she sounded like a little girl. Still, it seemed to have the desired effect, for Gildas flinched at her words, and when he looked at her, his eyes overflowed with regret.

"I suspected, my child. Nothing more."

"Why did you not tell me? You should have said something before… before…"

Gildas took one of her hands in both of his and turned to face her. "I could not, Seraina. For I could have just as easily been wrong and *you* could have been right. I wanted to say something, I truly did. But to do so could have caused an unraveling of the Weave, with dire consequences neither one of us could have predicted."

"And what of this?" Seraina pointed to the Habsburg army, thousands of men strong, spreading out before them as they spoke. Cooking fires were beginning to pop up like fireflies in the night. "Perhaps this is one of the dire consequences of which you speak."

She looked at Gildas. "This could be a war of my own creation. What if this is not the time for the Helvetii to fight back? Perhaps my people were meant to go into hiding and wait for another hundred years. If I have misread the Weave, thousands will die tomorrow and their blood will all be on my hands."

Seraina looked out at the fires again and tears broke free from both of her eyes. "I could not live with that," she said.

Gildas stepped in and put his arm around her shoulders.

"I too have misread the Weave, and you will again before this life is finished. No one can be expected to see all Her patterns, but do not be so quick to doubt your abilities. And besides. An occasional misreading of the Weave can have wonderful results."

He turned her head toward him and wiped her tears with his finger. "I think Thomas Schwyzer, Catalyst or not, would agree with me on that one."

Seraina rapped the old druid in the chest with the back of her hand. "How can you joke at a time like this?"

"Jokes should be strictly reserved for times like these," Gildas said, smiling. "Now, come here. Give an old man a hug and then we had best be moving on. Time is short."

Seraina made a show of resisting, but truth be told, there was nothing she wanted more. She would have stayed wrapped in the warmth of the old druid's arms for much longer, but he finally broke the embrace.

"It is time, Seraina."

"To the Mythen, then," she said, wiping her eyes once more.

Gildas nodded. "You go ahead. Someone must see that Thomas knows Leopold has reached Zug. I will stop by to warn him and then meet you on the mountain."

Seraina frowned. "I heard the alphorns, so I am sure they know by now."

Gildas nodded, knowingly. "You are most likely right. But since it is only an hour out of my way, I would like to make sure. Now go. The others will be waiting."

CHAPTER 23

IT WAS MID-AFTERNOON and Thomas was in his tent when the alphorns began. Seconds later, Noll ducked his head inside.

"You hear them?" Noll asked.

"How could I not," Thomas said. "What do they mean?"

"Leopold has reached Zug with a force eight thousand strong. Three thousand of them mounted."

Thomas nodded. It was no worse than they had been expecting. The Confederate forces numbered just over eleven hundred, with no cavalry to speak of. But Thomas had confidence in their defenses. The men had worked tirelessly at their drills. They would make Leopold's army bleed, of that he had no doubt. Whether or not it would be enough, that was another question.

An alphorn sounded again in the distance, and Noll looked in its direction.

"What do we do?"

"Make our rounds as usual. Check on the men, then eat a good meal and go to bed as early as possible."

"That is it?"

Thomas shrugged. "We have done all we can. The waiting is over. We are in God's hands now."

It was an hour past midnight when one of the Rubin brothers woke Thomas. He spoke in an urgent whisper.

"Sir, you should come to the front wall."

He could not tell whether it was Sepp or Marti, but Thomas knew neither one of them excited easily. He shrugged off his blanket and convinced his sleep-stiffened joints to get him on his feet. Without pressing the young man for further details, he followed him to the front gate of the wooden palisade.

Ruedi, Anton, and the other Rubin boy were already there, standing on the narrow ledge built halfway up the wall. They all stared at something in the darkness beyond. Thomas glanced at the brother walking beside him, and again at the one on the wall. He still had no idea who was who. When Anton saw Thomas approach, he hopped off the ledge to give Thomas room to climb up.

"What is it?" Thomas asked, as he stepped up the three split-log stairs to the ledge.

"A rider," Anton said from below. "Probably their advance scout come to survey the defenses."

"Evening, Cap'n," Ruedi said as Thomas slid in between him and the Rubin boy. The bearded man had rested his war bow between two of the sharpened poles used to build the palisade. The string was drawn, and a black bolt sat in its groove, waiting to be unleashed. Ruedi's fingers tapped the stock of the weapon tenderly. "Just say the word, and we can all go back to sleep."

At first, Thomas saw nothing. There was only a sliver of moonlight, but someone had already extinguished the nearby torches on their side of the wall, so he was able to separate out the shape of a man and horse from the darkness of the forest.

"He is too far out," Thomas said. "What is your count?"

Ruedi nodded. "The man knows his ranges. But I figure I

could find him with six of every ten bolts. Nine of ten if you just want the horse."

Thomas shook his head. "Hold, for now." *Six of ten* was a very long distance in Ruedi's measuring scale. The scout would not get much useful information from that far out. Especially, on a dark night such as this.

"How long has he been there?"

Ruedi nodded toward the brother. "He spotted him first. Rubin?"

Apparently, Ruedi still could not tell the brothers apart either.

"At least fifteen minutes, by now," the boy said.

"Any sign of a flag? Maybe he has come to offer terms," Anton said.

Thomas was just about to say that he would not be accepting any terms offered in the cover of darkness by Leopold, when Ruedi nudged his elbow and pointed at the shadow on the road.

"Here we go," Ruedi said.

The figure began walking his horse toward them, its hooves echoed off the hard packed road, carrying far in the stillness of the night. He nudged his horse into a trot, and the echoes sounded like a drum roll.

"That is no messenger pony," Ruedi said. "The man rides a destrier." He hefted his crossbow and placed it against his shoulder.

The black figure's horse broke into a gallop and both horse and rider began to emerge from the night and take form. He sits the saddle well, Thomas thought, just as the man let go of his horse's reins and raised a crossbow to his shoulder.

"He is attacking!" the Rubin boy said.

Ruedi sighted down the length of his war bow, following

the motion of the man and horse barreling toward them. They were almost within normal crossbow range now. Thomas scoured the woods, looking for others. But there was no one. What could he possibly hope to accomplish by attacking the palisade single-handedly? A young knight trying to make a name for himself? Thomas had certainly seen men do madder things.

"Cap'n...?"

Just as he was about to tell Ruedi to put him down, Thomas realized the man was not wearing armor. There was no glint of metal anywhere on him, and he shifted around much too easily on top of his war horse.

"Hold," Thomas said. "Get your head down, Rubin." He decided he liked Ruedi's efficient naming method for the brothers. The boy crouched over, but kept one eye high enough to see above the wall.

Still at full gallop, the attacker sighted down his crossbow, and, raising himself slightly in his stirrups to steady his aim, fired. The bolt thudded into the main gate of the palisade, and sent vibrations through the wood to where they stood. As soon as he let the shot go, he wheeled his charger around and galloped back into the night. Like the man, the hoof beats soon receded beyond the senses of everyone standing at the wall.

"Rubin," Thomas said. "Get me that bolt."

The boy did not move, but kept staring over the wall into the darkness. Thomas was about to tell him again, when he heard someone throw off the crossbar on the gate and pull it open. He leaned out over the wall and saw the other Rubin boy digging at the head of the crossbow bolt with his knife.

Maybe tomorrow he would figure out a way to distinguish between the two of them, but for now, Ruedi's system seemed to be working fine.

Seconds later, he came running back with the bolt in hand. Thomas jumped down and took it from him, then he and Anton looked it over in the light of a nearby torch.

"You think it might be a whistler?" Anton asked.

Thomas nodded, and held the bolt up to the light. "One that failed to whistle. Maybe a hastily constructed one." He found what he was looking for; he twisted the iron point and the head came off. The shaft of the bolt was hollow, and inside was a piece of parchment. He fished it out carefully with the tip of his dagger and held it under the torch. Now Ruedi and the two brothers also crowded around, craning their necks to get a better look.

The characters were slanted, the penmanship unskilled. Much like his own, really. It took him a couple of tries to fully understand what it meant. And when he finally did discern its meaning, he prayed he was wrong.

By the blood of Mary.

"What does it say?" Anton asked.

"Rubin! Bring Noll here. Now."

The two brothers looked at each other. "Which one of us, Sir?"

"Both! Carry him here if you must, but bring him now."

While he waited for Noll to show up, Thomas began arranging several lanterns and torches so that they bathed a wide circle of dirt in light.

"Someone get me another—"

"Lantern?" Gildas said. He held one out to Thomas on the end of his walking stick. "Will this one do?"

Thomas took a step back, and blinked. "Gildas? Where did you come from?" He immediately cast his eyes over the area behind the old man.

"She is not there, Thomas Schwyzer. You might as well

stop looking."

Thomas was about to ask who he meant, but something in the old man's eyes would not let the words come out.

"Where is she?" Thomas asked.

"Safe. Is that not enough?"

A thousand questions burned in his mind, but they would have to wait. For just then the boys came back with a puffy-eyed Noll Melchthal lagging behind.

"Sleep did not find me easily, this day, ferryman. But I was finally dreaming of soft hands and the most beautiful woman I have ever seen, and the next thing I know, Sepp and Marti's callused paws are shaking me like an apple tree."

Noll looked around and seemed to notice Gildas for the first time. "Who is the old fellow?"

"Some names are worth knowing, Arnold Melchthal. But mine is not one of those," Gildas said.

Noll glanced at Thomas.

"He is right. Ignore him for the time being. We have more important things to worry about," Thomas said.

Gildas nodded. "Agreed. Now, read us the message."

With everyone gathered around, Thomas unrolled the small parchment. "First, let me say that I believe this to come from a man well-known to all of us that served in Outremer. And while we have not always seen eye to eye in the past, I trust that he would not lead us astray. We must heed his words."

"Someone from the Levant? Who?" Anton asked.

"Sir Henri of Hunenberg," Thomas said.

Ruedi let out a whistle. "Henri? Is he still alive?"

Noll scrubbed his face with his hands. "Very much alive. And he rides against us under Leopold's banner. Go on. Read the note. Then we can decide whether or not to trust the man."

"It is direct and wastes no time, much like the man himself," Thomas said. He read it out loud then, though he had read it so many times to himself already, that he could have recited it from memory.

Thomas,

Beware the paths of Morgarten.

H.H.

Thomas looked first at Noll and then at Gildas. Noll's face was suddenly pale. Gildas stared at the moon and shook his head.

"Where *exactly* is Morgarten?" Thomas asked them both.

Noll cursed, and since he seemed to be the first to recover, Thomas turned to him. "It is a mountain range. Far to the east."

Thomas held out a long stick and pointed at the ground bathed in the orange light of lanterns. "Draw it," he said. "Mountains, roads, rivers, hills, and forests. I need to know everything."

Noll snatched the stick from Thomas's hand. "And you will. I may not understand the scrawl of monks, but I can read the lay of the land better than a man's face."

I believe you can. But whether or not it will be of any use, only God can decide.

The more Noll scratched in the dirt, the clearer Leopold's plan of attack became.

"Where is the last of our palisades?" Thomas asked.

"Here," Noll said, drawing an 'X'. "Just west of Lake Aegeri. To the east, on the other side of the lake, stands Morgarten. Leopold will march his army south, between Morgarten and Lake Aegeri. Here," Noll put his stick in an area south of the lake, "lies the town of Sattel. Just before Sattel the trees thin out and the land opens up. It would be the perfect location for Leopold to spread out his men and form up ranks."

Anton shook his head more with every scratch of Noll's stick. "From there he will be able to storm Schwyz, while bypassing every one of our defenses." A knife found its way into Anton's hand and he threw it at the palisade wall. It hit with a thump and quivered in the wood. "All these walls we spent months building, all our drills—useless."

Ruedi shrugged. "Gave us something to do, I suppose. Better than standing around waiting."

Noll pointed at the southern shore of the lake. "Normally, this area would be too marshy to march an army through—," he said.

"But not in late fall," Thomas said, finishing Noll's thought. *Leopold had put off his attack until now because he had been purposely stalling. Waiting for his bridge to form.*

Noll nodded. "The ground has already begun to freeze some nights. It will be hard and dry."

They had all been deceived, but none felt the blow harder than Thomas.

Leopold had disguised himself as a brash, overconfident general who favored a direct assault, where his overwhelming numbers would give him the advantage. And Thomas, seeing no further than Leopold had wanted him to, fell for it. He clung to his first impressions of the Duke as a young man of privilege, with little military experience, because that was the only advantage he could find in a hopeless war. He had eagerly accepted the notion that the Austrian army's weakness was its leader, when, in truth, Leopold was its greatest strength.

Thomas had underestimated the enemy. And now all those that depended on him were about to pay the Devil's toll.

As Noll kept adding to the landscape around the mountain of Morgarten, Gildas placed his hand onto Thomas's shoulder.

"You could not have known," he said, his voice carrying no further than Thomas's ears.

He refused to look at the old druid, or even acknowledge his words, but something in them, or his touch, quieted his fears enough for him to think. While staring at the dirt map, he felt a slim hope emerge. He took the stick from Noll's hand.

"We must attack them as they are stretched along the shore of the lake, where they have no room to maneuver. If we hit them hard enough, we could drive them into the waters where their own armor will do most of our work for us," Thomas said.

Anton crossed his arms and arched an eyebrow at Thomas. "Charge an army that will most likely outnumber us seven-to-one? And that would be seven *soldiers* to every *farmer*."

"It could work," Ruedi said. "If we come down off those hills and hit them in the flank like that."

The Rubin brothers perked up and glanced at one another. Thomas could feel the hopelessness, which had surrounded them all only seconds before, begin to lift like a morning fog.

"I have to kill that plan before it goes any further," Noll said. He held out his hand and Thomas surrendered the stick. "Lake Aegeri is very small. And very far. Leopold will march from Zug at first light, meaning even if we leave right now, the bulk of Leopold's army would already be well past the shores of the lake by the time we arrived."

He made one last, definitive 'X' between Schwyz and the lower end of the lake. "They would catch us here, out in the open, with not a rock to hide under. Leopold's knights would ride over us like a field of wheat."

Noll put the tip of his stick into the flame of a torch. He pulled it out and watched it burn. "There simply is not enough time," he said. He blew out the tiny flame and a delicate column of smoke rose into the air.

The fog was back. Someone cursed.

But Thomas was not yet ready to give up on his plan. "What is this here?" He pointed to a mark on Noll's map.

"A fork in the road," Noll said.

"Where does this other road go?"

Noll drew again with the stick. "It is the old road to Sattel. No one uses it much any more because it is in such poor shape and takes twice as long to reach the town."

"Is it still passable?" Thomas asked.

"I believe so," Noll said. "A small hamlet, called Schafstetten, is located here, so I imagine they still use it. But they would be the only ones that I can think of. At any rate, it is little more than a rough path, so we will only lose time by taking it."

"But how much would it slow down a large army?" Thomas asked. "If we blockade the main road and force Leopold to take the old one, would it give us enough time to get our men into position on the slopes above the lake?"

"Possibly, but we do not have the time or the numbers, Thomas. First, we would need to create an impassable barricade, which is no easy matter. Then we would need to get a sizable force to Schafstetten to hold back the Austrian advance until the rest of our army can get into place. They would be on open ground and unprotected."

Gildas stepped into the lantern-lit circle and stood right on top of Noll's map. He spoke directly to Thomas, as though he were the only one present.

"The plan is a good one. But no need to waste your men

creating a barricade. Leave that to me."

The men cast questioning glances all around.

"Uh, you are standing on my stick…" Noll said.

"The time for scratching in dirt is over, Noll Melchthal," Gildas said.

"Who the Devil are you?" Noll asked, raising his voice.

"He is a friend of Seraina's," Thomas said.

"Oh. Well, that explains a few things, but—"

"Can you really do it?" Thomas asked Gildas. "Erect a barricade by yourself?" *I am mad to even be asking.*

The old man nodded.

"Are you sure? I need to know for certain."

"Trust. That is all you truly need, Thomas Schwyzer. Nothing else," Gildas said.

Thomas let out a deep breath and stared at Gildas. Five thousand more men is what I really need, he thought.

CHAPTER 24

SERAINA CLIMBED IN total darkness. Eventually, the sun appeared upon the horizon, but its presence provided little comfort. In fact, she felt the lightening landscape was only time's way of mocking her.

She resisted the urge every few steps to twist and look over her shoulder far below in the direction of Zug. She knew she was too far away to see the Austrian army's base, but that certain knowledge did little to lessen her need to look. They would march soon, and weave their way through the mountain roads on their way to rid the land of the Helvetii. How many of her people could possibly survive?

She drove the thought from her mind, and instead focused on putting one foot in front of another. Her thighs burned, her calves cramped, and the elevation change was proving a challenge for her lungs. But she knew she must press on, for the others would be waiting. They would need her strength.

Finally, after what seemed like two eternities, Seraina stood upon the summit of the Greater Mythen. She sucked in full mouthfuls of the thin air and turned in a slow circle, gazing in awe at the land below, with all its secrets revealed through the majesty of the mountain.

A tremor ran through her body and her eyes glistened

with tears. There was power here; ancient and undisturbed for hundreds of years perhaps, but nonetheless it was here. She could feel it in the air, smell it in the thin layer of dirt dusting the solid rock beneath her feet.

Unlike the Greater Mythen's neighboring mate, this mountain had no trees on its summit; only rocks and scrub, and in its center a lone Christian cross three men tall. It was formed from two peeled logs, as thick around as her waist, notched and lashed together with cracked leather straps.

Seraina marveled at the willpower of whoever had hauled the logs up from the tree-line. It must have been a grueling and dangerous trip. But Christians were never ones to back down from the impossible. Thomas had taught her as much. They would have sensed the natural power in this place, just as the druids did thousands of years ago.

There were only a handful of the Old Religion's sacred sites left in the world, to the best of Seraina's knowledge, that did not have a church or cross built upon some ruins of a long forgotten people. Why should the fate of this place play out any different?

But those were concerns for another day. Another time. As of this moment, the past was not yet dead. The Helvetii were not just another memory, like so many others had become. Seraina swore that she would not let her people be washed away by the sands of time. Not while she yet lived.

With that vow upon her lips, Seraina walked toward the cross, and the twelve white-robed figures that surrounded it.

✧ ✧ ✧

Leopold had been in his armor for less than half a day and already it chafed his neck and hips. He could not wait to get out of it. When this day was over, he swore he would not don it again.

What was the point anyway?

He had no intention of being anywhere near the battle, if there even was one. The leather collars dangling from his horse's saddle were for show. Nothing more. The thought of trying to slip a strap around a sweating, bleeding, Schwyzer repulsed him to no end. Although, perhaps he could attach a line to his horse and drag the peasants behind. That would be good for morale when they entered Zug on their return trip.

Far away, the sound of another mountain horn called out. Two long, mewling notes, like a calf calling for its mother. The horns had been sounding all morning. Ever since they set out from Zug. Leopold closed his eyes and shook his head, which was beginning to ache.

When he looked up he saw a man. A very old man with white hair. Preoccupied with his thoughts, he had not realized that Klaus had brought the column to a halt. He had one hand on the bridle of Leopold's horse.

"What is this?" Leopold asked.

"It is an old man blocking the road," Klaus said.

"Ah, thank you."

It was not actually the old man who blocked the road, but rather, it was the score of felled trees crisscrossing it that made the way impassable. The old man just happened to be sitting atop that pile.

The old man wore a dull, colorless robe that may have been brown at one time. But his hair was white as bone and glistened when the sun's rays found it through the trees. He chewed on a long piece of grass and seemed to be completely unaware of the Austrians' presence.

✧ ✧ ✧

As Seraina approached the center of the Mythen, the white-robed figures encircling the cross began to chant. Seraina recognized it immediately. It was a lesser verse, called *A Greeting to the Weave*, and was a precursor for more powerful incantations.

One of the figures, an older woman, her blond hair heavily streaked with gray, broke away from the circle and stepped toward Seraina.

"Blessed be the Weave, daughter." She touched her forehead and her heart, and smiled at Seraina.

Seraina bowed her head and held her right palm over her womb. "Blessed be the knowledge of the Weave as passed through the Elders," she said.

"Do you remember me, child?"

"Of course, Elder Orlina. Gildas and I stayed with you often when I was young."

The woman placed her hands on Seraina's shoulders. "I should have known. You never forgot anything as a child. Why should that have changed?"

"Thank you for coming," Seraina said, her voice cracking.

Emotion swelled into the back of her throat. She looked at the circle of druids, the last of their kind, all come to help the Helvetii. As though they could read her thoughts, one by one, they turned and smiled at Seraina. They continued chanting. She recognized a few of the faces under the white hoods, but most were unknown to Seraina. The Weave only knew how far they had traveled to be here.

"Thank you…" Seraina said again.

Orlina shook her head. "Those who do the bidding of the Weave require no gratitude. We do what we do so that life can go on."

"Even though none of you are Helvetii?"

"We are all of the Old Blood, Seraina. We are all Celts. And today," she fanned her arm in the direction of the druid circle, "we shall all be Helvetii."

The chanting suddenly stopped. A cloud passed over the sun and a shiver that began in Seraina's stomach fluttered out through every limb.

"Come," Orlina said. "It is time to awaken the Mythen. We will need your strength, as you will have need of ours."

Orlina took Seraina's hand and led her to the edge of the circle. The druids there spread out to allow them room. Seraina looked at the base of the cross for the goat, for a ritual of this magnitude would need a sacrifice. But there was no tethered animal. Puzzled, she looked at Orlina.

The older woman pursed her lips and tried to smile, but her eyes crinkled with sadness. She gripped Seraina's left hand tighter, and the man on Seraina's other side took her right hand in his own. The other druids, likewise, grasped one another's hands, making a human chain around the cross. All save for two men opposite Seraina. They stepped aside, and Oppid padded silently into their center.

What is he doing here?

"Oppid!" The wolf looked at Seraina when she called his name. His golden eyes flashed and he whimpered once.

By Ardwynna's Word, no....

Seraina tried to shake her hands free, but the druids tightened their grip. She looked at Orlina, who only shook her head and stared at Oppid. "Orlina, no, please…"

Orlina closed her eyes, and her chest heaved with a heavy breath. "The Mysts will not come without a great sacrifice, my child. Balance must be maintained."

Oppid sat down at the base of the cross, next to a large, flat rock that someone had put there for a very specific purpose.

The druids began to sing. The melody slow and mournful.

"No! There must be some other way. Not Oppid… please, Orlina."

This time it was the older druid's voice that cracked.

"No, Seraina. *Not* Oppid."

Then Orlina's words failed her, and all she could do was thrust her chin out to point in Oppid's direction. Tears streamed down her cheeks. She shook her head and began to sing. Her voice quavered, but soon it was picked up and carried by the sounds of the others.

Seraina turned her head, and for the first time, noticed what was placed on the flat rock at Oppid's side. Folded ever so neatly was the white robe of a druid, and placed next to it was a walking stick. A peeled piece of oak, crooked and polished smooth with memories.

She screamed, her legs gave out, and she tried to curl into a ball. But Orlina and the other druid holding her hands would not let her fall. She stood there and cried, her body writhing, and still they would not release their hold, or let her fall.

Oppid howled.

Seraina answered the wolf with a scream. And sometime later, still wracked with sobs, Seraina began to sing.

✧ ✧ ✧

"You there!" Landenberg shouted. "What happened here? Who cut down those trees?"

The old man looked up and his eyes went wide, as though he had, until that very moment, been oblivious to the fact that an army thousands strong was less than fifty paces away.

"You came!" he said, pushing himself to his feet.

"What are you talking about? Come down off there," Landenberg said.

The old man chewed on his blade of grass, then pulled it out of his mouth and stared at it for a moment before throwing it away. Then he began walking down off the pile of trees, without once crouching or reaching out to balance himself by grabbing a branch. In a few seconds he stood on the ground, next to the exposed roots of a giant oak, and beckoned to the men to come closer.

"It is against the King's Law to cut down that many trees," Landenberg said.

The old man stroked one of the soil-covered roots next to him. "Do these look like they were felled with an ax, Vogt Landenberg?"

"If you know who I am, then you must know who this is as well." He gestured toward Duke Leopold.

"I do. And I have a message for your Duke," the old man said.

"Very well," Leopold said. "Go ahead. Tell me what you will."

The old man shook his head. "It is for your ears only, I am afraid."

Once again he gestured with his hand for Leopold to come near.

Leopold had already nudged his horse forward a couple steps before he felt Klaus's arm on his own. "My lord, it could be some form of trap."

Leopold blinked once and looked at Klaus. He was surprised that the two of them were already twenty feet away from Landenberg, Franco Roemer, and the other captains of his army. The old man beckoned again.

"Nonsense," Leopold said. "Look at him. He is even older than you. But accompany me if you must."

Leopold walked his horse forward. The old man smiled

and began taking slow steps toward the two men. A strong wind blew at the old man's back, whipping his hair and beard about his face. He closed his eyes, and his lips began to move. Something told Leopold to stop, and he yanked back on his horse's reins.

"My lord? Is something—,"

The old man's arms shot up toward the sky and the very air around Leopold seemed to scream. His horse reared up on its hind legs, its nostrils flaring in fear, and Leopold felt himself catapulted out of the saddle. He hit the ground hard and the air burst forth from his lungs.

He could hear laughter. A mad, gleeful cackle that ushered forth from the old man's lips. He stood there pointing and laughing at the Duke, while the wind swirled around the old man, plucking at his gray robe like dozens of giant fingers. Leopold pushed himself to his elbows. He wheezed and gasped, trying to coax even the smallest bit of life-giving air back into his body.

He became dimly aware of movement to his right. Klaus's horse ran by and mud from its hooves sprayed Leopold's face. The next thing he saw was the old man's head hitting the forest floor, the bloody stump of its neck picking up pine needles as it rolled. The laughter stopped and the woods went silent.

The headless body, however, remained standing with its arm raised and finger pointing at Leopold. Until Klaus yelled, and from his saddle, stretched out one of his long legs and kicked it over.

Klaus and several soldiers ran to the Duke, but Franco Roemer was already there, helping him sit up. Leopold's air returned, eventually, but the sunlight that had been streaming though the trees only minutes before, had deserted them completely. After a tense few minutes they had Leopold back in the saddle of a different horse. Leopold slapped at Klaus's hand as he attempted to steady his lord.

"Stop fussing over me! I am quite all right," Leopold said. He kicked his horse and began heading east, away from the deadfall.

The captain of the Sturmritter pulled up beside Klaus and asked, "What do we do with the old man?"

"Leave him to the wolves," Klaus said. Then he spurred his own mount ahead to catch up with Leopold.

CHAPTER 25

FRANCO FELT IT took forever for their long column to scramble over the poorly maintained road. Mountain streams regularly crossed their path, some of them so wide that Leopold would have to stop the entire column and send a scout on ahead to determine the safest point to cross. But finally, shortly after noon, the trees opened up, and they sighted the rebel forces.

Leopold signaled his army to a halt. Two mounted men waited in the middle of a lush, green field. One caught Franco's eye immediately, for he was dressed in a red tunic with the distinctive eight-pointed Hospitaller cross on his chest. Behind them, Franco could see a long line of men crowning a hill far in the distance. Their clothes and armor were the dull, motley assortment of grays and browns common in peasant armies, but Franco saw a few more of the bright red tunics amongst their number.

"What is a knight of Saint John doing here?" Franco could not stop himself from asking.

"That is no knight," Leopold said. "Only a pretender. A blasphemer dressed beyond his station. Pay him no mind, Sir Roemer."

That was easier said than done, Franco thought.

"Forgive me, my lord, but the Hospitallers are the Pope's holy soldiers. My men will have reservations, you understand."

Leopold turned on him. "They are no longer Hospitallers. The Order has discharged them all. They are deserters turned mercenary, and now they have sold their services to a rebel army. Tell your men that."

Leaving the column behind, Leopold, Franco, Landenberg, and Klaus trotted out to meet the two rebels.

Franco kept his eyes on the Hospitaller the whole time. He had never met one of the Black Knights in a tournament. He found himself wishing Leopold was wrong about this man being a pretender. The prospect of facing a Hospitaller knight on the field, especially one in his full red battle tunic, appealed to Franco's competitive spirit. A shiver went through his lance arm. It had been a long time since he had felt that sensation.

He watched the Hospitaller carefully as they approached. By the time they brought their horses to a stop in front of the two men, Franco felt he had a fair understanding of the man's abilities. He had no doubt the Hospitaller would prove a formidable opponent when his feet were planted on firm ground, but he was no horseman. His mount, a beautiful, spirited animal with the chiseled features of a true Egyptian breed, stamped its feet and threw its head around. The man was constantly jerking his reins, trying to keep the horse under his control.

"Hello Melchthal. I have been waiting for this day," Landenberg said, his lips settling into a twisted smile. He breathed noisily through his mouth, and Franco saw saliva spray through the cool air when he spoke.

The young rebel leader remained composed and did not reward the Vogt of Unterwalden with even a glance. Instead, he looked directly at Leopold. With no preamble, and certainly no respect for the fact he addressed a Prince of the Holy Roman Empire, he began to speak.

"These are our terms. Turn around and march back to your homes."

"You grossly overestimate your own worth if you think—," Leopold began.

"I am not finished. Before you leave, your men will drop all their weapons and equipment on the ground at their feet. We shall accept that as a toll for coming onto our land unannounced."

Leopold laughed and shook his head. "Still playing the part of a thief I see, eh Melchthal?"

The rebel kept speaking. His voice calm and detached. "You may keep your horses, so that your stink does not remain in our valley any longer than necessary. However, Berenger Von Landenberg must be turned over to us to be executed for reneging on his oath."

Franco started at the young man's direct words. He could not decide if he was brave or simply stupid beyond reason.

Landenberg was the first to respond. "That is *Sir* Landenberg, you whelp." He seemed to be more concerned about the rebel not mentioning his title rather than the fact the peasants wanted to execute him.

Leopold's lips spread into a thin line. "You have no idea how much I am going to enjoy this," he said. "Custom dictates I respond to your terms with a counter-proposal. Very well. These are *my* terms. Lay down your weapons and submit to be manacled by my slave handlers. You will be put to work in the quarries and mines until the Altdorf fortress has been rebuilt, to twice its original size, or until you die. Most assuredly, the latter."

It was the rebel's turn to laugh. "And you, Lord Leopold,

still playing the part of the tyrant?"

Leopold held up his index finger. "I am not finished," he said, smirking. "Your wives and daughters will be given to my men as a just reward for faithful service to their Duke. They may submit quietly, if they prefer, but to be honest, my troops would much rather take the women against their wills. They are fighting men after all. And is not a savage raping the only way to cool the heat in such a man's veins?"

Leopold cast his gaze on the man at Noll's side. "How do you prefer to take your women, Thomas? Willing, or defiant until the end?" He looked around, mockingly. "And where is your witch by the way? I do look forward to seeing her again. It will be nice to catch up where we left off."

The Hospitaller's eye twitched, and because he had a long scar at its corner, the movement seemed to tug up one corner of his mouth. But he most definitely was not smiling. "She is far away from here. And safe. Which is more than I can say for your blasphemous manuscript."

Leopold's face clouded over. His horse turned its ears back, feeling his master's rage, but the Duke was quick to regain his composure. He pointedly ignored the Hospitaller and began to exchange more unpleasant words with Melchthal. Franco took the opportunity to look behind the men at the lay of the land and the opposing force. The rebels in the distance were spread out. Probably to give an exaggerated impression of their number. Franco estimated no more than fifty men stood on top of the hill. Perhaps that many again trying to hide behind it. Did they really think they were fooling anyone? They were armed with pole weapons of some sort, and the postures of more than half of them betrayed that they had seen the passage of too many years.

What were they armed with? Homemade spears? Pitch

forks?

Franco shook his head. There would be little chance for glory in this battle. Something about the rebels' left flank caught his eye and he craned his neck to get a better view.

Just then the Hospitaller's horse whinnied, shuffled sideways, and then reared up on two legs. His master cursed and fought to regain control. Klaus spurred his mount forward in front of Leopold and had his sword half drawn, thinking his lord was under attack. However, it quickly became apparent that the rebel had simply lost control of his fiery mount. Klaus spit on the ground and backed his horse away. Franco was the first to speak once everyone relaxed somewhat.

"You have a fine animal," he said to the Hospitaller.

The man looked at Franco. His dark eyes stood out against his long facial scar like coal on snow. He nodded once, but offered no words.

"I would have you know that I intend to claim him when this battle is over. However, I will allow his return to you, if you can afford his ransom. Provided you are still alive, of course."

For some reason that Franco could not understand, Leopold found his claim to be humorous. He laughed, leaning low in his saddle.

The scar-faced man cleared his throat. "If you have my horse, there will be no ransom paid. For I will be quite dead."

There was something about the way the man spoke that made Franco want to take a closer look at him. There was no false bravado in his words, nor did he utter an idle threat, like so many men tended to do in order to quell their own fears. The Hospitaller's horse fidgeted some more, shifting from side to side, like he knew he was the topic of discussion.

"If it should happen otherwise," Franco began. "And you

find yourself holding the reins of my own destrier, I trust that you will afford me the same opportunity to buy him back."

When the Hospitaller spoke, his words were slow and deliberate. "We both know that will never happen. One way or another."

Leopold rolled his eyes and sighed. "If you two are finished sniffing out one another, I would like to call an end to these negotiations."

He performed an elaborate mocking bow aimed at the rebels. "It seems we have reached an impasse. Regrettably, the only alternative is war. Enjoy the afternoon, gentlemen." He squinted at the thick cloud banks rolling in. "Pity, it looks like rain."

Without waiting for anyone to respond, he wheeled his horse around and galloped back toward his army. Landenberg's face broke into a greedy grin. He raised his arm and pointed at the rebel leader, and then jammed his heels into his horse's side to take off after Leopold. Klaus, ignoring everyone, eased his mount away and walked after them, like he was in no hurry to be in anyone's company, friend or foe alike.

"I look forward to meeting you on the field," Franco said. He gave the Hospitaller a curt nod and trotted back toward his place at the head of the Sturmritter.

✧   ✧   ✧

"I think that went quite well," Noll said.

Thomas scowled as he reined his horse around. "What are you talking about? You were supposed to stall. Use up as much time as possible. Not send them galloping out of here, enraged like a kicked nest of hornets!"

"Well, maybe you should have done some talking then. For my first war negotiation I think I did very well."

"Very well? You virtually demanded they surrender and allow you to execute an Austrian noble in front of them. What kind of terms are those?"

"What has gotten into you? You are even more miserable than usual. Or is this just how you act before every battle?"

Thomas pushed Anid into a gallop. They did not have time to stand about arguing. Noll shouted something at him and followed close behind.

Though it pained him to admit, Noll was right about one thing. Thomas was more miserable than usual. And that was because he had met Franco Roemer. He had looked into the Austrian's eyes and where he had hoped to see a cocky, self-absorbed knight, he had seen a leader. An intelligent, experienced warrior with the most skilled knights in the western world under his command.

He leaned over and whispered into Anid's ear. The stallion leaped forward leaving Noll and his mountain pony far behind. He hit the bottom of the hill at lancing speed, but halfway up even Anid could no longer maintain a full gallop.

Good, Thomas thought. As long as they stayed at the very top of the rise, even the Sturmritter could not hit them with a full charge. Still, he wished he had had time to dig in cavalry pits and stakes to further slow them down and force them to break formation. But there was not enough time.

Time. The Devil's mistress. First, they could not get enough of it, and now, they had too much. How far away was the rest of his army? How long before they would arrive? How long could less than a hundred men hold back the might of the Holy Roman Empire? Was this really the best plan Thomas could have come up with?

Perhaps he could have done better. If only he had more time.

He topped the rise and his men opened up their ranks to let him through.

"Matthias!" Thomas called the boy to him as he jumped out of Anid's saddle. "You ride Anid and lead Noll's horse back to the men furthest away. Can you do that?"

"I could. But, Cap'n, I might miss the fighting."

"Then you better ride fast and run back even faster. And tell the men to double up on the horses."

The boy hesitated and glanced at the reins Thomas held out.

"That is an order, son. If you want to be part of this army, you must obey orders. Is that understood?"

"Aye, Cap'n!"

Matthias snatched the reins from Thomas's hand and was in the saddle before Thomas had to say another word.

"They will be here. I swear," Matthias said.

Noll finally appeared, and Matthias had his horse's reins before Noll's feet touched the ground. A second later he was galloping over the grassy slopes toward Schwyz, the soft, moist ground silencing the hoof-beats. Within seconds the mist enveloped both boy and horse and there was no sign that either had ever existed. The other horses had already been sent back. Thomas was well aware that four more men would make little difference, but knowing the boy would not be here when the fighting began, allowed Thomas to breathe a little easier.

Thomas stood at the bottom of the hill, the side furthest away from the Austrian army. He looked at his own forces: half were assembled on top the hill, in full view, and the other half crouched low behind its base. They had rounded up every last horse and mule available and rode here at full speed.

Eighty-nine mounts. Eighty-nine men. Handpicked by Thomas himself. Thomas had set quill to parchment yet again, and created another list. He glanced around him, seeking the Religion's red war tunics, and found his friends easily enough. Ruedi, Max, Urs, and Anton; they were the only survivors from the first list he had ever created. Both lists had started out with a similar number of names, and he could not help but wonder at the irony of it all.

Who was he to choose? Were the lists God's work, or the Devil's?

He closed his eyes and let out a deep breath. He reminded himself that on the other side of this hill, eight thousand Austrians wound their way toward them.

He felt a tap on his shoulder. Noll held out a water skin. "Better drink up," he said. "We might end up sweating a bit."

He grinned at Thomas, and more than a little surprised, Thomas found himself grinning back. Then Noll raised his voice so all the men could hear him. "That goes for everyone. If you have skins now would be the time to use them. Does not matter what is in them. No man in this army fights thirsty!"

Thomas took a long drink and was relieved that it was actually water, not wine. Cool, fresh water from one of the countless glacier-fed streams that quenched the landscape's thirst and kept the slopes covered in thick, green grass. Thomas thought of all the times he had gone thirsty over the years in the Holy Lands. Water was worth more than gold in Outremer. If he had possessed even a fraction of the water that now surrounded him, he would have been the richest man in the Levant.

He took one more drink and then he walked up the slope. Thomas took his spot between Anton and Max at the front of the square.

Seven men wide, seven men deep.

Behind him, in the second row next to Urs, Sutter called

his name. Thomas turned and Sutter held out Pirmin's great ax. Its heavy head glistened with the wetness of the fog. Through the small cross cut into its center, Thomas could see the outlying buildings of the small hamlet of Schafstetten. And far in the distance, although he could not see it, in his heart he felt the church of Sattel watching over them all.

"The big guy would be 'right pissed' if he missed out on this day entirely," Sutter said, his voice breaking ever so slightly.

Thomas took the ax. He was once again amazed at how light it felt in his hands. As he rotated the shaft in his grip, a sing-song Wallis accent sounded in his head.

"Do not fret none, Thomi. I would not make you carry it all by yourself."

The fog was building, and its moisture seemed to accumulate on Thomas's cheeks more than anywhere else. He drew a hand across his face and stared out at the enemy.

✧ ✧ ✧

"Captain Roemer!" Klaus called out.

Franco left his place at the front of the Sturmritter and trotted over to join Leopold, Klaus, and Landenberg.

"Your commands, my lord?"

"I want that hill with a single charge," Leopold said. "I see no reason to waste any time here."

"My thoughts exactly, my lord," Franco said.

"And I want my knights to be part of it," Landenberg said. He squished his helmet onto his head and gave it a slap, which made it ring. Steam poured out of the breathing holes in its long, metal snout.

Franco looked at Leopold. "With all due respect, the Sturmritter can do it alone, my lord. Perhaps Sir Landenberg's forces can ride them down as they run."

"Not bloody likely," Landenberg said.

"Stop it," Leopold said. "There will be more than enough Schwyzers to go around before the day is out. But remember this: each of your knights carries shackles enough for three men. Our goal is to get workers. We kill no more than necessary. Is that clear?"

"What about Melchthal?" Landenberg said.

"Yes, by all means kill him. And the Hospitaller as well. For that matter, kill every man who stands on that hill defying us. An example should be made. But stop there. Is that understood?"

Franco could not see Landenberg's face behind his mask, but when he spoke he could hear pure joy echo in his words.

"Perfectly, my Duke."

"Now, Captain Roemer. Take your force in for a frontal charge, but at the last, wheel around and take them in their left flank. I would like to see how quickly they can move their formation."

"Yes, my lord."

It was the exact strategy Franco had himself been considering. Of course he would never have presumed to say anything unless the Duke had asked for his input. The front of the hill was too steep for a cavalry charge, but the approach to the rebel's left flank was much less so.

"Landenberg. You will follow after Captain Roemer has crested the hill, and attack directly from the front. That should scatter them to the winds."

"Yes, my lord!"

It was a good plan. Franco was beginning to grow a healthy respect for Leopold's war skills. Perhaps he deserved the nickname people were calling him recently: the Sword of the Habsburgs.

"Today, gentlemen, we will teach these rebels what it means to defy God's Divine Order!"

Landenberg drew his sword and cheered. Other knights close enough to hear Leopold also let out some shouts and raised their weapons.

It was a good plan, Franco thought again. But as he stared back at the hill and saw the Hospitallers in their blood-red war tunics, he did not feel much like cheering.

✧ ✧ ✧

Seven men wide. Seven men Deep. To bide time, the square must hold.

Thomas watched the Sturmritter, perched atop their huge war horses, pull away from the vanguard. They came to a complete halt on open ground and remained motionless, like statues carved from mountains. Then, with their lances pointed straight up, they eased their mounts forward into a walk. Their timing and rhythm were impeccable; their movements exact copies of one another. Even the tall, blue feathers that crested each man's helmet seemed to sway in the wind to the same beat.

Thomas thanked God above that his forces commanded the high ground. Even still, it was intimidating to see such a perfect formation. A quick look at the men's faces around him, and Thomas knew his side was on the verge of losing this battle before it ever began.

He stepped out from the square and turned his back on the knights preparing to charge, and addressed his men.

"They are peacocks," he shouted. "Peacocks on horses, nothing more. They ride a fine show, but they cannot top this hill without their mounts stumbling. And once they do, their lances will be useless, and those plumed heads will be well within range of our axes."

He hefted Pirmin's ax into the air, and heard Urs let out a guttural holler. Max banged the flat of his sword against his own long-handled ax. They were used to these pre-battle pep talks. They knew the value of making noise to summon the battle furies and subdue fear. Fear that would otherwise rise up and consume even the bravest of men.

Anton whooped and other voices joined in.

Behind him, Thomas imagined the Sturmritter pushing their destriers into a trot. He did not look back.

"Those peacocks have come into our lands uninvited. Unwanted. And make no mistake, they mean to harm you and yours."

Thomas had to pause to let their shouts die down.

"Once they have killed you and me, they will march on Schwyz. After they have slaughtered your animals, burned down your homes, and raped your women, they will enslave anyone who manages to escape the initial butchering. Will you allow that?"

The men howled in outrage.

"Was any man here born to be a slave? Are you the fathers of slaves?"

"No!" Thomas clearly heard Sutter's voice over all others. Men slung the foulest of insults at the army before them, and screamed their defiance.

Thomas felt the ground shake with the approach of a hundred war horses. Still, he did not look back.

"I ask you again, because today you have a choice. Whereas tomorrow, you will not. Will you allow this?"

"NO!" The answer came as one deafening shout, as united as the Sturmritters' charge.

Thomas held up Pirmin's ax again and shouted, "And neither will I! God have mercy on their souls!"

The men went wild and waved their own weapons high in the air. Thomas turned in time to see the Sturmritter break into a gallop. They couched their lances, and as one, slowly lowered the deadly points until they were horizontal with the ground. Each man's knee brushed against the man's next to him. It was a perfect *conroi* in the making.

Thomas felt the earth tremble at his feet.

CHAPTER 26

ERICH SAT WITH his legs dangling over the edge of a small rock bluff. High above the Confederate army's position, he had a perfect view of the battlefield, so long as the clouds did not get any lower. Boots scraping on stone made him turn, and he saw the bald head of Reto push through the trees. He stopped well back from the cliff's edge, but tried to lean forward to get a better view.

That was the problem with men such as Reto, Erich thought. He wanted everything, but was willing to risk almost nothing to get it.

"Are the men in position?" Erich asked, turning back to the world far below.

"They are." Reto tipped a wineskin to his lips, swished the liquid around in his mouth, and then spit it onto the rocky ground to Erich's left. It stained the rocks there a rusty red. "But some of the men are grumbling. Been asking when they will get paid."

Erich pulled one leg up from the overhang and turned to look at Reto.

"You mean *you* have been wondering," he said. "Most of them have been with me long enough to know the answer to that question."

Reto took another drink as he stared back at Erich. "All right, then. I will not deny that. But I know I am not the only one."

"You will get your pay, along with everyone else. And the second you do, I want you gone."

"Some of the men might want to come with me," Reto said.

"You are welcome to any who do," Erich said.

He turned away and dropped his leg back over the ledge. As he did so, a fist-sized rock tumbled off into the abyss. He watched its long, silent descent until it disappeared from sight, and then Erich pushed himself to his feet. He stood there for a moment, with the tips of his boots hanging over the void, and watched as Leopold's cavalry began their charge.

It was time, he thought. Time to risk everything.

✧　✧　✧

As per Leopold's command, Franco led his men thundering straight at the hill. The men on top formed into a tight square and braced themselves for a head on attack that would never happen.

Franco raised his lance, pulled his destrier in a tight, right hand turn and galloped toward the enemy's left, curious about what he would see waiting for him behind the hill. Sure enough, as his mount started powering up the gentle slope to the side of the hill, a loosely formed mob of rebels appeared before him. They milled about, and seemed surprised to see the knights bearing down on them from this direction.

He released his reins and, guiding his horse with only his knees, pointed at the group on low ground. They would have to take this group first, and then climb the hill for the second. He shouted the command to change targets and, like a great flock of migrating birds, the Sturmritter adjusted their course without a single falter in the warhorses' strides.

"Lances!" Franco commanded. The knights' weapons came down once again, their iron-tipped points aimed straight ahead. The small group of rebels, who only seconds before appeared to be on the verge of fleeing, formed up into a square with what looked like short spears held before them.

The maneuver bothered Franco on some instinctual level. He remembered the Hospitaller, and his beautiful, but poorly trained mount. Why would a man ride a horse into battle that he could not control? Especially, a man trained by the Knights of Saint John. Some of the greatest horsemen in the world had come from their ranks.

The answer, of course, was he would not.

Franco reached up his hand and threw open his helmet visor.

It had been a diversion. The Hospitaller was drawing all eyes to him, because there was something he did not want Franco to see.

The men hiding behind the hill, perhaps?

The warhorses of the Sturmritter bore down on the rebels at full speed, their hooves tearing up great divots of the soft, grass-covered ground. The enemies' faces began to take shape. Franco flipped his visor back down. Impact was seconds away. Only thirty yards of grass separated the Sturmritter from their targets.

Thirty yards of grass that did not stand?

It was cut, and as Franco stared at it, very wet. As though brought there from somewhere else....

"Bog!"

Franco drove his legs back, commanding his horse to stop, but the animal's blood was up. It was bred for war, and once at full charge, stopping was the last thing on its mind. Desperate, Franco grabbed the reins and yanked on them, pulling his mount's chin to its chest. He slowed, but not much.

Several knights shot past Franco, and as soon as their horses' front legs sank into the mud, he heard a series of sickening cracks and whinnies of terror shot through with pain. The momentum of their mounts' rear ends carried them forward and over, spilling riders and horses everywhere. Packed so tightly together, there was little the knights following could do but trample their comrades, or try to leap from their saddles.

Franco fought to stay seated and save his horse from breaking its legs as it sloshed through three-foot-deep mud and over slippery rocks. He thought he was going to make it to solid ground, when an out of control knight speared his lance deep into his horse's flank. The horse fell, and rolled, with Franco still in the saddle.

He lay there thinking he should get up, but the mud was warm, comfortable, and a great weight was on his leg. He felt quite content to remain where he was.

Until he heard a scream. And another.

He turned his head toward the sound, just in time to see a peasant swing a long, heavy ax into the head of one of his men as he attempted to stand.

Unlike the others, no scream came from his lips.

✧ ✧ ✧

Thomas watched from the top of the hill as Noll's square charged the disoriented Sturmritter as they attempted to free themselves from the wetland marsh. Several were already on a firm piece of ground, and one of them blew a horn, summoning them all to that spot. They were recovering much faster than Thomas had anticipated. If enough of them managed to regroup, Noll would be in trouble. Thomas hated to give up the high ground so early in the battle, but the Sturmritter were far from finished.

"Square, left face!" Thomas shouted.

Every one of the forty-nine men lifted his ax to point at the sky and then pivoted to the left.

"Forward, slow."

As they began to walk, the first row lowered their axes to stomach height and the next row, slightly staggered from the row in front, aimed theirs slightly higher. The rest kept them pointed up.

"Three man front!"

The last three rows of seven men broke away from the square and ran to form a new front line beside the first. Thomas checked to make sure the line was straight, then he tightened his grip on Pirmin's ax.

"Forward. Full!"

Every single man let out a loud battle cry and the formation charged down the hill. They crashed into the knights, driving them back onto the marshy ground where their heavy armor became more hindrance than help.

Thomas pulled one of the few knights still mounted out of his saddle with the hook on the back of his ax and then speared him through the eye slits. He saw Sutter and one of the Rubin boys bring down another knight in a similar fashion. To his left, Urs exchanged blows with a knight covered in mud, but Thomas had to look away to bring his ax down onto a knight's arm as he attempted to crawl out of the marsh. Pirmin's ax slid into his armor's elbow joint and removed it cleaner than a surgeon's cleaver. He staggered back, screaming. A crossbow bolt appeared in his eye and he fell over.

Thomas looked for Urs again. He was gone, but a dead Austrian knight lay on the ground.

The screams became fewer, the sense of movement less. Men from Noll's square appeared, and Thomas knew the Sturmritter would not ride again. The thought saddened him, but that did not stop him from bringing Pirmin's ax down upon another one's head as he tried to crawl away.

His feet felt wet. Thomas thought he might be standing in blood, but when he looked down the earth was hidden by a thickening layer of mist.

Then it started to rain.

✧ ✧ ✧

Leopold's anticipation changed to confusion when he watched the Sturmritter go down. Then horror took over as he watched the two small squares of Schwyzers charge. A mist hugged the ground where they were, and blotted out some of the action, but the wind carried the screams of horses and men to his ears, leaving little doubt as to what was happening.

The Sturmritter, the finest knights in the known world, were being slaughtered to the man.

"God have mercy," Landenberg said.

Leopold turned on him. "Why are you still here?"

Landenberg did not seem to hear Leopold. He could not tear his eyes away from the axes rising and falling in the distance.

"Landenberg!"

"I, uh, I was waiting for Franco to appear on the hill. Only, he… never did."

"Get as many cavalry to the front as you can. We will hit them in the open, before they can climb back onto that hill."

Landenberg shook his head, his eyes still locked on the

dying men in the distance. A riderless Sturmritter warhorse, its eyes wide and nostrils flared, trotted past him looking for a new herd.

"Hornman!" Leopold called out and a young man ran to his side.

"Yes, my lord."

"Call up the rear guard cavalry as well."

The young soldier put his horn to his lips. The sound echoed all the way down the mile-long line of Habsburg forces.

Leopold took a deep breath and looked to where the rebels were reforming into squares.

"Now that you have sprung your trap, Thomas Schwyzer, let us see how you manage the rest of us."

CHAPTER 27

"FORM UP! FORM up!" Noll called out again.

So engrossed were his men with the grisly task of killing the last few armored knights flailing about in the marshland, that he had to run around and cuff several of them so that his orders registered. When they looked at him with eyes wild, but vacant, their blood-splattered features twisted, Noll hardly recognized them. He remembered Pirmin talking of how the battle furies could consume a man during times of war, and lend him strength. He watched the huge, but usually gentle, form of Hans Gruber run bellowing into mud up to his knees, grab a staggering knight by the plume on his helmet, and wrench his head around in a circle, throwing him back into the sucking muck from which he had just managed to free himself. He pinned the Austrian on his back with the butt end of his ax, and stomped on his helmeted head over and over, driving it deep below the water's surface. Gruber kept stomping long after the peacock feathers disappeared. Whether the man died from the crushing impact of the young man's blows, or drowned, Noll had no idea. But, he had long since ceased his struggles by the time Noll reached them.

"Gruber!"

He kept stomping until Noll shoved him from behind. The

young giant whirled around and Noll jumped back, not liking the way Gruber leveled his ax in his direction.

"Gruber, what is wrong with you? Form up!"

The big man blinked. Noll had to yell again before the man looked around sheepishly and, seeing half of his square already standing in the field, began wading through the mud to join them. Thomas's complete square stood there already. Noll saw Max and Urs, moving around the battlefield, shouting at members of Noll's square to form up ranks. Their red tunics made them clearly visible amongst the earth-covered dead and dying.

A minute later, Noll stood in the front line of his completed square. He could not remember the last time his lungs had worked so hard. But he felt strong and eager for whatever came next. Intermittent shouts and snarls erupted from his men telling him that they felt the same way.

Noll looked at the enemy for the first time since re-forming ranks. At least two hundred cavalry trotted toward them. Another five hundred milled about in a disorganized mass at the front of the army, trying to get into some semblance of attack formation. Behind them, tightly packed infantry, and more mounted knights stretched along the road and disappeared around the bend.

"God Almighty," Noll whispered.

"Ruedi, Max," Thomas shouted. "Take up rover positions on Noll's square. Anton, you and I will be ours."

"Aye, Cap'n."

Ruedi, crossbow in hand ran to stand to the left of Noll's square, while Max, his sword drawn went to the right. Normally, they would have seven to ten rovers per square, fast men with swords whose task it was to dart in and out of the enemy ranks, doing as much damage as possible when the two fronts collided. But, Noll reasoned, since this was a stalling mission, Thomas must have decided he would rather have the squares themselves as strong as possible.

Noll watched Thomas walk to stand outside his own square. He put Pirmin's ax on the ground and drew his short sword and mace. Next to him, stood Sutter.

Semi-transparent tendrils of mist wrapped around Sutter's ankles, as though rooting him to the damp ground. He stared defiantly at the approaching Austrians, with his ax held before him and his face grim. He looked more like some mythical warrior than a middle-aged innkeeper. The momentary illusion was shattered, however, by the old, patched, and mended vest that his wife had made him years ago. The same one that he had worn to serve Noll many a mug of ale over the years.

"Sutter!" Noll shouted.

"Sutter!"

The innkeeper turned around slowly, looking for the source of the call. He saw Noll waving and gave him a curt nod and a half smile, which was worth a full smile from any other man.

"I want to marry your daughter!"

Sutter's eyes went wide and then narrowed in the space of a heartbeat. Noll was suddenly glad he was separated from Mera's father by a score of armed men. He had not planned his words, but as soon as he said them he knew it was the perfect time, even as the men around him laughed.

"I mean when this is all over. And things have settled down a bit," Noll said.

Sutter's jaw clamped shut, and his eyes narrowed further.

He pointed at Noll. "Stay alive, boy. We will talk about this again."

Noll grinned. "That most definitely did not sound like a 'no'," he said.

"Time to get your feet back on the ground, Noll," Ruedi said, as the knights attacking broke into a charge. There were several flag bearers of Austrian noble families riding in the charge, but one in particular had caught Noll's eye: the red fist of Berenger Von Landenberg.

He tightened his grip on his own ax, and pushed all thoughts of Sutter and Mera from his mind. Out of his peripheral vision he saw Thomas rotating his mace arm to loosen it up.

"Squares, front face!" Thomas shouted.

The men in the front lines dropped to one knee, wedged their ax handle against their front foot, and pointed the spear tip of their weapons toward the enemy. The next line squatted and also stepped on the hafts of their halberds but remained standing. The next couple of lines completed the deadly wall by holding the points of their weapons parallel to the ground and over their comrades' heads. The men behind assumed a solid stance and placed one hand on the man in front of him to lend support, and to be ready to replace him when needed.

"Squares. Meet charge!"

This was no Sturmritter charge, Noll thought before the first horses hit them. Their front was not unified, and less than half of the knights attacking had lances. Most of them swung long swords that needed room to operate. And since the Schwyzer forces were so concentrated, the Austrians had to crowd together as they approached, cutting off a large number of the attackers. This forced them to slow down and follow behind the main force, waiting for their prey to run.

"Hold your ground!" Noll shouted as a horse penetrated three lines into the square before its rider was pulled from its back and hacked up by axes from the rear lines.

A swordsman slashed out and Noll saw Gruber recoil in pain, he dropped his ax and pressed his huge hand against his collar bone. Blood seeped between his fingers. Ruedi's crossbow clicked, and the young knight pushing into the square was lifted out of his saddle with a leather-fletched shaft punched deep into his breast plate. He fell under the hooves of the other knights pressing their mounts forward, trying to find an opening in the wall of axes. As soon as Ruedi fired, he ducked into the protection of the back lines of the square to reload.

Gruber found his ax. He hefted it up, and using it with one hand began pulling knights off horses like they were low-hanging apples. Once on the ground, the cumbersome armor of the knights was no match for the penetrating ax heads and the men who wielded them.

Another click from Ruedi's crossbow; another riderless horse crowding the front line. On the right, Noll caught glimpses of his other rover, Max. He seemed to be everywhere, with sword in hand, moving in and out of the square at will. Men, or horses, cried out every time Noll lost sight of him.

Noll had no idea how Thomas's square fared. Every time he tried to look he was confronted by a new enemy. He could see nothing but horses and knights' legs. He swung an overhead strike at a knight's thigh. His ax hit just above the knee, and even though it was covered in chainmail, he felt the end of the large leg bone crumble under the blow. The knight screamed, and fell forward, but managed to hold onto his horse's neck and break out of the throng around him. He went twenty feet before falling out of his saddle, and was promptly trampled by a riderless horse.

Within minutes, most of the horses immediately surrounding the square lacked riders. But the Austrians were so numerous, the horses could not escape. Terrorized, and many of them wounded, by the sharp spear points and the flashing ax heads, they stumbled around the outside of the square until they could force their way through the Austrians and gallop back to the main army.

Noll's arms were heavy, but he was not winded when the man behind him tapped his shoulder to initiate a line change. Noll dropped back, and Gruber stepped forward.

What is he doing behind me? That is not our regular formation.

As Noll stepped back he had to lift his leg over a body. One of his men. And another. The square held, but almost half his men had fallen. That was why Gruber was behind him, he realized.

He put his hand on Gruber's shoulder and rested his ax handle on the ground. He rolled his shoulder as best he could to relax the muscles. Gruber suddenly jumped. A long lance had been driven through his middle and stuck four feet out his lower back. Only Noll's quick feet stopped him from being skewered as well.

Gruber began to fall backward, but the point of the shaft stuck against the ground and would not let him fall. The big man looked around weakly. Noll leapt forward to protect him and maintain the front line. As he looked up, he found himself staring right into Landenberg's face.

The Vogt had a helmet with a metal snout, but his face mask was raised. Probably so he could breathe better, Noll thought. He pointed at Noll as he wheeled his mount around in a circle.

"I got myself a big one, eh Melchthal! And you will be next!"

Landenberg dug his heels into his horse's flank and barged through the other Austrian knights. Noll saw him heading straight to a lightly armored man with Landenberg's crest on his chest. He had three or four long lances, and held one out as the Vogt approached. Then, Noll had to focus back on the battle at hand. Someone had unhorsed an Austrian, and he rolled right in front of Noll like a sacrifice. He let the man push himself up to his hands and knees before beheading him. Then he stepped on his back while he used the hook on the back of his ax to help Sepp Rubin unhorse another.

Next to Sepp, working the front line with a borrowed ax in hand, was Ruedi. And next to him was Max. The rovers had taken up positions inside the square. The front line to be exact. This was not a good sign, Noll thought.

He risked a glance over his shoulder. There were only two rows of men behind him. Gruber was still standing, but the way his head and empty hands hung limp, Noll knew he could no longer count him.

The horses in front of Noll suddenly cleared, and for the briefest moment he thought the Austrians were retreating. But then, with his heart stuck in his throat, he realized that they had only pulled back to ready another charge. He saw Landenberg among them, lance in hand.

"Squares, form single! Seven men across, no rovers!" Thomas shouted.

The men pushed and jostled themselves into new positions. Noll found himself once again on the front line, touching shoulders with Thomas and Sutter.

"Square, forward full!"

Evidently Thomas too had had enough of defensive formations. Noll could not blame him. If they were going to die, they might as well die on the offensive. The men all seemed to agree, for the entire square raced across the open ground with renewed strength and war cries so terrible Noll wondered who was making them.

Landenberg tested the weight of a lance before handing it back to his squire and then took another one. He glanced over his shoulder, to see what the loud noise coming from the Schwyzers was all about, and had just enough time to lower his visor before the first charging rank was on him. He dropped his lance and drew his sword. Next to him, he saw his squire dragged from the saddle and his throat cut.

With no regard for maintaining formation, Noll pushed himself to reach Landenberg, cutting down everything in his path. But Sutter beat him to the Vogt. The innkeeper hooked his chainmail and pulled him half out of the saddle. Landenberg cursed and swung at Sutter's head, but he ducked and gave a final tug that pulled the Vogt down on top of him. The heavy man knocked the breath out of Sutter and he was slow to stand. As Landenberg stepped forward to thrust his sword into Sutter's guts, Noll hit the Vogt with the shaft of his weapon from behind and knocked him off to the side.

Landenberg turned and flipped open his visor. He smiled and his eyes lit up with mad intent, but he was too out of breath to speak. He swung his sword with both hands in an overhead strike at Noll's head. Still holding his halberd shaft before him, Noll lifted it and blocked the attack on the wood between his hands. Then he brought the bottom of the heavy pole across Landenberg's face. Spitting blood, Landenberg reeled back, but Noll kept his momentum going and, stepping forward, spun his ax over his head and sunk it deep into the side of Landenberg's head. His head bounced off his shoulder.

Noll shook as he looked down at Landenberg. His eyes, now as sightless as Noll's father's, stared up at the low clouds as the rain fell. It was hard to say what killed him first: the broken neck, or the heavy, flanged ax head lodged above his ear.

Noll felt rough hands on him.

"Noll, look!" Thomas said, facing him in the direction of the main army where at least five hundred more cavalry were readying to charge, and a long line of other knights were pushing their way up to the front through the ranks of infantry.

"No, there. On the slopes above."

Noll looked to where he pointed. A treeless slope. But a slope that was alive and in motion.

A score of giant logs, some of them covered in oil and burning, bounced their way down picking up speed as they went. Leaving a trail of burning oil on the green mountainside, they smashed into the horses and men gathered at its base. The scene instantly turned from what was already a frenzy into a full-blown panic. Horses' legs were swept out from under them and broken, some men were crushed, others burst into flames by simply being too close. Then, behind the logs and trees came rocks; large, jagged pieces taller than a man but round enough to roll faster than a horse can run.

Thomas stared at Noll, looking as surprised as Noll had ever seen him. "Did you…," he began.

Noll shook his head. "That is not my doing."

In the distance an alphorn sounded. Then another far, far away. Seconds later, more horns blared, but closer this time. Much closer.

Noll laughed and clapped Thomas on the back. "But those! Those are our doing!"

There was no longer any fighting around the men. The survivors of the Austrian cavalry that they had charged were racing back to the main army. Noll was not sure that was such a wise choice of destinations. For there were a great many screams coming from the main force as over a thousand horses tried to avoid the falling rocks and logs. Spooked, they threw their riders and trampled anyone in their path.

Thomas was watching the same turmoil.

"Now is the time," Thomas said. "We have to turn them on themselves." He placed cupped hands to his mouth. "Form up!"

"Form up!" Noll repeated.

"Square, face forward!" Thomas said.

They began to march toward the head of the largest army Noll had ever seen. Movement on the hillside caught his eye. A score of men were making their way down following the same route the logs had taken, shooting longbows and crossbows as they came.

No, not a score, Noll corrected himself. Twenty-seven men. Twenty-eight if you counted Erich. He grinned and could not help elbowing Thomas to make sure he saw them.

"Your outlaw friend has chosen a side, it seems," Thomas said.

"I never said Erich was my friend," Noll said. "But I must admit, I have never been so happy to see anyone."

Horns blew again, but this time one after the other in quick succession.

"Stauffacher is in place," Noll said.

Thomas nodded.

"Square, forward full!"

✧ ✧ ✧

It was raining, yet Leopold's world was in flames. He stared at the demons coming down the mountainside on paths of fire.

The acrid stench of burning soldiers and horse flesh clogged his nostrils. An arrow flew past his ear, but he did not notice.

"The Schwyzers are charging us my lord," Klaus said, drawing his sword. "We must move back into the ranks!"

Leopold's eyes remained focused on the mountainside and he seemed not to have heard Klaus.

"My Lord! We must leave. Now."

"What? No... that will not do... The men will think something is amiss," Leopold said. No sooner were the words out of his mouth than an arrow thudded into his horse's flank. She took it stoically, with only a short whinny, but then the pain came and she bucked madly until Leopold was thrown from her back.

"Leo!"

Klaus jumped down from his mount, but kept the reins wrapped around his hand so the horse could not bolt in the confusion. Men and horses were everywhere, and everyone seemed to be trying to go in the same direction. However, the road was too narrow, and neither the impenetrable forest on the one side, nor the steep hill on the other offered any alternative.

Leopold sat up, but his vision was blurred and he felt nauseous. He blinked and a bald-headed man kicked him in the face.

"Are you who I think you are?" the man said, his words echoed but Leopold was surprised at how they were so clearly audible with the shouts and screams of all those around him.

The man scrunched up his ferret-shaped face and his small eyes doubled in size. "Well, blackball me to—"

His blood was suddenly airborne and sprayed over Leopold's face, making the Duke squeeze his eyes shut. When he opened them, the man's body was on the ground; his neck cut half-way through from the rear.

Klaus reached down and grabbed Leopold by the scruff of his chainmail and hoisted him to his feet. Two more men brandishing swords appeared out of the fog. Klaus yanked Leopold behind him and pushed his horse's reins into his hands.

"Get on that horse, my lord, now."

Leopold heard the words but he could not move. He was not injured, but his feet seemed rooted to the spot. While Klaus fought for their lives, he found himself turning to look up the mountainside once again at the paths of fire. They were gone now, but they had been there only moments before. He was sure of it.

The demons had hid them, so none would know the truth. But I know....

Klaus ran one of the men through and jumped back to narrowly evade the other man's slash.

"Get on that horse!" Klaus yelled.

What horse?

Leopold again felt a tug on his chainmail, but this one was quick and from behind. The next thing he knew he was across a saddle on his stomach.

"I have him," Franco Roemer called out to Klaus. "Large groups of rebels are attacking all down the line!"

The mountains... they come from the mountains... and they are not rebels....

Klaus batted his opponent's sword aside and split the man in half with a two-handed overhand stroke.

"Get him out of here, Captain. I will follow as best I can."

Klaus managed to retrieve his horse's reins that Leopold had dropped and swung himself up into the saddle. Franco did not wait. He kicked his horse into a gallop and they weaved in and out of the press of men and animals crowding the road. Leopold thought his insides were going to explode, but as soon as they came to an open space, Franco stopped the horse and had Leopold sit behind him.

Klaus caught up with them. "Are you hurt, my lord?"

Is he talking to me?

"He seems fine," Franco said. "A little shaken, perhaps. But we can worry about that after."

On one particularly crowded section of road, fifty mounted knights struggled to regain control of their destriers in the midst of a group of infantry. War horses did not fight together with infantry, so any man not riding a horse, was an enemy in their minds. The snorting animals, trained to lash out with their hind legs, were kicking and trampling anyone that came too close and there seemed little their handlers could do to control them.

Franco tried to go to the left of the road, but there was a deep creek, and the ground around it was too soft. He opted instead for the sloped, but firmer, area to the right. They had to duck under tree branches and scramble along scree, but they were able to bypass the troubled section.

"Hold on, Duke," Franco said as he made his horse jump over a large boulder, dripping and dark with moisture, to get back on the road. No sooner were they on level ground, surrounded by their own infantry, than a horn sounded.

Leopold jumped.

A split second later, on the slope above, hundreds of howling demons brandishing giant axes erupted from the mist-shrouded trees.

Leopold screamed and covered his eyes.

The Schwyzers attacked at several points along the Austrian line, almost half of which was still marching along the shores of Lake Aegeri. Their panicked cavalry proved useless in such cramped fighting conditions, and some say the horses killed as many Austrians as the Schwyzers did. But, if truth be told, it was the lake itself that was responsible for the deaths of more men than anything. Encumbered with their expensive armor, thousands of Austrian nobles died that day trying to fight in water, or flee through it.

CHAPTER 28

COUNT HENRI OF HUNENBERG and the captain of the thirty cavalry troops Leopold had sent along with Henri and his knights, sat atop their horses and eyed the village in the field below. It consisted of a dozen thatched-roof huts and a common building. The one street was empty; all doors were closed. The villagers had seen them coming a long time ago. Just as Henri had wanted it. But the captain, a career soldier of the Holy Roman Empire, was beginning to suspect that perhaps Henri was not quite up to the task Leopold had charged him with.

"Shall we attack, my lord?" the captain asked.

"No. Not until we have word from Duke Leopold."

"We received his orders, and his blessing I might add, when we marched from Habsburg," the captain said.

"And I have ordered you to await confirmation from the Duke. If that is not to your liking, *captain*, then I suggest you find another Count to take orders from."

The man fidgeted in his saddle, making the leather squeak. "No, sir. Was just wondering is all."

Well, you will not have to wonder for very long, Henri thought, for in the distance he could see his messenger returning. Henri shielded his eyes to get a better look.

Something was wrong.

The man was bent low in the saddle, and his cloak billowed out behind him as he came at them full speed. His horse was foaming at the mouth when he pulled up before them.

"What is it?" Henri asked.

"The Duke's army, it is… it has been routed, my lord."

The captain let out a loud exhalation. "Come on, man. Talk sense. Routed by whom?"

The messenger looked at Henri. "It is true, my lord. The Schwyzers ambushed them on the shores of the lake. Thousands are dead, the rest are in full retreat."

"Who told you this?" Henri asked.

"I saw it with these eyes, my lord. The Duke's entire army scattered, running for their lives. I heard from one survivor, the Schwyzers are executing any man taken prisoner. Who could have predicted this?"

"What of the Duke?" the captain asked.

The messenger shook his head. "I saw no sign of him. They may have captured him. Surely the godless peasants would not execute a prince!"

Henri thought of Thomas and what he knew of the man. "You are wrong on both accounts. They are not godless, and yes, they are quite capable of executing a member of the royal family."

The captain turned to Henri. "This is dire news, but we should push on with our objective."

Count Henri stared at the man. "Take your men and return to your homes."

The captain looked at the defenseless village below. Henri could see him imagining the possible treasures that could be uncovered inside the simple buildings.

"I have been ordered by Duke Leopold to take this village,"

the captain said.

Henri shook his head.

"It seems Leopold no longer has any claim to these lands. But, as of this moment, that village is under the protection of the House of Hunenberg. You set one foot in there, and you will hang. The day is over, captain. This war is over. And if you set one foot in that village, your life is over."

Henri turned his horse and headed home.

CHAPTER 29

THOMAS KNELT BESIDE the Rubin boys. One held the other's lifeless head in his lap, while silent tears streamed down his freckled cheeks.

Marti. That was the boy's name. Had it really been that difficult to tell them apart?

Thomas put a hand on Sepp's shoulder and said a prayer for Marti. As he stood, he saw Ruedi leading two horses toward him.

"Cap'n, they found Leopold."

"Where?"

"A short distance to the west. I hear the men he is with is giving our boys a hard time."

Leopold. Thomas suddenly wished Seraina were there to help him decide what to do with the 'boy tyrant', as Noll so often called him.

"Lead the way," Thomas said, taking one set of reins from the crossbowman.

When Thomas and Ruedi arrived, twenty Schwyzers had formed a large circle around the three men. Leopold, his fine clothes and armor splattered with dirt and blood, sat on the ground at Franco Roemer's feet. The captain of the Sturmritter did not look as shiny as the last time Thomas had seen him.

Gone was his polished armor and peacock-plumed helmet. He wore simple cotton breeches and a sweat-ringed shirt that may have been white at one time. Now, it looked like it had been pulled from a pig bath. Beside him stood the hulking form of Klaus, his long sword held before him, daring anyone to come within its reach. His armor seemed intact, save for his helmet, which he had either lost in battle or discarded.

"Open a path," Thomas said. He drew his short sword and mace as he walked into the circle. "Throw down your weapons and surrender Leopold." He pointed his sword at Franco.

When Leopold saw Thomas, he screamed. His eyes bulged and he dug his heels into the soft ground to propel himself away backwards, but Franco held him in place with his knee planted firmly in the Duke's back.

"Stay where you are," Klaus growled at Thomas. His voice sounded like he was badly in need of a drink of water. Or, perhaps, he always sounded that way. Thomas was not sure he had ever heard the man speak.

Thomas kept walking, and soon discovered Klaus was not the type of man to warn someone twice. With a loud cry he charged at Thomas. His sword carved a murderous arc straight down at the Hospitaller's head. Thomas swayed his upper body to the side just enough for the sword to miss making any contact. Then he swung his mace hard against the side of the large man's knee. Klaus groaned, his leg buckled, and Thomas stepped in to slide his short sword straight through the man's throat. He pulled it out as quickly as it went in.

A fine spray added to the red of Thomas's tunic, but most of the blood was deflected by the older man's gray beard. It collected there for a moment, hidden from sight, but then it welled up and poured down Klaus's chest. Without even a whimper, he fell over backward, his body stiff when it hit the ground. His unseeing eyes stared at the clouds.

"No!" Leopold screamed and began crawling on his hands and knees toward Klaus, but Franco reeled him in and unceremoniously threw him behind his legs. Leopold fell over on his side, in a fetal position, and with his eyes clenched tighter than fists, began to moan.

Franco raised his sword and pointed it at Thomas.

"You will not find my throat so easily, Hospitaller." He cut the air with his sword. "Come. Let us duel for the Prince's life."

"Ruedi," Thomas called out, keeping his eyes on Franco.

"Cap'n?"

"Shoot this man."

Ruedi bent over, fastened the hook at his waist onto his crossbow string, and with a grunt, cocked the war bow by standing up straight. He pulled a bolt from his belt quiver and set it to the string.

Franco looked from Ruedi to Thomas, and his lips curled in disdain.

"You would have your man shoot me?"

"You have something I want," Thomas said.

"Then fight me for it! I took you for a man of honor when we first met. Will you prove me wrong now, here, in front of your men?"

Thomas felt his blood rising. Why should he care anything for honor?

"I was told my entire life that only the nobility and knights are capable of true honor. Well, as you may have noticed, I am neither." He waved his arm over the men surrounding them. "There is not a drop of blue blood in any one of us. But what we do have is loyalty. Loyalty to our countrymen, our children, our wives and husbands, our friends. So tell me, with all this, what need do we have of honor?"

Franco was quiet for a long time as he glared at Thomas.

"Your men have been executing prisoners. And do not deny it, for I have seen it several times already."

"I know. I gave the orders. From this day forward, any man who comes into our lands with intent to do us wrong, must expect to die if he is caught. That is our law."

"Peasants, yes, I can understand that. But a noble man's ransom could make you a rich man! It makes no sense to kill him."

"We do not want your kind's gold. We wish to be left alone. So why would we suffer, even for one day, the company of a man who comes to our door looking to take everything we hold dear?"

Thomas could see Franco weighing his words. Leopold tried to crawl away once again, but Franco stepped on his leg to keep him in place. He stared at Duke Leopold trapped under his boot, and then met Thomas's eyes.

"Very well. I will agree to lay down my sword and be executed, but only if you allow Duke Leopold to live."

"You negotiate a poor bargain," Thomas said. "This is my counter-offer. You will take Leopold from our lands and see him delivered safely to Habsburg. When his mind has recovered, you will explain to him that if he ever sets foot within our borders again, his life will be forfeit. As will the lives of anyone he brings with him."

Franco's eyes narrowed. "You would let us both go?"

"Someone must tell what happened here today," Thomas said. He pointed at Leopold cowering behind Franco's legs like a child hiding in his mother's skirts. "Since he is unlikely to remember many details, that someone must be you."

Franco sheathed his sword and pulled Leopold to his feet. He pushed the young Duke ahead of him, while he walked behind. He took a few steps and then turned around.

"This is not over. The princes will not let this stand. Sooner or later, one will work up the courage to march another army through your valleys."

Thomas remained silent. What could he say when he knew Franco was right?

"But when they come," Franco continued, "Do not look for me, Schwyzer. For I will not be counted among their number."

He turned back to Leopold and gave him another shove up the road.

✧　✧　✧

Seraina stood beside the sacrificial stone with Oppid at her side. The druids closed around her, chanting, while Orlina stooped and carefully picked up Gildas's white robe. The chanting became softer, and no more intrusive than the sound of a nearby creek.

Orlina held up the robe and slipped it over Seraina's numb shoulders.

"If we are to survive," Orlina said, "there must be balance." She pulled Seraina's head down gently and kissed her forehead. Without another word, she turned and began walking down the Mythen.

Each druid, in turn, followed Orlina's lead, and after kissing Seraina on the forehead, they too began winding down the rocky path. Soon, only Seraina and Oppid stood upon the Mythen's summit. She pulled the robe around her shoulders and knelt next to the white wolf. She wrapped her arms around his thick neck and stared at Gildas's walking stick until she could no longer feel her legs.

The trees told her where to go, but she took her time.

Seraina was in no hurry to see Gildas's body.

She arrived at the great pile of blown over trees, and scanned the area. There was no sign of him. She cringed. The Habsburgs took him, she thought.

But then, from the forest a short distance to the east, the wind carried to her a voice. A *singing* voice.

Seraina saw the white robe through the trees as she approached. The druid's hood was up and he stood over a low mound of rocks. He continued singing until Seraina was at his side.

His voice was soft and gentle, and the song was one Seraina did not know the words to, but somehow, she felt it was perfect. When the man turned to her and took down his hood, she was sorry the song had come to an end.

"Blessed be the Weave," he said. It was the man who had stood beside her in the circle. The one who had held her hand so firmly. He was pushing the far side of middle life, but his eyes shone with the wonder of youth.

Much like Gildas's, she realized. Uncannily so.

He smiled, and looked at the stacked rocks. "He was my elder brother," he said.

"I am sorry," Seraina said. "I never knew he had a brother."

The man shrugged. "Gildas was not one to talk about himself. Being an Eye of the Weave, I suppose he did not allow himself the time."

Seraina nodded, and she felt her throat constrict. "I never saw him much these last few years. He always seemed to be on his way somewhere, searching for new adepts."

"That is because he was the only one of us who could. We all have our part to play in the pattern, but Gildas was the only one who had the ability to identify talent at an age young enough to nurture it. As he did with you."

"But I have never found an adept before. I do not understand why Orlina thinks I can take over Gildas's duties," Seraina said.

"Because Gildas told her that you could."

"And if I cannot?"

The man chuckled. "Every thread in the Weave has an end. Time is sure to outlast us all, Seraina. But some threads twist and wind their way through the pattern of life in such a complicated and unpredictable manner, that it is virtually impossible to find where it finishes. I like to think our kind are one of those."

Seraina liked the sound of that. She had always felt in her heart that it was not yet time for this world to say goodbye to the Helvetii. She stared at the grave before her. Gildas had taught her so much, not just about the Weave, but about herself as well. She owed it to him to pass on as much as she could.

"I will leave you so you can say your goodbyes," the druid said.

"Where do you go now? What will you do?" she asked.

He scratched at a tooth with his index finger for a moment. "I think I will compile a manuscript."

"A book? Druids have never kept written records. What kind of book?"

"I think I would like... a white one," he said, laughing. "Yes! We need more white books to give our people hope for the future. There are more than enough dark ones already in the world."

Seraina could not help but smile at this. "Do you think it will work?"

He shrugged and held up his hands. "You should ask

yourself that question. Unlike you or Gildas, I do not have the sight to know what the future holds. My role, is simply one of support. If you are the Eye of our order, I am but one of many pieces of skin, trying to hold us all together."

"Will I ever see you again?" Seraina asked, hoping the answer was 'yes'.

He nodded. "Even if you do not want to."

He held up his hand in farewell, pulled up the hood of his white robe, and began to walk into the trees. As she watched the man leave, she noticed how small he looked. Speaking to him up close, he had given off the energy and stature of a much taller person.

Just before the druid disappeared into the forest, a soft breeze rustled his cloak, and as the same wind blew over Seraina, for the briefest of instants, she swore she could hear the tinkling of bells.

✧   ✧   ✧

Seraina waited until well after dark, until a time when she knew the celebration festivities in the Schwyz market square would be well under way. She put out her small fire and poured the cauldron of hot herb water that had been simmering over it into a wooden bucket.

Minutes later, with the bucket of warm water in hand, she eased open the flap to Thomas's tent. Still dressed in his red Hospitaller tunic, he sat on a stool with his weary head in his hands, staring at a single tallow candle on the small table before him.

He looked up, his face still streaked with dried blood and sweat. His mouth fell open, but no words came out. He made to stand, but when Seraina saw pain flicker across his face, she stopped him with a hand on his shoulder. She pressed him back down onto his stool and set the bucket down. Then she produced a clean cloth from the pocket of her white robe, Gildas's robe, dipped it in the water, and rung it out. The sound of the water falling echoed in the silence of the small space.

"Seraina, I—"

She cut him off by putting her finger over his lips, and then began wiping his face with the hot cloth. He closed his eyes, and she was thankful he did not speak. For she knew he would have so many questions. Ones that she could not answer because she simply did not know.

Why am I here?

She knew she should not have come. Thomas was the Catalyst, and his time had just begun. He would do things for her people, *their people*, that she would never dare dream. They were about to enter a new era, filled with much risk to be sure, but it would also be one which promised to set her people on a new path. One with opportunities the like of which they had not seen in a thousand years. So long as, no one came between the Catalyst and his gift to sense the Weave's patterns.

She knew the danger. And yet, she had still come.

She dropped the cloth into the bucket and a red cloud billowed out into the scented water. Slowly, she lifted his tunic over his head. Then she removed his chainmail vest and the padded cloth below. Finally, she unbuttoned his shirt and peeled it away. He winced every time she raised his right arm. His sides were covered in bruises but nothing was broken.

Seraina took out a fresh cloth and, starting at the hollow below his throat, washed down Thomas's entire body. When she was finished, they made love. Neither one of them uttered a single word.

Afterward, in the coldest hours just before dawn, with her head resting on his chest, Seraina began to speak. Her words were heavy with the power of her voice, and she hoped that with Thomas being so exhausted from the day's events, she would be able to make him forget how he felt for her. She would have to deal with her own feelings at another time.

She had spoken no more than a dozen words, when she felt Thomas's finger across her lips.

"I want to remember," he said. "I know you think you are doing me a kindness. But if we cannot be together, I do not wish to lose a single memory of you, Seraina. Painful or not, I should like to have them to look back on."

Seraina closed her eyes, but that did nothing to stop the tears.

A kindness. It was the perfect choice of words, she thought. For what is love, if not a *perfect* kindness?

CHAPTER 30

"ARE YOU JODOCK SCHNIDRIG?" Thomas asked, his voice rough from weeks alone on the road.

The question felt ridiculous, for even before the man nodded, Thomas knew the answer. Standing there with his arms crossed over his massive chest, his pose and stature rivaled that of the rocky peak of the Matterhorn towering in the background. His once blonde hair and beard were marble white, like the tops of the jagged crags that surrounded them on all sides. But his chiseled cheekbones and bright eyes made Thomas think that, in his youth, he had probably been even more handsome than Pirmin.

Several black-necked goats milled about the rocky yard of a small farmhouse nearby. Built entirely of stone, it looked as solid as the man who stood across from Thomas now. Even the shingles on its roof were fashioned from large flat stones overlapping one another.

It had taken Thomas over a month to make it to Wallis from Schwyz. The paths had been steep and dangerous, and he never would have managed it with his precious cargo intact if Noll had not procured for him a specially built alp cart that merchants used for traversing goods over the mountain passes. It was a narrow, two-wheeled, open wagon that was barely wide enough to hold the solid pine box that housed Pirmin's body.

Thomas cleared the dust from his throat. "I brought your son," he said.

"My boys are in Tasch," the man said. His eyes flicked to the box in the back of the cart. Thomas could see him begin to panic.

"No, not one of them," Thomas said quickly. "Pirmin. I have brought Pirmin home."

"Pirmin?"

The giant's eyes went suddenly wide and one leg buckled. He reached out to grab the side of the wagon. Thomas stepped forward and offered his arm, but the man held up his hand. He stared at the box for a long time before he spoke.

"You knew him?"

"Since we were boys," Thomas said.

He reached into the back of the wagon and dragged out Pirmin's great ax. He stood it on end and leaned it over to the older man. "This was his. I think he would have wanted you to have it."

Pirmin's father pulled his eyes away from the casket and looked at Thomas, the ax, then back at Thomas. He shouted out to someone in the house causing Thomas to jump.

"Mattie! Come out here and meet your brother!"

The door crashed open and a young woman half-walked, half-ran out to meet them. The speed with which she appeared, told Thomas she had probably been watching them the whole time. Her hair was the color of honey-dipped wheat, and where everything Thomas had seen so far of this land had been hard and cold, she was the exact opposite. She talked as she walked, the words bubbling out of her in the strong sing-song Wallis dialect.

"Well, I know you Daddy, and I know Mama too. And if this man is my brother, I swear I will milk the goats myself for a week!"

She stopped in front of Thomas and fixed him with a curious smile. Her eyes were the blue of a dawn sky, and her skin had the healthy glow of someone who liked to be outside. Her face was slightly flushed with excitement, which could have been due to the rare events of the day, but Thomas suspected she always looked like this. She was simply beautiful; like only Pirmin's sister could have been.

"Not *him*," her father said.

Did Thomas detect a hint of disgust at the thought?

"The one in the box."

Keeping one hand on the cart, the old man walked around to its side. He placed his massive hand slowly on top of the pine box and spread his fingers.

"His name was Pirmin. And I sent him away before you were born."

The girl's mouth opened as wide as her eyes. She glanced from Thomas to her father, and bit her lip, waiting for either one to speak. After a time, Pirmin's father looked at Thomas. The old man's eyes were wet.

"What is your name, friend?"

His tone, the way he looked straight at you when he spoke, the slight drawl to his words; Thomas saw so much of Pirmin in front of him a lump formed in his throat.

"You can call me Thomi."

"Can you stay with us a while, Thomi? I would like to hear about my boy."

And Pirmin would like nothing more, Thomas thought.

He nodded, and followed the Schnidrigs inside.

LEOPOLD'S FATE

WITHOUT RESOURCES, OR any real desire to face the Schwyzers in battle again, Leopold spent the next seven years focusing all his energies on helping his brother regain the crown of the Holy Roman Empire. Just when the war seemed to be going their way, Frederich the Handsome suffered a crushing defeat in 1322. Louis the Bavarian took Frederich, and over a thousand nobles from Austria and Salzburg, captive.

The Habsburgs were beaten. But Leopold continued to resist, and by leveraging his political connections with the other German princes, was a constant threat to the fragile Holy Roman Empire which Louis now ruled. After three years of captivity, to Leopold's surprise, Louis suddenly released Frederich.

The last leaves of fall were on the ground turning black when Leopold met Frederich's escort at the gates to Habsburg castle. The two brothers embraced and then Leopold stepped back to appraise his brother's condition.

For a man held prisoner for over three years, he looked exceptionally well. Better, in fact, than Leopold remembered. Frederich had put on some weight and his eyes were bright, but that could be the glistening effect of the tears of joy he was fighting back at being reunited with his younger brother.

"You look good, brother. Louis treated you well enough, I see," Leopold said.

"Of course he did. Our cousin is a fair man, and we were friends long before our disagreement over the crown."

Fair man?

Two foiled assassination attempts in the last year alone had Leopold believing otherwise. But he knew there would be no point in telling his brother just yet. Louis had had three years to shape Frederich's mind to his cause, and Leopold suspected it would take some time to undo the damage.

"No need to talk out here in the cold. Let us get you into the keep in front of a fire, and put some good Habsburg wine into your belly. Then you can tell me all about your time away."

Leopold took his brother's elbow to lead him through the gates, but Frederich pulled his arm away.

"What is it?" Leopold asked.

"I cannot go in just yet. We have something to discuss first."

"Surely that can wait until you have eaten some—"

"No. It cannot."

Leopold was afraid of this. Three years was a long time.

"Very well," Leopold said. "What would you have me know?"

"My release was conditional."

"On what?"

"I gave Louis my word."

Leopold felt his throat constrict. Louis knew Frederich's weakness too well.

"Go on."

"I promised to speak with you, and convince you that

Louis is the best suited ruler for the Empire at this time."

"You are the rightful heir," Leopold said. He tried to keep his voice low, soothing. But his throat burned with the taste of bile.

Frederich shrugged. "That no longer matters. We must consider what is best for the entire Holy Roman Empire. The German princes have been divided for too long, and as a result, everyone has suffered. Not just our family."

Leopold put his hand on his brother's shoulder.

"Come inside. We can talk more after you have rested."

Frederich shrugged his touch away. "No. I swore I would not set foot in Habsburg until you recognized Louis as the legitimate ruler. I know this is difficult for you, brother, but it really is best. For the Empire as a whole."

Leopold could take no more. "Listen to yourself! These are not your words. Your mind has been poisoned and turned against itself. Think of what you say."

"It is your own mind that swims in poison. Ever since Morgarten." Frederich shook his head and looked at Leopold with sadness in his eyes. "That battle did something to you, Leo. It turned you into a distrusting soul, jealous and petty. Here is a chance for you to let go of all that. To be a true Prince of the Empire once again."

Leopold felt his fist connect square on with the bridge of Frederich's nose. The cartilage gave way with a grinding pop and Frederich fell to the ground.

"Never!" Leopold's clenched hand trembled at his side.

Some of Frederich's escort drew their swords and held them pointed at Leopold, stopping him from advancing on his brother. Leopold's guards at the gate came pouring through, with weapons drawn, and pulled their lord behind them.

Frederich sat up on the ground. Blood streamed from his

broken nose and his eyes were wet with tears of pain and disappointment. He looked at his brother.

"NEVER!" Leopold shouted again from behind his men.

Frederich pushed himself to his feet. He mounted up and turned his horse away from the gates of Habsburg.

✧ ✧ ✧

True to his word, Frederich returned to Louis and confessed he had failed to win over his brother's obstinacy. He demanded to be put in chains. Legend has it that Louis was so impressed with Frederich's sense of honor, that he decreed they both should rule together. Louis the Bavarian remained the Holy Roman Emperor, but he agreed to give Frederich the title of King of the Romans.

Less than two months after Frederich the Handsome was crowned King of the Romans, his brother, Leopold I of Habsburg, died. He was thirty-five years old.

Frederich was so upset by his brother's death, that he immediately resigned his regency as King of the Romans and returned to rule over only Austria. Four years later, Frederich the Handsome, was also dead.

Louis the Bavarian continued to rule the Holy Roman Empire until his death seventeen years later.

###

Author's Notes

Swiss Halberdiers and Pikemen

By the end of the fifteenth century, Swiss mercenaries were the most feared and respected fighting units in Europe. They were ruthless, loyal to their employer, disciplined, and because of their exceptional mobility, revolutionized the use of the halberd and pike on the battlefield. Their ability to change up their formations quickly, turned the pike, which was traditionally used defensively to repel cavalry, into a fearsome offensive weapon effective against infantry as well. They were also known for not retreating from a battle. Of course, their practice of hanging the first man to run from his unit may have something to do with this. For over two hundred years, there was scarcely a battle fought in Europe where one side or the other did not enlist the aid of Swiss mercenaries. Even the Pope employed Swiss guards, and still does to this day.

Unlike other soldiers of fortune at the time, Swiss mercenary units were raised and trained by each canton (state or province). The canton arranged the contracts and received a cut from each assignment. The mercenaries themselves had strict rules they had to follow. These included: *Swiss do not fight Swiss, at harvest time we go back home to work the fields,* and *"no money, no Swiss".*

White Book of Sarnen

It is in the White Book of Sarnen that we first see any mention of William Tell. So named because of its expensive white parchment, it was compiled more than one hundred and fifty years after the Battle of Morgarten (1315). Most historians now believe William Tell was a fictional character created much later than the tumultuous times in which he was supposed to exist.

Helvetia

The official name for Switzerland is *Confederatio Helvetica* (the Helvetic Confederation), which is why its country code today is CH. Helvetia is the female personification of Switzerland. A peaceful, yet protective figure, she is usually depicted wearing a wreath in her hair and carrying a shield and sword. Her image currently appears on everything from Swiss Franc coins to postage stamps. In other words, the *Helvetii* are still going strong to this day. As for the *Druids of the Helvetii*, only one of their order could tell you of their fate.

ABOUT THE AUTHOR

J. K. Swift lives in a log house well off the beaten path in central B.C., Canada. He has worked as a school teacher, jailhouse guard, Japanese translator, log peeler, accountant, martial arts instructor, massage therapist, technical editor, and has called a few Bingo games. He gets his story ideas while traveling in Europe, feeding his chickens, and cutting wood.

He has written a prequel series to **The Forest Knights**, called **The Hospitaller Saga**, which follows the adventures of Thomas, Pirmin, and the rest of the Schwyzers as they grow up in the Holy Lands. You can learn more, or purchase, the first book (titled **ACRE**) here.
www.jkswift.com/books/acre

Go to his website to learn more or sign up for the New Releases Mailing List to be notified whenever J. K. Swift publishes something new.

www.jkswift.com

…a message from the author:
Thank you very much for reading my work. Reviews and personal recommendations from readers like you are the most important way for an author to attract more readers, so I truly am grateful to anyone who takes the time to rate my work. If you could take a moment to rate my story and/or leave a review where you purchased it, I would greatly appreciate it. It doesn't need to be long—a sentence or two about why you liked it or disliked it would be great. Feel free to contact me through my website and blog with any questions or comments. Thanks very much!

Sign up here for the **New Releases Mailing List** and be the first to know when J. K. Swift publishes a new story! Your email will never be given out to any third party and you will only hear from us when a new novel or short story is about to be released.
http://eepurl.com/hT8zU

If you enjoyed this story, you may also like:
HEALER: Keepers of Kwellevonne V.1 (short story series)

Why would anyone try to kill a healer?
Deenah's quiet life as an apprentice healer in the remote village of Brae's Creek is shattered when a stranger gravely wounds her master and flees into the wild. For all her skills, Deenah is unable to identify the strange forces at work on the injury. To save her master's life, Deenah must join the young Warder Kaern, and an aging veteran tracker, as they set out on a manhunt into hostile lands.

A 7000-word (28 pages) short story.

Printed in Great Britain
by Amazon